T0369493

Across the Wilderness

Journeys of Faith - Book 2

Jeanne F. Brooks

WestBow Press books may be ordered through booksellers or by contacting:

WestBow Press
A Division of Thomas Nelson
1663 Liberty Drive
Bloomington, IN 47403
www.westbowpress.com
1-(866) 928-1240

ISBN: 978-1-4497-0837-5 (sc)
ISBN: 978-1-4497-0838-2 (dj)
ISBN: 978-1-4497-0836-8 (e)
Library of Congress Control Number: 2010940408

Printed in the United States of America

WestBow Press rev. date:12/15/2010

Dedication

To my children
for helping me understand the
experiences of racially-mixed individuals
and the challenges they face in
choosing life partners

"And I will bring you into the wilderness of the people,
and there will I plead with you face to face."
Ezekiel 20:35

"For thou, O God, hast heard my vows;
thou hast given me the heritage of those that fear thy name."
Psalm 61:5 KJV

Acknowledgements

First and foremost, I give glory to **Jesus**, my Savior. His love carried me through life's trials. He is always foremost in my mind. As the scriptures say, His "strength is made perfect in [my] weakness" (2 Cor. 12:9). I pray that the stories I write help readers strengthen their relationship with Him.

Secondly, I thank the readers of my first book. I am blessed to be writing Christian novels. The queries of those readers encouraged me to complete this and the remaining books in this series, *Journeys of Faith.* The enthusiasm with which ***Through the Waters*** was received, affirms in me the desire to continue writing as long as the Lord gives me strength.

Lastly, I want to mention each of my beautiful grandchildren: **Lauren**, my love-bug. You are quickly becoming a beautiful young lady. **Zaire**, my little man. You are growing into a handsome, spirited young man. **Savannah**, my little butterfly. I look forward to seeing you soon. **Peyton**, my sweetie-pie. You are a talented, particular, and wonderful little girl. **Taryn**, my lil Dykstra. You are a challenge… so much energy, so smart. **Xavier,** my little fella, I hope you find what those faraway looks are seeking. **Israel**, I see in your pictures strength and brilliance in your eyes, so like your father. And finally, **Noah**, another I have yet to meet and nickname, but no less loved by this grandmother and the same goes for your little brother, Samuel. And last, but not least, my newest little granddaughter, Adalyn, so tiny and precious.

Prologue

College graduation marked a new beginning for best friends, Maddie, Taylor, Isobel and Ashley. Each had a different plan for their life beyond academia; each one had studied and graduated in a different area for their major. Now, as they squealed and hugged, they recognized that they might not see each other for a long time, and tears of sadness mingled with tears of joy.

Always traditional, Maddie was going to be a schoolteacher of elementary grades and Ashley had trained to be a nurse. The less traditional one in the bunch, Taylor, had dreams of a career in the Gospel music industry. Isobel was the unusual one in the bunch. She never wanted a professional life beyond graduation. She longed for the type of family she hadn't known as a child. She had fallen in love, and looked forward to marriage and family life.

Time would tell how each one's career would work out, and only God knew where their spiritual growth would lead, but for now, Isobel was excited for her future. She wanted to support Jason through his remaining educational endeavors and be the kind of wife he needed to be successful. She still had one major hurdle toward that goal… meeting his parents.

Chapter 1

Anxiety and anticipation possessed her body; her hands were damp and her heart racing. *What would they be like? Would they like her?* Isobel had never felt this apprehensive.

As if reading her mind, Jason put his arm around her, drawing her closer as they walked down the gangway toward the plane. "It's going to be alright, sweetheart. I love you, and they will, too." He sounded convinced. *Or was he trying to convince himself?*

They soon found their seats and settled in for the long flight from Omaha to Boston. Isobel flashed her brilliant smile at Jason attempting a show of confidence she didn't feel, trying to put Jason's mind at rest. It seemed to work; he shrugged the navy blue, fleecy blanket around his shoulders, tucking the tiny pillow between his shoulder and the window. He was dozing before the plane reached cruising altitude.

Isobel rested against him and daydreamed of their future together and all the plans they had for the days ahead. She looked tenderly at the young man asleep in the seat next to her. Youthfully muscular, at 6'2" he towered protectively over her when they walked together, although she was 5'10". Asleep, his dark lashes rested gently on his cheeks and contrasted sharply with his blond hair. His high cheekbones and strong, square jaw lent an air of confidence, even as he slept, an occasional soft snore puffing from his pursed lips. She was overwhelmed with love, smiling as she remembered how they'd reconnected two years ago.

☙

She'd been working at a bookstore when Jason, the jock from high school, walked in and asked for her help finding a book. She never did find the book. They made plans to meet after she finished her shift, and their relationship flourished despite their differences in upbringing. She, like the rest of their class, knew Jason came from old money, and Isobel was just an orphaned daughter of a military man, working her way through school. That disparity alone had kept them from dating in high school but, in college, their shared faith overshadowed everything else.

As Isobel looked down at her sleeping fiancé, she couldn't help but smile. All her assumptions about Jason had been proven wrong. He was going to be a doctor, but only because it was what *he* wanted, not because his father had planned for it. And he hadn't attended his father's alma mater after all, choosing instead the same college as some of his Academy classmates. As for surgery, the elder Dr. Armstrong's specialty, Jason said no to that, too, in favor of Family Practice. Jason stirred, and Isobel reached over to smooth an errant curl back off his forehead. He'd locked horns with his father over so many things.

She couldn't help but wonder what would happen later today when Dr. and Mrs. Armstrong were faced with Jason's latest rebellion. He was supposed to have kept women at arm's length until he finished medical school. In fact, Dr. Armstrong held such a hard-line rule on that issue, that Jason hadn't told them about Isobel until just before graduation. She wasn't sure she liked the idea, but Jason always had one reason or another for delaying things a bit. Now—

"Ladies and gentlemen, we've begun our descent into Boston…"

Jason woke and, looking her way, smiled and took her hand as he said, "Well, here we go…"

Isobel looked out the window. *Here we go, indeed.* He'd said his parents hadn't been angry on the phone. In fact, he'd been surprised by what seemed to be "quiet acquiescence." He meant it to be reassuring, but Isobel could tell by the way he said it that he was worried and now, as the landing gear lowered with a rumble, Isobel wondered if a tirade on the phone might have been better than silence. For better or for worse, she was about to find out.

By the time Isobel and Jason were standing at the baggage carousel, waiting for their luggage, Isobel's stomach was in knots. *At least they were going to the family's country cottage out on Cape Cod. That would have to be more relaxed… wouldn't it?* She couldn't shake her uneasiness over meeting Jason's parents and, once again, he seemed in tune with her anxiety.

"Believe me, Izzie," he spoke earnestly, holding her hands to his chest. "It's going to be just fine. They just need to get to know you like I do…" Her eyes followed his head movement as he looked over the crowd for his parents.

It wasn't difficult to find the senior Armstrongs in the crowd. Dressed in perfectly tailored suits, they stood slightly apart from the blue-jeaned, T-shirted throng making its way toward reunions accompanied with delighted cries and emotional hugs. Isobel saw Jason's mother frown slightly and then whisper something to her husband as she searched the moving mob for… *anyone but me.*

Isobel held back, relieved when Jason took the lead greeting first his father... *They shake hands?!* "Thanks for coming, sir. We could have caught the shuttle…"

"Nonsense, son, we've been looking forward to meeting your young lady. Now, where is she?" His voice was warm, but Dr. Armstrong looked right past her, too, as Jason bent to kiss his mother's cheek before slipping his arm around Isobel's waist and drawing her close.

With a broad smile, Jason said, "Mother, Father, I'd like to introduce Isobel Kirk, my fiancée."

Isobel would never forget the next few seconds.

Mrs. Armstrong gasped audibly and grabbed her husband's arm. Dr. Armstrong covered his wife's hand with his own and patted it as he gazed – *or was it a glare* – at Jason. It was as if the entire airport stood still. For a few brief seconds, Isobel was aware of only these four people, frozen in time.

Dr. Armstrong regained his composure first and reached out to Isobel. "It's so nice to meet the girl who finally captured our son's heart." He glanced at his wife before continuing. "Jason hasn't shared much with us about you," he paused emphatically and nodded at Jason, "*or* your family."

"We'll have time for that later, Father, when we get home." Jason turned and looked meaningfully at his mother. Finally, Mrs. Armstrong offered her hand.

"How do you do, Miss… uh… *Kirk*, is it?"

"I'd rather you call me Isobel." The woman's hand-shake bore all the enthusiasm of a dead fish.

"Yes… of course." She took a deep breath before offering an all-too-bright smile.

"Well, now. Aren't *you* a surprise?" She arched one eyebrow at Jason, "And *you*, young man, were to avoid entanglements until you'd finished your training." She turned to Jason's father. "We should be going now." Without another word, she turned and walked away.

Chapter 2

The drive to Barnstable was long and quiet. When Jason's parents met his attempts at conversation with one syllable answers, he stopped trying, instead meeting silence with silence. He reached for Isobel's tiny hand hoping to communicate a calm he didn't feel. *What would Isobel think when they got to the "cottage"?*

As they drove up the curving drive towards the ivy-framed entrance, Isobel exhaled sharply and withdrew her hand. When he looked her way, her mouth was fixed in the shape of an O. She looked at him with an expression that was part surprise, part terror. He leaned close to whisper, "It's okay; it's just a house," momentarily distracted by the fragrance of her shampoo. "It'll be fine. Don't worry."

When his father stopped the car in front of the carved, double oak doors, Jason opened his own door and pulled Isobel after him. His father popped the trunk open, but showed no intention of helping them with their luggage. Taking Mother's arm, Dr. Armstrong led her up the wide, stone staircase toward the house.

They'd barely gotten inside with their luggage when Mother called from the stairs; she was already retreating toward her room, apparently.

"Show your guest to her room, Jason. We still dress for dinner and it is served at six sharp, *as usual*." She turned and climbed the stairs like a queen, her hand gently gliding along the banister. Once on the landing, she glanced down one more time before retreating into her bedroom. Father had witnessed the entire scene from where he stood in the doorway of the library, but when Jason turned toward him with a pleading look, all Father did was nod and retreat. When he closed the door without a word, Jason turned to Isobel. Her eyes glistened with unshed tears.

"Come on; let me show you to the guest room." He lifted her suitcase and led the way to the nicely appointed guest room complete with fresh cut roses from his mother's garden.

❧

Isobel felt suffocated by the atmosphere in the house, despite the obvious personal touches in the guest suite. Lavender perfumed the linens on the plush bed, and the open windows allowed sea air to freshen the room. However, the superficial beauty contrasted sharply with the deeper ugliness of snobbery. *I never saw a hint of arrogance in Jason.*

Even as a letterman athlete in high school driving the BMW he received on his sixteenth birthday, he maintained a grounded attitude. He was one of the most down-to-earth people she knew. He talked often of his desire to help others, and she thought he had learned that compassion in his home. Now she realized his kindness must be an anomaly in his family. Suddenly, Isobel became aware of Jason's voice.

"Izzie, I'll leave you to relax and change for dinner, OK?" He set down her suitcase and carry-on near the bed.

Isobel nodded, avoiding Jason's questioning look. Not waiting for her response, he left her alone to decide on appropriate dinner attire. *Would a fresh outfit do the trick? Or should I pull out one of my fancier dresses to satisfy his mother?* Isobel sat on the bed pondering her dilemma, helpless and saddened at the cool reception. *Will she even notice what I wear? She tried her best not to see me…* Tears welled up and finally the dam broke; she gave in to her disappointment. She threw herself onto the plush bed, hiding her tears in the fluffy pillows, hoping to muffle her cries of sorrow from the rest of the household.

Once she cried herself out, Isobel washed her face and tried to refresh her makeup, hiding the evidence of her tears. Although, she normally needed little makeup to enhance her exotic beauty, today she used face powder to cover her reddened nose and cover-up for the circles under her eyes. Unfortunately, she couldn't hide the bloodshot appearance of her eyes. Gazing at her reflection, she wished for blond hair and for round or oval blue eyes instead of her distinctive almond-shaped brown eyes. *Maybe then I would have passed muster with Jason's folks.* She thought wryly.

She took her time dressing, but still had at least 30 minutes before she needed to be in the dining-room. *Postpone the inevitable,* Isobel decided, carefully sitting on the edge of the chair in the corner so as to not wrinkle her outfit. At 5:55pm, with one last glance into the mirror, and satisfied her efforts, Isobel opened the bedroom door. She glanced to the left and then the right. She didn't see Jason, and didn't know which room was his, so she hesitantly made her way toward the stairs. Loud voices echoed upward from the main floor, drawing her in that direction. The closer she got, the louder and angrier the voices. *Mrs. Armstrong really sounds mad!*

Then Isobel heard her name. She held back, not wanting to intrude, yet wishing she could see what was happening in the library. When she saw Jason approaching from the direction of the kitchen, she tucked herself in closer to the stairwell. He opened the library door, and the words and voices became more distinct, clearer.

"*Isobel*! Why, even her name sounds foreign! James, what on earth could be going through that boy's head?" Mrs. Armstrong paced around the desk in the library. "How could he bring home that… that…that *Italian* or *Mexican*, or whatever she is?" She emphasized each ethnicity with scorn. Her eyes flaming, she stopped in front of the desk. She looked at her husband who sat calmly in his easy chair with his fingers tented under his chin. "She's definitely NOT American, I can tell you that much…!" shaking her finger at his expressionless face.

"Now, Catherine..." James kept his voice even-toned trying to soothe his wife, but she reacted with more anger.

"Don't 'now, Catherine' me!" she stopped beside his chair. "I demand you do something about this -- this *travesty*!"

"Catherine, it isn't all that troubling. Think calmly for just one minute. How long has he dated this girl? Two years, right? And when do they think they will get married? ...surely not until he finishes medical school. So we have four years to work on this problem."

"No, James, we need to do something now! They *have* been dating two years! That is two years too long, and the longer it is allowed, the worse it gets. We *cannot* have our good name sullied in the rumor mill and smeared all over the society page because of some *POOR immigrant* girl!" She said 'poor' as if it were a dirty word and 'immigrant' as if she were cursing. "We need to nip this thing in the bud!"

Just as she finished her tirade, she heard a sound from the doorway and turned to see Jason entering the room. He looked from one parent to the other and said nothing for a moment.

"Jason, son," his father started to speak to break the oppressive silence, but Jason held up a hand to stop him.

"No, *Dad*," he'd never called his father by the casual moniker and it sounded disrespectful, even sarcastic. "Don't patronize me with explanations. I heard enough to know... oh, and *Mom's* behavior at the airport?" Again, his use of an informal nickname displayed his scorn. "Yeah... *I think I get it*."

As Jason spun on his heel to leave the library, Isobel's eyes met his. She stood helplessly on the stairs. Her red-rimmed eyes spoke volumes, but the slump of her shoulders revealed even more. She had seen and heard the entire tirade, feeling Mrs. Armstrong's contempt. Isobel also took in Dr. Armstrong's passive agreement with his wife's position.

Isobel didn't know if to run back up the stairs or out the door. She just knew she wasn't wanted in this home, and she wouldn't stay where she wasn't welcome. The sadness in Jason's eyes restrained her from choosing. She knew he loved her and, despite his parent's attitudes, he wanted to marry her. As he moved toward her with his hands outstretched, she backed away, just a step.

"Izzie, please, don't..."

"Don't what, Jason? Don't get upset? This might have been avoided if you had told them sooner... *or* if you'd told me how *prejudiced* they are!" she looked pointedly over his shoulder at the Armstrongs, but saw no remorse in their expressions. Looking back at him, she softened her voice, "I got the message, Jason. They are not happy with your choice of a fiancée. So, where do we go from here?"

Helpless, Jason shrugged his shoulders, "We follow our plan, Isobel. You know how much I love..."

Just then Mrs. Armstrong came sweeping out of the den, "Enough of this drama... We have dinner waiting for us." She looked at Isobel's casual outfit, "Dear," using a condescending tone, "I did say 'we dress for dinner', did I not?" She looked meaningfully at Jason. "And where do you think this 'plan' will fit into *our* society, Jason?" She did not wait for an answer, but led the way to the dining-room where the staff had an elegant, formal dinner table laid out.

Jason took Isobel's hand and walked in silence to the dining-room with his father following on their heels. Whispering in her ear, he sought to reassure her, "Your outfit is just fine, Isobel. You are dressed just right for dinner; she just wants you to doubt yourself."

And doubt herself she did. Isobel felt like shrinking under the table instead of sitting in the chair Jason indicated was hers. As he adjusted the chair under her, Jason leaned forward to peck her cheek, as if a kiss could undo all the hurt she'd experienced in the last ten minutes. Then he circled the table and sat across from her giving her a feeble smile as he picked up his napkin and placed it in his lap.

Isobel recognized the signal and followed his example. She was surprised that they started dinner without saying grace. Despite the lack of religion in her home before Aunt Betty, over the last few years she had slipped into certain habits. Blessing a meal and reading the Word were two practices she continued through her Academy and college years. Jason, too, evidenced his faith in outward behaviors, so she assumed his parents were the source of his commitment to the Lord.

Dinner in the Armstrong home was a silent affair. *At least this dinner was,* she thought. Isobel watched as Jason kept his eyes on his plate and Dr. Armstrong buried himself in the news of the *Boston Globe* as he took bites of his meal. Mrs. Armstrong seemed oblivious to the tension at the table as she directed the staff in serving the food. Isobel couldn't wait for the ordeal to finish so she could escape to her room. She needed to think. *What do I do about his relationship with his family? It wouldn't be right to come between them… maybe we need to reconsider…?*

Chapter 3

Mrs. Armstrong signaled for the removal of the remaining dishes, and rose to leave the table. Always the perfect hostess, she saw to the minutest details; however, tonight she neglected her manners with regards to Isobel. Throughout dinner, Isobel felt invisible, totally ignored. What conversation occurred was aimed at Mr. Armstrong or Jason, and even that was minimal. Now, as she spoke to the staff, she extended more courtesy to them than she had to Isobel. Her dismissive demeanor also made it clear that she wasn't interested in after dinner socializing.

Dr. Armstrong followed her lead, as he routinely did, and headed back to his library with only a cursory excuse. The library was obviously Jason's father's haven in their stormy household. Once in his library, the family did not bother him; his sanctuary was sacrosanct, especially for the children. Jason had told Isobel that he and his cousins always spoke in hushed tones when outside the door, for fear of disturbing his father's 'work'. To Isobel, Jason was still that scared kid, afraid to disturb his father's peace.

With dinner finished, and the elder Armstrongs gone, Isobel sat with her eyes downcast, her hands clasped in her lap. She didn't speak when they left; she shrunk into her chair at the table as if unseen. She knew Jason was waiting for her cue. With no hint of what she was thinking, no clue to her hidden emotions, she quietly rose from her chair and, without a word, headed toward the stairs intent on retreating to her room.

"Izzie," Jason pleaded with her, "come walk with me in the garden…"

Isobel interrupted him with a gentle shake of her head. Soft as a whisper she replied, "I just need to be alone for now," and headed up to her deceptively beautiful guest room and the privacy of her thoughts.

Isobel found the solitude of her room strangely soothing. She could think more clearly with distance between herself and Jason's parents, if only by walls and halls. Although summer temperatures kept the evening warm, she settled into the easy chair by the window, wrapping up in the cozy quilt to ward off the cold she felt in this home.

Could she consider marrying into this family when it was obvious they would never accept her as a daughter-in-law? *How can I not marry the man I love? Then again, how can I be the cause of a rift between Jason and his parents?* Would he regret it one day, and blame her for the chasm in his family? Would he eventually need to return to his parents, leaving her broken-hearted?

Isobel knew from her days at the Academy and years in college with Christian friends, that she should pray for an answer to her dilemma, but she wasn't convinced that God would hear her. Her spiritual life was one of ritual rather than commitment. She used prayer as part of her daily routine, but didn't feel them in the same way that her friends, Taylor and Maddie, did. They talked to Jesus as if He was their best friend. She never joined the talk of Jesus, because she hadn't had a 'born again' experience. Isobel was a Christian by habit only, but right now she wished she had listened more, followed their example, and understood what they tried to share. She longed for the comfort they seemed to get from their faith; it had helped her friends through many trials, and she yearned for that kind of help, from somewhere, anywhere.

Sleep finally rescued her from her worries. Isobel sank into a fitful slumber, and woke in the chair early the next morning, still in her dinner clothes, not feeling at all rested. Her mind immediately rushed back to thoughts of Jason and his parents, but she also woke convicted with what she had to do.

With the sun barely rising in the morning sky, she quickly bathed and dressed, repacked her bags and, using the phone in her room, called for a taxi. Isobel took her bags downstairs, quietly slipping out the front door. Isobel hurried down the driveway, not looking back; she wanted to meet the taxi at the entrance rather than risk waking someone in the house with its horn or engine running.

❧

Jason did not sleep well that night, either. He wondered and worried about what Isobel was thinking. He had already made his choice between her and his parents when he asked her to marry him. He solidified that choice when inviting her home with him; however, he had not anticipated the hostile reception. He knew his parents wouldn't immediately welcome her into the family, but had hoped that once they gave her a chance, they would love her as much as he did. He never thought his mother would be outright rude and discourteous; that went against all he learned from her about 'correct behavior' in a social setting. Politeness was the foundation of appearing in control and superior in high society, and she had always been a model in that arena.

The house was still and quiet when Jason got up that morning, but the sun shined brightly through his bedroom window and he could hear the staff fixing breakfast in the kitchen below. At his window, he could smell the biscuits baking and the scent of meats and eggs wafting up from the kitchen. Hoping to head off a sour breakfast reception, Jason went to Isobel's door and knocked gently. When he got no answer, he knocked a bit harder. Hesitantly, he reached for the door-knob. He didn't want to open the door in case she wasn't up, or was in the middle of dressing.

Just then the maid came out of a side door to the guest bathroom. "Looking for the lovely miss, sir? So sorry, sir! I was just in her bath to freshen her towels, and found she's not in her room. The bed was quite nicely spread off, and a note lay on the pillow, sir."

"A note? Did you pick it up?"

"Oh, no sir, I thought I best leave it for you or your mother. I did right, didn't I?" She seemed to fear her job was in jeopardy.

Knowing that many a maid had been fired for minor infractions in the Armstrong household, Jason reassured her, "It's OK," he replied. "I will get it. I'll not tell my mother and I'd rather you said nothing, either. Go ahead with what you were doing."

The maid appeared relieved and hurried off with her armful of towels. Catherine Armstrong held tight reins on the staff, and expected no less than perfection. Jason knew that she would have preferred the maid bring the note to her, rather than letting Jason see it first.

Dreading what he would read in her note, Jason picked up the single sheet of paper. His heart dropped to the pit of his stomach as he opened the paper, anticipating the worst:

Dearest Jason,

I'm so sorry. I never meant to be a wedge between you and your parents. I love you so much and just want you to be happy. I am afraid that you won't be if we get married. Please forgive me for leaving without saying good-bye, but I know you would try to talk me out of leaving, or worse still, you would leave with me and hate me later for making you choose between me and your parents. I don't know where I am going or what I plan to do, since our plans were all I had, but don't worry about me. Go on to medical school and make your parents proud. I know you will make a wonderful, caring doctor. I will be OK, although I will miss you, and will always love you. Be happy. My heart is forever yours.

Izzie

Jason's heart sank as he read her tear-stained note, knowing how hard it had been for her to write it. He smiled wryly at her use of his pet name for her. Would he ever use that term of endearment again? His stomach felt sick at the realization of her departure. Emotions roiled in his heart mixing anger and resentment, and then sorrow and despair; it was hard to hold on to his Christianity in light of the revulsion he felt toward his parents. Anger at his mother's cruelty incensed Jason, and he seethed at his father's impotence to stand up to his mother.

But Jason's anger at his own ineptitude in handling the entire situation burned even hotter in his chest. *Why didn't I have the foresight to know how they would react? Or did I? Was I trying to deny the truth, postpone the inevitable? How could I lead my precious, gentle Isobel into this mess?* In his mind's eye he saw the stark contrast between the classes, more aware of the chasm than ever. He saw no point to the rigid rules of society and had hoped to break out of those constraints without alienating his family, but now saw how difficult that was going to be. He had to find Isobel and make it up to her. He had to convince her that they still had a future. *But first…* He searched out his parents, sitting on the patio for their breakfast.

"*She's gone, you know!?!*" He tried to hold back his fury, but his parents saw it in his eyes.

"Son, why don't you sit down… join us for some coffee or juice, at least." His mother did not acknowledge his statement. She acted like every other summer morning in his life – brunch on the patio and small talk to start the day.

"*Mother*, did you *hear* me? Isobel has left!"

"Really, dear? I had no idea." Her drawn out 'really' sounded phony and forced.

Looking up from his *Wall Street Journal*, Dr. Armstrong glanced at Jason over his reading glasses on the tip of his nose, "Now, Jason, surely she's just in the house somewhere…"

"No, *Dad*, she's not! She left a note! Mother was probably hoping for this, after the way she acted toward Isobel last night!" Jason knew he was on the verge of disrespect, but he didn't care. He didn't recognize himself and the anger he felt; it was as if a stranger had taken over his body.

"*Honor your father and your mother…*" The words of that command suddenly came to mind as if spoken by an Unseen Force. And just as quickly, he began to argue with God. *How could he honor his parents when they had dishonored his choice for a wife?* He wondered if God really required that of him. *Was this a test of his faith, a test of his Christianity? What was God really requiring of him? Should he give up Isobel to honor his parents?* Jason shook his head, physically trying to dismiss the urgings of the Spirit.

"Jason, just calm down. Let's talk this over. You must realize *the girl* isn't suitable marriage material..." once again, his mother's tone irritated him.

"*The girl*'s name is Isobel, *Mother*! And I *do not* see that she is unsuitable!"

"Now, son," his father cut in, "you have medical school ahead of you. Now is not a good time to consider marriage. You know this; we've spoken of this many times. Before you get seriously involved you need to finish your training. Then you'll meet a suitable spouse. Now, a little fling doesn't hurt..."

"Father! How could you suggest such a thing? You know I am a Christian! I would never disrespect a woman that way!" Jason knew he needed to leave; he had to find Isobel; he had to get out of his parent's home before he said something he would regret. He spun on his heel, went inside the house, grabbed his car keys and wallet and headed off to Logan. He had to try to stop Isobel. Maybe she hadn't found a flight yet. He expected Isobel to fly home, to her Aunt Betty, her only remaining relative.

As far as he knew, she had no other options, so he began by asking about flights to Kansas. Because of security issues, not one of the ticket agents was willing to tell him if Isobel had made a reservation or caught a flight. He didn't see her in the ticketing area, and wasn't allowed near the gates to see if she was waiting, so he picked up a phone and asked for a page.

"*Passenger Isobel Kirk, please meet your party at the Ticket Counter. Passenger Isobel Kirk, please meet your party at the Ticket Counter.*"

Jason sat down, hoping, waiting for Isobel to come walking toward him. He thought she might be waiting for his page, expecting him to follow her. Ten minutes passed, and he tried again, calling for a page.

"*Passenger Isobel Kirk, please meet your party at the Ticket Counter. Passenger Isobel Kirk, please meet your party at the Ticket Counter.*"

Unable to sit still, Jason walked up and down in front of the counter. He paced for another ten minutes, and then realized she wasn't going to answer the page, *if* she was still in the airport. He sat down and put his face into his hands. He shuddered to think of Isobel leaving forever. Just the thought of what pain she must be feeling, of the hurt his parents had inflicted on her, caused him to consider jumping on the next flight to Kansas.

One problem prevented him from doing just that. He had no idea where in Kansas her Aunt Betty lived, whether Kansas City, Topeka, Wichita, or maybe in the country. He didn't even know if her Aunt Betty shared her last name! What could he do? How could he find her Aunt Betty's phone number?

It was all so hard, so painful, and he couldn't give up. He had to find Isobel before he headed out to medical school. Despite any arguments his parents might give, he would use all his resources to find her and make it right. He wouldn't give up on their love and commitment!

Chapter 4

When the taxi put Isobel out at Logan International, she stood for a moment pondering her decision. Then, resolutely, she grabbed her bags and headed toward the airline ticket counter. Without advance notice, the flight was expensive, but she was left without a choice. Either she stayed where she wasn't welcome or she left her dreams behind to search for a new plan. The only direction she knew was back to Aunt Betty, like Dorothy in *The Wizard of Oz*, back to Kansas.

She didn't check her second bag. She headed directly to the gate; the boarding had already started when she heard a distant page in the terminal calling her to the ticket counter. "*It has to be Jason.*" Desire to return to him fought with the sorrow of leaving. She continued down the passageway, ignoring the page. Her heart raced as she searched for a seat. Holding back the threatening flood of tears, she excused herself as she bumped a passenger already seated.

A brown-skinned young man with straight black hair who looked to be about her age or slightly older sat in the aisle seat of a nearby row. With two open seats next to him, Isobel was surprised to see passengers walk by as if he was invisible. From her own experiences, Isobel recognized bigotry for what it was. She asked if the seats next to him were taken, and received the expected answer. By his features, Isobel thought he might be Hispanic, but his deep, clear voice resonated without an accent.

"No, they're open. You're welcome to sit there, if you like," and he got up to allow her access to the window seat. Isobel tried to lift her carry-on suitcase to the overhead bin, and he promptly took it from her, easily placing it into the bin. She nodded her thanks and inched into the window seat, placing her other bag under the seat in front of her. The seat between them remained open as passengers went on to other open seats.

Settling in, Isobel felt her heart return to a normal rhythm. She eased back into the seat, thinking of the flight ahead. With her seatbelt fastened, a blanket over her lap, and a pillow on which to rest her head, she was ready for the flight, but not ready for the future. Isobel prayed for sleep so she wouldn't have to make small talk with her neighbor. Unfortunately, the young man had a different idea.

"I'm K. C. Fox," he reached his hand out to shake hers.

At first she hesitated, and then she shook his hand briefly. "Casey? Like Casey up at bat?" She maintained a nonchalant, disinterested expression, hoping to discourage further conversation. She couldn't smile, even if she wanted to, and her eyes reflected her pain and reticence.

"No, K period and C period, like the initials, like the city." He smiled broadly. "My real name is kind of hard to say, so I use my initials." She nodded, and then turned her face to the pillow not offering up her name or any further conversation. Before long, the plane was in the air and she was dozing, forgetting the man next to her, instead dreaming of her lost love.

Isobel woke to the announcement from the flight attendants. *"Please fasten your seatbelt and place your tray-tables and seats in the full upright, and locked positions."* She hadn't undone her seatbelt during the flight, so she just straightened herself, neatly folding the blanket and placing it and the pillow on the seat between herself and the young man. She'd already forgotten his name, and he seemed preoccupied with a book, for which she was grateful. *At least I don't have to make small talk.* She gazed out the window watching the ground get closer and closer as the plane landed at the distant end of the runway. Isobel didn't turn from the window as they taxied toward the terminal; thinking of Jason, she had no desire to encourage conversation.

When the plane stopped at the gate and everyone rose to gather their baggage from the overhead bins, Isobel had no choice. *Great! I have to ask him to bring down my suitcase.* He stood tall enough to look into the bin without stretching and too tall to remain in front of his seat; he was already standing in the aisle. Before she could open her mouth to speak, he was reaching for her carry-on.

"There you go," he said as he placed the bag on the seat he previously occupied. He turned to get his own backpack, smiling as he turned away. "Are you changing planes, or is this your final stop?"

Again with the small talk. She tried to act as if she hadn't heard his question.

"I'm glad to be home," K. C. tried once again to engage her, looking at her for a response.

"Mm-hmm." Isobel hoped he would get the message.

"Yeah, you too, huh?"

The crowd was inching its way off the plane and he was jostled along. A kindly gentleman from the row behind hers held the line, allowing Isobel to move in behind K. C. with her bag in tow, as if he thought they were together. She acknowledged his courtesy and moved along with the other passengers. Proceeding up the gangway toward the terminal, she was deep in thought. Sensing someone ahead, she looked up to find the same guy had paused midway up the gangway to wait for her.

"Are you collecting luggage from Baggage Claim? I don't have any other stuff, but I could help you, if you do."

Trying to accept the overture as mid-Western friendliness, Isobel gave up ignoring him and decided to talk. "No, I don't have any other bags," she replied. "I travel light." And she gave him a quick smile, although it did not extend to her eyes.

"Now that's what I'm talking about. I was wondering if you'd lost your voice. And I didn't know if you could smile, either."

Isobel knew he was teasing her and tried to hide the second smile that made its way to her eyes, this time. "I'm sorry if I've been rude. I just have a lot on my mind."

"I could tell that from the sad look in your eyes. Do you feel better since you got a rest on the plane?" His kindness and concern was refreshing, and Isobel relaxed a bit as they walked side-by-side through the terminal toward Ground Transportation.

"Oh, I'll be alright in time." She let out a deep sigh which caused him to look at her more directly.

"Did you lose a loved one or something?" his rich voice softened with empathy.

"Not really, but in a way, I guess." Her answer was off-putting and this time he got the message. He walked silently and the comfortable sound of their feet along the tiled floor was calming, in a strange way. *Jason and I will never walk side by side like this, again.* All the long talks and casual walks were in their past, and from now on, she would be alone.

Isobel's eyes filled with tears and she gulped back the emotion threatening to erupt. K.C. saw her struggle; refraining from further questions, he walked in silence beside her until they reached the terminal median shelter where they were to wait for the Grey Car Rental Shuttle bus.

"Which rental car service do you use?" he asked just to make conversation without broaching a sensitive subject. When Isobel told him, he smiled. "Great minds *must* think alike... I am headed there, too." That said, K.C. once again helped Isobel get her luggage situated on the shuttle as she took her seat near the front of the bus. He sat opposite her seemingly expecting more dialog, but Isobel kept her gaze out the front window, effectively thwarting any efforts from him.

K.C. was intrigued with the sorrowful, yet beautiful young woman. There was something familiar in her bearing or features; he just couldn't figure out what it was. He wasn't sure how, but he wanted to find a way to get to know her better. She resisted his meager attempts at conversation; small talk had never been his strong point. K.C. could sense distrust and fear, yet he longed to ask her for a phone number, an email address, or some way to contact her. He thought about it all the way to the rental car agency, and as they waited to get their cars.

Could I just follow her? No, that would look too much like stalking! How could I even consider that? K.C. wondered if he was losing it. There was something about that exotic creature that touched him deep inside. She reminded him of the young women in his home community, with her long black hair and smooth brown skin. Even the curve of her nose and elliptical shape of her eyes were reminiscent of the girls he grew up around.

He was proud of his Native American birthright. If, and when, he decided to marry, he planned to take a wife from a native tradition, one who could appreciate the richness of the heritage and customs of their culture. But this woman intrigued him. She might even be part Native American, but he wasn't sure. *She is a puzzle just waiting for me to decode.* And how he loved a challenge!

Suddenly, K.C. roused from his musing and realized she was heading out to the car lot with the associate. He still had paperwork to complete before he got his car, and in dismay, he watched as she shook hands with the young man who had helped her into the Taurus she just rented.

K.C. turned back to the guy at the counter, signing and initialing the contract and finished the transaction. He took a set of keys from the board and showed him to his rental. After the usual walk-around, he shook the girl's hand and slid into the driver's seat. Then, when K.C. started the motor, he looked up and saw the beautiful young woman driving away toward I-70.

Chapter 5

"Isobel, my dear, what are you doing here?" Aunt Betty swung open the rickety screen door and embraced her niece. "You're supposed to be in Boston, meeting your future in-laws…" She pulled back and stopped short looking into Isobel's tear-filled eyes. "Oh, dear, what's happened? It can't be all that bad, now. Come, come, let's talk this through and see what we can do to fix it." *I don't remember her being so kind,* Isobel thought. She only saw the authoritarian side when she was a teenager.

Aunt Betty put her arm around Isobel's shoulder and gently brought her through the kitchen and into the living-room. Sitting on the burgundy, velvet davenport, she patted the cushion beside her, encouraging Isobel to sit down to talk. The hominess and warmth of Aunt Betty's farmhouse wrapped Isobel in love. *What a difference between this middle-American, simple home and the elegant, old-moneyed mansion I left in Boston!* The contrast was glaring to Isobel.

"Auntie, it was awful!" Between gulps and tears, Isobel told her story. "You wouldn't believe how condescending his mother was… and then, when she called me a 'poor immigrant girl' and told Jason to 'nip it in the bud', I knew I couldn't stay…they hated me!" The last phrase was awash with grief.

Isobel talked on, crying at times, hiccupping with sobs as Aunt Betty patted her hand and allowed her to grieve her lost love. Betty didn't have a lot to say at first. She knew Isobel just needed to share her sorrow and vent her frustrations about the imaginary lines of social class and financial status that had come between her and her beloved Jason.

When she sensed Isobel was running out of steam, she knew it was her opportunity to share and commiserate. "I just want to show you why I never married," Aunt Betty said as she pulled out old photo albums with black and white pictures mounted with tiny triangle corners on crumbling black paper pages. Isobel always knew it wasn't due to her aunt's appearance. Aunt Betty's youthful photos showed an elegant, beautiful woman, obviously high-spirited and fun-loving. There were pictures of her enjoying the fellowship of her youth group at church, and others of Betty and her girlfriends out for picnics or frolics.

Isobel saw several pictures of one particular young soldier. Of all her friends, he was the only non-white – he appeared to be Native American. She had seen these same pictures a long time ago, but never put two and two together. Now, on her own, Aunt Betty shared her personal experience of lost love. In a time when interracial relationships were frowned on, Aunt Betty had fallen in love with a boy from a nearby reservation.

"Tommy Running Bear… I truly loved him," Aunt Betty's eyes twinkled with moisture, "and we planned to be married in Hawaii on his R & R. I never expected to get that call, the one where they told me he had been injured just days after arriving in Viet Nam. He was in a military hospital, unconscious and missing his legs. He had stepped on a land mine in an attempt to save a child walking through a mine field." She paused for a long moment, and then continued, "He never came out of the coma, and for that I am grateful, because I know he would have hated to live in that condition. But the worst part was the reaction of his family, when I arrived at the hospital." Her voice was thick with emotion.

Isobel wondered if her aunt would continue the story. She touched Aunt Betty's hand, "It's OK, Auntie. You don't have to tell me anything else."

"No, dearie, I must, because then you will know that I do understand what you've been through." She twisted the handkerchief she had pulled from under the cuff of her dress sleeve. "His parents told me I had no place at his bedside. They didn't want me there, and they stayed with him most of the time. The only time I could visit was when I knew they had returned to their hotel. But I stayed beside him as much as I could, every opportunity. And God was gracious to allow me to be there when he passed. They weren't able to take that from me."

Now Isobel was tearing up. She could only imagine a youthful Betty Kirk holding the hand of her beloved as he breathed his last breath. As painful as it was to hear the story, how much more so it must have been for her aunt to experience that loss. She reached out to her aunt and the two cried in each other's arms, one for a distant loss and the other for her recent rejection.

Suddenly Aunt Betty pulled back and reached for Isobel's hand, "Come now! Just look at the two of us. Blubbering away like some silly ninnies. Let's go to the kitchen. I'll make us some hot chocolate and I have some of your favorite cheesecake in the fridge. We need some cheering up!" She tugged Isobel to her feet and hand in hand they went to the bright yellow kitchen with its black and white checkerboard floor. With the 1950's styled metal dinette set, with its speckled gray, vinyl seats and chair backs, and its shiny, black laminate table surface, it harked back to an era of simplicity and strength.

Isobel always loved this kitchen; to her it was the heart of Aunt Betty's home. It was where she spent the most time grieving the loss of her father, while Aunt Betty fixed some delicious treat meant to chase away the blues. It was her aunt's way, to feed the spirit with high calorie foods and rich chocolate drink topped with whipped cream or marshmallows. Isobel always marveled that she didn't gain a hundred pounds during that first year after losing her daddy.

This is good! I made the right choice coming back to Aunt Betty's. Realizing how estranged they had become, especially during her difficult teen years, Isobel now looked forward to closing that gap with her aunt, now as one adult to another. The evening yielded up previously unspoken secrets, and she knew Aunt Betty would share even more, given half a chance. She didn't know what her future held, but she slept well that night, determined to be strong and proud of her heritage, not ashamed the way she'd felt after Jason's mother's hurtful words and behavior.

❧

Jason did everything he could to find Isobel. Contacting friends from school wasn't easy. The dorms were emptied of all residents since graduation. He did manage to locate several from their group, but not one had any idea where Isobel might be. Isobel had never talked to them about her family, and had always stayed on campus during breaks.

Finally, realizing that was a dead-end, he started trying to find the elusive Aunt Betty. He began with the Internet, searching for Betty Kirk in Kansas, and found eight women with the last name of Kirk. Some were named Betty and a few of them were named Elisabeth, but might have used Betty as a nickname. Not knowing where she lived, Jason decided to start calling down the list until he found the right one...

"Yes, ma'am, I understand. Sorry to have bothered you…" Jason felt foolish being chastised by yet another elderly matron, for calling her home. It was his sixth call to Kansas, and each time he had received a similar response. He had tried to explain his mission, but it seemed farmer's wives and stoic mid-westerners were unsympathetic to his pleas. *In this day of telemarketers, nobody trusted strangers calling, especially asking personal questions…* If only he could get past their natural suspicions. He knew that, in general, a story of unrequited love touched the heart of elderly women like none other.

Dialing the seventh of the eight numbers, Jason was disheartened and weary, but unwilling to give up. He had to find Isobel. He was jarred from his thoughts when the ring was abruptly interrupted by another older female voice.

"Hello? Hello…uh, hi… my name is Jason Armstrong, and I am trying to locate a Betty Kirk with a niece named Isobel. Please,

please don't hang up..." and then Jason realized that she was still listening; she hadn't hung up!

With her hand covering the mouthpiece on her phone, Aunt Betty turned to Isobel sitting at the breakfast table. "It's him!" she whispered. Isobel's hand stopped in midair with her mug trembling until she replaced it on the table, spilling hot chocolate on the way down. She shook her head and mouthed the single word, "NO!"

"Dear, you need to speak with him. After all, he loves you! He must have wondered when you just ran off."

Hesitating only a second longer, Isobel slowly pushed her chair back from the table. She stood just as slowly and walked to where Aunt Betty was still holding the phone with the receiver muffled against her chest. Isobel reached for the phone and smiled grimly at her elderly aunt.

"Yes...hello?" Isobel spoke softly, resisting the urge to start telling Jason how much she missed him. She longed to speak and hear the words of love they had so recently shared. *Was it really just two days ago?*

"Izzie! Oh, Izzie, I thought I'd never find you! I've been calling all over trying to find your Aunt Betty, hoping you were there. Honey, why did you leave me? You know I love you? Why, Izzie, why?" Finally, Jason paused, taking a deep breath.

"Jason, you know why." Isobel spoke quietly, yet firmly. "I don't want to come between you and your family, your parents."

"You know I don't care what they think..."

"Jason, stop. I know you love me, I do! But think about it..." she paused briefly, took a deep breath and continued, "You love them; they are your parents. And you need your parents help to become a doctor. It's your dream, and I don't want to be the reason you don't reach that."

"Isobel, can I come there so we can talk in person? It's just too hard to talk on the phone..."

"No, Jason. I need time and space. For now, let's agree to stay in touch, to be friends. Go on to medical school and do your best. I'll find something to do and, God willing, we can see each other from time to time. But I need to think about our relationship. I need to find a goal of my own, so your parents won't think I am just after your money or status. I just need time!"

Now Isobel's voice rose in a crescendo, trying desperately to convince Jason that she was truly saying what she wanted, even though it felt like a lie. She wanted nothing more than to be with him, to feel his arms around her, comforting her, but she needed to persuade him to give her room to think. Evidently, she convinced him, because Jason finally agreed to her request. She gave in a little, when he asked if he could still call, '*just to talk*'.

Once off the phone, Isobel felt her knees weaken and Aunt Betty guided a chair under her so she could sit down. Grief-stricken, she looked up at her aunt with tears sparkling in her gentle brown eyes. "I did it, Auntie, and I think he understands." Then the dam holding back her tears gave way and she wept as Aunt Betty held her, patting her back, whispering words of comfort.

Chapter 6

K.C. couldn't get his mind off the beautiful young lady he had met on the plane. His thoughts wandered back to the brief conversation with the young woman as he drove the four hours to Macy, Nebraska. He loved the openness of the plains and listening to the local Christian programming on his radio as he drove. Usually, the music and drive let him meditate on his way home, but today was different.

The pain and sorrow in her eyes still haunted K.C., and he breathed a prayer for her as he remembered those hypnotic brown eyes. He wondered if their paths would ever cross again and wished he had at least gotten her name. K.C. shook his head. '*Why can't I get her out of my mind? It was just a chance meeting. I know nothing about her, not even where she was headed or if she's married!*' He thought, '*I can't get distracted at this stage in my career.*'

He was on the verge of launching his professional life as a lawyer. He still had his bar exam to pass, so decided to spend time on the reservation with his family while he prepared for the test. He felt confident he would be offered a position once he was through that process, although he did wonder if his ethnicity would factor into whether or not they choose him. Sometimes he wished the affirmative action laws were not in place; then he would know he was chosen for his abilities alone.

Heading home felt good. Renewing his bonds with the people he grew up around and getting in touch with his roots always felt right. He needed to remind himself of his goals and the plans he had to help others along the way. His visit might be short so he needed to make the most of the few weeks ahead. K.C.'s visits usually entailed helping a tribal member with some legal issue or helping his mother around the house. Mrs. Fox relied on her only son more and more as he matured and as she aged.

Growing up on the Omaha Reservation in northeastern Nebraska, K.C. was well aware of his mixed tribal heritage of Lakota, Apache, and Omaha. K.C.'s full name, Kwsind CrowDog Fox, reflected that legacy, but K.C. recognized the need to fit in when not on the 'rez', which was why he used his initials. He beat the negative expectations for kids on the rez and finished high school as valedictorian of his class, which earned him a scholarship for college. K.C. supplemented that by working at various on-campus jobs to earn money for clothes and other personal needs. K.C. was determined to succeed for the sake of his family and for the honor of his people.

School holidays and spring breaks were spent on the reservation, not off in Cabo San Lucas or Miami with his friends and classmates. K.C. took his responsibilities as man of the house seriously, responding to family emergencies and being available to counsel his sisters when they were in trouble. Unfortunately, try as he did, he couldn't stop them from getting pregnant or getting into drugs.

As firstborn, K.C. set the tone for his sisters. His moral fiber, built through his mother's faith and guidance, never faltered, even in his youth when so many on the 'rez' went astray. Sometimes this strength of character placed him at odds with his peers on the reservation, but he was steadfast throughout his school years and on into college. Someday, he hoped to provide better for his mother, whether on or off the reservation.

It wouldn't be easy to convince her to leave their home in Macy. She still felt responsible for Skyla, Talitha, and Shyne. The older two lived on their own and depended on their annual allotment from the tribe and welfare for income; each had a couple of children under school-age. Meanwhile, his mother still had Shyne and her baby living at home.

One of K.C.'s ultimate goals in practicing law was to help improve life for the youth on the reservation. With alcohol and drugs, early pregnancies and early deaths from risky lifestyles or poor health, he knew more could be done. He wanted to work toward changing the laws that put kids in jails instead of offering them rehabilitation and education. But before he could pursue that objective he needed to establish himself in the legal community, actually practice of law, and find the best way to make change happen.

K.C. saw his exit just ahead and began signaling. As expected, Macy hadn't changed since his last visit. He drove another 30 miles, beyond the town limits, turned down a rarely traveled dirt road, overgrown with weeds and wild grasses. Like a homing pigeon, he knew where to turn, but a stranger might have missed the barely visible tire ruts leading through the fields to his mother's home.

K.C. expected to see his mother sitting on the porch, in the old bentwood chair his grandfather had made many years before, but she was already on her feet, having seen the dust cloud created by his car. Wiping her hands on her apron, he noticed how much smaller she appeared; her back curving more with each visit home. She took off her glasses and cleaned them with the corner of her apron, then dabbed at her eyes as she realized that it was K.C. coming home.

"Kwsind. Kwsind." She said his name almost as if breathing a prayer. "You've made it home, again!" Mrs. Fox stepped gingerly down the twisted board steps, warped from weather exposure, holding a rail that shook as she leaned on it for support.

"I need to fix that before she falls," K.C. thought. *"Wow, the house could use paint, too..."* He glanced around at the unkempt yard before he bent down to give his mother a hug. Again her fragile frame caught his attention. Her hair had more gray than black, too, aging her beyond her years.

"Ma," he said her name like a goat bleating it greeting, "Have you not been eating well? You've lost more weight."

Mrs. Fox laughed and patted his arm, moving away as if embarrassed at his observation. "You always say that. I'm doin' jes' fine, now, don't you worry."

Movement by the curtain at the open window caught his eye. Then the door opened and Shyne came out with her little boy sitting on her hip. "*She is so tiny. She looks like she should be playing with dolls, not holding her own baby.*"

"Hey, sis, how's it going," K.C. affected a casual attitude. Talking to Shyne was like walking on eggshells; she took everything as criticism.

"Fine," her short reply was meant to put him off.

Shyne hates when I show up. She used to brag about my accomplishments, and planned to go to college just like I did. Like K.C., Shyne was quite smart, but her dreams came to a screeching halt when she decided she was old enough to have a boyfriend. …when she decided she was in love. …when she became pregnant. And when the boyfriend took off to join the army to avoid fatherhood. All her dreams died back then, and every time K.C. visited, he reminded her of dashed hopes.

Shyne looked up at her handsome, older brother with glistening eyes.

Lifting the baby from her arms, K.C. caught a whiff of ammonia that took his breath away. "Now what's this little guy's name?" He reached out to put his free arm around his mother's shoulder and nodded to Shyne to join them in the house.

"He is called, 'Tadi Hotah', but I just call him Tad or Taddy." Shyne looked at her brother for approval and reached for the baby so she could change his diaper.

"I like that. 'Wind' sounds like freedom and 'White' because…?" K.C. raised his eyebrows in question, as he smiled his approval at his little sister.

"You know…his father…" Shyne's voice dropped off.

To ease her discomfort, K.C. feigned distraction and raised his nose in appreciation of the fragrance of stew cooking. "Ma, you always got a hot pot on when I come home!" Food in the pot was one constant he could count on, no matter what else was going on.

K.C. enjoyed the warm meal and after cleaning up for his mother, he joined Shyne and Mother on the porch, taking his seat on the rough-hewn boards near Ma's rocker. He watched as Shyne stood at the other end of the porch, trying to get her little one to sleep with a bottle in his mouth. *Why don't the girls nurse their babies and save the money spent on formula*? He thought.

"Hey, Shyne, is Taddy growing OK? Have you been taking him for check-ups?"

Shyne appeared annoyed at his question. "Why take him to the clinic if he ain't sick?" She jiggled the baby as she rocked him, trying to hurry him to sleep, but it wasn't working. He rubbed at his eyes and struggled in her arms. "Come on, now! Just settle down, wontcha?"

Hearing the impatience in her voice, he offered to take little Tad and Shyne eagerly relinquished the baby, sitting down on the step nearby. She was more herself when not caring for the baby; having a baby was harder than she expected. *I wish I could ease her burden.* K.C. pondered as he rocked his nephew to sleep. *But this was a journey she has to make on her own. Motherhood isn't a job; it's a lifetime commitment.*

Wishing he could share the love of Jesus in words, for now, K.C. could only be His ambassador, showing her the unconditional love he knew from the Lord. Only Jesus could truly lift her burden, and only He knew how to reach her heart.

Chapter 7

Isobel awoke with a start! *What woke me up?* She listened intently. All she heard were the soft, puffing snores coming from her aunt's bedroom. *This old house creaks and groans so much…that must be it!* She felt wide awake even though the clock said 2:00am. Isobel got out of her warm bed and went to the kitchen for a glass of water. Looking out the window over the sink, she saw an image, maybe just a shadow, dart across the yard toward one of the outbuildings.

She tried to clear her vision, rubbing her eyes, and tried to focus on the barn door. Nothing moved. *Maybe I'm seeing things…* she shook her head, placed the glass on the counter beside the sink, and turned to go back to her room. Then, in her peripheral vision, she saw the barn door swing open, and she spun around toward the window. Her heart raced; nothing moved. Isobel stared as hard as she could toward the barn.

A barn swallow whipped low from the window below the rafters of the barn's roof accompanied by several bats. Isobel took a deep gasp; she had been holding her breath without even realizing it! *Just the usual creatures!* She thought. *The wind must've grabbed the door.* Suddenly she felt silly and chilled.

She went back to the bedroom and climbed between the now cool sheets and shivered. Pulling her knees up to fetal position, Isobel tried to get warm again. Despite her fatigue, Isobel couldn't shut of her thoughts. A thousand thoughts kept chasing each other through the recesses of her brain…Jason's phone call at the forefront. Once again, tears threatened, but she fought them back. *Somehow, I need to move on with my life. I need to find a new path…*

Finally the weariness took over, and she fell into a fitful sleep. The pillows weren't right; she punched at them. The blankets wouldn't cooperate, either. Isobel's body moved from one side of the bed to another, dragging the blankets along, and then pulling them over her to the other side.

By morning, she woke nearly as tired as she'd been the night before. The rays of sun sneaked between the yellowed venetian blinds at the window, heralding a bright, beautiful day. Isobel didn't feel it. In her chest was a weight of grief and anxiety. It was as close to the physical pain of a heart attack as she could imagine. She sat on the edge of the bed with her head in her hands. Tears of fatigue flowed like a release valve, easing the pressure in her chest, but bruising her eyes and face with their salty burn.

When Isobel finally got up and looked in the bathroom mirror, her eyes were puffy and her face red and blotchy. She took a washcloth and wetted it with the coolest water from the tap and dabbed at her face. She put it under the faucet again, this time folding it several times as the icy stream washed over it. She laid it gently onto her eyes. The soothing chill eased the puffiness of her eyes as she repeated the process over and over.

She cleaned up and, following the smell of fresh-brewed coffee, joined Aunt Betty in the kitchen. "Good morning, Auntie."

"Isobel, my dear. Are you doing better this morning? Did you sleep well?"

Her aunt's genuine concern warmed her heart. "I'm doing alright, but…"

Aunt Betty's eyebrows lifted, like question marks, in Isobel's direction, "What is it, dear?"

"I woke during the night and came out for a glass of water, and… I thought someone was out by the barn."

"I've been fooled by shadows and noises on this old farm many times!" Betty Kirk chuckled.

Isobel relaxed a bit, though she wasn't fully convinced. "I did see some birds fly out of the barn, and the door swinging in the wind…"

"You see? It's nothing! It will take you a while to get used to this open country living, I imagine."

Isobel gave her frail, elderly aunt a warm hug and sat down at the table to more food than she usually ate for breakfast. She was surprised to find she had an equally large appetite this morning. She loved her aunt's cooking. *I need to help around the house, too, to ease Auntie's burden.* She cleared the table and sent her aunt to sit down while she took care of the dishes.

A knock on the door interrupted her work. She opened the door surprised to see an elderly gentleman at the door.

"Fitz, you old dog, come on in," Aunt Betty spoke behind Isobel, inviting him to sit at the kitchen table.

"What happened to your car?" his question took Isobel by surprise.

"What do you mean?" she looked at his face, noting the concern in his eyes, she headed toward the door.

"I just drove up to check on Betty, and saw it sitting out there…"

All four tires on her car were flat! "What on earth?? It was fine when I parked it yesterday!"

"Are you sure you didn't drive through some glass or nails or something?"

Isobel shook her head, still staring in shock at the damaged tires.

Betty Kirk drew her inside and closed the door. She introduced Dr. Cameron Fitz-Randolph, the country doctor serving their community, and Isobel realized he spoke of concern

"Dr. Fitz, I did see something during the night." Isobel went on to tell him, as she had told her aunt, about the noises and shadows she'd witnessed. "Who would want to damage my car? I haven't even been here long enough to make enemies!" *Was it a just prank or…?* Isobel couldn't let her imagination head down that road.

Dr. Fitz urged Isobel to call the Sheriff's office and waited with them until Sheriff Jones arrived and then he headed back to town. Sheriff Jones walked around the barn and other outbuildings to see if anything else was out of place. He spent a long time in the barn and stopped beside her car, then leaned down and picked up what appeared to be a tool.

Looks like a screwdriver, Isobel thought. She saw him kick at the tires, and stop to look around, almost like a hound smelling the air for a scent. Sheriff Jones moved out view as he walked to some of the other outbuildings. After about twenty minutes, he knocked at the back door.

"What is that, Sheriff Jones?" Isobel invited him inside.

He placed the items on the table. "Well," he drawled, "this here tool is what poked the holes in your tires…" he held up an ice-pick.

"Who would want to do this?" Isobel dropped into the chair behind her. "…and why?"

"Don't rightly know, miss. Ain't got an answer for you on that, but I aim to keep lookin' into this." He paused for a moment, and then he pointed to another item on the table. "This here is a broken stick from out behind the barn. There were several others all the way of the back pasture. Made like a path through the bushes. Guess that's where they came in, whoever they were." He looked at Aunt Betty with a question in his eyes. "Betty, anybody been bothering you lately?"

Aunt Betty took her time answering. She busied herself at the stove, pouring him a cup of coffee and cutting a generous slice of coffee cake for him. "Now, Sheriff, you know how it is around these parts. Kids like to play pranks, you know… There just isn't enough to keep young folk busy these days." Her evasiveness was obvious to Isobel and she wondered if the Sheriff picked up on it, too.

Sheriff Jones nodded and chatted for a few minutes while enjoying his coffee and cake, and then, as he rose to leave, he instructed both Aunt Betty and Isobel to keep their eyes open. He needed to find the trouble-makers and hold them responsible for the damage to Isobel's rental car, but he was also concerned they might do something even worse the next time.

Isobel nodded and escorted Sheriff Jones out to his car. It was then that she saw her rental close up. Her shoulders drooped with the weight of thinking someone hated her that much. *But whoever did this might not even know me or Aunt Betty.* The tires been punctured as Sheriff Jones said, but someone had also keyed the sides of her car. Three long scrapes on each side.

Isobel watched the cloud behind the Sheriff's car get smaller and turned back to the house to call the car rental agency. While on hold waiting to speak to a human after going thru several computer prompts, she thought of Aunt Betty's vague answer to the Sheriff's questions. *If she's had other strange things happen and not said anything…* Once again, Isobel was glad she had come to live with her aunt.

Life settled into a routine at Aunt Betty's. Isobel enjoyed reconnecting and getting to know her aunt better. Aunt Betty welcomed her presence in the home and seemed at peace with the arrangement. There was no talk of Isobel finding work or leaving; finally, Isobel felt loved and needed. Days and weeks turned into months, the seasons changed, and Isobel grew to love Aunt Betty more and more as one year melded into the next.

Isobel thought often about Jason; he called about once a week '*just to talk*', and she enjoyed those conversations. But she had not wavered in her decision to not marry him, at least not yet. She, and he, both needed time to work out the pain that caused their split and their family issues. He needed to mend his relationship with his parents, and she had a growing love for her aunt to nurture.

Her aunt often shared childhood memories with Isobel. She talked of growing up with Isobel's father, some of the mischief they got into, as well as school days and the challenges of growing up in such a rural setting. Farm life had built both strength of character and physical stamina in the Kirk children that helped them as they navigated their youth into adulthood. Through Aunt Betty's stories, Isobel came to understand her father differently than she had as a child. He became somewhat of a hero through Aunt Betty's descriptions of the times he stood up for her, and when she talked of his military service.

Chapter 8

K.C. found being at home both restful and frustrating. He slept well in the familiar surroundings of his tiny bedroom. His old trophies still sat on the bookcase, and academic awards papered the wall above the bed. His quilt – gifted to him from his grandmother on the occasion of his birth – still covered the single bed. His well-worn, straight-backed chair sat in front of the small desk. Although somewhat musty from lack of use, the room welcomed him, allowing him to relax and find a measure of peace.

Every morning he got up just as the sun rose over the horizon, to begin the day with his family. This morning Ma was already up with her bed neatly made. As he passed the bedroom used by Shyne and Tad, he noticed she still slept while Tad played in the playpen she used for his bed. His diaper was soiled and soaked; the odor emanated from the room. *I'd sure like to clean him up, but Shyne is so sensitive about her mothering skills.*

He walked on down the hallway to the front room where he found Ma seated with her Bible open on her lap. Her eyes were closed. *Is she dozing?* Then he saw her lips moved ever so slightly as she breathed a prayer. He sat down, quietly waiting to join her worship time. She looked up from her meditation and smiled seeing her eldest sitting nearby.

"Kwsind, how nice…."

Before she could finish her sentence, they heard the noise of a truck driving up to the house. The motor was loud, sounding like it had no muffler, and they looked out to see a barely drivable truck. Its paint was sun-bleach and the back end was a homemade contraption of wood and metal to allow hauling of large loads. With loose, dent-hammered bumpers, it looked like only the rust was holding it together.

K.C. and Ma moved to the front door to greet the visitor only to realize it was his second sister.

“Hey, Ma!” Skyla jumped out of the passenger side in a pair of tight, cut-off jeans with faded and worn areas over the thighs and buttocks. Her top was also too tight, for obvious reasons. Driving the truck was an older guy, about thirty-five, with scruff on his chin and colorful tattoos covering his one visible arm. He spat dark brown juice from chewing tobacco out the window and sneered at their questioning looks.

“Hi, Sky,” K.C. spoke first, and she looked at him suspiciously.

“Uh, yeah, K. What you doin’ here? Thought you had some big time lawyer job off in the world somewhere…”

“Skyla, girl, come give your mother a hug,” Mother stepped off the porch toward Skyla, but she only allowed a sideways hug from her mother before pulling away. “You know your brother comes home to help us whenever he can.”

“Yeah, my brother, the big-shot. He couldn’t wait to leave the rez, and all of us, behind!” The scorn in her voice gave away more than her facial expression. She quickly changed the subject.

“Ma, I got a problem and I need some help,” she started, and then stopped short, not wanting to talk in front of K.C. “Kin we talk inside… away from…” she jerked her thumb in K.C.’s direction.

“Anything that needs saying can be said in front of me, sis. Ma probably can’t do much to help anyway, but I might be able to.” K.C. watched in silence, always suspicious when one of his sisters showed up unannounced and spoke of a ‘problem’. It usually involved money, which his mother did not have to spare.

“Yeah, right, the guardian angel! The man with the solution! I am so tired of your holier-than-thou attitude every time you show up! I just need to talk to Ma!" By now Skyla's voice raised several levels and had wakened Shyne who came out carrying little Tad with his diaper still smelly and soiled.

"Hey, little man! You stink! Shyne, why don't you change that boy before you come out here?" Skyla pinched her nose in disgust. Shyne pushed out her lower lip in defiance and stood up straight to look her sister in the eye. "I'll change him when I am good and ready! He is *MY* child, not yours!" and then she marched into the house to get away from her big sister.

Self-satisfied, Skyla turned once again to her mother. She took her mother's upper arm and leaned in, "Ma, I *really* need to talk to you... *in private*!" She looked pointedly at K.C. as if she wanted him to leave, too. *Here she goes, asking Ma for money, again!* Skyla pulled her mother to the other side of the front porch and whispered to her.

"Ma, I'm in a bad spot and I need some cash...*fast!*"

"Now, Sky, what trouble are you in this time? And who is the man in the truck?"

The man in the truck said nothing and made no movement to get out; he watched the family interaction with a smirk of amusement, tapping his fingers on the steering wheel impatiently, waiting for Skyla to finish her business.

"Don't worry 'bout him, Ma. He's just a friend..."

"He looks too old to be your friend, dear. Is he partly the reason you need money?"

"Come on, Ma, no more questions...just give me some cash. I gotta get goin'. He's waiting for me."

Mother looked over Skyla's shoulder toward K.C. and raised her eyebrows, pleading for help. She had trouble saying 'No' to her girls. Unfortunately, she helped them out of the trouble so often; it was now a vicious circle.

"How much do you need?" K.C. asked as he walked over to them.

Skyla scowled at him. She preferred to deal with her mother because she hated how guilty she felt around K.C. It was like looking in a mirror and seeing an ugly reflection, and she didn't understand why she felt like that around him. *Life was just fine when he wasn't around!*

"I need five hundred." There, she said it.

"What on earth could you need that much money for?"

"I just need it, OK? I made a bad investment and lost the money..." she tried to sound like a businesswoman, but the attempt fell short.

"Investment?" K.C. scoffed. "More like you had some drugs to sell and used them instead, and now you owe your dealer..."

"Yeah, whatever! I just need the cash, *now*, Ma!" Skyla turned back to her mother, who held her head down in shame.

K.C. hated seeing his mother's pain. He pulled out his wallet and a wad of bills. "That should be enough. Now, don't come back bothering Ma for money. She doesn't have it!" K.C. took Skyla's elbow and steered her toward the truck.

Speaking in the direction of the driver of the truck, K.C. warned, "And whoever you are, you better not get my sister into more trouble!"

The man displayed his yellowed, broken teeth in a broad grin, but still said nothing. He revved the engine with a loud rumble and a cloud of black exhaust. Once Skyla was inside, he reversed the truck so fast K.C. thought he would lose control, and then he spun it around in a circle and sped down the rutted path to the road, bouncing and jerking all the way.

K.C. turned back to his mother and saw her dabbing her apron at her eyes. "Ma, it isn't your fault..."

"Kwsind, I only wanted the best for my girls and you. I don't know what I did to make Talitha and Skyla stray so far from God."

"Ma, sometimes kids just have to test the waters, try the forbidden fruit. Look at Adam and Eve. They walked with a perfect God and yet they disobeyed." He put his arm around his mother's shoulder and guided her into the house and back to her Bible. "Let's pray for them and leave them in God's hands now." K.C. sat beside his mother, clasped her hands in his larger, firm grasp and began to pray. Together they implored the Lord to watch over Talitha and Skyla and to be with Shyne as she seemed to be heading in the same direction. They prayed for protection to encircle Shyne and Tad to keep them from the temptations on the rez.

❧

Shyne overheard them praying as she stood in the hallway with Tad on her hip. She had bathed him and dressed him in a clean diaper and T-shirt and cleaned herself up, too. She was glad that Skyla left. Her older sisters scared her; they could be angry one minute and laughing the next. Or they just acted weird altogether, and that was even worse.

Now, hearing her mother and brother praying for her touched a tender spot in her heart. She tried to play tough, but inside she hurt deeply. The poor choices she made along the way had forever changed the direction she hoped for in life. Watching K.C. go off to college had inspired her to strive for good grades, too. She wished she could have continued in school, but pregnancy put a stop to her education. Now she had a child to care for and she doubted she would ever go back to school.

❧

K.C. and Mother finished their prayers and looked up to see Shyne coming into the room. Her eyes looked moist; her face appeared softened, gentle.

"Hi, little sis. Can I hold my nephew?" He reached to take Tad from her and she gladly released the baby into his uncle's arms.

Shyne sat next to K.C. and looked timidly at Mother's Bible. "I remember us doing worship each morning before catching the school-bus." She looked at Ma. "Maybe I could join you sometime, Ma?"

Ma smiled broadly, her brown eyes glowing for the first time since K.C. arrived home. "I would welcome you into my prayer garden." Shyne reached over and embraced her mother warmly, and Ma nodded to K.C. over Shyne's shoulder and tucked her face into the curve of Shyne's neck, snuggling her little girl again.

Later in the day, as K.C. worked on some of the projects around the house, and while Tad napped, Shyne offered to help K.C. She was curious about life off the rez; she left the reservation only once - to visit Henry Doorly Zoo for a school field trip. She plied K.C. with questions, and he could see why she did well in school. She had a thirst for knowledge that was only briefly quenched. He wanted so much for this young woman, and breathed a prayer of thanks to God for working on her heart.

Life gradually became routine and after doing various tasks and errands each day, K.C. used evenings to study in preparation for the bar exam. He still didn't know in which state he would test. He thought about taking the bar in Nebraska and practicing at some small town lawyer's office rather than a large law firm. Despite his Harvard degree and excellent grades, it might be the better choice, given the challenges Ma faced in dealing with Skyla and Talitha.

Chapter 9

Aunt Betty took daily afternoon naps, leaving Isobel opportunities to read or write in her journal. Throughout the year, at least once a week, Jason called to touch bases. He shared stories of school, but he also still talked of the future showing he still hoped that they could get married. Isobel tried to make her feelings clear, even though she didn't fully understand them herself. Her heart longed for lost dreams, but her logic responded firmly, still recoiling from the hurt and rejection from his family.

As usual, summer heated up with temperatures rising to 100 degrees and higher. Prairie grasses were dry and brittle, and the evening news included burn ban warnings and stories of forest fires in Colorado, California, and New Mexico. Isobel worked the garden earlier in the day, staying indoors and protected from the blazing afternoon sun. With the heat, Aunt Betty seemed even more tired than usual. In addition to her afternoon nap, she fell asleep in her chair mid-morning and occasionally turned in much earlier than her 8:00pm bedtime. It seemed to Isobel that Aunt Betty spent more time sleeping than awake, and she began to worry that her Aunt might be ill.

"Auntie, when's the last time you went to the doctor?" Isobel asked one morning over breakfast. It was late August now, and temperatures had finally cooled down to the 70s and 80s, but Aunt Betty remained as fatigued as when it was hotter. She continued taking frequent naps, and was short of breath even with minimal exertion.

"Oh, dearie! I hate seeing a doctor… you know how it is… they just make you sick!" She winked at Isobel.

Isobel giggle and Aunt Betty joined in with a chortle. "Honestly, Aunt Betty! They don't *make* you sick; they just tell you what is wrong, and you know it!" Isobel tried to straighten her face.

"I know nothing of the kind. Isn't it the same thing? I mean, if the doctor never tells me I'm sick, am I really?" Aunt Betty turned away and gazed out the window overlooking the wide open fields, and then she looked back at Isobel quizzically. "I've lived a long, happy life, my dear, and we all have to die of something." She sat down in a kitchen chair with a deep sigh and pulled her handkerchief from her cuff.

Isobel knelt beside her aunt, tenderly taking one gnarled hand into her own. "Auntie, I feel like I am only now getting to know you. I don't want to lose you, yet. Please don't speak of dying… let's just make an appointment for my peace of mind." She kissed the misshapen, wrinkled hand and released it as she stood to her feet. "I can call for you, if you'd rather..."

Aunt Betty shrugged, relinquishing her power. Dabbing at her eyes with the lacy kerchief, her aunt looked helpless and vulnerable. Suddenly it was clear to Isobel. Perhaps God's reason for the split between herself and Jason was so she could care for her elderly aunt during her last days on the earth. "*The parent becomes the child and the child the parent…*" she thought. If this was God's plan for her life, she welcomed it; her love for Aunt Betty had grown, filling the void left when her father died. They finished their breakfast in silence, and Aunt Betty left the table to sit on the screened porch to enjoy the fresh air.

Isobel cleared the dishes and tidied the kitchen before she called for the doctor's appointment. The phone number was on the little-used list of emergency numbers that Aunt Betty kept pinned to the wall above the phone. After explaining her aunt's fatigue and depression, the nurse was able to fit them into an appointment later in the week. The nurse also ordered basic lab work, an ECG and a chest x-ray. Apparently, according to the medical records, Aunt Betty hadn't had an exam in several years. The nurse instructed Isobel where to take her aunt for the lab and other tests, so it would all be available for the doctor at her appointment.

Isobel went to tell her aunt of the appointment, but she found her dozing in her rocker, her head nodding forward onto her chest. "Auntie, come, lay down inside so your neck won't hurt."

Betty pushed herself up from the rocker, steadied herself and then moved over to the wicker love seat. She pushed a cushion up to the arm before she lay down on it, and Isobel gently pulled a handmade afghan over her aunt's legs for modesty's sake. Before Isobel even stepped aside, Aunt Betty was gently puffing snores as she dozed. Isobel went into the house to write in her journal. Lately she found herself focusing on her spiritual growth as well as her concerns for her aunt, and journaling was her outlet for her thought.

"Hmmm, Ms. Kirk," Old Dr. Fitz looked up from the lab results, "it seems we have some issues to address."

Isobel sat forward on her chair, "Doctor, what is wrong? How bad is it?"

The gray-haired physician looked from the vibrant young woman to the handsome elderly woman sitting on his right; the contrast was remarkable. The older woman's floral shirtwaist dress belied the emaciated frame hidden beneath. Her reticence evident, she was clearly at this appointment against her will. Ms. Betty Kirk was not interested in further diagnostic work-up. She had been stubborn as long as he knew her. Leaning back in his chair, his hands tented in front of him in contemplation, He gazed at the once stately woman, wishing he had better news.

During his examination, he was surprised to see how thin she was in the exam gown. She managed to hide her weight loss by wearing loose dresses well below her knees with long sleeves, but the gown offered no concealment. Her color was also off, although not noticeable to the untrained eye. It did not take a trained physician, however, to see the fatigue: the blue circles under her eyes and the slump of her shoulders.

"Miss Kirk..." he nodded toward Isobel, "Ms. Kirk..." this time looking directly at Aunt Betty. "The test results do not look good. You are severely anemic..." He rambled on, speaking in medical terms, trying to list all the indicators, both negative and positive, though there were few of those.

"What are you saying, Doctor?" Annoyed at his talking over their heads, Isobel redirected his attention, "Is my aunt sick or not? And if she is, just what is wrong with her?"

Dr. Fitz-Randolph looked from Isobel to her aunt. Betty Kirk sat silent with her hands in her lap twisting a handkerchief. Turning back to Isobel, he tried to answer very delicately.

He began cautiously, "given the severity of her anemia and the spot on the x-ray, I must be honest...I am concerned of the possibility of cancer."

Betty Kirk lifted her eyes to him and suddenly he recognized the expression as one of acceptance. "*She knew*!" he thought. "*Of course! Her quiet acceptance of her niece's prompting made sense now.*" Once again, he proceeded with care.

"We could admit you to the hospital for further testing, if that is easier for you..."

Aunt Betty shook her head. "No, I'm going home. I've been blessed with a long, beautiful life, and I won't finish it in a hospital bed. I need to be in my own home."

"This doesn't necessarily mean..."

She interrupted him, yet again. "Fitz, now how many years have you known me? And why do you think you can bamboozle me at this point in my life? You know how old I am. Sooner or later I, like everyone else, must die. The difference is that I am prepared: I know my Saviour, and am not afraid of death. I have the blessed hope, after all."

"Now..." she rose from her chair and picked up her purse, "Isobel, are you ready to leave? I am, and I'd like to go now..." and she started toward the door. Her feebleness was even more apparent to Isobel as she watched Aunt Betty reaching out to steady herself.

With each step, she rested her hand on furniture, the back of a chair, the edge of the desk, then another chair, slowly making her way toward the door.

Isobel hadn't said a word during the exchange between Dr. Fitz-Randolph and her aunt. She watched as her aunt spoke to him, as if they were well-acquainted beyond a doctor and patient relationship. And she had been under the misconception that her aunt hadn't been to the doctor in ages. Evidently, she knew him well enough to put him in his place. It did leave her concerned for her aunt's health, however.

Should I force her to get more tests? Do I just let her go home? How do I force a grown woman to do something against her will?

For now, Isobel knew she could not argue with her aunt who was already on her way to the car in the parking lot. Isobel pulled out her keys and quickly joined her aunt by the car, unlocked the doors and helped Aunt Betty in on the passenger's side, and then she slipped into the driver's seat. They drove home in silence, each in their own thoughts. One thought about how to extend the life of her loved one while the other pondered how to finish out her life gracefully.

"Auntie," Isobel began gently as they made their way from the car toward the back door of the house. "Can we discuss the tests Dr. Fitz-Randolph wants to do?"

"No, child, we will not discuss them! I've heard it all before, just one more test, and then another, now surgery, a little time to recover, then more tests… I will not be put through the ringer and spend my last days in the hospital trying to prolong a life that only the Lord has control over!"

"But Aunt Betty, there may be some medicine to help…"

" What if the cure is worse than the curse? Do you want to see me die peacefully in my own home, or would you rather I be hooked up to tubes and machines in a sterile hospital room? Here…" she motioned toward the open prairie, "I can enjoy the fields, the birds and the serenity. A hospital is not a place for peace and restfulness. They wake you every couple of hours just to make sure you're still alive! Please understand, Isobel. This is my choice."

Recognizing the strength of her argument, Isobel realized Aunt Betty wanted to stay in control. Aunt Betty obviously had thought this through and had her mind made up. Isobel's only wish was that she had a better understanding of Aunt Betty's faith.

For the few weeks following her doctor's appointment, Isobel and Aunt Betty continued their routine of early morning breakfasts, Aunt Betty's frequent naps, and Isobel taking on more of the household chores, including the gardening and laundry. She managed to work Aunt Betty's old wringer washer and hang clothes on the clothesline (a task she hated as a teen; back then it seemed old-fashioned and tiresome). She no longer wished for a modern washer and dryer, choosing instead to give thanks for having time to share her auntie's burdens.

Aunt Betty turned in earlier and earlier as the weeks went by. When the weather permitted, Isobel sat on the porch to journal or read on those quiet evenings alone. If rain or temperatures prevented her use of the porch, Isobel would sit on the window-seat in the bay window of the living-room. Still able to gaze out over the farmyard, she felt at peace until one evening, a flicker caught the corner of her eye.

Sensing something was terribly wrong Isobel jumped up and saw yellow flames shoot from the upper window on the barn. She ran outside in time to see a neighbor's truck pulling up the drive. She quickly recognized Mr. Alder and his oldest son. "We saw the flames and came right away," he yelled as he parked and they jumped out of the cab. He ran for the garden hose. "The best we can do is wet down around it so the fire doesn't spread to the other buildings."

Isobel ran around to the side of the house to grab a second hose she knew was coiled there. She turned the faucet on as fast as she could and pulled the hose back toward the barn. Other neighbors were arriving with various tools to help thwart the fire: axes, picks and shovels. They began digging a trench around the barn while the Alder's kept the water on the structure. Another grabbed the hose from Isobel and started filling the trench.

Isobel set about fixing cool drinks for the workers and serving them whenever one took a break or traded off with another volunteer.

They worked late into the night fighting the fire and were successful in preventing its spread. However, the barn was a total loss, as were the contents. Besides stored hay, the barn only held an old tractor, several saddles and harness sets from days gone by and miscellaneous furniture that Aunt Betty wanted to keep, but didn't want in the house. As far as Isobel knew, there was nothing of real value in it, but she would need to ask Aunt Betty. Whoever did this was either intent of destroying everything in the barn, or they just wanted to send another scary message to Aunt Betty or Isobel.

She was surprised that all the commotion had not awakened Aunt Betty. Her bedroom light had not even turned on so Isobel was certain Aunt Betty had slept right through the fire. *She must be worse than I thought, if she is so exhausted...* Isobel didn't have time to think any further; the Sheriff approached, wiping his forehead with an old bandana. He adjusted his hat on his dampened hair.

"Well, young gal. Seems coincidences just keep happening since you came to town..."

Isobel looked at him in disbelief. "You know that my aunt was not surprised by the first incident, so I am sure things happened before I got here!" Isobel felt defensive and angry at the suggestion that trouble followed her. In college, she was the one who avoided risky situations, who never got into messes like so many other college students did.

Sheriff Jones acknowledged her statement, and took a few minutes to explain how he would have to come back to investigate the fire. Despite fire-fighting techniques, the ashes and embers remained too hot to sift through. Some of the neighbors promised to keep drenching the structure to cool it down and prevent flares.

"I'll pop back 'round here sometime tomorrow to take a look, if that's alright with you and yer auntie." Isobel saw him to his vehicle and returned to the house to check on Aunt Betty. She needed to shower off the dust and soot of the fire, too, before she turned in for the night and she only had a few hours before dawn. The kitchen and dishes would have to wait until morning.

Chapter 10

K.C. had taken the entire year to prepare for his bar exam while he continued fixing up the homestead and cleaning around the property. It had been months since they last heard from Skyla; she hadn't come back to borrow money since the episode last summer, but she had called a few times, at first. Talitha, his other sister, had not visited, but they always knew where to find her. She lived in public housing in Omaha, if you could call it living, and had her two children with her. K.C. wished that Sky would be more responsible. She often left her children with Talitha for days at a time while she was off with one boyfriend or another.

This older man she had looked like trouble and K.C. wondered how long before he dragged Sky down with him. One sweltering summer morning, the answer came in the form of a phone call from Omaha County Jail. Skyla and her friend had been arrested. The 'friend' had decided they needed more money and to get it, he chose to rob a bank. Skyla sat in the truck, supposedly unaware of the reason for the visit to the bank, and police said she drove the getaway vehicle, so she was equally responsible for the crime. The robbery would have been bad enough, a Federal offense, but her friend also shot a bank guard who tried to stop him. The guard died on the spot, thus the charge of murder. She was being charged with first-degree murder!

K.C. knew immediately that he could not leave his little sister in the lurch. He needed to find some way to get her off or at least get her sentence minimized. His mother was devastated with the news and he could not abandon her either. She needed both emotional and spiritual support, as well as help traveling from home to Omaha for the trial. He was accustomed to his sister's and their problems, but this was more than a pregnancy or drug problem.

Nebraska's law on first-degree murder allowed the death penalty or life imprisonment without parole; this was a matter of life and death. K.C.'s first order of business, after hearing of Skyla's predicament, was researching just how he could assist in her defense. He soon found out that he could not visit without meeting certain requirements, one being that Skyla needed to mail a visitor request form to him.

While waiting for word that his visit was approved, K.C. continued to study for the bar exam focusing on the Nebraska law since it appeared he would not be leaving this area. He was scheduled for the bar exam in just weeks, but decided to delay until the February cycle because focusing on both Skyla and the exam would be too much. His mind wasn't settled enough to study well, either. He worried about Ma's reaction to Skyla's arrest and he worried about Skyla sitting in jail waiting for a court-appointed attorney to plead her case.

"Sky, how you doing?" K.C. sat on one side of the table and Skyla sat across from him wearing traditional prison garb. She was wearing her usual make-up and her hair was drawn back tightly from her face in a rubber band at the nape of her neck. She seemed years older than her age; her gaunt face showed fresh acne on her forehead and chin. Reeking of tobacco odor when she walked in, it was obvious that she had been smoking, probably more than before.

"K., I'm not so good. They said my kids are gonna go to foster care. I thought Tali was taking care of them, but according to my lawyer, she can't qualify as a foster parent… too many issues, just like me!" She dropped her head in shame as she said the last words.

K.C. took her hand in his and patted it to comfort her. "Sky, we'll get through this, together, as a family. We won't abandon you or the children. If necessary, I will take the children, but we won't lose them to the system. Too many from the rez are lost to foster care and adoption. We will protect your babies, somehow!" He was vehement in his assertion.

Reassured by her brother's strength, Skyla perked up. Their visit was too short for K.C. to gather as much information about the crime as he wanted. He needed to know as much as possible in case there was some loophole to help her. Anyway, K.C. believed that she really did not know what her friend had planned. She did not know of his plan to rob the bank; she thought he had money to withdraw. And she was horrified that he had actually killed someone. She was raised with a reverence for life and would never willingly choose to be with a man capable of murder.

As K.C. left the jail, heading for her lawyer's office, he thought about his future plans. He remembered a verse from his childhood, somewhere in Jeremiah, about how God had good plans for us and not bad plans. He trusted God to make *ALL* things work together for good.

"Mr. Jeffers, what can I do to help my sister?" K.C. had listened to her lawyer's explanation and plan for her defense.

"I'm afraid there isn't much to be done. The state has a pretty good case. The law is clear when it comes to a death caused in the commission of a felony. The best we can hope for is to get the lesser sentence of life without parole since she did not pull the trigger."

"I understand that. But there must be some extenuating circumstance that could change it to a lesser charge…?"

"I'm sorry, Mr. Fox. I sympathize with your family and your sister. What my advice is to you all is to look out for her kids. Those two little ones are going to grow up without their mother, unless a miracle happens, and they will need all the family they have to keep them from following in their mother's footsteps."

K.C. was more than a little frustrated at the system right now. The process of gaining custody of Skyla's two toddlers seemed just as difficult as her trial. Nebraska's Division of Child & Family Services required them to jump through hoops to qualify as a foster home. The term itself grated on K.C.'s nerves. They weren't trying to be a foster home; they were already family to the children. They only wanted to have the right to raise them within their family circle and not allow them to be reared outside the traditions of their ancestors.

❧

"Ma, you've got to perk up. The folks from welfare are coming to interview us today. If they see you so down in the dumps, they will never give us custody of Brya and CeCe. At least clean up a bit, put on a fresh apron and tidy your hair."

K.C.'s mother looked much older than her 53 years. The furrows in her brow were accentuated by the fly-away gray strands of hair hanging into her eyes. She didn't have the energy to even brush it off her face. His heart ached for her; she hadn't been reading her Bible or praying like she used to. Her eyes were so far away that even the suggestion of worship didn't move her. She rarely spoke, and then only to whisper a request or answer with single-syllable words.

While preparing for the home inspection, K.C. and Shyne had finished fixing the farmyard and had painted the house. From the exterior, their home appeared perfect for raising children. Now he was trying to give the inside the same appearance. He swept every room and tidied the bedrooms. They had placed two extra toddler beds in Ma's room for Brya and CeCe, and bought a few toys to brighten their corner of the room.

Shyne had the kitchen sparkling, clean and bright; the only negative K.C. could see was his mother's depression. He wasn't sure how the Child Protection folks viewed placing children in a home with someone suffering with a mental illness and he didn't know how to help his mother get better.

A cloud of dust along the driveway announced the arrival of the social worker and case worker from the Division of Child and Protective Services. K.C. took a final look around the room and called to Shyne to pick up Tad and take him off to her room during the interview. He answered the knock on the front door and greeted the couple, inviting them into the humble Fox home.

The interview seemed to last forever, and K.C. was glad to see the welfare officials leave. It went better than he anticipated, and even though Ma sat in the corner not contributing to the conversation, they seemed prepared to allow the children to live with their grandmother, aunt and uncle. They were pleasantly surprised at the preparations made for the children and approved of Shyne's care of her son, despite her youth.

"In the opinion of the state," they said, "keeping families together is our goal. Let's give it a try!"

K.C. nearly jumped up to kiss them when he heard their decision. Even Ma seemed to brighten a bit at the announcement. Her eyes gleamed with unshed tears and K.C. squeezed her hand. Finally, Ma turned to him and asked him to pray a prayer of thanksgiving and together they praised the Lord for working out one of their problems. Now they only had to see to Skyla's court case.

Skyla's children were delivered by the agency social worker about a week after their initial visit to the Fox home. Three-year-old Brya and two-year-old CeCe adapted well to the routine in the home and Shyne took them under her wing. Together with Tad, they made a happy circle on the outside. They didn't seem to miss their mommy much; Shyne poured out her love to them and they soaked it up like a sponge.

The frustration of not being able to help Skyla was eating at K.C. Without his law license, he had no standing in the legal community, not even as much as a paralegal. And without his license, he couldn't contribute to the household expenses. He and Shyne continued doing what they could for Ma, cleaning the house up, working the garden and keeping the yard tidy.

Despite the grandchildren in her home, Ma seemed to be slipping into a depression like K.C. had never witnessed. She sat around in her bathrobe all day long, crying and fretting about her little girl. She didn't cook; she wouldn't eat unless they placed food right in front of her and helped her get started. She didn't bathe except when Shyne ran her bath and led her to the bathroom. It seemed she had taken the problem with Skyla deeply and didn't have the strength to bounce back.

K.C. and Shyne tried reading the Bible aloud to their mother, hoping she would find strength in the faith she had held for so long. Ma nodded her head as they read, affirming her faith in the words, but when they stopped, she once again slumped into her chair, an immovable force. K.C. couldn't convince her to go to the doctor, and she refused to visit with Skyla, instead moaning about her lost girl.

On the day of Skyla arraignment, Shyne and Tad joined K.C. for the drive to Omaha. They wanted to show family support, but knew that their mother's absence would be felt more than their presence. The little ones were going to spend the afternoon with their Aunt Tali while they went on to the court house. The brief stop at her house gave K.C. a glimpse into the lives his two sisters led away from the rez.

The house was barely livable… inside wall paint peeling as well as the woodwork. The floors looked like rough-hewn wood with no finish. It had splinters at the well worn areas and spaces between the boards where ants crawled in. Ragged, rough-edged sheets of fabric hung from nails at the windows. Talitha's couch was broken down in the center as if a giant had sat on it; the cushions had lost all fluff.

K.C. was saddened at the site of his niece and nephew sitting on the floor on a blanket. When Shyne sat Taddy, Brya and CeCe next to his cousins, his heart hurt all the more. He wanted so much for his family, so much more than this.

At the courthouse, K.C. and Shyne took their seats just behind the bar on the defendant's side of the courtroom. They were greeted by the clean smell of freshly vacuumed carpets and newly waxed wood fixtures. K.C. looked at the tables set up for counsel, all the electronics available and thought of the day he might be a part of that side of the courtroom, rather than acting as an observer.

The small number of observers consisted of mostly news reporters. With restrictions on cell phones and electronic devices in the gallery, most were limited to notepads for note-taking. Not that this proceeding promised many surprises. From K.C.'s understanding of the law, he knew that arraignments were usually short and to the point. Without a jury present, the judge formally charges the defendants and takes the plea of guilty or not guilty from the defendants. They are informed again of their right to counsel and the specifics of their indictment are available for the counsel at this time.

K.C. also knew that once this part of the process was taken care of, the case moved ahead more quickly. There would be the jury to pick, the defense to prepare and finally the actual trial. He dreaded hearing the details of the crime for which his little sister sat in jail; for the first time, he was glad Ma hadn't come and wasn't here to hear them.

The county prosecutor and court appointed attorneys entered the courtroom and took their assigned seats. They spent time organizing their notes, plugging in electronic equipment and, in general, getting ready for the proceedings.

At nearly 11:00am, the time her arraignment was set to begin, Skyla entered the courtroom from the holding cell area accompanied by a female guard. She wore a typical jailhouse orange jumpsuit and, although her hands were cuffed and attached to a chain around her, her ankles were also shackled. Her companion in crime, William "Bill" Short, followed her similarly dressed and constrained.

The guard escorting him maintained a safe distance between the two defendants and they were seated at two separate tables, although they were co-defendants. They had no interaction, not in glances, not in body language, and definitely not in words. If K.C. didn't know they were co-defendants, he would have thought they were total strangers. *Amazing how much trouble you can get into with a total stranger!* K.C. thought.

Just then the bailiff entered the room and made the usual announcement, "All rise. The court is now in session. The Honorable Judge Howard Franklin presiding." And the lawyers, defendants, and everyone in the gallery stood until the judge sat in his chair, pounded his gavel and said, "Order in the court!" The court officer said, "Be seated" and the rustle of everybody taking their seats filled the room for a brief moment, and then all was quiet.

Judge Franklin looked over the papers in front of him and looked out into the courtroom toward the prosecutor's table. "I see a motion from the prosecution… a plea agreement?" He looked over his reading glasses at the young lawyer who immediately rose to speak.

"Yes, your Honor. We have reached an agreement with one of the defendant's counsel."

"And the terms of the plea are acceptable to the defendant?" This time Judge Franklin looked toward the tables with the court-appointed defense attorneys.

K.C. was worried. He hadn't heard anything from Skyla's lawyer about a plea agreement; could Bill Short be turning on her, taking a plea to put the blame on her? It didn't make sense. She sat in the truck the whole time. He didn't know what to think about this strange turn of events. If Skyla was thinking of a plea agreement, he hoped she would talk to him first… not just jump at the first offer, which might not be the best they could do for her. K.C. was getting a headache running these thoughts around in his head.

"Yes, your Honor," it was Skyla's lawyer who spoke first. "My client is willing to accept the terms of the agreement at this time."

"You understand, Miss…er…Skyla Fox, is it?" she nodded, "that you will need allocute, that is, make a statement here before the court, of your involvement in the case. …and that, although the prosecutor has offered a lesser sentence in exchange for your testimony, it does not release you from punishment under the law?"

"Yes, your Honor," she stood to her feet as she spoke softly, but clear enough to be heard throughout the courtroom.

"The terms of the agreement state that you will testify against your co-defendant…" the judge was interrupted by Bill Short jumping up and lunging toward Skyla.

"Why you little tramp!" Thankfully, the tables were far enough apart that he was unable to reach her, but he managed to send papers flying off the desk, knocking over his chair and crashing to the floor because of his ankle shackles. The court officer subdued him quickly and Bill was hauled out of the courtroom to the holding cell while the judge called for order in the courtroom.

Skyla was obviously shaken, but immovable in her decision, it seemed. Shyne nudged K.C. and whispered to him, "What does all this mean? I don't understand…" K.C. motioned for her to be quiet as the judge began to speak again, now that the courtroom had settled down. "I'll explain later," he whispered back to her.

"Miss Fox, are you ready to allocute?"

The silence was deafening in the gallery as all waited to hear her side of the story. She was required to take responsibility for her part in the robbery and murder, and the reporters wanted to hear all the gory details.

They were somewhat disappointed, however, when Skyla told her side of the events for the day of the robbery. She told how she didn't even know Bill Short for more than a couple of days before the crime. Skyla also told how she tried to help him by stopping to get money from her brother, but that Bill wanted more. By the time she understood his plan, they were outside the bank, and she didn't know how to get out of the situation, so she just sat there. She couldn't describe what happened inside the bank; all she could do was to share what they did after the robbery until the arrest. She hung her head as she finished and K.C. saw her shoulders shake as she sobbed quietly.

The judge was less than sympathetic. He gazed at her for a minute, waiting for her to get herself under control. Impatiently, he cleared his throat and she looked up. Her attorney stood beside her indicating they were ready to complete the process by accepting the terms of the plea agreement. But Judge Franklin seemed to have other ideas.

"Young lady! You are old enough to know the difference between right and wrong…" Skyla started to answer, but the judge stopped her. "You've had your chance to speak; now it is my turn, and you WILL listen." He nodded for emphasis, and she shut her mouth tightly.

"Yes, you know the difference. And what else did you expect when you parked by a bank? That he was going to withdraw a tidy sum to get more dope for you?" He held up his hand as Skyla made moves to protest.

"I am not sure you understand the gravity of what happened. A man's life was taken from him; his children and grandchildren will have to go on without him. A bank robbery is not just a simple felony. It was Federally-insured and thus becomes a Federal offense. I am not accepting the terms of the plea..."

Skyla cried out looking at her lawyer, "Can he do that?"

"I can do as I please, young lady. This is MY courtroom, and you WILL be quiet. That is the last warning you are going to get. As I was saying... I think the prosecutor negotiated too light a sentence for the crime. Rather than the 10 to 12 years, I am sentencing you to 20 years hard time. You MIGHT get out by 15 for good behavior, but I wouldn't count on it. If I have any say on your future, you will spend the full sentence in the custody of the Federal Bureau of Prisons." He slammed his gavel down and dismissed the court.

Skyla sat down, shocked and stunned at the turn of events. Twenty years away from her children; they would not even know her when she was released. She looked over her shoulder at K.C., and tearfully asked him to care for her babies.

K.C. could do little more than agree at this point. He was also stunned. Not only was she not going through a full trial, she was on her way to some prison for the next twenty years, and he could see no way to help her. He fully understood the proceedings, and knew that the judge was within his legal rights to do what he did. His concern now was how he was going to explain all this to his mother and to his little sister, Shyne who understood just enough to be standing next to him in tears.

The female guard returned to lead Skyla away. Meanwhile, the reporters had scurried out to meet their deadlines with the news. They would have to wait for another day to witness the trial of Bill Short, and to hear Skyla testify against him.

K.C. and Shyne left the courthouse in silence. The drive home was long, tedious, and heartbreaking. Shyne didn't want the explanation K.C. had promised earlier. She just wanted to turn time backward. She wanted her childhood back; she longed for days long gone when she and her sisters laughed and played without a care, long before they had kids or drug and alcohol problems. She wanted her childhood back so much her heart ached.

For his part, K.C. realized the burden of the family had become his. He didn't have school as an excuse, or a career set in stone. His life was in flux, and he was the only one able to carry the load. He was the oldest, educated and most likely to find employment once he passed his bar exam, which was just around the corner. With mother's depression, there was no way she could take care of Sky's babies; DFS would take them away immediately if they knew of her condition.

K.C. made up his mind, on that long, silent drive, to take care of his family. Perhaps this was the plan God had for his life. His altruistic dream might have changed course, but he knew he could serve Native Americans right there in Nebraska even without apprenticing in a large firm. Omaha had some fine legal firms that he hadn't explored in his job search. Yes, he could follow God's lead, and work in his own corner of the world, for the good of his people.

Chapter 11

Isobel watched Aunt Betty weaken by the day until, early in October, she sat waiting for her aunt to join her for breakfast. Hearing a rasping cough coming from her aunt's room, Isobel knocked on her door. "Come in…," Aunt Betty called out weakly. *She looks so tiny in that old four-poster bed.* Pillows puffed out around her head and shoulders and several quilts up under her chin indicate that she was cold despite the warm Indian summer weather.

"Auntie, are you alright?" Isobel knelt on the braided rug beside her aunt's bed. She rested her head on her crossed arms on the bed beside her aunt.

"Isobel, dear, I'm afraid I cannot join you for tea this morning." Aunt Betty rested her thin, frail hand on Isobel's head. "My old bones just aren't cooperating." With a catch in her voice, she coughed a bit to clear her throat. "I think we may need to take a trip into town to see Dr. Fitz… perhaps he can give me something for the pain."

"Auntie! I knew you were tired, but pain?" Isobel's head jerked up; her eyes searched Aunt Betty's face.

"Honey, don't fret at me. I just need a bit of help to bear the discomfort…. You've been such a blessing… God is so good to have provided me with a loving niece when I was unable to have children of my own." She stopped to catch her breath, but the racking cough took over.

Pointing to the glass and pitcher on her bedside table, her hand shook. "Please…?" Once again she broke into a paroxysm of coughing. Isobel reached for the water and, when the coughing receded, she helped Aunt Betty sit forward to take tiny sips from the glass. Worn out by such a small effort, Aunt Betty rested back onto her pillows and Isobel tidied her bedding around her. "I will call Dr. Fitz right away, auntie. We'll get you something for the cough as well as the pain." Tenderly she touched Aunt Betty's hand. *She is so frail, so thin.*

Isobel spoke with Dr. Fitz-Randolph's nurse, explaining the need for a visit and the nurse promised to call her back in a few minutes. "*Curious*," thought Isobel. "*Last time she just gave me a time to come in…*" Just then the telephone rang, jarring Isobel from her musings.

"Hello?"

"Miss Kirk? This is Dr. Fitz-Randolph's office."

"Yes, do you have an appointment for my aunt?"

"No, actually, Dr. Fitz says it isn't necessary for her to come into the office. We will call in a prescription to the drug store for both her cough and the pain, if that is OK with you."

"Doesn't he want to see Aunt Betty?" Isobel was puzzled.

"It isn't that, dear. Dr. Fitz wants to spare her the trouble of coming in; he can come out there on his way home from the office this evening. He wants her to remain comfortable, rather than using her energy to come in here."

Isobel thought of Dr. Fitz's consideration and wondered at his kindness when her thoughts were once more interrupted.

"He says if you cannot get to the pharmacy, he could bring out the medicines, too…?"

"No, I'll take a few minutes to get her medicine this morning," Isobel replied. "She needs the medicine soon as possible."

Finishing her conversation with the nurse, she went to tell Aunt Betty that she was stepping out for a few minutes, but her aunt was fast asleep again. Town was close; it only took about 15 minutes one way, so she got back before Aunt Betty woke from her nap.

Isobel checked in on Aunt Betty as soon as she returned from town, and Isobel was glad to see that, for the first time since the doctor's visit, Aunt Betty seemed to be sleeping peacefully. Over the weeks, Isobel heard her aunt moving around in her room, restless, trying to ease the cough or to find a position of comfort so she could get a bit more sleep. It was common for her to awaken several times a night. Now she seemed at peace.

Isobel went outside to sit on the broad front porch and contemplate her future. Looking out over the unkempt farmyard, broken-down fences, and overgrown pastures of hay sadly in need of mowing, Isobel wondered how Aunt Betty had managed for so long on her own. The distance to the nearest neighbor alone kept her isolated. Other than the rented out portion of land, the remaining farm buildings sat in disrepair and needing paint, new roofs or tearing down altogether.

Isobel was certain her aunt had little time left, and Isobel wasn't sure Aunt Betty had put her affairs in order. Not that Isobel was hoping for any kind of inheritance. She was pretty sure there wasn't a nest egg stashed away, and the rented land from the farmstead barely paid the taxes. No, she was just worried that Aunt Betty might have little treasures she would want to leave to other relatives, however distant. Isobel had only met a few cousins over the years, but she did not know what Aunt Betty's relationship was with them.

For now, Isobel felt paralyzed by fear of being alone, sorrow over her lost love, and the greatest sense of aloneness. *When Aunt Betty dies, I will be totally alone!* Bible stories from childhood came to mind: Abraham leaving Ur for an unknown place away from family and friends, Joseph in Egypt, and the Israelites later on, wandering in the wilderness.

"*Yes,*" thought Isobel, "*I, too, am in a wilderness of loneliness,*" and she wished again for a closer walk with the Lord, as Maddie, Taylor and Ashley had demonstrated when they hung out together.

Aunt Betty's health continued to decline and her pain increased. Isobel did whatever she could to keep her comfortable, but it was a losing battle. The cancer had taken over; fighting the pain took more and more medicine. Dr. Fitz-Randolph finally prescribed morphine.

He made a home visit to make sure she understood how to give it and what to watch for. He also wanted to ease the burden from Isobel, if possible.

When offered hospitalization or a long-term care facility, Betty Kirk remained adamant. She would die in the same home she had lived most of her life! Isobel hugged her aunt as tears filled her eyes. Dr. Fitz also choked a bit as he tried to maintain his professionalism. "Well, then, we will just leave it this way. Let me know if you need anything further" and he placed his hat on his head as he moved toward the front door. "I will check on you if you don't call," he nodded and let himself out.

Isobel followed the doctor outside. "Dr. Fitz, how much longer does she have?"

"My dear, there is no way of knowing when she will close her eyes for the final time. I can take a guess, if you like. Maybe a week or two… no more than a month, I'd say. She's very weak and morphine tends to depress the breathing, especially as she needs more to cover the pain. Be careful, but don't let her suffer."

He reached out and held her hand for a brief second; he gazed into her deep brown eyes. "You know, I've known you since infancy, held you as a baby, and you've grown into a beautiful young woman, Isobel. Your kindness to Betty means a lot to me…" It seemed he had more to say, but then he released it suddenly, like he received a shock, as if he'd come to his senses just in time. "We can talk later," he said in closing and stepped off the porch toward his car. "I'm sure you will have many questions in the weeks to come."

Isobel was puzzled by his enigmatic statement. What questions? What could he know or want to say that needed to wait? Her curiosity was piqued, but Aunt Betty was sleeping when she went back inside, so she sat down to journal her thoughts and his comments before she forgot the strange way he left things.

As the morphine kept her pain at bay, Aunt Betty slept more and talked less. She awoke to take care of personal needs only to doze off again. The loneliness of not having someone to talk to enveloped Isobel. Her journal became her companion throughout the following weeks while watching her beloved aunt deteriorate. In it, she shared her hopes, wishes and dreams for the future. But most of all, she wrote of her fears: fear of being left alone when Aunt Betty was gone, fear of the handling of Aunt Betty's business, as well as concern about Dr. Fitz's answers to questions. *I wonder what questions those might be…*

Dr. Fitz returned to visit Aunt Betty one week after starting the morphine. He listened to her lungs and checked her blood pressure and heart rate. She barely roused enough to greet him, and then dozed off again. "Betty is resting well?" he turned to Isobel.

She nodded her head, afraid to speak because of the lump in her throat.

"Her blood pressure is low, but that is to be expected with this medicine. Is she having any breakthrough pain?"

This time Isobel gulped and composed herself enough to speak. "No, if I see her restless or grimacing, I give her another dose. She's just sleeping so much that we don't get to talk much, anymore." She looked at Dr. Fitz with a question in her eyes, but he didn't pick up on her cue. She still wondered about his earlier statement, but hadn't thought of any questions to ask.

"No, I don't 'spect you get to talk much… Betty used to be quite a story-teller."

"How long have you known her, Dr. Fitz? She said you knew her for a long time…?"

"Well, now, I guess we met sometime in high school. She and I were in the same class, and she was the older sister to my buddy, your dad. We hung out here quite a bit until I went away for college and medical school, and your dad joined the military. But when I came back and decided to practice here, Betty was still on the farm. Your dad had moved on, of course, but she was always here." He mused over the thought for a moment, then shook his keys and said, "I gotta get goin' now… call if you need anything." And he stepped off the porch before Isobel could probe any further into the strange friendship between her aunt and this kindly doctor.

Aunt Betty hung on longer than predicted. On rare occasions, when Isobel was preparing her medicine for her, Aunt Betty tried to speak, but her strength limited her to whispers. One evening, before the morphine sent her back to sleep, she surprised Isobel with a request.

"Dearie," she whispered, "don't... hate your... father. He did... the best... he could. "

"Auntie, now don't struggle to talk. You know I love my daddy. I would never hate him."

"He... wanted... to tell you... I wanted... to tell you... he couldn't... I... didn't know... how..." Betty slipped into sleep as the medicine began its job, and once again, Isobel was left wondering at a puzzling statement, this time from her aunt. She didn't know these would be her aunt's last words.

Isobel noticed Aunt Betty wasn't rousing to use the toilet, or to take meds, and Dr. Fitz had his nurse come out to put in an IV for medicine and fluids and a Foley catheter for urine output. She took time to teach Isobel how to care for them. She also offered to come out several times a week to help, and Isobel appreciated the help.

Although caring for a bedridden family member took a lot of work and could be stressful at times, Isobel used her time wisely. She read the Bible to Betty and talked to her even though she couldn't reply. She told her aunt how much she would miss her, and how much she loved her, not knowing if she could even hear the words.

Aunt Betty gradually slipped into a coma, nonresponsive to pain. But Isobel continued to talk to her every time she repositioned her or tidied the bed. Turning Aunt Betty and changing her bedding was not easy on her own, so between nurse visits, she managed the best she could with waterproof pads and mattress protectors. When the nurse came out, together they cleaned Aunt Betty much better, giving her a full bed-bath and changing the linens completely.

Indian summer broke with a wild storm across the prairie late in October. The rain pelted down on the roof when Isobel woke up, but the house was otherwise quiet. She had taken to checking on Aunt Betty every two hours through the night, just to make sure her IV was OK and to change her position from side to side.

Isobel lay in her bed listening to the rain, relaxing for a few minutes before getting up to start the day. She was beginning to feel the effects of being a caretaker. Lack of sleep and weariness from worry was taking its toll. She wished she could just sleep a bit longer, but it was nearly time for Aunt Betty's medicine, and she didn't want to risk her feeling pain.

Pushing back her bedding and slipping her feet into fluffy pink slippers that sat beside her bed, she pulled on her matching bathrobe and headed for the bathroom. She stopped suddenly outside Aunt Betty's room. Her heart raced; she could feel it thumping into her throat. Something wasn't right. She didn't know how she knew, she just did.

"Auntie?" Isobel made her way into her aunt's room. "Auntie?" this time her call became a cry, followed by a gasp. She could tell right away that her beloved aunt had died in her sleep. She looked peaceful for the first time in weeks, no furrows in her brow, no restless movement from pain. "Oh, Auntie, not yet! Please, not yet," she knelt beside her aunt's bed and rested her head on the bed, giving way to her tears and sorrow. "No, Auntie, I'm not ready… I can't do this on my own… Please, oh, please…" Although she didn't have a relationship with God like her friends and her aunt had, she knew she needed comfort. Isobel cried out for Someone to ease her pain, and felt an urging in her heart that He heard her plea.

Chapter 12

K.C. worried all the way home after picking up the little ones from Talitha's home. Despite the small ones chattering and Shyne trying to keep them under control, his mind kept wandering. *How can I tell Ma about Sky taking a plea?* After talking with Skyla's lawyer, he understood she made the best deal she could. By testifying against Bill Short, she would be able to vindicate herself to some degree. K.C. felt guilty, too. *What if I had asked her not to leave with Bill? Maybe if I hadn't given her any money…* Then he caught himself. … *no, it still would have happened.*

K.C. understood that God has a plan for each of his children, but that He also gives everyone free choice. So even if God's plan was for good, not for evil, as it said in Jeremiah 29:11, each person was free to choose whether to follow God's roadmap. K.C. realized that first Skyla would need to accept the Lord as her Saviour, and then God could help her make something good come from this awful situation.

K.C's greatest concern was how Ma would take the news of Skyla's conviction. Ma had always held so strongly to her faith, but somehow this had hit her exceptionally hard. Like a ship adrift, she was unable to find that Anchor on whom she had always depended. K.C. prayed all the way home that he would be able to soften the blow and guide her back to her safe harbor, back to her faith in God.

As he drove down the rough path leading to their house, Ma sat on the porch in a chair near Mrs. Charbanneau, the neighbor who stayed with her for the day. The two seemed engrossed in something on Ma's lap. K.C. was happy just to see Ma cleaned up, dressed and out of the house. But to realize she had her Bible opened on her lap, and seemed to be discussing it with Mrs. Charbanneau gave him hope.

"Hi, Ma… Mrs. C." K.C. called out as he got out of the car. He circled to the other side where Shyne was trying to gather up the babes like a hen with her chicks. He picked up Brya and CeCe, one in each arm, and she took Taddy out of his car seat and grabbed all the bags they had taken along. As they got to the porch, Ma spoke… a sweet sound to K.C.'s ears.

"Now children, come and give Granny a hug," she moved her Bible to a spot beside her chair and reached toward K.C. to take Brya and CeCe onto her lap.

K.C. looked over at Mrs. Charbanneau with a question in his eyes; she nodded in response, neither speaking for fear of breaking the moment. Ma petted on the little ones as if seeing them for the first time. Shyne stood to the side with Taddy on her hip.

"Ma, you're looking better today," she spoke softly with a question in her voice.

Ma nodded her head. "Dear Sister Violet here helped me out of my abyss. She just kept praying over me and sharing promises from the scriptures until the enemy had to flee. Thank you, Jesus!" She raised her hand and looked to the sky for a brief moment, but instantly refocused on the grandchildren.

"And my Skyla, son, what's to become of her?"

This was the one topic K.C. hoped to avoid, but knew he must address. He took a seat on the step near his mother's feet and touched her knee.

"Ma, she took a plea bargain."

"Does that mean she will be coming home soon?"

"No, I'm afraid not. She was present when a crime was committed and it resulted in the death of a man, so she has to be punished. She took the plea to lessen her sentence, but she will still have to spend time in prison. We don't know for sure how long..." Knowing wouldn't help Ma, so he chose to be vague about the sentence.

K.C. watched for his mother's reaction. Would she dissolve into depression once again?

"Hmm...um hmm... yes, Lord." She seemed to be praying silently or hearing the Lord in her mind, but at least she didn't break down. "So, we need to pray for her, hope for her and visit her. The scriptures tell us that by visiting the prisoner in jail we are serving Jesus, so we will visit her." She looked directly at K.C. "Where will she be held?"

"I'm not sure, yet but, as soon as her lawyer knows, he will inform us and help us set up a visitation program. The children can be taken to her for visits, too, so we need to help make that happen... for Skyla's sake as well as theirs."

Ma nodded as did Mrs. Charbanneau and Shyne. They were all in agreement, and a burden was lifted from K.C.'s shoulders as he watched his mother respond as she used to when a crisis came to the family. She seemed back to her old self, if not totally, at least 80% there. Unfortunately, it didn't last. After Mrs. Charbanneau left, and as Shyne began fixing food for the family, K.C. sensed Ma's withdrawal. She didn't move from her chair once Shyne took Brya and CeCe to put them down for their naps.

Instead, she stared out over the long driveway as if watching for the return of a prodigal, watching for Skyla. When K.C. attempted to get her for dinner, she resisted, sitting down firmly in her rocker and pointing toward the road. He didn't understand how she could be calling on the Lord one moment and less than an hour later, unable to speak, unwilling to move.

Maybe she needs a psychiatrist.... During his time away from the reservation, he was exposed to non-Native treatments for a multitude of problems. In college, students often went to the counseling office when they were over-stressed, and on occasion they went to the health center and got medication to help them. He saw how both counseling and medication helped people with serious depression or anxiety issues, and was beginning to think he should find a doctor for his mother.

It went against their cultural beliefs to see psychiatrists; Native Americans, in general, preferred to find help through one of the tribal shamans using traditional purification rites to heal the mind. Even those who professed Christianity had a hard time not using traditional healing for taboo areas, like mental health. They didn't see a conflict between their religious conviction and the healer's methods. But somehow, K.C. had to convince Ma to get outside help for her depression.

Early the next morning, K.C. headed toward Omaha to find a mental health specialist. He also planned to spend a few hours studying, if he could get focused on his studies. His thoughts raced, and he wasn't sure how effective his studying would be.

Suddenly he pulled the car to the side of the highway. He put his head in his hands and wept. He wept for his little sisters, each with their own problems, but especially for Skyla. He wept for his mother and her sorrow. He grieved at the absence of a father to talk to and who would carry the family burden. And most of all, he cried because he had forgotten to pray over the issues he was facing.

"Oh, Lord, forgive me." He prayed. "Without Your help all my efforts are useless. Lord, you know what I need before I even ask, but now I come to you pleading on behalf of my family. Help me to help them. Help me find a Christian counselor who will help my mother and get to the source of her pain. Please, Lord, I need you now."

When finished praying, K.C. felt the burden lifted and realized that the Lord was carrying it, too. He started the car again, and drove with peace in his heart. He was always amazed at how all-encompassing God's love was. He was astonished at how he could lay all his burdens at God's feet and be assured that 'all things would work together for good'.

K.C. arrived in Omaha with a fresh sense of purpose. He first went to the library where he could take care of his own business, but also do a search online for local therapists that recognized value in traditional healing arts as well as present day medicines. He needed to be sure that his mother's beliefs would not be ridiculed, but that she would receive acceptance as both a Christian and a Native American. He laughed to himself as he thought of the old advertising mantra "let your fingers do the walking." He was going to let God do the walking; He would guide K.C. in his search for a doctor.

By the time he'd finished his business at the library, K.C. had the name of several Native American Christian therapists, he finished his application for the bar exam, and he obtained information on review classes scheduled on the campus of the University of Nebraska in Omaha. He also found out that he could volunteer at the Legal Aid Society, not to work as a lawyer per se, but to assist people with advice, telling them where they could get the type of help they needed and put them in touch with the right agencies.

Best of all, K.C. found the address for Pastor Jim. Pastor Jim led the youth group he attended before leaving for college. He was surprised and pleased to find that his pastor-mentor still lived in the Omaha area. *Thank you, Lord, for knowing what I would need even before I thought to ask….*

"Is Pastor Jim in?" K.C. asked the church secretary who was busy preparing leaflets for the mail.

She nodded and asked him to wait just a minute. She knocked softly on the door of the pastor's office and was answered with, "Enter." She stepped inside just long enough to inform Pastor Jim that he had a visitor. She opened the door for K.C. and returned to her desk to continue stuffing envelopes.

"Why, K.C., look at you, all grown up!" Pastor Jim, on the other hand, had aged since K.C. last saw him. His hair was grey at the temples and crow's feet at the corners of his eyes evidenced his smiling, cheerful spirit. He reached out his right hand to shake K.C.'s and clapped him on the back. "What have you been up to? Come on into my office and fill me in…" He walked toward a pair of easy chairs, still shaking K.C.'s hand.

For the next hour and a half, K.C. shared the recent events in his life. He didn't focus on himself, but asked Pastor Jim to keep his little sister in prayer. Pastor Jim promised to visit Skyla as long as she was still in a local facility. K.C. also asked Pastor Jim to pray with him regarding his mother's care. Pastor Jim offered to look over the list of counselors and to help K.C. choose a trusted therapist for his mother. He even made the phone call to set up the initial appointment for K.C. to meet the psychotherapist. They talked of old times, reminiscing about the Youth Group and the great times they had. K.C. told of his college experiences and his plans for the future. All in all, the time was well-spent and K.C. left feeling uplifted and encouraged.

With the appointment set for the next week K.C. drove back to the farm and found Shyne struggling to keep the children under control. Ma had allowed Shyne to get her cleaned up and dressed before she sat on the porch. K.C. sat next to her, wishing he could say the right thing. Instead, he sat in companionable silence, smoothing her skirt on her knee.

After a few minutes, she reached out and touched his hand. He told her of his visit with Pastor Jim. "You remember him, don't you, Ma? He used to visit our chapel when I was a kid… Pastor Jim, do you remember him?" She didn't answer; she went back to staring toward the road. He told her of the appointment he had scheduled for the following Monday, and was pleased to see her nod ever so slightly, acknowledging his efforts on her behalf, and he trusted the Lord to work it all out once they took the steps needed toward her recovery.

Chapter 13

With her tears spent, Isobel went to the bathroom, washed her face with icy cold water, and took a deep breath. She dialed the all-too-familiar phone number.

"Dr. Fitz, this is Isobel Kirk… yes, she's gone…"

At the other end of the line she heard the strangled sound of the doctor trying to compose himself. His voice was choking and he said he would be right over to confirm her death. He also said that he would call the coroner and take care of all the details, for which Isobel was grateful because she didn't have a clue of the process of reporting a death in the home.

When he arrived, Isobel could see from his red-rimmed eyes and the flush of his cheeks and nose that Dr. Fitz-Randolph had been crying. She never knew a physician to care so much for a patient, and she wondered at his sentimentality. *Perhaps,* she thought, *it is time for him to retire, if he gets this emotional at the loss of a patient.* He entered the house at her invitation, and went directly to the bedroom without speaking. He stood in the doorway looking at Aunt Betty with his hands clasped at his chest.

"Could I have a few minutes with her?" he asked Isobel quietly.

"Unh, sure, I guess… do you need me to do something else?"

"No. I'll just be a few minutes, and then we can talk." He moved to close the door behind him, indicating his desire for privacy.

Isobel was left confused, standing in the hallway, so she went to the kitchen to fix coffee. She brought out a small loaf of banana bread that she'd baked the day before to avoid throwing out some over-ripe bananas. Cutting generous slices, buttering them, and placing them on a serving plate served to busy her hands and mind. She couldn't face what was coming: the wake, the funeral, burial and finally, the aloneness.

Dr. Fitz came out of Auntie's room and gently closed the door behind him. "I tidied up a bit, so the coroner could get to her bed…" he said nodding his head in the direction of the door. "I didn't move anything personal, just adjusted the bedside table and made a bit of space…" With each sentence, his voice faded at the end as if the effort of speaking was too much.

"Come, sit here," Isobel pulled out one of the metal and vinyl chairs by the table.

Dr. Fitz-Randolph sat with a deep sigh. "I suppose you're wondering why Betty's death hits me so hard." He lifted his eyes to Isobel's. She nodded, but did not speak. Pouring coffee into the mug for him helped calm her just a bit. She offered the bread and he took one slice onto his saucer.

"Betty was a lovely lady. I fell in love with her as a teen with nothing to offer her. I didn't tell her anything, but held out hope that she might come to love me once I came back to town as a doctor." He took a sip of the rich, black beverage. "I thought my successful completion of my studies and setting up practice where I could support her would win her heart. The problem was, I didn't know she had already lost her heart to another. When she fell in love, she fell hard; she never got over her first love, and I never got over her. I hoped for years that her heart would soften toward me…"

Again the tears formed in his eyes, and by this time Isobel was just as moved. Thinking of her own lost love and the love story Aunt Betty shared with her, as well as Dr. Fitz's unrequited love, made Isobel wonder if ever love won out. *Was it possible to find happiness in love, or was that only in fairy tales?* She wondered.

"Is this what you meant about questions I might have in coming weeks?"

"No, my dear. You have much to discover and I cannot break a confidence because of my doctor-patient relationship with your aunt. I can only hope you are strong enough to deal with what you learn."

Isobel wondered that he could so easily tell her of a secret, of his promise to keep it, and pique her curiosity in such a gentle manner. She could read compassion in his action, but felt angry at being kept in the dark. "Doesn't that relationship end with the death of the patient?" she asked harshly.

"One might think so, but I take the promise seriously, so I am sorry, my dear. I will be glad to answer questions once you discover the secret, but I cannot tell you what has been kept from you by my patient and her brother."

Isobel thought back to Aunt Betty's request that she not hate her father, and realized it was all a part of the same puzzle. Longing to ask more questions, but not knowing where to start, she let the conversation lapse. They both stood to their feet as they heard the coroner's hearse drive up.

Isobel sat at the kitchen table while the coroner and his assistant moved Aunt Betty from her bed onto the gurney. She couldn't bear to watch them zip closed the black bag, preferring to see it wheeled out with the white sheet covering her.

"Where will he take her?" she asked Dr. Fitz as the coroner drove away.

"Your aunt made all the funeral arrangements several years ago, realizing her age was creeping up there. She will be taken to the Meier Funeral Home and her burial will be at the Final Rest Cemetery just outside of town."

Isobel nodded, knowing the small town had few choices in such matters, anyway.

"Will you be alright? I need to leave now, to finish up the paperwork…"

"I'll be fine," she answered halfheartedly, knowing she wouldn't be, now that she was alone in the world. After showing him to the door and watching him drive off, Isobel felt more alone than ever.

She sat for a moment wondering at her future, now as she moved beyond taking care of her aunt.

❧

Isobel was roused from her daydreaming by the loud ring of the old telephone.

"Hello?"

"Izzie, it's Jason."

Isobel hadn't heard from him in a couple of months. She figured he was either too busy or had moved on, maybe dating someone else. Afraid to find out, she never called him to ask.

"Hi, Jason, how are you?"

"Well that sounds kinda subdued. Are you OK?"

"My Aunt Betty died in her sleep last night… I guess I am just processing everything… trying to figure out what to do next…"

"Oh, Izzie, I am so sorry. I wish I could come and be with you during this time, but…"

"No, Jason. You coming here would only confuse me more. I need to get through this time on my own and tie up her loose ends. I need to let people know… There's the visitation, funeral and all, then I guess there will be a reading of her will… I need to find out if any distant relatives are around to notify and figure out what I am going to do now that she is gone…" Isobel's voice cracked as she said the words aloud. *Gone… she is gone.* Despite having had months to prepare for this loss, the reality seemed weird, almost dreamlike. It felt as though Aunt Betty were just in the other room needing to be turned. Or that she was out of the house at the store, or something. *Gone? How does someone just stop living? How does a body stop functioning? What happens afterwards? Is there a heaven or hell to float off to?* Isobel's mind continued on various tangents until Jason's voice brought her back.

"Izzie, did you hear what I said? I want to be there for you. I am waiting for you to be ready to see me again. Just let me know and I will come to you. I don't care what my family thinks… I am in love with you and will always love you. Remember that!"

For a second Isobel longed for the safety and comfort of her relationship with Jason. But then she remembered why she was at her aunt's house in the first place.

"No, Jason. We can continue as friends, like I said before. But you need to focus on your studies. Chase your own dreams before you try to complicate them with a partner your parents won't tolerate. Please, let's just be friends."

"Isobel, I keep you in my heart as I study every day. If it makes you happy, I will settle for friendship for now." And before he could say more, Isobel made an excuse to get off the phone, her heart thumping into her throat, and tears threatening her eyes.

Isobel moved through the next few days in a fog. Many of the details had been taken care of through Aunt Betty's instructions, just as Dr. Fitz had said. Food began arriving within hours of the news of Aunt Betty's death getting out: casseroles, bread and pies, cakes and cookies. So much food was delivered that Isobel began freezing what could be frozen to prevent spoilage and waste.

The same elderly women who had accompanied Aunt Betty to her graduation came to the house and made short work of cleaning it, focusing on the bedroom, taking out anything that spoke to Betty's illness and death. Isobel had not been able to go into the room since the hearse had carried her beloved aunt away, so she was grateful for their help.

She was surprised at the number that turned out for the wake. She had not found any phone numbers or addresses of relatives, so she had to assume that there were none to contact. However, several people came up to her at the visitation to say that they were distantly related… third cousins or something… and how touched they were by the loss. *Where had they been during her life, and throughout the illness?* Isobel thought, and then felt bad at thinking such mean things. It seemed the whole town, and several neighboring communities turned up for the funeral. The cathedral-like community church was filled, with some even sitting in the choir loft above the main floor of the sanctuary. Several men stood in the back, while the mother's room was crowded with women, but few children. Dr. Fitz joined the pastor on the platform, and spoke on behalf of 'family member's'.

Isobel felt conspicuous sitting alone in the family pew at the front, staring at the blond wooden casket with brushed nickel handles and latches. Atop the coffer sat a photo of Betty taken in her younger days, when most of the congregants would have known her. She preferred, according to her instructions, for people to remember her like that rather than seeing her after the illness had ravaged her body. Even Isobel had not viewed the body as was tradition; she chose to remember her aunt living and vibrant, as well, glad that she had said her good-byes while Betty was yet living.

The pastor gave a moving eulogy and several close friends also spoke. The choir sang two of Betty's favorite hymns, *Peace like a River* and *Blessed Assurance*, and the congregation stood together to sing the old standards *Amazing Grace* and *Shall We Gather at the River*. Isobel couldn't sing along; the words caught in her throat and she was still struggling with her belief in God and the idea of a hereafter. But the tunes did seem comforting both in words and their melodies and Isobel felt more at peace as the service came to a conclusion.

They filed out of the church with Isobel leading the procession, as she followed the elderly pallbearers carrying the coffin. She got into her seat as they place the coffin into the rear end of the hearse. A long parade of vehicles followed the leader out to the cemetery. It took longer for the people to assemble around the burial plot than the actual graveside service.

Isobel was given the seat of honor at the side of the plot, under a green tent. Still moving as though on auto-pilot, Isobel stared at the equipment on which the casket was place. It was a contraption used to lower the box into the ground safely. The pile of dirt from out of the hole was piled to the side with an artificial turf covering to camouflage it.

As the pastor spoke briefly of the blessed hope of eternal life, Isobel mind drifted to thinking of the last funeral she had attended. It was days before her fourteenth birthday; her father had suffered for a year and a half with cirrhosis of the liver caused by his years of drinking. He had not been a mean drunk; he was a slobbery sentimental man when drinking alcohol. He would cry and tell her how sorry he was, how he loved her and her mother.

Now his words made more sense, although Isobel still wondered just what the secret was that he and Aunt Betty shared. *Why did Aunt Betty die before telling her? What horrible thing was she supposed to forgive her father for?* Dr. Fitz obviously knew more than he was willing to share. She would continue to ask him questions, keep probing until he satisfied her curiosity.

Realizing the pastor had finished, and that the crowd was dispersing, Isobel rose from her seat. The rest of the day passed in a haze… the reception at the church seemed more like a party; everyone smiled as they talked of Betty Kirk. The gathering felt oppressive. Isobel was glad when all the formalities finished and Dr. Fitz dropped her back at the farm. She entered the kitchen hesitantly, knowing she was once again alone. Recognizing her good friend loneliness, she sat down at the table, head in her hands, and wondered if she would always feel so empty.

Chapter 14

Jason had trouble concentrating on his studies after he spoke with Isobel on the phone. He wanted nothing more than to comfort her, to wrap his arms around her and wipe the tears from her beautiful eyes. He couldn't bear the fact that she was grieving alone. More than ever before, he wanted to be with her.

He had his commitment to school, which was also important to him, but his heart yearned for Isobel, and nothing his parents could say or do would change that. They had insisted on his not following her when she left last summer. He wanted to even though she told him not to, but his parents, especially his mother, stood firm. If he left to chase after *that girl* they would cut off his support for medical school, and he would be on his own.

What choice did he have? If he wanted to become a physician and help hundreds of *poor, immigrant* people that his parents so vehemently disapproved of, he needed their help. So he found himself sitting in a dorm at medical school at Harvard, while Isobel grieved alone in Kansas.

Walking to lectures one day, several weeks after speaking to Isobel, he saw a tall, elegant young lady walking confidently across the Quad. Her dark hair hung down her back, swaying as she walked. "Isobel?" He ran after her, "Izzie?" When he touched her shoulder, she turned around, but it wasn't Isobel. Her face was pale with black lipstick and heavy eye makeup. Her hair obviously dyed to create a Gothic look, totally opposite Isobel's natural exotic beauty.

"Oh, so sorry, I thought you were someone else,"

Apparently it wasn't unusual for guys to approach her; she laughed at his confusion. Then she asked if he wanted her phone number, telling him she thought he was cute. He told her, no, and backed away as she laughed all the more at his discomfort.

What on earth am I doing? Am I going crazy? I need to buckle down and focus! Jason gave himself a silent tongue-lashing as he headed back toward the lecture hall.

Jason found a way to refocus and got into his studies with a vengeance. He was determined to finish top of his class, if only to prove to himself that he could. He heard the part in 1 Corinthians 10:31 "whatsoever ye do, do all to the glory of God" as if it was spoken into his ear. He knew then that he had to continue working toward his goal. He wasn't looking for special consideration for a residency program; he only wanted to use his God-given talents to the honor of his Lord and Saviour.

Studying kept his mind busy, but Jason refused to give up on Isobel. He kept her picture on his desk to remind him of their goals for the future, the plans they'd made while dating. Although he had yet to disappoint his father with the news that he did not want to be a surgeon, his energy went into building the broad knowledge-base needed for Family Medicine. Even if he ended up in Kansas, rather than in practice with his father in Boston, he would be happy providing he and Isobel were together.

Chapter 15

Isobel wandered around the big farmhouse, wiping imaginary dust from the old sideboard, straightening doilies on the burgundy, velvet couch and easy chair. It really wasn't necessary. The ladies from Aunt Betty's church had just cleaned the day before. They came each Wednesday to make sure all was in order and ended up staying the day tidying and cleaning. They always left with the promise of returning even though she hadn't asked them to, and they asked nothing in return. When she offered pay, they seemed hurt at the suggestion.

By the time they left, Isobel felt like a whirlwind had attacked the place; the house was spotless, everything was where Aunt Betty kept it, and nothing was out of place. Isobel knew they were only helping, but it only served to remind her of her loss. She missed conversation and morning tea with Aunt Betty, and she missed having her there for advice. The ladies meant well, she knew that, but it couldn't continue. She needed to decide what to do with her life, where to go, how to support herself.

The first week after the funeral had been spent tying up the loose ends of Aunt Betty's estate. The reading of the will, looking at her finances, closing out accounts: all these needed to be addressed right away even though Isobel was still grieving and couldn't seem to think clearly. Dr. Fitz helped some, always sitting nearby when she had to attend to business, just so he could make sure she understood things. Isobel depended on him probably more than she should have.

"Well, Miss Kirk, it seems you are both fortunate and unfortunate. I'm sure your aunt felt she was doing something good in leaving everything to you. At the time she wrote her will, I believe her farm was doing better, as were her finances. However, the picture changed significantly over the last few years." The lawyer leaned back in his seat and put his hands together in a church-steeple under his chin. He seemed deep in thought, but Isobel was sure he already knew what he was going to say next.

"Miss Betty Kirk, your aunt, was a fine woman… um… not a brilliant businesswoman, though. She was often too easy on farm hands and entered into agreements with tenant farmers but didn't always hold them to the terms of those agreements." He paused for effect and Isobel sat patiently, looking at her hands in her lap, waiting for him to make his point.

Dr. Fitz-Randolph, on the other hand, had little patience for the lawyer's dramatics. "Just say what you mean, Sorenson. The girl doesn't need all the details of her aunt's life. Just give her the facts, so we can work on solutions, if there are problems."

Mr. Sorenson seemed annoyed at the interruption. He resumed where he had left off, as if Dr. Fitz hadn't spoken. "She just was too soft. As a result, your aunt left little beside the farmhouse, the land and outbuildings and farming accoutrements, such as they are. Her bank account has little more than enough to pay for her outstanding bills with the local stores." He nodded for emphasis. "She does have a life insurance policy. The payout is $100,000.00. Now, that can sound like a lot of money to a young woman, but it really isn't all that much. Betty has a mortgage on the farm…"

"Now, wait a minute, Sorenson. She paid that farm off years ago…" Dr. Fitz-Randolph leaned forward toward the lawyer.

"Yes, that she did, Dr. Fitz-Randolph. However, when things got rough a while back, she took out a reverse mortgage to take care of some necessary repairs and to send for tuition payments for Isobel at that *boarding school* she was at." The scorn in his voice reflected his disgust. Mr. Sorenson felt that private schools were responsible for the decline of quality in public schools, and that all those supporting private education were against 'the American way'.

Dr. Fitz sat back into his chair, stunned. Isobel was only starting to grasp the significance of their communication. Her aunt left all to her, but all also meant debts as well as assets, and it sounded like the debts amounted to more than the assets.

"How bad is it?" Isobel asked softly. Perhaps if she spoke soft enough, the answer wouldn't be so loud, so devastating as she expected.

"Quite bad, I'm afraid," Mr. Sorenson responded equally soft, trying to ease the blow.

The three sat in silence for a moment, Isobel looking at Dr. Fitz and he was looking at the lawyer. Mr. Sorenson watched the two of them, waiting for signal that they were ready for the rest of the bad news.

"It's just that Betty had some bad investments over the years that…"

"Now, Sorenson, let's not rehash old business…"

"But it isn't old to me, Dr. Fitz…" Isobel protested, but he cut her off.

"Isobel, Betty wouldn't want this. Let's talk about this later, OK?" He turned back to Mr. Sorenson. "So, the long and short of it is, Isobel inherits everything, is that correct? But, aside from the real estate, there are debts to be paid, right? Now let's get down to brass tacks… exactly how much debt?"

Mr. Sorenson shuffled his papers, moved the paperweight on the corner of the desk over to the other side, and then he reached out with a single paper in his hand. Dr. Fitz took the paper, looked at it briefly and handed it to Isobel.

"So that's that then. We can talk later, and I'll bring Isobel back later to sign any papers that need doing." Dr. Fitz-Randolph got up from his chair, not waiting for Isobel to speak. He motioned for her to get up from the chair, and guided her by the elbow to the door of the office. The secretary looked up as they passed, but neither spoke. Dr. Fitz just continued leading Isobel out of the law firm and to his waiting truck.

As they drove back toward the farm, he didn't try to open conversation and Isobel kept staring at the paper in her hand. $-\$58{,}000^{00}$. She'd never seen numbers like that; she'd never earned money like that. Her paychecks at the bookstore had been in the $200-$500 range. She'd never even held a thousand dollars in her hands before. And she hadn't earned enough to file income tax, let alone that much money. How would she ever take care of her beloved aunt's debts?

She couldn't understand how the God her aunt talked about so much could allow this to happen. How could He allow Aunt Betty to die; how could He allow her to have it so hard that her debts ran up that high? How could He put this kind of burden on her shoulders? She wasn't ready for this. She only just lost her aunt and now she had to deal with this? She'd only just graduated college and life was supposed to be just starting for her. But here she was, in debt for thousands of dollars and she didn't have a clue where to get a job, not a clue! No wonder she hadn't committed to God – He didn't seem to care for her!

Dr. Fitz watched Isobel out of the corner of his eye as he drove toward the farm. He could tell she was worried, scared, angry, hurt. So many emotions seemed to be running through her as she sat folding and unfolding the paper from the lawyer. The dampness from her hands caused the paper to wilt more with every fold.

"Hey, don't worry yourself." He put on a relaxed affect as he pulled up the driveway to the house. "We can take care of this…"

"How can *we* take care of this? I don't have that kind of money. I doubt you do, and anyway, you don't have any obligation here, do you?" Isobel's statement put Dr. Fitz in his place, but he didn't let it go.

"Debts are cleared by having estate sales… we see them quite often out in these parts. Families that don't want to come home to the old farm just sell off as much as possible to cover the debts and that's that! You don't have to carry the debt on your shoulders, unless you plan to stay on the farm…" he left the question hanging as he pulled up her driveway. Isobel didn't try to answer, either, as she got out and headed for the house. She hadn't thought that far ahead.

Tears streamed down Isobel's cheeks as she watched kindly Dr. Fitz drive away. She knew she had been mean, but at this point she didn't care. Her heart hurt so deeply with the losses she'd experienced first, the pain of rejection from Jason's parents and breaking it off with him, then the loss of her only remaining relative, and now this burden on top of it all. She felt so alone, so very alone.

Dropping the curtain over the window, she turned to the kitchen that had once been her haven of rest when visiting with Aunt Betty. Isobel felt duped. She nearly fell for that God thing that her aunt spoke of so lovingly. She had even come to enjoy listening to Aunt Betty read the Bible and prayer. But now she was so angry with God that she wanted nothing to do with Him.

Reaching over to the table where Aunt Betty kept her Bible and devotional materials, Isobel picked them up and pushed them into a drawer on the bureau. She couldn't take the constant reminder and she certainly wasn't going to use them. *There was no way on God's…* She laughed at herself. *Why say 'God's green earth' if I don't believe in Him?* She turned from the bureau and picked up the paper with all the numbers on it.

What should I do? She wondered as she looked over the numbers once again. *Could I raise enough money to pay off this debt?* Then she wondered if she should even try. *Do I even want to stay on this farm? Why would I want to?*

Isobel thought for a moment and then decided that she needed to talk to a different attorney. Maybe Mr. Sorenson hadn't told her all the details; maybe she wasn't responsible for her aunt's debts. She decided find a neutral lawyer, one from the city. Looking around, she found the Yellow Pages book and began searching for the name of a lawyer to call or for the Legal Aid phone number.

Chapter 16

That same week was much better for K.C. On the morning of the appointment set up by Pastor Jim, K.C. woke feeling optimistic for the future. He had spent the week focusing more on God's messages from the Scriptures; he claimed promises and spent time in prayer for his family and his future. He wanted to take care of them and lift the burden from his mother's shoulders. For too long, she had carried the burden. She may have even felt abandoned when he went off to college. But he planned to change that.

Through his devotions, he came to realize that his first priority should be his family… *"But if any provide not for his own, and especially for those of his own house, he hath denied the faith, and is worse than an infidel." (1 Timothy 5:8KJV)* was the verse for yesterday's devotion. He had always equated the first part of the verse with his choice to practice law helping other Native Americans, but it was more than that.

His family deserved his focus, not just reaping financial rewards from his career. With his father dead and the man that fathered Talitha, Shyne and Skyla out of the picture, K.C. knew he needed to step up to the plate, to be the man of the house. He needed to provide spiritual leadership and a physical presence, as well as financial sustenance, to his family. He started having his devotions at the dining-room table rather than staying in his room. Before long, both Shyne and Ma were joining him at the table.

Ma was still withdrawn and quiet, answering in subdued tones only if she felt able to. More often than not, she would look blankly at whoever asked a question. K.C. kept her lifted up in prayer hoping she would regain the strength she used to have. Somehow, losing Skyla to incarceration had affected her like losing a child through death. He vaguely remembered his mother being depressed when he was quite young, although at the time he had no name for her tears. Now he wondered why she hadn't gone for help years ago. Perhaps she felt she was doing fine, but this time was definitely worse. Whenever she had challenges in the past, she leaned on her faith in God and pulled through. K.C. held on to the hope that the Christian counselor would guide her back to her Anchor.

Shyne was living up to her name. She was bright and lively, trying to keep the children under control and urging Ma to get up and come out to join the family each day. Ma did brighten with the grandchildren playing at her feet; she leaned forward to watch them, although she said little. Shyne had taken to motherhood and was thriving in her role as auntie/caregiver to Skyla's kids.

Taddy loved the attention from Brya and CeCe. They acted like he was a doll for them to play with, except when he got in the way of their games. Then they didn't get mean to him, but instead cried to Shyne to get him out of their way. Taddy giggled at their cries, and found many ways to get the same result.

"What's on your plate for today, Shyne?" K.C. looked over his breakfast to her.

"Well, since you are taking Ma into the city, I thought I might visit with some of my schoolmates." She glanced his way, "No, not one of the bad girls! It's Cassie."

K.C. relaxed knowing that Mrs. C's daughter was a Christian, like her mother. She rarely went out with other teens, unless they were from her church. "Is she coming over?" He asked.

"Well, I don't have a way to haul these kids now, do I?" She smiled at him, taking no issue with the question. "Maybe you can help me get my license one of these days, just in case of an emergency when you aren't here…?"

K.C. grinned at his eager little sister, "Sure, kiddo. I'd love to." He turned to Ma.

"Ma, we need to head out now."

"Oh, where are we going?" she asked softly.

"Just into the city for an appointment," he replied, trying not to say anything that might upset her. If he mentioned a doctor or therapist he was afraid she would bolt, or just not cooperate.

Ma looked almost excited as she asked, "Are we going to see my Skyla?"

"No, Ma, you know we can only visit her on scheduled visitation days…"

Her affect flattened again, but she allowed Shyne to help her out to the car. It was obvious she needed help to deal with having a child in prison. Shyne buckled the seatbelt and pecked Ma's cheek with a little kiss. "Be good now," she admonished Ma as if she were the parent instead of the child.

K.C. got in the driver's seat and buckled up. He looked over at Ma as he started the car and saw the same blank look so often in her eyes these days. She sat like a bag of potatoes with her shoulders slouching, her chest down on her tummy, barely recognizable as herself. His optimism waned slightly, but then he breathed a prayer for strength, claimed a promise and turned the car down the drive toward the highway to Omaha.

He turned on some soothing, classical music and Ma seemed relaxed. She closed her eyes where always before, on their outings to Omaha, she would take in the scenery and changes since the last drive. *Hopefully, she will stay relaxed when she sees it is a therapist she is visiting*, he thought.

Dr. Pearson was prompt with his appointments, and one of his patients just leaving as K.C. and Ma drove up. K.C. helped her out of the car and guided her toward the office entrance. Painted on the door, in bold lettering was Donald J. Pearson, MD. Under his name, however, were the words K.C. had hoped would not be there: Adult and Family Psychiatry. Thankfully, in her near catatonic condition, Ma paid little attention to the door and allowed K.C. to open it and direct her inside to a chair. He went to the counter to check her in, finding that it would only be minutes until Dr. Pearson called for her.

Initially, Dr. Pearson would interview the patient alone, the nurse had told him. Then, once he established the course of care, he would call in K.C. to discuss treatment options. According to the nurse, by doing it this way, the patient feels their privacy is protected. Otherwise, K.C. figured, Ma would think they were talking about her, so it was just as well she go in first.

The nurse appeared at a side door and announced that Dr. Pearson was ready for DeeDee Fox, and K.C. assisted her to the door. The nurse took her by the elbow and nodded her thanks to K.C. as she guided Ma inside the doorway and closed the door behind them. K.C. felt out of control, unsure of his choice to bring Ma to a therapist. He bowed his head and prayed silently, asking for peace and guidance with the many issues on his plate. He continued talking to the Lord throughout the 45 minutes of Ma's visit with Dr. Pearson. He lifted his head only after hearing the nurse's voice, calling his name.

"Yes?" he responded quickly, hoping he was answering on the first call. He didn't want her to think that he also had mental problems. *There you go, worrying about what others might think,* he reflected. *If I can't overcome my concern, how can I expect Ma to accept counseling?*

"The doctor will see you now," and she opened the door wide enough for him to enter the narrow hallway. Along the walls, he noticed unusual artwork: Disney© collector prints of cartoon characters framed to look like film frames. *How strange,* he mused, *I would expect to see these in a pediatric clinic…*

They arrived at the door of an expansive office. Inside, the room was furnished with quality dark wood furniture: a desk, several bookcases filled with the requisite books and journals on Mental Health and Psychiatry and a credenza under the window with several expensive-looking pieces of statuary. Also, at the other end of the room, encircling a fireplace, sat several cozy chairs and a large sofa. He looked around, missing the stereotypical couch. The expensive furniture and décor had K.C. wondering if this was the right place for them. Although Pastor Jim recommended Dr. Pearson, from all appearances, his fees would be outrageous. *Well, we're committed for this visit,* he considered, *we can always go to a different, less expensive clinic next time and start from scratch...*

"Come on in, Mr. Fox," Dr. Pearson reached out to shake his hand.

"Uh...Thanks," His manner was warm and welcoming; K.C.'s first impression was definitely positive.

Dr. Pearson motioned to one of the overstuffed armchairs near the glowing fireplace. "Let's sit down and talk for a bit."

It was then that K.C. realized his mother was already seated in another of the armchairs; she was so short, he hadn't seen her before. "Ma, you ok?" He looked into her eyes anxiously.

"Kwsind, I'm going to be ok. Dr. Pearson told me he can help." Her tone was still somewhat flat, but at least she had answered, so K.C. was hopeful. He looked to Dr. Pearson for confirmation of his mother's statement.

"Let me be honest. Your mother is clinically depressed, but I'm guessing you already figured that out, since you've brought her here..."

K.C. nodded.

"Right then. We have several treatment options and I'm hoping we can agree on one of them." Dr. Pearson explained everything from counseling alone to hospitalization as means of helping Ma. When K.C. asked him specifically for his best recommendation, rather than a list of care modalities, Dr. Pearson got right down to the plan.

"I suggest outpatient therapy with medication and shaman assistance. Would you know a medicine man on whom we might call?" he asked of K.C. and Ma both.

Ma nodded. "There is one on our reservation, but he doesn't approve of my faith."

K.C. responded, too. "Yeah, I spoke with Pastor Jim, and his recommendation was that you could help in that area, Dr. Pearson. We don't know too many that have a positive sense toward what they call 'the white man's religion'-Christianity."

"Well, yes, I can assist, but I do not perform the ceremonies myself. I prefer to maintain a separation between my counseling and the homeopathic methods used by the healers. I have no objection to their incorporation into the treatment plan, but I do not have the skills that they have." His honesty and openness was impressive.

"What I'd like to suggest is that Mrs. Fox think about how she wants to approach her treatment," he nodded in Ma's direction. Surprisingly, Ma shook her head in agreement. K.C. was pleased to see her engaged in the process. "Mrs. Fox, I would also like to suggest that you talk to your son about some of the issues we discussed."

Ma held her head down as if ashamed, but nodded her head again, in agreement with Dr. Pearson's instruction. "It won't be as difficult as you think," Dr. Pearson tried to reassure her. "Your son will not judge you harshly; he is also a Christian, right?"

K.C. acknowledged that he was a born again Christian and held fast to the teachings of Christ. He used the opportunity to assure his mother that he would be open to listening to anything she had to share. "Ma, you know I am always there for you! Haven't I taken care of you, stayed with you during this trying time, and always tried to help the girls?" She nodded. "So, I will listen. Don't ever feel that you can't talk to me."

Once that was established, K.C. wondered how to broach the subject of fees, but Dr. Pearson got to it before he could ask.

"I'm sure you are concerned about cost of treatment. Pastor Jim spoke to me of your need and, as I frequently do, I agreed to keep the fee within whatever you feel is adequate. I sometimes take on patients for no-fee treatment, but I know that goes against your culture. I appreciate that you do not take charity, and want to pay for services, so let's say, $10.00 a visit. Would that work for you?"

K.C. couldn't speak; his heart was full with gratitude to both Dr. Pearson and to his Lord and Savior for working this out before he even knew to ask. He reached out to shake Dr. Pearson's hand, and Ma also shook hands with the good doctor. He escorted them to the waiting room and spoke quietly to the receptionist before returning to his inner sanctum.

K.C. and Ma stood at the reception desk, and the girl smiled at them. "That will be a co-pay of $10.00, please." She spoke as if this was an everyday occurrence. K.C. paid the fee and he and Ma left with a weight lifted. Ma already seemed more alert and interested in looking around her environment instead of hiding in her shell. She watched the scenery pass by as they drove back home, and K.C. said nothing to upset the balance. In his mind, he wondered what his mother had to share with him, and when she would choose to share it.

Chapter 17

K.C. stopped at a pharmacy near home to fill the prescription that Dr. Pearson had written for Ma. Ma stayed in the car, but a noticeable improvement in her posture reassured him that Ma was better after just that first visit for therapy, although she had something on her mind that was interfering with her functioning. He wondered at the doctor's instructions to Ma and when she might share with him whatever it was she had on her mind. Dr. Pearson had cautioned him against forcing the issue. Instead, he told K.C. that gentle encouragement and support would give her the confidence to open up when the time was right.

When they arrived home, Ma took the initiative to undo her seatbelt and climb out of the car unassisted. She smiled when the grandchildren squealed their greetings to their grandmother, and even leaned down to give Brya a hug. K.C. was pleased to see his mother opening up to the grandchildren. Since it was likely that Brya and CeCe would be with them until adulthood, it was important that they feel loved and accepted in their home. He left Ma with Shyne and the kids and went to his own room for some much needed privacy.

K.C. realized, in the quiet of the drive home, that he had the bar exam coming up in February. He still needed to pass the test and get his legal profession back on track. The volunteer time with the Legal Aid Office kept his mind busy, but did nothing for bringing in an income, and his savings was getting depleted. He needed to balance his studying with ma's appointments and ensuring that Shyne did not feel overloaded

In the privacy of his room, K.C. took time with the Lord. Whenever he felt overwhelmed or uncertain of the future, prayer calmed his spirit. His Bible opened to his favorite verse from Jeremiah 29:11. *"For I know the plans I have for you," declares the LORD, "plans to prosper you and not to harm you, plans to give you hope and a future."* He had claimed this promise many times over his years of studying, assured of his call to work in the Native American community. Never in his wildest dreams did he think the Lord would lead him right back home. He opened his review material and set his mind toward passing the bar exam in six weeks.

Around dinnertime, K.C. came out of his room to find Ma helping Shyne in the kitchen. The two were talking softly, but not secretively, and looked up frequently to check on the toddlers playing on the living-room floor. He smiled at the domestic picture and breathed a bit easier seeing Ma pitching in. "What's for dinner, ladies?" he kissed his mother's cheek and squeezed Shyne's shoulder.

"Look at you! Hiding in your room all afternoon and now you want food?" Ma was actually teasing him.

"Hey, you know how it is…gotta study to pass the boards, and gotta pass the exam to work, and …"

"I know! You gotta work to eat!" She smiled proudly at her son towering above her.

He pecked her other cheek and moved out of the kitchen to where the children were playing. His gaze rested on Taddy's flushed face. "Is Taddy sick?" He reached out to the little boy's forehead and felt heat radiating before his hand before he even touched it. "He's got a fever!" He picked up the quiet little one who had been sitting away from the other two children.

Just then Taddy coughed a rough, hacking cough, rattling deep in his chest, and his nose began to run with thick, green mucous. His body felt limp when the coughing stopped; the spasms of choking on congestion brought up from his lungs racked his little frame.

"Shyne, we need to take him to the doctor or the emergency room!"

"No, I won't take my baby to that place. I heard people go there to die. I'm not putting Taddy in danger!"

"Aw, come on, sis. You don't believe those stories, do you? We live in the modern world, not back in the dark ages."

"K.C., you don't understand! The rez doesn't get the kind of care you saw out there in the big cities! We get the leftovers, the docs nobody wanted to hire… I just can't take the chance." She lifted Taddy out of K.C.'s arms, "You help Ma finish up. I'm gonna put him in a cool bath to bring down the fever…"

"What about that cough? He might need antibiotics… or it might be one of those flu bugs we hear about this time of year…they can be deadly for little children!" K.C. felt panic in his chest. They didn't need another crisis. And what of the other toddlers? Was it contagious? Would they also get sick? The weight on his shoulders got heavier by the minute, then he heard a still small voice, *my son, I won't give you more than you can bear…* He recognized the voice and thanked the Lord for His reminder.

Shyne was caring for Taddy for now, so he did as she asked, and helped Ma finish serving up dishes of food for the little ones. He took them out to the table, and put the children into chairs by their dishes. Ma brought two plates of food out, one for him, the other for her. They sat with Brya and CeCe and Ma asked K.C. if he would say grace over the dinner. They reached out to hold hands in a circle with the children, and bowed their heads.

"Lord, we thank you for answering our prayers before we ask. We thank you for caring for us from day to day, and now we thank you for the blessing of having Ma better and of having this food on our table. Be with Shyne as she cares for Taddy, and help him to get stronger to fight this illness." He closed the prayer in the customary way after presenting several other requests before the Lord.

"Uncle, why we have to ask God if he already give us answers?" Three-year-old Brya had obviously listened closely to her Uncle K.C.

"Well, God likes us to talk to Him. It's like when you ask for food, even though you know we have food in the house. Jesus wants us to tell Him what we worry about, so He can help us not worry." K.C. wasn't sure if she could understand his explanation and he wasn't used to explaining things to toddlers.

Brya just nodded. She was satisfied that Uncle K.C. had taken time to give her an answer. She picked up her fork and started eating without further ado. CeCe needed a bit of help, since he was only two-years-old. Ma had cut his food into bite-sized chunks and now showed him how to poke the food with his baby fork and take it up to his mouth. Watching her brought back memories to K.C. of the days when his little sisters were much younger. She seemed like her old self once again.

Suddenly he heard Shyne cry out for help. He rushed to the bathroom to find her holding a limp, unconscious Taddy. "He was just coughing and couldn't stop…then he passed out. He's turning blue around his lips…!"

K.C. grabbed the child and laid him on the floor. He took his index finger and swept the boys mouth and throat, clearing thick phlegm from his airway. He leaned over and breathed into the child's mouth the way he had learned in CPR class, and was relieved when Taddy responded with a deep gasp for air. "Now, Shyne, we have to take him to the emergency room! No questions, no arguments. Grab a few things and let's go right now." He turned to where his mother was standing watching the events.

"Ma, are you ok to watch Brya and CeCe, or should I go get Mrs. C?"

"I'll be fine, son. You go take care of that one. If I need help, Sister Violet will come on over. Don't you worry about me, now, just take care of my Tadi Hotah, and I will pray."

Shyne came out with a diaper bag overstuffed with clothing, diapers and bottles. Taddy sat on the floor, bleary-eyed and flushed. Once in a while a little whimper escaped his lips, otherwise he sat motionless. K.C. lifted him and guided Shyne out the door with a parting glance toward Ma to reassure him that she would be fine.

They drove to the nearest hospital to the Macy area, a PHS Indian Hospital in Winnebago. He dropped Shyne and Taddy off at the Emergency Department entrance and went to park the car. By the time he reached the reception desk, Shyne had been taken into a triage room, so he sat and waited and prayed. After what seemed like an eternity, the nurse came out and told him that he could go in to the screening area where they had already started an IV and had little Taddy in a giant sized metal crib.

"What are they saying, sis?"

"They want to admit him," she gulped, "they say he has pneumonia! How could he have pneumonia? Where did he get that? I don't understand…" she broke down and cried against K.C.'s chest.

"Sis, the good thing is that we got him here. He is still alive. He could have died back there when he stopped breathing, but he is still with us. Let's trust the doctors to make him well, and not try to figure out where his illness started." In his mind, K.C. wondered if Brya and CeCe had been ill recently; perhaps they brought the bug with them. Then his mind went in another direction, praying that they didn't get sick as well.

After the necessary paperwork was completed, Taddy was admitted to the hospital, and arrangements were made for Shyne to sleep in his room. K.C. needed to get back home, so he left her looking tiny and forlorn. *She was so young to have to deal with a sick child*, he thought. He tried to maintain his speed to the speed limit on his way home, despite his desire to rush back to Ma and Brya and CeCe. But when he got home, he was thankful to find the little ones had been bathed and tucked into bed, and Ma was sitting quietly working on beadwork to keep her hands busy.

They turned in early that evening to prepare for the busy days ahead. "Ma, don't forget to take your new medicine." He reminded her as she headed toward the bedroom.

"How often do I have to take it?"

"It's just once a day for now, Ma, and it will make you feel better."

"I heard the pills they give for mental problems make you numb."

K.C. tried to assure Ma that the medicines were better now. He had a battle on his hands convincing her of the benefits of taking pills, but he knew she would be better taking the antidepressant.

Ma's problems, Taddy's illness, Skyla's legal troubles and his upcoming test combined to make a heavy burden for a young single man. K.C. wondered about his study schedule. He would have to act as chauffeur for Ma to her appointments, as well as visits to Taddy until he was discharged healthy. The bar exam weighed heavily on his mind with just six weeks left to review. He also needed to attend a review session in Omaha in a couple of weeks. It all seemed like too much to deal with. The last thing he remembered before falling asleep was breathing a brief prayer…

Chapter 18

Isobel put off calling the Legal Aid number she found in the phone book; her nerves were frayed and she felt emotionally fragile. Until the financial issues began to seriously impact her life, she wanted to deal with more immediate issues. The first detail to take care of for Aunt Betty, was sorting through her possessions. Isobel knew she could not keep Auntie's clothes, nor did she want to. What she did want to do was to give the best items to Aunt Betty's church for distribution to the poor and needy. *It was what Aunt Betty would have wanted,* she thought.

As Isobel held up one dress after another, looking at the quality and condition, she thought of the various times she had seen her aunt wearing the garment. Some of Aunt Betty's perfume lingered in the fabric; Isobel breathed it in as she held one dress to her face. Suddenly her resolve crumbled.

"Oh, Auntie. Why, just when we were growing so close? Why did you have to go?" Tears welled up in her eyes and she sat on the edge of her aunt's bed, clutching the dress, rocking as she cried. "I just miss you so much! I know you are at peace, no more pain. But I miss you."

"Hello? Isobel, are you here?"

Isobel heard the familiar voice of Dr. Fitz. Quickly she dried her tears with her sleeve and straightened her clothes. A quick glance in the mirror reflected the dark circles under her eyes. *Oh well, nothing to do about them*, she thought. Otherwise, she looked acceptable. "I'm here, Dr Fitz," she called out as she opened the bedroom door and headed toward the kitchen where he usually landed when visiting.

"Ah, Isobel. I was driving by and just wanted to check in on you. How are you doing, my dear?"

Isobel looked at the kindly old gentleman and saw that grief had taken a toll on him as well. He appeared to have aged in the few weeks since Aunt Betty's death; his hair seemed greyer and his face drawn.

"You know. I'm doing as well as I can. Trying to tie up loose ends and decide what to do with my future."

"Well," he paused for effect as he looked over his glasses at her, "I might have some help for you on that count..."

"Are you talking a job possibility? Cause that's what I really need about now," Isobel replied. "But I don't know how my degree could translate into a job in this area... It's in International Business, you know?"

"Yes, you have a specialty in International Studies, but the foundation of your degree is Business Management or Administration, isn't that right?"

She nodded and looked at him quizzically. In such a rural region of the state, Isobel could not see an application for her degree, unless he was hoping to get her into managing the local grocery or one of the restaurants, neither of which appealed to her.

"Look, my office manager needs to take a leave of absence. Now..." he raised his hand to silence her protests, "I know it isn't what you had in mind, but it would be something until you get Betty's affairs in order, don't you think? It isn't difficult work, and I'm not a hard task-master." He smiled gently at her with a nod of his head.

Isobel gazed down at her feet for a moment, and then realizing how few her options were, decided it could work. After all, Dr. Fitz knew better than anyone all the struggles she had been through, and what was on the horizon. He would understand if she needed a day to take care of legal battles or to clear financial burdens. On top of that, she knew he would be a great reference for her next effort at finding employment.

"I'll do it," Isobel said looking him straight in the eye. "Do you know how long she will be gone?" referring to his office manager.

"Not exactly, but we can play it by ear. If she comes back before you are ready to move on, you can stay on as her assistant for a bit. But if you need to leave before she comes back, I hope you will give me adequate time to round up another…?"

"Of course, Dr. Fitz, I wouldn't leave you in the lurch, not after you've been such a great support to me."

"Good. Then it's all settled. Except one detail…when can you start?"

"When do you need me?"

"Yesterday would be nice, but if you can make it tomorrow, that will do," Dr. Fitz smiled at his joke. Isobel shook his hand, and he made to leave. "Gotta get back, now. I never know when I'm needed, but I stand ready when called." And he saluted like a soldier and left the same way he'd entered, through the back door.

Isobel stood for a moment, watching him pull out of the driveway. She wondered why Dr. Fitz would worry about her. Why was he trying to help so much? He acted like she was his family. Surely it wasn't just his sense of duty to Aunt Betty, but what then?

Then she thought of the job offer. Not in all her dreams had she thought of settling in such a rural area. *Actually, this would be just a steppingstone toward my career,* she thought, *nothing permanent.* She shivered at the thought of staying in rural Kansas between White Cloud and Highland, towns most people never heard of. Isobel was certain her future lay somewhere far from this bump in the road. She headed back toward the bedroom to resume work on sorting auntie's things.

The dresses lay on the bed where she'd left them, but something in the corner of the room caught her eye. It distracted her from sorting clothing. Sparkling on the bureau, reflecting the single beam of light that slipped between the mini-blind and the curtain, a ring she hadn't noticed before. It amazed Isobel that, as many times as she had been in Aunt Betty's room, as many hours she spent sitting with her beloved aunt, she never saw this beautiful piece of jewelry.

As a matter of fact, she never saw her aunt wear rings or earrings. She remembered a chain auntie wore around her neck and tucked into her dress. Isobel had never had a reason to ask Aunt Betty about it; it didn't seem important, but now she knew its secret... It held this ring close to Aunt Betty's heart! Yes, the ring lay on the bureau with a slender gold chain threaded through it and carefully placed on a piece of velvet fabric on the dresser.

Isobel could only assume that this ring was the final remnant of Aunt Betty's youthful romance. It might have been her engagement ring, although the setting was nontraditional. It was beautifully designed with leaves and tendrils twisting on either side of the stone, lifting it off the ring just enough to highlight the flower design with a round-cut ruby for its center. The gold was what caught the light – it was brighter than any Isobel had seen, and she knew it must be high quality. Isobel recognized unique colors in the gold...green leaves and softly pink tendrils – indicating it was Black Hills gold from South Dakota.

She held the delicate ring in her fingers as she walked across the room to the window, turning the ring and looking at every detail. Isobel imagined a younger, beautiful Betty and her beau anticipating their life ahead as she and Jason had done, and she wondered if she would become a lonely spinster like her aunt. She loved Jason still, and saw no point in the future where she could open her heart to another. It seemed impossible right now; she couldn't even consider it.

Looking around the room, Isobel wondered what other secrets lay hidden amongst Aunt Betty's belongings. Knowing there had to be clues or an answer to what secret Aunt Betty and her father kept from her, Isobel had chosen to start where it was safe...sorting clothing. Certainly no clues could be among the shirtwaist dresses and blouses and skirts in her aunt's closet, although there was no telling what might be in her bureau. *People were known to hide all sorts of things in their underwear drawer*, she thought and she glanced back at the bureau.

Isobel shook her head as if the motion would enforce her resolve. *I need to finish the clothes, and then I can move on…the mystery will have to wait for now.* She marched back to place the ring on the bureau and stepped over to the bed to look at more dresses. *There really aren't many left to check out,* Isobel mused, *and what I do next is totally up to me!* And with that, she pressed forward finishing the task at hand by the time lunchtime rolled around.

After thinking about it all through lunch, Isobel decided to sort through the items in the chest of drawers. *Only four drawers, after all,* she thought. *What could be so hard about sorting her nighties and underwear?* Although, deep inside she felt apprehension akin to anxiety, as if her heart told her the information she was wondering about would be in there.

She found nothing unusual in the top drawer…bras and panties, an old girdle and several packages of new pantyhose. Along one side lay several pair of sports socks and a used ACE bandage from some previous sprain. Isobel's heart relaxed a bit, slowing its pace and she began sorting the second drawer contents.

Again, just the usual nighties and pajamas one would find in possession of an elderly aunt. A couple of lightweight nightgowns were still in gift boxes; Aunt Betty liked to use old items until they were well-worn before breaking into new, even if they were gifts. The ribbons on the gift boxes showed age in both color and condition, so Isobel didn't even know how old the gifts were. She was sure these would be welcome additions to the bundle for the church to give to the less fortunate.

The third drawer held a jumble of items. It had more than just clothing. As a matter of fact, it seemed to be more of a junk drawer to Isobel. Aunt Betty was ordinarily very organized, but this drawer must have been her surrender to disorganization. It held everything, from a couple of tools: hammer, screwdriver, pliers and tape measure to several lengths of fabric, possibly for dresses she planned to make. A small sewing kit lay near the fabric probably for emergency mending, and a shoeshine kit sat beside that. Underneath all of this, the drawer was lined with newspaper, or so it seemed. An entire newspaper from back in 1968, a couple of years before Isobel's dad joined the military, covered the bottom of the drawer.

It didn't take long for Isobel to realize that this paper had more significance than just lining the drawer. The front page gave a lengthy news report of various battles in Viet Nam, and referred the reader to the back page for a list of wounded, KIA and MIA. Knowing Tommy Running Bear was probably on the list, she laid it aside. Isobel paused before going on to the last drawer. Her heart was doing flips again, and seeing the newspaper reminded her of her own search for clues.

Sitting on the edge of the bed, Isobel stared at the bottom drawer of the bureau as if it held a snake or some monster. The anticipation and anxiety was overwhelming. She felt her heart pulsing in her throat and found it difficult to breath. Finally Isobel took a deep breath and collected her nerves enough to continue. *After all,* she thought, *what could be so bad in there?* Deep in her heart she felt a foreboding, ominous sense that her world was about to change dramatically.

Opening the bottom drawer, she saw a stack of papers tied with a blue ribbon tucked into the back corner on top of all the other stuff. She could tell the papers were old. Cracks, like spider webs, crawled over the printed words and the amber color of age varied from barely beige in the center to nearly brown on the edges of the paper.

She held the bundle carefully, reverently, as she sat down to the kitchen table. She knew Aunt Betty was gone, but somehow untying the ribbon seemed like an invasion of her aunt's privacy. Her fingers shook as she loosened first one bow, and then the other. Separating the twist of ribbon and laying it flat on the table, she picked up the first paper.

There at the bottom was the name of Aunt Betty's one true love, Tommy Running Bear. But between Darling Betty and Forever in my heart, he wove his words into a beautiful tapestry of love. Obviously, he loved Aunt Betty as much as she loved him; his letters left no doubts. Isobel couldn't stop the flood of tears as she read the words on the page. She thought of Jason and the love they had shared and wondered…

Isobel put the first page back on top of the others without reading anymore. She would save the letters but, for now, wanted to leave them alone out of respect for her aunt. Maybe someday she would read more and try to honor that love in some way; it just couldn't be now. She had too much on her plate right now and had to focus.

As she placed them back into the bureau she saw another previously unnoticed package. It appeared to be a handkerchief box, flat, no more than three-quarters of an inch deep, and about 12 inches square. In Aunt Betty's neat, delicate script, Isobel saw her name written across the front. There was nothing else on the box, just her name, looking just the way Isobel felt, alone.

Isobel was overwhelmed with anxiety; she replaced everything into the drawer and closed it. She let out a breath, as if holding it the entire time and felt weak-kneed. *I'll get back to this later,* she thought. *I need time to think, maybe even ask Dr. Fitz some questions to prepare me for whatever the drawer holds.*

Chapter 19

K.C. awoke the next morning with the determination to carry his family through the many crises they were facing. But first, and foremost, he needed to focus on reviewing for his law licensing exam. He needed to have an income if he was to support the family, and that meant successfully passing the exam on the first try. He would continue his volunteer days in the Legal Aid Office and he planned to make good use of the time. Whenever there was a break between clients, he would use their law library to study his review materials. They could always call on him if he was needed, but he needed to carve out minutes here and there to make the best use of his study time.

It was difficult to focus when he was at home, and in the evenings, for now anyway, he needed to be available to Shyne. He was thankful for one thing, that Ma seemed to be well enough to care for Brya and CeCe. If she wasn't able, he didn't know how he would have managed. He breathed a short 'thank you' to the Lord for working out that problem for him. *It was wonderful knowing Someone had the solution before you even know the problem,* he thought.

That week passed quickly. Taddy was released after four days in the hospital, and K.C. never saw anyone as relieved as his little sister when she signed the discharge papers. He helped her carry Taddy and his stuff to the car, and she seemed reluctant to let him go even long enough for K.C. to fasten the car-seat in place. She just kept watching Taddy while he responded to her gazes with coos and bubble blowing. "He's ok, now, little sis," K.C. tried to reassure her, but she just watched him most of the way home. Taddy still needed to finish his antibiotics, and Shyne wouldn't be satisfied until he had.

K.C. was just happy the child was coming home with them. It was one less worry. With Taddy on the way to recovery, and Ma taking her medicine and doing better, he had only to worry about his exam coming up. He couldn't help Skyla right now, but perhaps down the road, he could find some exception or ruling that could get her sentence decreased.

He did have one other thought that kept creeping into his mind lately. He was beginning to yearn for a wife. He would prefer to wait until he was established in a law practice, but wouldn't mind having someone to share his life. He watched his nieces and nephews and looked forward to the day when he would have children of his own. Right now, all he could do was to leave it in God's hands, though, because he had no social outlet, no way of meeting young ladies since leaving school.

On rare occasions he would meet someone at the Legal Aid Office, someone of his culture and traditions who attracted his attention. But he had high standards, and too often they came to the office because of serious legal issues. They were usually married, or already had children or both. And the strongest criterion he was waiting to find was a godly woman, someone with whom he could share his faith.

K.C.'s days began melding together in a pattern of monotony: volunteer work at the Legal Aid Office, studying for the bar exam, and returning home to care for the needs of his family. He had just a couple of weeks left before his test, and felt unprepared.

"Ma, I need to take some time away from home to prepare for the bar exam," one evening he opened the subject with his family over dinner. "I thought I might stay with Pastor Jim in Omaha for the last two weeks before the test, just so I can focus and make use of the libraries at the college there… what do you think?"

Ma had been doing so much better. While Taddy was in hospital she took care of Brya and CeCe and maintained the house, including fixing meals. She seemed almost like her old self. K.C. had taken her for her weekly counseling sessions and she continued to take her antidepressant when he reminded her each evening. Only one thing bothered K.C. She still had not opened up to him; she avoided telling him what she had shared with the doctor. *Perhaps it isn't all that important,* he considered. *As long as she is doing better, why rock the boat?*

Ma smiled in response to K.C.'s inquiry; he respected her opinion. "Son, things are fine here. Shyne and I can manage for that time and she can be my evening reminder."

K.C. realized she had been reading his mind. "Thanks, Ma. I appreciate that." Then he turned to Shyne quietly feeding Taddy and not weighing in on the subject. "What about it, sis? Are you ok with the plan?"

"Will you have a number we can call if we need you," her eyes expressed her apprehension.

It was then that K.C. realized how much they had come to depend on him. Despite his long absences in school, they still needed to know there was someone on whom they could depend. "You can count on it! I'll make sure I give you contact information, just in case."

That being settled, Shyne smile her agreement and nodded. "We'll be ok, then."

K.C. set about making arrangements with Pastor Jim. He knew from his youth, that Pastor Jim always kept a room available for times like this. Whenever he was approached by one of the young people needing solitude or a retreat, his house was open. It was quiet and located near the law library, so K.C. knew it was the perfect solution.

Pastor Jim welcomed him with open arms, and quickly showed him a tidy bedroom off the kitchen where he could stay for the next two weeks. Pastor Jim made him feel at home and K.C. quickly relaxed. He set his books on the desk, turned on the desk lamp and immediately set about reviewing. Law school taught students how to think like lawyers, but did little to instill specific cases and precedents in the minds of future lawyers. This review time was important for that very reason, and K.C. was determined that, if he did his best, the Lord would carry him through.

Chapter 20

Several days went by before Isobel had the courage to open that bottom drawer again. She started working in Dr. Fitz's office the next morning, as planned, and focused on learning how to schedule appointments, the billing system, and how the filing system for the medical records was organized. Dr. Fitz hadn't moved into the computer age, yet, so all medical records were color-coded binders. The office manager would be gone for an undetermined amount of time, so for now all responsibilities for the office fell squarely on Isobel's shoulders. Fortunately, the office was quiet which gave Isobel time to review and remember all the tasks she needed to take care of. Almost immediately on that first day, Isobel knew this job was not her choice for a career.

The office manager was something of a 'jack-of-all-trades' responsible for filing test results, typing, and receiving and sorting correspondence, acting as a liaison for referrals to either Kansas City or Omaha, as well as making sure support staff came in on the correct days. Since Dr. Fitz's schedule was rather random, they only had a medical assistant most days with a nurse two mornings a week for drawing blood and assisting in specialized exams.

Her education had prepared her for the corporate world, not a rural clinic. She felt out of place in her business suit from her internship summer in college. So, on the second day, she dressed down in casual slacks and a short cardigan sweater over a slightly longer shirt, with the cuffs turned back to allow her to work freely.

On Friday Dr. Fitz usually took a half day. He liked to have a bit of extra time for the weekend and, since he was on call all the time, it really didn't make much difference in terms of serving the community. He gave Isobel the choice of leaving early, as well, or staying to tie up loose ends.

She opted to leave at lunchtime. She still had things to take care of at home, namely, finishing going through Aunt Betty's things. The bottom drawer of the bureau continued to play on her mind, and she knew she needed to just finish up Aunt Betty's business. With the estate matters still unsettled, Isobel didn't know how long she had to complete everything.

After changing into work clothes, Isobel stood for a moment staring at the bureau. What did that little box hold for her? Again, she found her heart thumping and her palms sweating. She wrapped a scrunchie around her long pony-tail, pushing loose strands off her forehead. Then Isobel sat in front of the chest of drawers. If she didn't sit, she was afraid she might faint, so high was her anxiety level.

Right now, finding what may be the clue to some mystery about herself, with no one to answer her questions, Isobel felt abandoned. She couldn't have felt more alone if she were on a desert island or out in the middle of the wilderness. First her mother, then her father, and now Aunt Betty... all gone! Then Jason's family rejected her effectively thwarting any morsel of confidence she might have had in God. She had no one to help, no one to lean on, and no one on whom she could depend. Most of all, Isobel wondered if her questions would ever be answered; worse than that, she didn't even know what to ask!

As Isobel pulled the drawer out, her eyes were drawn again to the sweet bundle of love letters. Gently lifting them and putting them on the bedside table, she once again saw her name written in auntie's old-fashioned script on the front of the flat handkerchief box. She reached for it, her breaths shallow and her pulse rapid. Isobel gently lifted the lid from the box, recognizing that age had weakened the corners.

She set aside the lid and lifted apart the tissue paper inside revealing an official-looking document…her birth certificate. Isobel had never seen this previously. Each time it was needed for school registration or to get her driver's license, either her father or Aunt Betty had been along to hand it to the official. She never questioned the reason; it just seemed normal to her that they maintained control of legal documents.

But now, looking at the rectangular certificate with the raised stamp in the lower corner, she began to understand their protectiveness of the paper. It recorded all the pertinent information of her birth: the name of the hospital, her weight, length, time of birth and date. Her father's name and occupation (military) were recorded correctly. But, in the place where her mother's name should have been was the name of some stranger, a Delfina Beaupre. It was a name unlike any in the family. She turned it over looking at the back as if some explanation would suddenly appear. Had her mother used this other name? But she was Japanese, and this name definitely wasn't Japanese!

What could this mean? Her father had married her mother in Japan, about five months before her birth. *She had seen their marriage certificate, but not this…* she thought. She once asked them if she was premature, and recalled her father showing discomfort at the question. His response was that she was an unplanned, but welcomed blessing in their lives. There weren't any other openings for her to ask again and, as she got older, and understood more about couples and premarital relations, she assumed the obvious.

But then, it seemed whenever she asked about her mother after the accident, he would deflect. When she was very young, he would just hug her, saying, "Mommy isn't here". As she got older, he changed the subject or just went quiet, so she soon learned to not ask. *It was just his reaction to grief,* she had thought. But now, Isobel wished she had been more persistent. Although there were other old papers in the box, none seemed to apply to her, so she just put the certificate back in the box and replaced the lid wondering what else Aunt Betty had hidden in her bureau drawer.

Then another package in the drawer caught her eye. Isobel sat staring at the fat, yellowed 11x14 envelope. It was the type with bubble protection inside, aimed at preventing breakage or damage. Without realizing it, she realized she had been staring at the envelope for several minutes, looking at her name carefully printed in the address block. She had taken in nearly every inch of the package that she could see without turning it over. Would this package hold the answer to her questions or cause more doubts about her mother?

She took a deep breath and cautiously reached out to the envelope as if it would burn her. Picking it up, she turned it over to see the self-sealed flap. Isobel took it to the kitchen table to open it. Although the gummy glue might have held well for shipment at one time, age must have degraded it, because it easily released when she lifted the flap. She expected to find papers, maybe more letters, but was surprised when looking inside she saw three seemingly valueless items and, deeper in the envelope, a thin book.

She brought out the first of the trio, a tear-drop shape with crisscrossing, colorful threads forming a beautiful web in the center. From the bottom of the tear hung two feathers, one long and white, the other brown and much smaller. On the threads between the tear and the feathers sat several glass beads. The whole thing was delicate and beautiful. She placed it on the table and turned back to the other items.

The second of the trio that Isobel pulled from the envelope was a ring, an Air Force ring with a blue stone in the center. She had seen similar rings on some of her father's friends when she was a child. She once asked her daddy why he didn't have one, when she was admiring the ring on his best friend's hand. He had laughed it off, saying his wedding ring was more important to him.

The last trinket that Isobel found inside the package was a doll. It wasn't like the mass-produced dolls in the stores. It was about six inches tall and appeared to be an old-fashioned corn cob doll, complete with corn-silk hair. Isobel had seen dolls like this in collections in the area. The early settlers used what was available to make toys for their children, and in Kansas, it was corn. The unusual part of this doll was its dress. All the dolls Isobel had seen were wearing long dresses that replicated the styles worn by early settlers in the region. This tiny doll was dressed in Native American attire: leather with fringe and beads.

The book turned out to be a baby book. Not the mass produced type she'd seen at baby showers or in department stores, the cover on this one was soft, golden leather and the spine held together with shoestring-like darker leather strips. Lettering carefully burned into the front cover said: *For this child I prayed… 1 Samuel 1:27.*

Isobel carefully lifted the supple cover revealing rough, handmade paper imbedded with tiny pressed blossoms. Each page was a different, pastel color of the textured paper, the edges rough and uneven. On the second sheet the same information from her birth certificate had been carefully transcribed. Although there were no lines on the paper, the lettering was flat-bottomed as if written against a hard edge, like a ruler.

Leaf by leaf, she glance through the book obviously put together with love. In the very back she found a greeting card with a baby on the front. Inside, handwritten in the same style as the rest of the book, she read: *My darling little girl. The wind blows the prairie grasses, and your brother grows strong, but you do not. I fear you won't survive. The sickness shakes your body and I have no strength to give to you. Forever, my heart yearns for you. Again we will meet, of that I am certain.*

Isobel touched her cheek and felt the familiar moistness of tears. Was this a message from Delfina Beaupre? From her mother? The beauty of the book and the words in the card revealed the love of the creator, she thought. Suddenly, Isobel felt a chill wash over her. The thought might have been spoken by Aunt Betty in reference to the Bible as the words of the Creator! *How strange*, she mused, *that God would come to mind at a time like this.*

Again, she pushed the thoughts aside, feeling overwhelmed by the many events of the last few weeks. She wrapped her arms around herself, rocking and crying, feeling so engulfed in grief, anger and loneliness that she wasn't sure what to do next. She thought of just boxing up all of Aunt Betty's things until some other time. Each new discovery seemed to open more wounds for Isobel, and she wasn't sure how much more she could bear.

Looking inside the envelope again, Isobel hoped to find an explanation for the items, but there was nothing else in it. She shook it out just to be sure. Nothing. Confused, Isobel looked at the three items on the table. They didn't tell a story; they didn't give a complete picture. The book, dream catcher and doll indicated Native American heritage. But the ring was out of place. *They have to mean something*, she thought, *there must be another clue somewhere.*

Anger and helplessness overwhelmed her. She couldn't believe that, suddenly, she was a totally different person than who she grew up thinking she was. Her heritage was totally different from what she had believed for her entire life! Even the forms she had filled out for college entrance were all lies. Isobel gathered everything into the envelope and put it back into the bottom drawer to get back to later.

She felt betrayed, exposed as a fraud, stripped of all she had known about her family heritage, and alone, so lonely. Suddenly, she was glad that Jason's family had rejected her. *What if we had married and then his family learned all this new information? They would have felt justified in their awful attitudes.* How horrible it would have been to be so exposed!

But then she wished she could call Jason. She knew he would be sympathetic. He would listen and show compassion. He might even offer to come to her aid, to help her find her mother. But she couldn't risk that. She loved him too much to involve him in what seemed to be a family scandal. She couldn't reach out to him, not now, maybe not ever!

Isobel moved through the day as if sleep walking. She continued to clean out cupboards and closets, mindlessly sorting Aunt Betty's belongings. Most would go to the church for distribution or discarding, so Isobel was mostly boxing up everything. Occasionally, something too worn or outdated went to the rag bag, and one or two items with sentimental value set aside for her to keep, but nearly everything found its way into one of the boxes by the end of the day.

That was when she remembered the handkerchief box and the unexplored papers in the box. Finding the bureau behind several boxes of clothing and linens, she opened the bottom drawer. Inside was the handkerchief box where she had placed it, slightly askew, but intact. She lifted it onto her lap and once again began taking out one article at a time: the offending birth certificate…

Another paper caught her eye as she was about to pull the letter out of the envelope. It appeared to be a war bond. Scrolled borders around the edges and beautiful script with lines filled in with hand-written information. Two signatures on the bottom looked very official. She picked it up and looked it over, front and back. Although she'd never personally seen a bond from World War II, she had seen pictures in school when they studied the war in history class. It was dated 1943.

Couldn't be worth much, she thought, *after all this time, surely Aunt Betty would have cashed it in if it was worth anything at all.*

Isobel put the paper over into the lid with the birth certificate. Again, after a deep breath to prepare for whatever she might find, Isobel reached for the next paper in the box. The paper she held appeared to be written by her aunt. Maybe she would finally have the answers to her questions.

> *Dearest Isobel,*
>
> *I'm sorry for you to learn of your heritage in this way. Your father tried, as did I, to tell you, but we were cowards, trying to pretend it didn't matter. Randy had a girlfriend before he went in the military and she was pregnant when he left. Delfina didn't tell him; she didn't want him to worry. You were born just a month before he came home on R & R, but we still didn't know about you.*
>
> *Your mother brought you to me when you were 3 months old, because you were ill. She had no trust for hospitals and doctors, but she knew me. You see, she*

was sister to the man I loved. Because of my love for Tommy, she felt she could trust me with her precious daughter. I had you until your father came back from Japan some six months later, married to Naoko. She was wonderful to agree to raise you as hers. You were beautiful and even looked as if you could have been her child.

Your mother was a lovely woman, Isobel, so please don't judge her harshly. She hoped to come back for you, if you lived. And I promised her that if she couldn't, then I would tell you of her when you were grown. She wants you to find her. She said she will long for you until you return to her. I don't know where she is now; I lost touch with her and I don't know what became of her, if she remarried, had more children or is even still alive. Just know that she loves you and hopes to see you again.

I love you too, my dear, and hope to see you at the great reunion when our Lord returns to claim His own. Your loving aunt,

Elizabeth Kirk

Isobel stared at the letter. She finally realized that she really wasn't part Japanese; she was part Native American. How she could trace a woman from over twenty years ago? Who knows what her name is now? *Where would I start*? She didn't have time for the search right now though she wished she did.

Isobel was weak with fatigue. Emotionally wasted, she just wanted to sleep. She took a long shower, crying, pounding on the walls of the shower, venting her anger and pain. *Who was she? Who was her mother? She wasn't even adopted, so there were no adoption records to trace. The name on her birth certificate was probably no help if her mother remarried.*

The loneliness, the alone-ness, a more empty feeling she had never had in her entire life. Drying her skin with a fluffy terrycloth towel, she pulled on a flannel nightgown, brushed her teeth, and curled up in her bed. Sleep came quickly, but dreams chased her throughout the night. By morning she was exhausted, unable to recall her dreams and wishing she didn't remember her reality.

Chapter 21

Isobel went to work at Dr. Fitz's office on Monday only to find that his assistant had returned from her emergency leave of absence. She had conveniently had her 'emergency' over the Christmas holiday season, and now that it was the New Year, she was back. Evidently her family hadn't needed her as badly as she thought, and she was happy to come back to work so quickly. Isobel, on the other hand, was a bit confused. Although Dr. Fitz had assured her that she could stay on, she knew there just wasn't enough work in such a small practice to keep two people busy. She was also anxious to clear up things at the farm, and a day job kept her from reaching that goal.

After staying on for one more week, Isobel gave Dr. Fitz notice, and he agreed that she was not obligated to give the usual two weeks. He seemed disappointed, but fully understood her reasoning.

"Just be sure you let me know if you need anything," he told Isobel on her last day. "Have you heard anything on the investigation into the fire or your car's damage?"

"No," she answered, although puzzled by his query. From past experience, she knew that he was usually the first in town to hear any news, and that the Sheriff would have talked to him before he even spoke with her. "Why do you ask?"

It was Dr. Fitz's turn to be surprised, and his discomfort was apparent. "I…uh… no, well… you know, I am just concerned that they find the culprit or culprits that would do something like that."

Isobel let the conversation drop, figuring that she may have overreacted to his interest. After all, he had cared about Aunt Betty, so it was reasonable that he might be protective of her niece. At least, she hoped that was it. She would hate to think he had an ulterior motive in asking about the search for the guilty party. But what motive might he have, other than interest in her welfare. *Sometime soon*, Isobel thought, *I need to ask him the questions I have about my heritage. I wonder just how much he knows.*

Still worried about finances and the legalities of inheritance, Isobel broke down and called the Legal Aid Office in Omaha so it would be far enough from Mr. Sorenson's connections in Kansas City. She drove up to Omaha on a Tuesday and was shocked when she entered the Legal Aid Office, to see a familiar face in the rear of the room sitting across the table from an older woman. He smiled his recognition of her, and she returned his greeting, and then turned to the receptionist. "I have an appointment...Isobel Kirk?"

"Oh, yes, Ms. Kirk. If you could just fill out these forms for us, Mr. Fox will be seeing you today." She looked up at K.C. and he nodded. Uncertain whether this was a good idea, she hesitated for a moment.

"Ms. Kirk, if you are worried about confidentiality, everything here is just as private as if you went to your personal lawyer. No need to worry." The receptionist had read her body language correctly, and Isobel relaxed with her guarantee of privacy.

She sat on one of the old, hard plastic chairs and held the clipboard on her knee to work on the paperwork. *It was surprising how much information was needed to just get a little advice*, she thought. When she had completed the forms, she sat back down and waited for K.C., or Mr. Fox, to finish with his client.

"Ms. Kirk, would you like to come on back?" K.C. approached the reception area as he saw his other client out.

Isobel felt awkward. She remembered how stiff and unfriendly she had been when last they met at the airport. So much had happened since then; so many changes in her life that she felt like a different person. She followed K.C. to the rear of the room and took the seat the woman previously occupied. She looked at the bundle she'd brought with her: her aunt's will and the financial statements from Aunt Betty's lawyer. For some reason, she had also brought along the old war bond, just in case it might be worth something.

"Now, Ms. Kirk, how can I help you," K.C. opened the dialogue.

"First of all, Ms. Kirk reminds me of my elderly aunt. I prefer Isobel, if you don't mind."

"And I prefer K.C. as I once told you," he smiled. His white teeth practically glowed in contrast to his rich, brown skin tones and full lips. Isobel blushed. *Now, why am I noticing things like that?* She thought, annoyed by her tendency to show embarrassment on her face.

"OK, K.C. I'm here because of a couple of issues. First, my only living relative recently died and left everything to me."

"Well, now that doesn't sound like a problem!"

"You don't understand. When I say everything, I mean debts included. And her lawyer told me that the debts outweigh the assets by about $58,000.00. What I need to know is what my responsibilities are. Am I required to pay off debts when there aren't enough assets to cover them?"

Before he gave her an answer, K.C. asked for more information. The fact that her issues were in the state of Kansas complicated matters a bit, since state laws varied. And he needed to research the property and financials to see if there was anything left out. He took a look at all the documents she came with, although he passed over the war bond at first. Then, just as he was putting the papers back into her manila envelope, he saw it again and picked it up.

"This might be the answer to your problem," he said, turning it over and holding it up to the light. "If this is still valid, it may provide you a way to pay off those debts. I tell you what I'd like to do. If you could give me a week to do some research, I might have the answers you need." K.C. looked at her for affirmation.

"I would need to come back here, then?" She asked.

"That would probably be best. But I take my bar exam next week, so could we make it the week after? I don't think anything will happen between now and then."

"If you think it will be ok." She just wished she could get a straight answer from Mr. Sorenson so she wouldn't have to ask a stranger to do the work like this.

They agreed to an appointment time two weeks away, and Isobel left, not feeling much better about things, but at least hopeful that K.C. might find her an answer. As he walked her out to the lobby, his hand touched the small of her back and an electric shock went through her. She knew it meant nothing to him, just a gentlemanly way of guiding a woman, but since Jason, it was an unfamiliar sensation to her.

He opened the door for her and watched as she got into her car and drove away. *No time for distractions,* he thought. But the sense of having known her before, that 'déjà vu' thing people talked about continued to haunt his mind. He finished the afternoon volunteer work and returned to the law library for an intensive study session aimed at chasing one beautiful young lady out of his thoughts.

Chapter 22

Isobel drove home from the Legal Aid, taking her time and musing over the encounter with K.C. Fox. How was it possible that they would meet again like that? With all the law firms and lawyers in the area, how was it that she *just happened* upon the one place where he was volunteering? It seemed too coincidental to Isobel, but she couldn't consider that God had a hand in their meeting. She was still too angry to consider the God of her Aunt Betty as anything other than absent and unhelpful.

Aunt Betty talked of how He got her through the rough patches in her life but, to Isobel, He was the source of her problems. After all, if He was so great, couldn't He have prevented all this trouble? If He truly loved people, like Aunt Betty said, wouldn't He have let her have Aunt Betty just a little longer? Wouldn't He have given her time to tell Isobel all about her origins, about her birth mother? Then her thoughts drifted back to the unexpected encounter.

K.C. is certainly a handsome man, Isobel thought. *He probably has a committed relationship… Anyway, why should that matter? I don't plan to date anyone for a long time! I have too many questions, too many problems to solve, to complicate it with a boyfriend.* Then she thought about Jason, and all the plans they had for their lives. Their relationship had seemed so solid before her visit to his parent's home. Isobel wondered what might have happened had she not left the way she did. What if she hadn't broken up with Jason, but had stood her ground with his parents? Would they have come to accept her? Might she and Jason be married by this time?

All her daydreaming had carried her down the highway without noticing how far she had driven, and already it was time to turn off for her back road drive to the farm. She needed to pay better attention to the road; the twists and turns required it, and the last thing she needed right now was an accident. Isobel kept to the speed limit and made her way home refocused. It made no sense to wonder about Jason or to think whether to begin dating again. For now she needed to focus on settling Aunt Betty's business so she could get on with her life.

As she drove down the long dirt drive toward the house, she was surprised to see a vehicle driving toward her. The driveway wasn't made for two vehicles to pass; the ruts were deep and parallel, just wide enough for one car, so she slowed her car wondering if the other would stop, but it didn't. And it wasn't a car. It was an old truck she'd seen parked behind the clinic on several occasions. She wasn't sure, but she thought it belonged to Dr. Fitz. Instead of stopping, it swerved onto the field alongside the driveway and went around her. Because the truck was a four wheel drive, the cab was too high for her to see the driver, and it sped off toward the road before she could see the license plate.

Isobel continued toward the house wondering if she was going to see another outbuilding burning, but was grateful when all looked calm around the farmyard. She parked in her usual spot near one of the smaller sheds, locked her car and headed for the back door. That was when she realized the screen door was ajar, and the back door was wide open.

Was Dr. Fitz just here? Maybe he just forgot to close the door... she wondered as she pushed it open wider and made her way indoor. *What if a burglar is here, still in the house?*

Nothing looked out of place in the kitchen or living-room. Isobel was beginning to think her imagination was getting the best of her. After vandalism of her car and the burning of the barn, she was more than a little on edge. She looked around and everything was as usual, until she went into Aunt Betty's bedroom. It was there that everything was out of kilter.

Drawers were pulled out of the dresser and bedside tables, and the contents thrown all over the floor. Even the few clothes left in the closet were askew with some falling off their hangers and others right on the floor. They had been pushed apart as if someone was trying to find something behind them. Strangely, the jewelry box sat untouched, and that held the most expensive items in the room!

Isobel stood looking around and wondered what to do. Maybe she should call Dr. Fitz and ask him outright if he'd been there rummaging through Aunt Betty's things. With his unusual interest in the previous crimes, she wondered if he were responsible for all these attacks. She hadn't lived in the area long enough to really know who to trust. Maybe his interest in Aunt Betty wasn't as loving as he described. Did she owe him some debt or have something belonging to Dr. Fitz-Randolph? What if he held a grudge against Aunt Betty?

Should she call the sheriff? He had told her to call if anything else went wrong, so Isobel went to the phone only to find it wasn't working. She looked down and saw the phone cord to the wall had been cut. She thought of going into the bedroom where the other telephone was, but quickly saw that it too was damaged and nonfunctional.

Now I wish I had a cell phone, she thought. *At least then I wouldn't feel so cut off…* Isobel heard a noise outside the window of the bedroom. Rather than going to the window, she rushed outside just in time to see someone running away from the house, across the same field the sheriff said was used as an escape from one of the earlier attacks.

It appeared to be a young man, maybe in his early twenties by the way he ran, dressed in typical farmer overalls and a plaid shirt. She couldn't tell what color his hair was because he was wearing a straw hat. *What a stereotype! Could be any farmer's son*, she thought. *At least that let's Dr. Fitz off the hook,* Isobel breathed a sigh of relief. *But why was that truck driving off, and if it was Dr. Fitz, why didn't he stop to talk?* Without a telephone, and seeing the young man running off, Isobel was undecided whether she should get back in her car and drive into town to talk to the sheriff or just start straightening up the mess. She closed the door behind her and stood assessing the damage and trying to make up her mind, when she heard vehicles pull up into the farmyard.

Half afraid to look out, yet needing to know, Isobel peeked from behind the curtain to see the same truck that had sped past her earlier. Her heart thumped uncontrollably in her chest until she saw the second vehicle was Sheriff Jones' car. Dr. Fitz jumped out of the cab of the truck and met Sheriff Jones as he got out of his official car. They walked together, apparently seriously discussing the break-in.

Isobel let out a deep sigh and went to open the back door, greeting Dr. Fitz with an uncharacteristic hug given out of a huge sense of relief. She was happy that he wasn't the culprit but, instead had gone for help. At least she could relax a bit, not wondering if everybody was suspect. *I should have never doubted him*, Isobel thought. *He acts like a father to me and has never given me reason to suspect him.*

"Well, young lady. It seems you've had a bit of trouble again," the sheriff got right to the point.

Isobel indicated to the chairs in the kitchen, inviting them both to take a seat. They gladly accepted her offer of coffee. She set about making the coffee, listening as they talked, surprised to hear that they already had a suspect in mind. Setting the coffee in front of each man, Isobel pushed the creamer and sugar between them. She went to the pantry for a plate of cookies to give them. Only then did she allow herself to relax enough to ask questions.

"Why didn't you tell me about this feud between Aunt Betty and her tenant farmer? At least I might have been better prepared when things started happening around here!" The tone of her voice gave evidence to her annoyance.

"We couldn't be sure, and really, we still aren't sure. It's just an idea we are tossing around..."

"Well, let me help you! Does this farmer have a son in his late teens or twenties that runs around in coveralls and a straw hat?"

They both looked at her in surprise.

"He hasn't been here while you were here, has he?" This came from Dr. Fitz; his concern was quite apparent. "He didn't hurt you, did he?"

"First you need to answer my question. Is that young man connected to the tenant farmer?"

This time Sheriff Jones chimed in, "Yep. That'd be Old Jacob's youngest, Joshua. He's a bit thick, but he does whatever his pa tells him to do."

"Well, I saw him here when I first got home and found this mess. I was looking for a phone to use, and heard him outside the bedroom window. When I went to the door, he was running off in the same direction that the sheriff had found the path through the brush."

Sheriff Jones looked pointedly at Dr. Fitz. As if rehearsed, the two men gulped down the last of their coffee and then stood to go. Dr. Fitz picked up his hat and placed it on his head while Sheriff Jones took a quick look at the phone cords and in the bedroom, at the mess. They told Isobel that they would get back with her later and together they drove off in their vehicles.

Isobel looked at the disarray in the bedroom and laughed. *I guess I needed this to jump-start me into getting rid of more stuff.* She realized that nearly everything that was tossed about could actually be thrown out or given away. The vandal had actually helped by emptying the drawers. At least all she had to do was gather the items into large bags to give to either the church or the trash. Isobel smiled at the irony and started gathering the clothes into piles. A verse her aunt used to quote came to mind, *"All things work together for good..."* She didn't know the rest, but it sure seemed to fit this situation.

Isobel kept working, picking up and tidying up until everything seemed back in place. She thought it strange when she saw the handkerchief box with all the items out of it on the floor. The papers had been crumpled and the baby book looked as if it had been tossed aside. If the vandal was looking for something, he didn't find it there, because nothing was missing...except the war bond she'd left with K.C. with the other documents! *What if that boy, Joshua, was looking for that?* Isobel wondered. *What if it really is valuable?*

Chapter 23

K.C. found that Pastor Jim allowed him total freedom to study. He was able to spend late evenings at the Law Library to study for his bar exam. The two weeks passed quickly and, all too soon, K.C. was staring at the last hours to test day. He thought about taking a last visit home to see his mother and sister…to reassure himself that all was well on the home front.

Shyne called him regularly to check in and update him on Ma's progress. Ma steadily improved with the medication getting to therapeutic level, and Shyne said she was like before Skyla's troubles. She said that Ma even spoke about Sky without slipping into that daydreamy look she used to get. She didn't sit on the porch watching the road, either. Instead, Ma was fully involved with Taddy, Brya and CeCe. The trio played well together, and Ma often laughed at their antics.

After her usual call, K.C. put the idea of going home out of his mind. Beside the distance, he knew the time was precious minutes that could be spent in studies. The sun woke him with its brilliance on the morning of the test. Without hesitation, he was up preparing for the day and praising God for the beauty all around him. He even broke into a song while showering, and Pastor Jim greeted him warmly when he went to the kitchen for breakfast.

"Thought I'd fix you a 'test day breakfast'," Pastor Jim grinned as he turned from the store. He was wearing a chef's apron and holding a spatula. K.C.'s nose tingled with the scent of turkey sausage, hash browns, and pancakes already sitting on the table. In the frying pan, yellow, fluffy scrambled eggs were nearly ready. Pastor Jim gave them a final turn to make sure they were cooked, and carried the pan to the table where K.C. had taken his place.

"You really didn't have to go through all this trouble, Pastor!"

"Son, you are one of my success stories, and I sure want to see you over this hurdle. What kind of father figure would I be if I send you to take a test on an empty stomach?" as he scooped out another spatula of eggs.

K.C. conceded and stopped Pastor Jim from filling his plate with eggs. "I need to eat some of the other stuff, or you're going to be eating hash brown and sausage sandwiches for the week." K.C. joked with his friend.

Pastor Jim sat at the table and the two men prayed together, asking for a blessing on the food. More importantly, they asked that God would bring to remembrance, those things that K.C. needed to recall to pass the exam. His heart was warmed at the sincerity of Pastor Jim's plea on his behalf. He added his words to the prayer, giving thanks for the opportunity for fellowship with his surrogate father, and for the many blessings provided him over the years.

On arrival at the test center, K.C. set about the business of focusing on the exam. He could not allow distractions to take his focus off his ultimate goal-to care for his family. He knew that many did not pass the bar exam on the first effort, but he was determined to do the best he could to be in the numbers that were successful on their initial attempt. Time seemed to crawl; the day was protracted by the quiet sound of future lawyers scratching answers onto paper, sighing deeply when stumped by a question, and scraping the floor with their chair as they rose to take a bathroom break.

Finally, after hours of blocking out the world, K.C. emerged from the test center without a good sense of whether he had actually passed. Parts of the test were subjective and parts objective, but in the end the key was scope of knowledge. Another key component was not just knowing cases and examples, but knowing where to look for answers. K.C. had a good sense of research and case studies.

He was careful, though, about feeling over-confident. Instead, he chose to be cautiously optimistic as he headed home.

K.C. drove up the driveway to his home, he realized how much he'd let slide as he studied. He noted cosmetic needs on the house, despite the time he and Shyne had put into fixing the house and yard. The work never ended, and he wondered how his mother had kept up over the years while he was away at school.

"K.C.!" Shyne squealed at him as he got out of the car. She ran to him and gave him a hug unlike her usually reserved greeting.

"Hey, sis! What's up? Is everything ok?"

"Oh, yeah, all's well here… I'm just glad to see you. Kinda got used to having my big brother around, you know!"

K.C. smiled. It was good to see her so happy. It was suddenly apparent how necessary he was in her life. She needed to have a man in her life that would provide a positive image. Maybe he could help prevent her spiraling into a dismal existence like Tali. They hadn't heard from Talitha since Skyla's sentencing, and her phone had been turned off due to nonpayment of the bill. *Soon, we need to drive up and visit her*, he thought. *She needs to know she is important to us, too.*

He walked into the house to see Ma sitting on the floor with the little ones. She was showing them how to stack blocks and build little houses. Taddy was still too young to understand, but he loved knocking the blocks over after she stacked them. Ma grabbed him around the belly and snuggled her face into his neck.

"You little monkey! How can I show Brya and CeCe how to build things if you keep pushing them down?" Her question was met with the giggles of a happy, healthy little boy tickled by grandma's lips on his neck blowing raspberries.

"Hi, Ma."

Ma turned and saw her handsome son standing in the doorway. "Well, K.C., you finally decided to show your face…"

K.C. could tell she was joking, and just the attempt made him smile.

"OK, so I'm back. Now what trouble have you been getting into?"

"Me? Trouble?" she smiled. "Oh, just the usual…"

K.C. helped her up after she set Taddy down near Brya who put her arm protectively around his shoulder. She gave K.C. a warm embrace and walked over to the table to sit down with him. They sat for some time, just filling each other in on the events of the last two weeks, until Shyne interrupted. "I need to set the table, folks," she was holding a dish in each hand. "Stew for everybody, tonight!" K.C. got up and helped her with the dishes, and then he followed her into the kitchen to assist with serving out the smaller bowls for the children.

"So, what you gonna do now that you did that test?" Shyne asked as they worked quietly together.

"Well, I still have my volunteer time at the Legal Aid until I find a job. I can't really do much until I get the results."

"I mean, when the report card or whatever gets here, what you gonna do? Are you moving on now that Ma is ok? I know that was your plan before Sky messed up."

Ma joined into the conversation as they set the three little bowls in front of the children, already seated by Ma in their usual chairs. "Shyne, you shouldn't put pressure on your brother. If he needs to move on, then he needs to move on."

"Now, Ma, you know I'm not going to desert you guys. With two more children in the house, I think you and Shyne have your hands full. I plan to stick around, maybe practice in Omaha if I can find a law firm somewhere willing to take on a rookie lawyer. Anyway, don't worry yourselves. I'm here, and I'm not planning to go anywhere for now."

They seemed satisfied with his reassurance, and all ate their dinner quietly discussing upcoming events in the region, local politics with the tribal council, and some of the elders on the rez who were ill. K.C. told them of his meeting with the exotic woman on the flight home and seeing her again at the Legal Aid Office.

"If she's so elegant, what's she doing using Legal Aid?" Shyne asked.

"Well, beauty and style don't equal money. It's just that she carries herself with pride and it comes through in her confidence."

He shared a little of her issues, trying to not break confidence. He just wanted them to have a visual of Isobel, just in case…

Again with my mind wandering in the wrong direction, he thought. *I can't allow distractions, yet. Keep to my plan…results for the exam, find law firm, establish career,* ***and then*** *consider dating. Besides, I don't even know if she is involved. The subject didn't come up, again, and probably won't either.* He shook his head, annoyed with his daydreaming. *I need to maintain a professional relationship!*

Chapter 24

K.C. spent the weeks after taking his exam busy researching the cases he had taken on at the Legal Aid Office. He tried not to focus on Isobel's case until he cleared his desk of all other issues. He wrote a letter to the utility company to ask forgiveness for an overdue bill for one client. For the next, he drafted a letter to the courts about a husband who had broken a restraining order. Finally, he was able to give good news to one client in reference to her concerns about her taxes. Fortunately, the error was on the part of the government and, instead of owing money, she would receive a refund.

Although not the type of law he wanted to practice, there was a certain fulfillment he had whenever he found a positive outcome for a client. He only hoped he could work something good for Isobel. He briefly reviewed her documents, and everything seemed in order. He saw no conflict between what Sorenson had said about Betty Kirk's finances and what was in the papers. He did think it odd that Betty would allow her finances to be in disarray and not warn her niece.

Fortunately, unless Isobel intended to keep the farm, an estate sale would take care of some debt, and the remaining was written off. Heirs were not required to pay off debts unless they rejected the estate sale in favor of retaining the real estate. In such a case, their obligation was offset to a degree determined through probate. But Isobel seemed to feel a moral obligation to pay the debt regardless.

K.C. admired this, but worried at how she could manage $58,000 in debt when she wasn't even employed.

K.C. turned his attention to the war bond. He thought it unusual that it would be kept in a handkerchief box in a drawer rather than in a lock box, *if* it held any value. That thought led to another... what if there were more where this one came from? Or what if Betty Kirk had a lock box somewhere with other bonds or savings? K.C. put aside the bond. He leaned back in his seat and thought about Isobel.

There was something alluring about the young woman. He still could not put his finger on what the attraction was aside from the obvious. She was truly a beautiful woman, but he sensed something even deeper drew him to her. Maybe it was the sorrowful way she looked when taking the plane trip from Boston. Perhaps it was something inside him that made him want to rescue a lovely lady.

He refused to think of her as a possible romantic interest. Besides the fact that she was a client, he wanted to find a wife who shared his cultural background. He had nothing against those of other ethnic groups; he just wanted to raise his children with pride in their unique Native American heritage. No, he would not consider her as a potential partner. Instead, the best he could hope for is that she would be a friend, and perhaps a friend to his sisters to encourage them to strive for better. Once again, Tali came to his mind.

When he got home that evening, K.C. was welcomed once again by his mother taking an active part in the household. Shyne was changing Taddy's diaper and Ma had Brya and CeCe outside showing them plants and insects. All was as he hoped it would be. Inside the house he smelled food cooking and saw a tidy, well-ordered house. He went to his room to change, and went out to the front porch to watch Ma and the children. She soon sent the children in to clean up for dinner and sat in her rocker next to K.C.

"Son, you seem to have something on your mind," she was very astute.

K.C. shared with her his concerns for Talitha. "Ma, we haven't heard from her in a while, and I'm worried."

Ma nodded. "I too have been thinking of her and praying for her. Shyne is a blessing, but I can't neglect my other children. Talitha has her challenges, and I surely don't want to see her turn out like Skyla. That would break my heart!" She nodded again, "Yes. That would truly break my heart." She seemed to slip into a daydream, but quickly looked up at K.C. as if to reassure him that she was alright.

Once again, K.C. wondered just what it was that Dr. Pearson wanted Ma to share with him. He hadn't pressed the issue; he just kept taking her to her weekly appointments, hearing Dr. Pearson remind her each time. Just when Ma seemed ready to open up, she would go quietly into her private place in her mind. He could see it in her eyes. Not vacant, exactly, just distant, as if remembering long ago.

"Ma," she looked up at him again, "Ma, when will you trust me enough to tell me what Dr. Pearson wants you to tell me?"

She smiled at her fine-looking, intelligent son. "Soon, son. Very soon."

K.C. had to be satisfied with that for now. At least it was a start. Perhaps if he could just be patient, she would finally open up to him. Shyne called them in for dinner and he helped her stand so they could go together. Shyne was doing well with dinner preparations these days. She never complained and seemed quite comfortable in her role in the household.

"Hey, little sis, wanna go with me to see Tali tomorrow?"

Shyne looked over at Ma who nodded indicating she was fine with the idea. "Sure, I'd love to see her…will we be bringing the kids along?"

"No, I thought we might just visit her alone. I'm worried about her. If things aren't going well, I don't want to expose the children to more confusion."

They ate the rest of their dinner quietly talking about Tali, discussing how his research for the Legal Aid Office was going, and comparing notes on the children and their development. K.C. thought that this was how he had envisioned the perfect family. The only missing link was a father. He knew his mother wasn't interested in finding another husband. Two had been more than enough, so it was up to him to fill that void in the home.

The next morning, with Taddy on Ma's hip, and Brya and CeCe on either side of her, K.C. and Shyne drove down the dusty driveway to the highway. Heading north toward Omaha, they had to go only about 5 miles to the turnoff for Tali's house. Little had changed from the last time they were there. The house was still unpainted, and raggedy curtains still hung at the windows. There didn't seem to be any sign of life, and K.C.'s first thought was that the house was abandoned. Perhaps Talitha had moved. How would they ever find her if she didn't contact them?

Shyne got out quickly after K.C. pulled the car to a stop. He tried to prevent her from a futile try, but she was determined to check for Tali. She knocked on the door and looked into the windows. "She's in there, K.C. She's sitting on the couch, but not answering the door."

K.C. got out the driver's side and hurried onto the front porch. "Tali, open the door. It's K.C. and Shyne…come on, open the door."

Just then the door opened. Talitha stood passively before them in a dirty T-shirt and jeans, smelling as if she hadn't bathed in weeks. Behind her the two children sat on the floor, looking just as dirty with matted hair and snotty noses. Their big eyes looked pathetically up at the adults as they entered the room.

"Tali, what's going on here?" He took her hands and looked into empty eyes reminiscent of Ma's eyes just weeks ago. "Tali, honey, what's wrong?"

"K.C.?" Shyne called to him, "These babies are hungry. I wonder when they ate last." She happened to have some mints in her bag that she was sharing with them.

"O.K. That's it. Let's take Tali and the kids home for now. We can worry about this place later. Right now, they need help."

Shyne went to the bedroom but found nothing clean to bring along for her niece and nephew. K.C. couldn't find anything for Tali, either, so they just grabbed a blanket to wrap around the children and their mother in the back seat of the car. Once they were settled,

K.C. drove as fast as he could without breaking the speed limit, to get them home. Although he wasn't happy about Tali's condition, he knew that Ma needed to feel needed; perhaps this was just what the doctor ordered.

All the way home, K.C. prayed for wisdom and understanding. He also prayed for Tali and the children's health. He wondered if they were sick or just malnourished. What he did know was that Tali needed professional help, just as Ma had. *Do mental issues run in our family?* He wondered. It seemed more than coincidence that both Ma and Tali reacted to stress in the same manner. What was different was that Ma seemed to have a secret working on her mind. Did Talitha also have a dark secret haunting her, or was it just despair over her lack of help and money?

Chapter 25

Ma immediately recognized the signs of trouble with Talitha when K.C. helped her out of the car. Ma came off the porch to give her daughter the heartfelt hug of one who understood the pain of depression. She guided Tali into the house and took her straight to K.C.'s bedroom. Although they hadn't discussed where Tali and her children would stay, K.C. knew before he started toward home with his sister, that he would be relinquishing his room. After all, he was just one person; Tali and her children needed a space to call theirs.

K.C. brought in the few things Shyne and he had gathered from Tali's house. Ma was sitting on the bed beside Talitha talking softly to her, trying to comfort her. Tali's face showed no sign of recognition or joy. She seemed like a pose-able doll, sitting where she was place, unresponsive to questions. *It's like Ma's illness all over again,* K.C. thought and the irony didn't escape him. *Perhaps it's a case of not having the coping skills to deal with life's stresses.*

He went to look for Shyne realizing that two more children had been added to the mix. Talitha's daughter, Tamila, and her son, Kerron, were standing in the bathroom waiting for Shyne to finish running a bath. Tammy was five and Kerron was six, so Shyne decided to bathe them together so she could supervise them. Brya, CeCe and Taddy were napping so she was able to devote her energies to getting Tali's children clean and fed. K.C. decided to help out by fixing a meal for the little ones.

He decided to do simple peanut butter and jam sandwiches with glasses of milk. He cored and sliced an apple into wedges and divided it between them. By the time he got lunch prepared, Shyne had finished scrubbing Kerron and Tammy, washing their hair and toweling them dry. K.C. took Kerron while Shyne led Tammy to Ma's room to dress in some of Brya and CeCe's larger clothes. Although the clothes were a bit snug, the kids looked a whole lot better than when he found them at home.

When placed in the chairs at the table, it was all K.C. could do to stop them from attacking the food. They were ravenous! His heart broke as he wondered how long Tali had been like she was, how long since these children had eaten. All too soon, he realized they could probably eat more, but he wasn't sure that was a good idea. He didn't want their stomachs to reject the food, so instead of making another sandwich, he gave them each a cookie for desert.

Neither child had said a word; they ate quietly and quickly, hardly looking up from the food. When they finished the last drop of milk and ate their cookies, Tammy looked at K.C. with her large brown eyes partially hidden by her bangs.

"You are Uncle K.C." she stated in a firm voice, older sounding than one would expect from a five year old. "You are Mommy's brother. She said you would come."

Kerron nodded his head, still chewing on his last bite of cookie. He wiped his mouth swiping his sleeve across his face and said, "But you took a long time." His voice growled out the words, raspy and rough as if he had a sore throat.

K.C. knelt between them. "I'm sorry I took so long to come for you. We are going to help your mommy get better, ok?" Both children nodded in agreement and K.C. thought he detected a tiny smile on the corner of Tammy's mouth.

Shyne sat on the couch watching the exchange. Her face reflected her concern; she wasn't her usual smiling self.

"You ok, little sis?" K.C. couldn't afford for another casualty to emotional distress.

"Oh, yeah. I'm fine. I've just never seen Tali so sick. I'm used to her being my stronger, older sister. While Skyla messed up, Tali always seemed to land on her feet. It kinda scares me. What if I fall apart like that someday? I don't want to be like that, K.C.!"

K.C. did the best he could to reassure her. But even as he told her she would be just fine, he wondered. God was his anchor in life's storms, but what did his sisters have to hold onto? And was faith enough? Ma had her challenges despite her trust in the Lord. He knew that doubt came from the enemy, and he needed to keep his heart fixed on God or he, too, could fall into the trap of hopelessness.

The next morning, K.C. had to leave Ma and Shyne to deal with the five children and to watch Tali. He needed to research war bonds so he could advise Isobel with regards to her financial concerns. He also wanted to talk to Ma's counselor about Tali. He didn't think she was in any condition to accept help; he didn't know how to handle her situation.

He drove into Omaha and went directly to Dr. Pearson's office. He asked the secretary if Dr. Pearson could find a few minutes for him. She checked and was happy to tell him that Dr. Pearson could see him when finished with his current patient. K.C. sat in the waiting room and picked up a well-worn magazine from the table next to his chair. The choices were the usual sports magazines, Newsweek magazines, and those dedicated to beautifying the home or garden. The dog-eared copy he picked up at random happened to be a medical journal which only a doctor could probably understand. He thumbed through it absentmindedly and placed it back on the table. His mind was preoccupied with the mental health of his family. He wondered if there was a genetic cause for Ma and Talitha's breakdowns, or if it was due to the despair of living on the reservation. He rested his head in his hands willing his mind to quiet down.

"Mr. Fox? Dr. Pearson will see you now." The secretary opened a side door to the hallway leading to the plush office that K.C. remembered from his previous visit.

"Thank you. I really appreciate this."

"Mr. Fox." Dr. Pearson did not seem put out by his unscheduled visit. He reached out to shake K.C.'s hand. "What can I help you with? Your mother is doing well, I hope?"

"Oh, yes, this isn't about Ma. I have another issue that I need advice on..."

K.C. proceeded to explain the events of the past 24 hours to Dr. Pearson. He tried to describe Talitha's condition, and Dr. Pearson asked pointed questions aimed at getting a better picture of her case. It wasn't long before Dr. Pearson interrupted K.C.'s discourse.

"I hate to say this, but I believe she needs hospitalization."

K.C. was shocked at Dr. Pearson's statement. "How can you suggest that without even seeing her?"

"Because I recognize the description you've given of her condition. She doesn't move independently, doesn't respond to questions and does not initiate or participate in conversation. You must realize that this is serious. She probably won't eat unless fed and your mother is still working on her own recovery. She cannot be responsible for a catatonic daughter, as much as I know she will want to. This type of depression is not easily handled at home, especially living as far from town as you do. She needs intensive medication and care to get her through this."

K.C. realized that what he was saying was true. It just went against their beliefs to release control to a medical facility. They saw hospitals as a place to die, not somewhere to get better. How could he convince Ma to let him bring Tali to Omaha for treatment? He looked at Dr. Pearson who was giving him time to digest what he had told him.

"So that's it, huh? Hospitalization? For how long?"

"That will depend on how she responds. Medication helps most, but sometimes we need to try other measures. Be assured we will do nothing without informed consent."

K.C. was fully aware of that term. He had studied malpractice law as part of his review, and knew that treatments needed to be signed off on by either the patient or a guardian or parent. He nodded, and thanked Dr. Pearson for the time. He made arrangements with the receptionist to bring Tali in so Dr. Pearson could evaluate her and admit her to the hospital for her treatment.

Leaving Dr. Pearson's office with a heavy heart, he tried to shift gears. He needed to complete the research for Isobel's case to ensure she would not be left penniless by inheriting her aunt's financial problems. He headed to the University Law Library and claimed a computer on which to do his research. He opened his briefcase and brought out the notebook he used to keep track of his sources. He still wasn't totally sold on using a word processor for his records; it was easier for him to refer to his own handwritten notes when doing research.

K.C. spent the major part of the day trying to find information on war bonds. It was much harder to find out the current value of a war bond from World War II than he thought it would be. Finally, he decided to contact a local historian to help him. He made an appointment to meet the elderly gentleman later in the afternoon. The Internet yielded many sites dealing with current day bonds and trading of stocks and bonds, but to find specific information on war bonds seemed elusive.

He looked forward to his conversation with Mr. Jurgensmeier, the historian specializing in documents. K.C. picked up all the loose papers and his notebook and placed them carefully into his briefcase. The last item to go into the attaché case was the yellowed bond. He looked closer at the document and realized it was not a war bond. It was a municipal bond, purchased for a whopping $100, a tidy sum for anyone in 1943. He wondered if it would matter in the big scheme of things. A war bond or a municipal bond, either one was a fascinating subject. K.C. doubted he would come across a similar issue anytime soon in his legal career.

Chapter 26

Sheriff Jones, with Dr. Fitz-Randolph following, returned to Isobel's farmyard. As she looked out the window, Isobel noticed that they both appeared relaxed as they got out of their vehicles,. She greeted them at the door and Sheriff Jones held up his hand as if to stop questions before they started. She looked over his shoulder toward Dr. Fitz and he just shrugged his shoulders and motioned with his head toward the sheriff.

"Ms. Kirk, let's have a seat and talk for a few minutes."

Isobel took the nearest chair, feeling for the seat and slipping into it carefully; she felt like the sky was about to fall.

"We went over and talked to old Jake and his son, Josh and, as they pointed out, we have no proof of anything and they aren't 'fessing up to anything." He looked at her over his glasses. "Old Jake swears he ain't up to nuthin'. And his boy there is dumb as a rock. He just does what daddy says, so we can't get a thing out of him."

"But what do you think? I mean… you must have a reason for suspecting them?"

Dr. Fitz chimed in for the first time, "we do have reasons, but it won't help for you to know them right now, Isobel!"

"Why not? Why can't I know who is threatening me? Why can't I understand what's behind all the things that have happened? I'm scared! I need to know if I need to get a guard dog, or move away from this house, or what I should do!"

Sheriff Jones wiped his forehead with his old kerchief and stuffed it back in his hip pocket. "Girl, you just need to listen. When the time is right, we will tell you. I don't think they'll be doing anymore tricks now that they know we're on to 'em. Old Jake looked scared enough when I started talking jail and the like. Nah, I don't spect they'll be coming round anytime soon." He looked at Dr. Fitz for affirmation.

"He's right now, Isobel. They were scared. I wouldn't tell you that you're safe if I thought there was a chance that they'd do you harm. I made a promise to your aunt that I would watch after you when she was gone, and I plan to keep that promise." He gave her a meaningful look, "Now, you can rest easy and sleep well at night. Old Jake and Josh will stay away for now. Meanwhile, Sheriff Jones needs to keep looking for evidence to link them to the arson, the car damage and this break-in. Once we have proof positive, they can be charged. Until then, you need to keep doing what you've been doing."

Isobel looked from one man to the other. She could tell they were sincere, but she wasn't convinced. Anybody willing to burn a structure so near the house as the barn was dangerous. And why was that kid looking into the window of her bedroom? Would he have hurt her if she had walked in on him? What if Old Jake and Josh *weren't* responsible for the attacks? What if Sheriff Jones was on the wrong track and the *real* criminal came back to finish the job?

They talked for a few more minutes, just small talk, and then both men excused themselves and left, one to his medical clinic, the other to his investigation. Once alone, Isobel sat in the quiet of the house, once again wondering what she was going to do. It could be harder to sell the property with the rash of vandalism. Until Sheriff Jones had a suspect arrested, Isobel decided she would continue down the path she'd chosen: clear the estate and move on. Dr. Fitz had said he would send out a repairman to fix the telephones. She did not expect to hear back from K.C. about the inheritance issues for a while, anyway. But without telephone service, she felt vulnerable and scared.

Sheriff Jones had not shared, with Dr. Fitz or Isobel, all the information he already gathered. He had been watching Jake and Josh for several years, ever since Aunt Betty told him of a couple of strange happenings on the farm. They both knew that Jake and Josh were responsible, but there was nothing concrete to use against them. He needed to talk to some of the sheriffs in surrounding counties to see if they had any ideas on how to go ahead with this case. He wondered if Jake and Josh had ventured outside Doniphan County. Something told him that their crime spree on the Kirk ranch wasn't their first.

The telephone repair van pulled into the yard and parked near the burned out barn. The repairman, with his low-hung belt filled with wires, cables and miscellaneous connectors, as well as a mobile phone, looked about her age. Isobel wondered if she had attended school with him when she first moved in with Aunt Betty. Isobel opened her door for him and he took a quick look around to survey the damage.

"Well, he sure did a number here!" he said as he looked at the dangling wall plate. "He didn't just cut your wires; he pulled the line right out of the wall. That's unusual! Normally, a cut wire to prevent the phone call is all a burglar will do. But in this case, it seems he wanted to plain make your life difficult, as well!"

He went outside to check out the connection coming into the house and came back with another report. "He didn't mess with the line out there, funny enough! But, your aunt hasn't had this service updated in a long time. The connection box is an old style one that predates our current NID box. If you're alright with it, I'll just switch that out while I'm here… no charge."

It sounded good to Isobel, since she didn't know what NID meant or how important all that was. She just needed her phones back in case of an emergency. She agreed to have him update the system, and do whatever was necessary to secure it against vandalism. Unfortunately, Isobel soon found out from the repairman, that phone lines were vulnerable. There really wasn't a means of locking the NID; it could be easily opened with a screwdriver.

The young man worked steadily until he had the NID installed. Both inside boxes were exchanged for the current modular type so the phones could be easily unplugged for replacement. When he'd finished, he was meticulous about cleaning up any mess he had made. Then he turned to Isobel to discuss total cost and for her to sign the work order.

"I thought I recognized you," he said when he saw her signature. "We went to school together many years ago." He reached out to shake her hand, "Jeff Newell, at your service."

She smiled. "I wondered about that, when you drove up," she replied.

"Hey, uh…, would you like to go for dinner some time? We could drive into the city and get away from the small town gossips…"

Isobel shook her head, "I'm sorry. I'm not ready to date."

Assuming she was referring to her aunt's recent death, he played off his disappointment with a quick grin. "Well, when you're ready, send up a flare or something, and I'll show you a good time."

That said, and all papers signed, Jeff left and Isobel was once again alone to mull over the direction of her life. As usual, her mind wandered toward Jason, wondering what he was doing, wondering how he was doing. She missed him so much that at times she felt a pressure on her chest causing her to have difficulty breathing. The discomfort usually went away when she did relaxation exercises. She had the same sensation when she thought of her Aunt Betty.

She missed Aunt Betty more than she thought possible. She came to realize how much she had started depending on her aunt's strength in her life. Her wisdom and compassion had made all the difference when she split up with Jason. At that time, she had nobody else she could turn to and now she recognized that she truly had no family. Every day it became more apparent how alone she truly was. Then, she remembered the puzzling comment Dr. Fitz had made shortly before Aunt Betty's death. He had told her to contact him when she had questions in the upcoming weeks. Up until now, he hadn't reminded her of that conversation, but Isobel decided it was time. She had so many questions; maybe Dr. Fitz could answer at least some of them.

She picked up the phone to call him, and just then saw a figure darting across the field just beyond the burned out barn! Quickly placing the phone back in its cradle, she ran outside and yelled into the distance, "Why don't you just show yourself and tell me what you want? Why can't you leave me alone?" Nothing moved. She sat on the step and just watched and waited. Not a sound, not even the birds chirping. The quiet was deafening! Isobel got up, brushed off her backside, and went back in to call Dr. Fitz.

"Dr. Fitz? It's Isobel," she started, but before she could say much more, Dr. Fitz was telling her he would be right over. "But, nothing's wrong, I just…" Once again, he cut her off. He told her that he needed to talk to her about something important, and then said good-bye. The next thing she heard was the dial tone after he'd hung up the phone.

Dr. Fitz must have driven faster than usual, because he arrived in record time, as if he had already been headed out to her place before she called. Jumping out of his car with the energy of a much younger man, he seemed excited. "Hey, Isobel," he leaned over and kissed her cheek, "do I have news for you!"

The bewilderment on Isobel's face must have clued him in to her total confusion. She was expecting him to turn up with bad news, but he seemed thrilled to bring her whatever news he had.

"First, sit down, little lady," he guided her to a chair. She was moving under his direction because she didn't know what to think. She sat at the kitchen table where so much bad news had passed over the last few months.

"I don't want you to think that I'm interfering in your business, but… well to put it bluntly, I know someone that may be interested in buying your farm!"

Isobel did a double take. "I haven't even finished settling Aunt Betty's estate, Dr. Fitz! I haven't put it on the market for sale. How can they want to buy it when I don't have a clue of its value?"

"Whoa, there! One question at a time! Now, we didn't talk numbers. They just indicated they were looking for a farm about the size of this one, and I thought of you. And you know, with the recent vandalism episodes, you may not be able to get top value…"

Again, Isobel was flabbergasted. Here she thought Dr. Fitz was looking out for her interests, yet, now he was trying to tell her to not ask too much for the farm. He knew how much debt Aunt Betty left behind, and he knew of her sense of duty. *How could he suggest she ask less than market value for the farm*? Isobel thought. It made her wonder if Dr. Fitz had a connection to the sabotage on the farm. Had he known that it would lessen her property's value? Was he responsible for old Jake and Josh's efforts at scaring her? Suddenly, she wasn't sure she could trust anyone, even Dr. Fitz.

Chapter 27

"Kind of you to meet with me today, Mr. Jurgensmeier. Here is the item I discussed with you on the phone," K.C. laid the bond on the glass display cabinet between he and the elderly historian. "I think I told you it was a war bond, because the date was 1943. But when I looked closer, well…"

"It's a municipal bond, son. And in mighty fine condition, too." He turned it over, looking at all the markings and scrollwork border. "Yep, mighty fine condition. And it appears to be authentic. All too often these old things are reproduced and sold to folks who just like the looks of 'em. Then some heir to the estate begins to think the phony is worth something. But I believe you got a live one here, son."

K.C. stood silently, watching Mr. Jurgensmeier as he inspected the bond and talked. The historian pulled out his vintage eye loupe to magnify the signatures and other markings as he continued talking. He cleaned the lens with his handkerchief and then placed it carefully to his eye while holding the document up for close inspection. Then he stopped talking, put the loupe onto the cabinet, wiped his forehead with the same handkerchief from his back pocket and looked at K.C.

"Now, what did you say your connection is with this paper?"

"Actually, I didn't," replied K.C. cautiously, "why?"

"Well, I was jest wondering how you came to be holding such a valuable piece of paper! After all, you come from the rez, don't you?"

The nasty tone of prejudice that K.C. had experienced throughout his childhood punctuated the statement from Mr. Jurgensmeier. Obviously, the elderly gentleman wasn't much of a gentleman. He made no secret of the disdain he held for the Native Americans from the reservation, despite calling K.C. 'son' when he first entered the shop. He probably figured the document would be a fake, so K.C. was not a threat. But someone from the 'rez' had no right to things of value.

"Mr. Jurgensmeier, I thank you for your assistance and opinion on this document. I will take it back to its owner now..."

Mr. Jurgensmeier moved slightly as if to avoid K.C.'s reach for the bond. Then, realizing he could not prevent him from taking it, the elderly man grudgingly handed it over to K.C. "You jest be sure the rightful owner gets that back!" Even when losing, he had to give the last jab.

K.C. took the municipal bond and placed it into his briefcase. He looked at Mr. Jurgensmeier one last time, debating whether to tell the man that, if his bar exam came back with good results, he would be a lawyer. *He's not worth it! He probably wouldn't believe me, anyway, without the paper to prove it!* He took his leave the same way he'd come in, and wondered where the nearest authority on municipal bonds could be found.

Back at the Law Library, K.C. sat in front of a computer trying to find more information on municipal bonds. He used Google and Bing and still came up short. Trying to figure the value of old bonds was difficult and required an expert. Not only did the value vary according to which municipality issued the bond, but also by the percentage of increase initially assigned and the frequency of maturation and rolling over to reinvest. Some bonds held up under the changes of time, but if the municipality went bankrupt between 1943 and present day, the value could be zero, other than to a collector of World War II memorabilia.

Accounting and finance was never K.C.'s strong point, which was one reason he went into law rather than the sciences or business. However, from what Mr. Jurgensmeier had said, and from what little he could find on-line, he was certain that Isobel held a windfall in this municipal bond, providing the issuing municipality was still functioning under the financials that had been responsible for issuance of the bond. He did wonder how many bonds were issued, and how that affected the overall value.

He sat back in his chair and rubbed his eyes. He hated being indoors so much, and he especially disliked staring at computer screens. Research was necessary in the legal profession, but K.C. looked forward to the day when he would have an assistant, a paralegal or something. He relished putting cases together, but would be happy to leave the busy work to someone else. Unable to reach a conclusion on the value of the bond, he opted to try once again to talk to an expert. This time, he thought he would ask other lawyers for references rather than randomly pulling a name from the on-line list as he had with Mr. Jurgensmeier.

K.C. went to the offices of the professors for the School of Law first, thinking they would be a good resource. They did not have any recommendations, since they were not actively working in the field and had not need for specialists in antique documents. But they did advise him to talk to several of the local law firms that often provided guest speakers for the specialty law classes.

At Fischer, Price and Associates K.C. found several aging attorneys with a small, specialized clientele: those in need of help with wills, trust funds and other inheritance issues. Although they couldn't advise him regarding the bond, they were able to clarify the inheritance laws in Kansas. Just as K.C. had found in his research, Isobel would not be liable for her aunt's debts. The assets would be sold and those funds applied to cover as much of the outstanding debt as possible. Beyond that, the various creditors would write off the remaining debt as bad debt.

Knowing Isobel's sense of duty, he realized that would not solve the quandary she found herself in; she would still want to make good on the repayment of all that was owed. K.C. hoped that the value of the bond would turn out to be enough to cover any outstanding liability left from the estate. He thanked the old gentlemen and shook their hands. They were gracious and did not seem concerned by his ethnicity as was Mr. Jurgensmeier.

K.C. had better luck at the second law firm he visited. The firm of Franklin, Frederick and Sons was another well established legal office, but evidently the sons had taken over from their fathers. The younger men appeared to be in their late thirties or early forties. Somewhat intimidated, K.C. approached with caution only to be welcomed warmly and invited into one of their offices.

"So, you are hoping to become a lawyer?"

"Actually, I've already sat the bar exam. I'm just waiting for the results, and then, hopefully, I'll be in the market for a job." K.C. knew he shouldn't be hinting for employment, but he was also fully aware of his family's quickly dwindling resources.

Not taking the bait, or being deliberately elusive, the apparently younger of the two quickly changed the subject, "We understand you are in need of some professional guidance?"

"Well, yes," K.C. wasn't offended at their dodge. He did need their help, so he returned to the subject. "I need help with valuation of a bond issued in 1943. I'm doing some volunteer work, and one of my clients brought it to me with a bundle of other documents related to her inheritance. Would you have the name of anyone that specializes in antique documents? It's a municipal bond…"

"We don't know of someone that may be able to help," the older brother finally spoke. "The question is, what is in it for us?"

K.C. looked at them perplexed, "I thought you understood that all I need is a name…"

"That's all well and good, Mr. Fox, but we are in a business, not a charity." Both men looked smug as K.C. gazed at them flabbergasted at their boldness.

"I can see I've come to the wrong place," K.C. started to rise from his chair. "My client is not wealthy enough to have her own lawyer. She came to the Legal Aid Office for help, not to be raked over the coals. Now, gentlemen, thank you for your *valuable* time!"

He stood and headed for the door without another word. He didn't even shake their hands.

The search for a professional to assist him was more complicated than he anticipated. He wondered if he would need to travel to a larger city to find a resource to answer his questions. K.C. couldn't believe the barriers he'd encountered in his own profession. There was only one other law firm recommended by the professors at the law school. Hopefully he would have better luck with the next law group.

On a side street several blocks from his starting point at the Law Library, K.C. found the last lawyer on the list. The office was small and unobtrusive; if he hadn't been given the address, he would never have found it. The name was on a hand-printed sign hanging in the window. *Not the stuff the law profession was made of,* K.C. thought. It looked amateurish and crude. As he opened the door he heard a tinkling of the bell hung over the door, triggered by the movement of the door.

A middle-aged man in a tidy, though out-dated, suit came from the back room. "Can I help you, son?"

K.C. smiled at the expression. He'd heard the term 'son' more times that he could count since he started this investigation. From Mr. Jurgensmeier it was a term of derision rather than respect. From this gentleman, the word sounded warm and friendly. K.C. looked into his kindly blue eyes and recognized a glow of joy. He smiled. Although, unless he asked, he couldn't be sure, his heart told him that Mr. McMillen was a Christian. His demeanor and warmth spoke to the love of the Lord.

"Mr. McMillen. So good to meet you. I am K.C. Fox; I believe you may have received a call from Professor Jeffries about my problem?"

"Yes, and I know just the person to help you, Mr. Fox."

"Please, call me K.C. Mr. Fox sounds old to me."

"OK, K.C. In Kansas City is a specialist in the field of antique stocks and bonds. She loves a challenge, and will be glad to help you. I already called and spoke with her. Here is her card; she will be available at your convenience."

K.C. was speechless. He thanked Mr. McMillen and they sat down and chatted for a while. K.C. had nowhere else to go that day; it was too late to drive down to Kansas City, so that would have to wait. Meanwhile, he wanted to find out what opportunities there might be in the Omaha area for a new lawyer fresh out of school. He was surprised when Mr. McMillen suggested that, once the results came back from his bar exam, K.C. should give him a call.

"I've been looking for a partner. As you can see…" he motioned around the office, "I don't have a lot, but I do need help. I frequently get cases that are too much for me to handle, and a second lawyer would be welcome. Let's get together and talk more, later, ok?"

Agreeing to call after he received his results, K.C. left joyful. Not only did he have the name of a well-respected expert, he had a job possibility. It amazed him how God was always working in the background. He breathed a prayer of thanksgiving and continued heading for home with a smile on his face and a song in his heart. He anticipated the challenges ahead with Talitha, but at least he was assured that God was in control.

Chapter 28

Isobel decided that she needed to move forward with the sale of the property. Even if K.C. found a solution for her financial questions, she did not plan to stay in Kansas. She wasn't sure where she would move to, but was certain that there were no opportunities for her to use her degree in this rural region of the country. Isobel was considering a move to the Pacific Northwest, either Washington State or Portland, Oregon. The discussion of opportunities for international business degreed students predominantly included coastal cities; Los Angeles and New York always came up.

She had no desire to live in such huge metropolitan regions. While working on her degree, she hadn't even considered job options because her focus was on her wedding, on her marriage to Jason Armstrong. He seemed to pop into her mind whenever she was stressed. At one time, she would have turned immediately to him for advice and assistance. *Would it be wrong to call him?* She considered the idea and quickly dismissed it as a sign of weakness.

Isobel concluded sorting through Aunt Betty's belongings several days after Dr. Fitz's visit. It still puzzled her how he could have an interested buyer for the farm. Why did it seem he wanted her to move on? He needn't worry. She wanted to leave the sadness and memories behind just as bad as he seemed to want her to go. She wanted to start fresh; she just wasn't sure how or where to do that.

One morning, several weeks after the break-in, Isobel was awakened by a knocking on the kitchen door. She wrapped her robe around her tightly to ward off the cold air of winter and warily approached the back door. Relieved, she saw Sheriff Jones standing at the door, blowing on his hands and stomping his feet to stay warm.

"Sheriff Jones. Come on in and warm up." She opened the door widely. "I haven't started the heat yet this morning, but come on in. It won't take long to take the chill out of the room. Would you like some coffee?" She finally stopped to take a deep breath.

Sheriff Jones smiled at her energy. "Sure, young lady, I'll take a cup of your coffee. I reckon it's about the best I get in these parts." He lowered himself into the same chair he took each time he visited. "I got some news for you. But I guess you figured that when you saw me."

Isobel looked up from her task of setting up the coffee maker and nodded to encourage him.

"We'll we made an arrest..."

Isobel squealed, "You what? You mean you found who did all those things to me?"

"Now, don't get too excited. We took in Josh for his part in the break-in and the damage to your car. He admitted that he was trying to scare you with the car incident, and was searching for some paper that his pa had sent him to look for. But he didn't 'fess up to the barn burning"

Isobel was confused. She assumed all the events were tied together, but it sounded as if more than just Josh and old Jake were to blame. "Do you know who else might be doing some of these things?" Tentative, Isobel wasn't sure she wanted to know who he had in mind.

Sheriff Jones took a bite of one of the cookies on the plate she had rested on the table. He seemed to be measuring his response, as if to not get her any more upset. "I do have another suspect in mind, but I can't prove anything right now. I'll keep you informed as new information comes up." He took a sip of the coffee she had just put in front of him. "Whew! That's hot!"

Isobel smiled wryly. "It's supposed to be hot; it was just made fresh." She wrung her hands and looked up, "Sheriff Jones. Is Dr. Fitz a suspect?"

Her question took him by surprise. Whether because he assumed she was clueless about the crimes or because he did consider Dr. Fitz a suspect, Isobel couldn't be sure. She only saw the surprise in his eyes.

Sheriff Jones gulped down the hot coffee, grabbed another cookie and rose from his chair. "Guess it's time I get out there and chase some criminals." He avoided answering her question. "I'll keep you informed, little miss." And with that, Sheriff Jones went out the door without a backward glance.

His exit did little to restore Isobel's trust in Dr. Fitz. Sheriff Jones hadn't indicated whether or not he considered Dr. Fitz a threat. As she cleared the table, she reviewed the events of the last few months. Like a movie, each major event since her aunt's death ran through her mind like individual scenes and she wished she could turn off her memory. Over and over, the scenes ran on and it exhausted her to keep rehashing everything.

Isobel wondered when she would hear from K.C. Fox. Her next appointment was scheduled a week away, but her anxiety level was rising and she needed to make plans for her future. She picked up the phone and called the number for the Legal Aid Office.

"Is K.C. Fox there today?" she asked the young woman who answered the phone.

"No, Mr. Fox isn't scheduled to be here until next week. Can someone else help you?" "So he won't be in for the next few days?"

The girl replied once again that he wouldn't be there until the next week. She also repeated her question if another volunteer could assist.

"No, I need to talk to him. He's handling my case," Isobel replied, trying not to sound too disappointed. "I already have an appointment set for next week; I was just getting anxious, that's all." She closed out the phone call as politely as she could, but in her heart she was let down. She wished she had gotten his personal number so she could check on his progress.

Isobel called the local real estate office and scheduled an appointment for that afternoon. She decided to list the property, not knowing how long it could take to sell in the depressed housing market. Despite Dr. Fitz's mention of a potential buyer, she wanted to hold out for the best price she could get, so she could pay as many debts as possible with the proceeds. She would need to pay off the mortgage first, but if the farm sold for enough over that loan, perhaps she could take care of some other outstanding accounts as well.

Judy Harrison, the real estate agent, was thrilled at getting the listing. "We can definitely move this property," she assured Isobel. "There's been a lot of interest since Betty Kirk's death."

"Oh, really? Who has been showing interest? Local folks?"

"Well, I can't really divulge that information. Just in case they want to make an offer, I have to maintain neutrality. After all, I am one of just a few realtors for this county, so more than likely, I will be working for both the seller and the buyer. You did see that release in the contract information, didn't you?"

Isobel had no experience with property sales, and realized that she should wait to ask K.C.'s advice before proceeding with the contract. "Is it ok if I take this with me to have my lawyer look at?" Isobel looked up at the realtor who was more than a little surprised.

"Mr. Sorenson knows my work. He knows I don't do anything underhanded. I always represent my clients the best I can."

"Oh, I'm not going to Mr. Sorenson. I have another lawyer who is helping me."

Judy couldn't hide her confusion. "But he's the only one in town…"

"Exactly! That's why I went out of town for advice. I'll bring these back as soon as he's reviewed them and advised me." Isobel nodded to Judy who had no choice but to agree.

Judy placed all the papers into a manila envelope and slowly opened the little metal clamp to seal it. She handed the package to Isobel without smiling. "We don't take kindly to going to outsiders for help." It sounded almost like a threat to Isobel. She took the envelope and left without further discussion.

Once home, Isobel sat wondering who she could trust. She didn't know who she could turn to. She had never felt more alone since Aunt Betty's death. She thought again of calling Jason. He was the one person she could count on. But what if he had found another girlfriend? Could she handle hearing that he was finding happiness and moving on? Could she handle not knowing? She made up her mind to call him that evening when he would be back in his dorm room.

"Jason? It's Isobel…"

Before she could say more, Jason interrupted her. "Are you alright, Izzie? What's wrong?"

"What makes you think something is wrong?" She smiled realizing he always could read her voice.

"Darling, you know I know you by heart! What is it? How can I help?"

Isobel started carefully telling him of the events before and after the death of Aunt Betty. Jason listened without interrupting her. When she talked of the fire, she heard a quick intake of breath at the other end of the phone line, but he didn't stop her. However, when she shared the story of the break-in and how Josh had looked in the bedroom window, Jason couldn't keep quiet.

"Izzie, you need to move from there! It isn't safe, and I don't want anything to happen to you!"

Isobel went on to tell him of her plans to sell the property to pay debts and how awful the inheritance looked. Then she explained her concerns related to listing the farm with Judy; she told him of Dr. Fitz's reference to interest in the land. He kept listening, taking it all in, and Isobel knew he would give her a logical, unbiased perspective. His analytical mind always impressed her.

"Isobel, do you want me to come there?"

"No! You need to stay in school. I don't want you to jeopardize your academic career and your future. No, I'll handle this. I just needed to talk to someone I could trust."

"You know you can always call me, dear. I will always be there for you. There's no room in my heart for anyone else. Please know that what I said before still stands. I want us to marry someday. All you have to do is say the word. I will wait as long as it takes!"

After talking for a while longer, Isobel felt relieved. Her strength of character was revived just from hearing his voice, but her conviction that she was doing the right thing was confirmed more by his words.

She began to look forward to her meeting with K.C. and, hopefully, to selling the farm. She needed a fresh start, of that she was sure. Her conversation with Jason opened up new avenues, new hopes for her future, although she still didn't see a way around his parent's prejudices. She was startled from her daydream when Jason asked her if he could pray with her.

"I haven't been down that road much these days, Jason," she replied. "It seems that God has forgotten me."

Jason asked again, and she couldn't deny him the chance to exercise his faith. Jason prayed fervently for Isobel. He asked God to touch her heart, to soften it and mold it for His work. He asked that the enemies be held at bay, to prevent injury to Isobel and to allow her to move from the area without harm falling on her. Jason said all the right things, and talked to God as if he were talking to a Friend.

Isobel felt warmed by his concern, but also felt a softening in her heart toward the Lord. Maybe, just maybe, things would be easier to deal with if she allowed Jesus to carry some of her burden. By the time Jason finished his petition, Isobel was also moved to pray. She didn't say much, except to thank God for putting Jason in her life, and to work their relationship or friendship for His glory. She wasn't brave enough to commit to a new start for them, but she was open to the possibility.

They said their good-byes and Isobel got off the phone feeling more hope for her future. She would be glad when all was settled and done, and she could move on with her life, whether with or without Jason.

Chapter 29

K.C. decided to contact Isobel before driving to Kansas City. Since he would be driving right past her corner of the state to get there, he thought perhaps she would want to go along. After all, his efforts were pro bono; she should have a vested interest in appraisal of the bond. He didn't need her assistance, but he certainly wouldn't mind spending time with her, getting to know her better. He called her home phone number and was pleased to hear her voice on the other end.

"Ms. Kirk?"

"Who is calling?" Isobel didn't recognize the voice at the other end of the line. She was still receiving telemarketing calls for Aunt Betty, so she didn't take it for granted that the call was for her.

"Ms. Kirk, this is K.C. Fox…"

"Oh, K.C., I'm sorry. I didn't recognize your voice."

"No reason you should," he replied. "After all, the only time we've talked was in the office. What I was calling for was in reference to the bond you brought with all the other papers."

"Did you find out if it has any value?"

"That's what I'm calling about. There is an expert in Kansas City who may be able to provide us information on whether it holds any present day value. I was wondering if you'd be interested in driving there with me…we could make a day of it, or just a quick drive there and back… it's up to you."

Isobel was a bit surprised at his suggestion. Other than Jason, she had never spent time with a young man, especially not on a drive to another town. It seemed rather intimate to sit in a car with someone for a couple of hours of driving.

K.C. sensed her hesitation and understood. From their discussion in the office, he knew of her broken relationship, as well as the loss of her aunt, and realized she felt vulnerable. Doing his best to reassure her of his honest intentions he made a suggestion. "If you would rather meet me at the office of the lady that was recommended to me, I'm ok with that, too. I don't want you to feel obligated or trapped by driving with me."

She laughed with relief at his suggestion. "Now, that would be silly, to drive two cars all the way to Kansas City. What if mine broke down? No, I need to stop being impractical and childish. I appreciate what you are trying to do for me. I'd be glad to ride along with you. And, since I've never really seen Kansas City, I'd enjoy a day on the town." She thought, *at least it wasn't like a date in the evening.*

K.C. was please that she was quick to agree. And he looked forward to the idea of making friends with Isobel. She seemed like a lovely young lady, and it had been a long time since he'd allowed himself the opportunity to socialize with the opposite sex. Although he wasn't looking for a long-term relationship, the thoughts of a friendship appealed to him. They finalized the arrangements and decided to take the drive on the following morning.

Isobel looked at the phone in her hand, heard the dial tone, and wondered at her boldness in agreeing to going with K.C. Here she had just spoken with Jason, on this same phone, the evening before, feeling so close to him, and was now planning a day out with her 'lawyer'. *Was this the same as being unfaithful?* She wondered. She could rationalize the outing as a business trip, strictly business. But once they finish the visit to the expert, and toured the town, it was no longer just business, it became pleasure. She was sure Jason wouldn't like her having a date, however inconsequential, with another young man. *But we aren't in a committed relationship anymore,* she argued with her heart. Unwilling to call K.C. back, she left the plans set, but determined to have K.C. bring her home immediately after their morning appointment with Ms. Cassidy, the expert in antique stocks and bonds.

Isobel slept fitfully throughout the night. Each time she opened her eyes, darkness greeted her, and her heart dropped. How could she sleep with a guilty conscience? But why did she feel guilty? She kept wrestling with the plans for the day. Even driving for two hours seemed more time than she wanted to invest in a guy at this point in her life. How could she get out of it? Should she try? Isobel dozed off again and again until finally sunshine filtered through the blinds, stinging her eyes with its brightness.

She went to wash up and faced herself in the mirror. Her eyes were bloodshot and the eyelids puffy, as was her face. She splashed cold water on her face and looked again. The sudden chill against her skin tightened her skin and helped decrease the fullness around her eyes. A couple more splashes and she felt awake and looked nearly normal, except for some residual redness in her eyes.

Isobel went through her morning ritual, getting ready for the day despite her misgivings. She ate a light breakfast consisting of yogurt with a little granola mixed in and a cup of black coffee. She knew if she ate more she might get car sick. Tidying up took just minutes, and by 8:00 she was sitting at the table watching and waiting for K.C. to drive up. Needing something to occupy her hands, Isobel reached for Aunt Betty's well-warn Bible.

Opening the cover for the first time since Aunt Betty's death, she recognized her aunt's handwriting listing verses, on the inside cover. She flipped through the dog-eared pages worn thin from years of use, yellowed with age. The pages fell open to the book of Jeremiah. Isobel looked at the pages and saw some verses were underlined in red and others in green. Occasionally, the lines under the words were black or blue. She didn't understand her aunt's code for underlining, but knew that each verse was special for a different reason. One verse in particular was not just underlined; it was highlighted with bright, neon yellow. Isobel read it aloud, "*…thou hast given me the heritage of those that fear thy name.*" She paused, thoughtful.

Isobel recalled the closing lines in Aunt Betty's letter, and her dedication to her faith. She wondered about her birth mother. Did she also believe in God? Did she trust in a personal Savior? If she did, she would be disappointed to know that Isobel had only gone through the motions in high school and college. Then she thought of Jason and his prayer for her, and how she felt moved to pray as well. *Perhaps God was reaching out to me,* she thought. She quickly put her musings aside as she heard a car pull into the yard.

K.C. looked around at the tumbledown farmstead. He saw the burned out barn still waiting to be cleaned up. Then he looked at the house and saw a beautiful face gazing out the window. He waved and headed for the back door where Isobel met him, purse in hand and jacket over her arm. Before he could say 'good morning' Isobel was speaking.

"I decided that I need to return straight home after our appointment with Ms. Cassidy. I hope that doesn't inconvenience you, but I think it's for the best." She didn't make eye contact but headed for the car; K.C. opened the passenger's door. After she settled in and had her seatbelt on, he closed the door and went around to the driver's side. Before starting the car, he turned to Isobel. "Could you tell me what changed between last night and today?"

"I think it's too soon for me to be out and about with a guy. I'm just not ready, for even a casual friendship. I'm sorry. You probably think I'm silly and making more of the plans for today than they warrant…"

K.C. put up his hand to stop her apologizing. "It's alright! No need to explain further. I understand. Let's just take it one step at a time, ok? Let's just get to know each other as we drive there, and then you can decide how you want to spend the day. No strings attached, mind you. Just a friendly outing, *IF* you decide to do it, that is." His straight, white, evenly spaced teeth shone between his full-lipped smile. The contrast between his teeth and skin was amazing to Isobel, and his honest smile melted some of her reserve. She nodded and K.C. started the car, satisfied with the compromise.

Conversation was inhibited at first. The usual small talk followed by brief questions went nowhere until they were off the country road and headed toward the city on a major road. It was then that Isobel visibly relaxed, almost as if she was concerned about the reaction of her neighbors. K.C. wondered if Isobel had issues about his ethnicity. He couldn't place hers in any box, and didn't want to ask such a personal question, so he put that thought in the back of his mind.

She initiated conversation asking K.C. questions about his career path and how he happened to go into law. K.C. openly spoke of his heritage and his family. He told her of the recent challenges related to Skyla's legal defense, as well as briefly touching on the reasons he still lived on the rez, despite his education. Isobel seemed touched by his concern for his sisters.

"You have no brothers?" she asked.

"No. I've been blessed with nephews, but I am the only male of my generation, so that gives me the responsibility to care for the women: my mother and sisters, as well as their children."

"That must be quite a burden to bear?"

"Not really." He replied. "I am blessed to have the skills and abilities to take care of them."

With that comment, K.C. opened the door to a conversation about religion. Isobel asked many questions aimed at whether God truly existed, and why bad things happen. She couldn't reconcile a loving God with the horrible events that happen on earth, along with the tragedies she had personally experienced. K.C. tried to answer carefully but honestly, breathing a prayer for wisdom before each response. He could tell that she had had exposure to basic Christian beliefs, but had never internalized them, and he hoped and prayed that his answers would guide her closer to the Lord.

After reaching an impasse in the discussion, K.C. decided to move the conversation toward Isobel's goals in life. By discussing the temporal, he hoped to help her see the value of the spiritual. Focusing on the development of a well-rounded person, healthy, happy and holy, he hoped to open her mind to the possibility of allowing God into her heart.

"So, you studied International Business? What did you have in mind when choosing your major?" he asked her.

"Mostly, I was thinking of the fact that my mother was from Japan." Isobel gulped, and K.C. looked to see her tearing up. "Now, I know that she wasn't my real mother, and I don't know what my background is."

K.C. wondered at the statement, but seeing her fragile emotions exposed he tried to move to more solid footing, returning to the subject of college majors and plans. "Did you have a job in mind after graduation? I know your aunt's illness and death put your plans on hold, but what do you plan beyond clearing her estate?"

"That's just it! I don't have a clue! I thought I would be getting married shortly after graduation, but that fell through..." K.C. was astute enough to not delve into that subject with her. "...so now I am trying to figure out where to go for the best job opportunities."

It was about this time that they pulled into the parking garage of a tall office building in the middle of downtown Kansas City. Isobel had never been up into a building that stood over four stories, so pressing the button for the twenty-second floor set butterflies swirling in her stomach. They stepped off the elevator into a well-decorated lobby surrounded by dark wood door frames and smoky glass windows with names etched into them. It looked like an expensive firm, and Isobel looked at K.C. with concern.

"You know I have no money to pay for this kind of service," she wondered at the wisdom of this trip.

"Don't worry. Ms. Cassidy assured me that our first consultation was free. Charges are only incurred if she needs to take time for research and title searches or verification of ownership." He took her elbow and guided her through the door with S. Cassidy Investigations, LLC engraved on the window. They were soon escorted to the inner sanctum of Ms. Stephanie Cassidy.

Isobel was surprised at the youth of the private investigator who claimed expertise in document verification and valuation. She thought the woman would be matronly, elderly, gray-haired and wearing wire-rimmed glasses. Instead, they were met by a petite, well-groomed professional in a pin-striped ladies business suit. Her hair was neatly coiffed in the stylish stacked cut with highlights, and her glasses the chic, rectangular, tortoise-shell frame by a well-known fashion designer. Isobel immediately realized that Ms. Cassidy ran a profitable agency, and once again worried at her ability to help them without cost.

K.C. took charge of the meeting, while Isobel sat in her chair silently watching and listening. From his briefcase, K.C. produced the bond after explaining his own research and the difficulties he had verifying its value.

Ms. Cassidy sat up straight in her chair when she saw the bond. She reached across the desk and slid it toward her until she could pick it up gently between two fingers. She touched the stamped seal, held it up to the light as if searching for watermarks that wouldn't have existed in 1943, and read the words and signatures under her breath. She reacted in much the same way that K.C. had when Isobel first showed it to him. Isobel wondered if Ms. Cassidy had any more of a clue to its value than K.C. had.

Ms. Cassidy sat back, still holding the bond lightly between two fingers. She put it onto a plain sheet of paper on the side of her desk and looked from Isobel to K.C. in puzzlement.

"Do you know what you have here? Have you any idea?" This was spoken directly to Isobel.

Isobel shook her head 'No' and then spoke quietly. "Is it worth anything?"

Ms. Cassidy looked at her in amazement. Then she turned to K.C. "Is this for real? Did you really not figure out the value of this thing?"

K.C. flushed at her insinuation. "No, that is why we came to you, Ms. Cassidy. I would not hide something like that, had I come across something telling me its value."

Stephanie Cassidy relaxed and leaned forward. "You have a windfall here, Ms. Kirk!"

"How much of a windfall?" Isobel was afraid to hope for enough to clear her aunt's debts.

"Well, I can't be certain until I research the exact numbers on the bond…" Isobel sighed. *Yep, here we go with the costly research,* she thought. *I knew this was too good to be true. Nobody does anything for free!*

K.C.'s voice interrupted her thoughts. "Just get to the point, please, Ms. Cassidy. Ms. Kirk has been through a lot in the past year, and we need to help her with this current issue, so she can get on with her life."

"Well, I estimate, and mind you this is just an estimate… This bond is potentially worth $1.5 million dollars…"

Isobel gasped and grabbed K.C.'s arm for support. He asked for a glass of water, and Ms. Cassidy buzzed her assistant who brought in a crystal pitcher with three matching glasses, all sitting on an equally beautiful silver tray. Once Isobel had a refreshing drink, she turned back to Ms. Cassidy who was once again looking over the bond.

"Yes, Mr. Fox, Ms. Kirk, I believe this bond is valued between $1.5 and $1.75 million. I can verify the exact value, if you like. It would make the process much easier for you to cash it out, if I verify it and confirm ownership."

Isobel and K.C. spoke briefly in whispers, but then agreed to Ms. Cassidy's offer of assistance. She asked them to come back after lunch, when she could have a contract ready for signatures. There could be no confusion as to the terms of their relationship, and the percentage Ms. Cassidy would receive. If the value was indeed as much as she indicated, her cut was worth her services.

Chapter 30

K.C. took Isobel to lunch at a nearby cafeteria-styled deli. It was less intimate than a traditional restaurant and less threatening for Isobel. He knew she had hoped to be on her way home by this time. She was quiet and obviously uncomfortable as they found a table. It seemed she was looking around for anyone that might know her, afraid of giving the wrong idea about K.C. and her relationship.

Always the gentleman, and without a second thought, K.C. held Isobel's chair for her to be seated. She pulled it in rather than waiting for him to push it, giving another signal that she wasn't looking for male attention. She hung her purse over the back of her chair and unfolded her napkin in her lap without saying a word. Then she finally spoke.

"K.C., I appreciate all that you are doing for me. And I appreciate where we are right now with Stephanie. I hope she is right with her estimate, but even if the value is half of what she estimates, it will be a lot of money, and for that I am thankful. What I want to say, what I *need* to say is that I am not looking for more than a professional relationship. Even a friendship seems too much for me to deal with at this point in my life. I have no focus, no plan, and I can't jump into another relationship in hopes of rebuilding my prior plan for my life."

She paused. This was a long speech for someone not known for being talkative. K.C. wanted to say something, but he could tell she still had more to say, so he held his peace. He just looked at her serious, deep brown eyes, wishing he could reassure her that he was not looking for more than friendship. He knew that his timetable may not be God's plan, so he left the issue at the throne when he prayed each morning.

She gazed back at him, wishing with all her heart that she could be more open to his offer of friendship. She needed someone in her life to trust. Right now, with the Sheriff's investigation and insinuations, she wasn't sure who she could count on in that little town. Was Dr. Fitz truly keeping her best interests in mind, or did he have an ulterior motive? And there was the barn… Who hated her enough to set it afire? No, she couldn't depend on those in the area around the farm, but could she depend on K.C. for more than legal advice?

"Please realize that, first and foremost, I need to clear my aunt's estate. Beyond that, I just don't know. I will need you to advise me, legally speaking, and I hope you are ok with that."

At last, K.C. heard an opening for him to speak. "I do understand. And once again, I want to assure you that I am fine with your request. I have some complicated concerns going on at home, too. I just feel some sort of connection with you, but I only want to get to know you better. I can back off to a purely professional relationship, if that's what is necessary to preserve future opportunities." Isobel nodded assent and they set about eating their food with little further discussion or conversation.

Returning to Stephanie Cassidy's office, Isobel was apprehensive about signing a contract. This was all new to her, never having done business on her own. Isobel was off-balance by being thrust into the adult world with her aunt's death left. She was out of her element. The one thing she was grateful for was that all this was preparing her for her future. Had she married Jason as originally planned, she probably would have been dependent on him for these matters. Instead, she was learning to be an independent woman.

"Come on in! I'm so excited to see you back," Stephanie Cassidy was positively animated. "I did a little work while you were gone and I was able to determine the exact value as of today's market."

Isobel looked at K.C. in shock. Was this a dream? How could this be happening so quickly? Stephanie obviously had good news. Isobel slid into the nearest chair before her legs gave out on her. K.C. took the chair beside hers and reached to squeeze her hand to give her courage. She smiled wryly at K.C.'s attempt, too anxious to relax.

"I was amazed at how easily I was able to verify ownership by one Ms. Elizabeth A. Kirk who purchased the municipal bond in 1943 for a price of $\$100^{00}$. She evidently either forgot to cash it out, or retained it hoping for this particular outcome. Either way, it has continued to gain value as the economy has grown. The current cash value is a bit less than I originally estimated…"

Isobel sighed. She had concerns that it was too good to be true, and here it was.

"Now, don't get discouraged. It isn't bad, just not as good as I thought. Current calculated value is \$1.25million." Isobel gasped, her hand flew to her mouth! "With my costs removed up front, you would take away \$1,025,000.00. How does that sit with you?"

Isobel was speechless so she looked to K.C. He nodded with a question in his eyes, and she responded with a nod and a smile. She could take care of the debts and get off to a fresh start with that amount of cash, and still put aside a good nest-egg.

"Ms. Cassidy, we appreciate the speed with which you were able to resolve this for Ms. Kirk. She is quite satisfied with the results. What do you need to complete this process?"

Stephanie Cassidy explained the contractual procedure which was required to protect both Isobel and herself. She needed to recoup her costs, as previously agreed to, and was required to enumerate the actual expenses and commission costs. It all required notarizing and registering for tax purposes and to prevent fraud. She showed K.C. everything in writing and he passed the required documents on to Isobel for her signature. When all was said and done, it was arranged that the money would be deposited directly into an account established for that specific purpose in Isobel's name. From that account, Isobel could reinvest funds, write checks off the money market portion, and retrieve enough to pay the debts on Aunt Betty's estate.

It all seemed too much for Isobel to take in. She felt like she had been holding her breath throughout the process; she inhaled deeply of the fresh air as they exited the office building. What an eventful day! She could hardly believe all that had transpired. She wanted to pinch herself to make sure it wasn't a dream.

K.C. broke the spell once they were in the car. "Have you considered what you will do beyond this point?" He started the car and backed out of the parking space and headed out of the parking garage.

"I don't know. I want to move on as soon as possible; I need to sell the farm since I will never be a farmer." *Plus, I don't know who to trust in that community…*

K.C. let her talk for a while, and then he broke in with a suggestion. "Have you thought of going back to school?"

"School? Why would I want to do that? I've got my degree, already."

"Your degree is somewhat limiting, if you don't mind me saying that. It would limit where you could live, since it isn't very marketable in the Midwest."

"I know. I was thinking about that for the past few months, every time I tried to decide what to do after the estate was settled. I don't know that I want to live on either coast, but what would I do in the Midwest? I don't know… school? Do you mean, like a graduate degree? In what?"

"That's what I wanted to talk to you about. Have you considered studying law?"

"Law? Well, no, not really. I mean, Jason and I were going to do something for people of modest means. Once he got his M.D. we were going to serve people who really needed help. Law sounds like such a cushy job. It doesn't really sound altruistic, if you know what I mean."

K.C. grinned at her naïveté. "Actually, it depends on what area of law you study. Now, like me… well, my goal is to help my people. I am not trying to get rich from being a lawyer."

Isobel considered the idea and what he had said. It was certainly an interesting thought, but… "I guess I just need to take my time and think about it. I really don't have a clue, but thanks for trying to help. And, by the way, thank you so much for all the help you've given me. Is there any way I can repay you? I know the Legal Aid Office doesn't allow payment, but surely there is something?"

"How about your friendship? Is that up for negotiation, yet?"

This time it was Isobel's turn to smile. He was nothing if not persistent. "OK, you've worn me down. We can be friends." They continued the drive in companionable conversation with none of the earlier stress.

Chapter 31

Isobel considered K.C.'s suggestion about going to law school quite seriously. Because her focus beyond graduation from college was a life with Jason, she felt like a boat without a rudder to steer it, drifting with the currents, unsure of how to get a grip. Now K.C. had offered her an option, a way to make use of her college degree without settling for a job she might not enjoy. Throughout the drive home, the small talk kept her mouth busy, but her mind kept working in the background, wondering at his suggestion.

At home, inside the house, Isobel felt safe. The day's events actually scared her. She never saw the amount of money talked about today, let alone being responsible for how it would be used. It was so overwhelming that all she wanted to do now was take a nap. It was as if her body was exhausted from hard work, rather than her mind exhausted by the sudden reprieve from all her concerns. She sat on the side of her bed and realized her hands were shaking.

Curling up with the homemade afghan she kept on her bed, Isobel dozed off almost immediately. She wasn't sure how long she slept, but the sun had gone down, and the house was chilly. Pulling the afghan around her shoulders, she sat up when the phone suddenly rang.

"Hello?" she answered tentatively.

"Izzie? It's Jason. Are you ok?"

"Oh, yeah. I'm fine, why?"

"You sound funny…kinda far away and soft."

"Jason, I'm so glad you called. I need your advice."

Isobel told Jason about the inheritance, the bond, going to Legal Aid, and everything that came out of that visit, including the value of the bond and K.C.'s suggestion about law school. Throughout her discourse, Jason asked few questions, just enough to keep her on track. He asked her why she hadn't asked him for help sooner, and didn't seem satisfied with her response.

"I could have helped you get a decent lawyer," he said.

"K.C., I mean, Mr. Fox, has been very helpful. He is going to be a full-fledged lawyer when he gets the results of the bar exam…"

"But he isn't now, is he? And what's with K.C.? That doesn't sound very professional. Why would he have you use his first name? Just how old is this K.C. fella?"

Isobel didn't like the tone of jealousy she heard in Jason's voice. He had never shown this side of himself to her before. "Jason, he is just helping me with Aunt Betty's estate. And yes, he is young, but it doesn't matter. I am certainly not looking for anyone right now."

"Right now? You mean you might be in the future? Izzie?" Now his voice sounded subdued. "You know I am still hoping we can work things out."

Isobel sighed. It was so complicated. She wanted to ask Jason's advice, but they still had so many issues between them. But who else could she turn to? Dr. Fitz? No, Jason was her anchor when she needed strength. "Jason, really, can we put all that aside for now? I need your help now. I need your advice. What do you think of the idea about going for a graduate degree? What can I really do with my current degree?"

Jason switched gears and talked with Isobel about options. As much as he hated to admit it, K.C.'s suggestion might be a good one. She could go to law school while he finished his medical school. It would keep her busy and focused.

"As long as you decide to do it for yourself and not because you owe him anything. I think it might be a good idea. You know you have to take the LSAT to apply to law schools."

"I know. K.C. told me all about the process when we were driving home today."

"Mmhmm. I'll just bet he did." Jason hated when he sounded snide. It wasn't in his nature to be unkind or sarcastic. But for some reason, he felt threatened by the unknown K.C. Fox. After all, K.C. had access to Isobel and he didn't. What if K.C. moved in on her when she was vulnerable? What if he was just after her money now that he knew she was inheriting so much? He wanted to protect her from 'the Fox'.

"Jason, there's no need for that tone. K.C. isn't even what I would consider a friend, yet. We have been working on my aunt's estate. That's all. Please don't feel threatened. You know I still love you. That hasn't changed. I just can't be the cause of an estrangement between you and your parents. Until something happens to change that, I have to look toward my future without you. But I still value your opinion on my choices."

If Isobel could see Jason, she would have seen his sheepish expression. He felt thoroughly chastised and realized he needed to work on his own issues. The green-eyed demon threatened his fragile relationship with Isobel, which was exactly what he did not want. He still had hopes of them marrying one day. It all rested squarely on his parent's ability to accept Isobel as well as his own ability to be patient.

Jason switched gears and started discussing the pros and cons of graduate school with Isobel. They talked long into the evening, weighing her options, discussing their futures both separate and the possibility of together. They didn't run out of topics; it seemed just as when they were dating, constant conversation. Isobel missed that part of their relationship, so she enjoyed their moments on the phone. It refreshed her need for companionship and her mind wandered briefly to K.C.'s offer of friendship. Pushing those thoughts aside, she refocused on what Jason was saying.

He shared his current life with her, living in the dorm and studying medicine. Jason would soon start his rotations through the various medical specialties. He was enjoying medical school more than he had anticipated. Always before, his career plans were guided by his father's expectations. But now he knew that medicine was the right direction for him. Jason reminded Isobel of their plans to help the impoverished and shared his enthusiasm that hadn't diminished over time.

Isobel had an idea that she didn't share with Jason; she thought of establishing a charity to help Jason with his unselfish endeavors. *I need to talk to K.C. about how to do that*, she thought. *At least that is one way I can feel ok about using that money.* She smiled at what she anticipated Jason's reaction would be when she sprung it on him.

In the end, Jason weighed in on her educational goals. He suggested that, if she decided on law school, she try to apply to Harvard so they could be together. This wasn't exactly what Isobel had in mind, no matter how tempting the thought. She figured that they needed the distance between them in case his parents never come around. Unless they changed their attitude about Isobel, she could see no way for Jason and her to be together.

Finally, when Isobel's stomach reminded her that she needed to fix dinner, they closed their conversation with a prayer and a promise to talk again. By now, the prayer was less uncomfortable. It actually seemed right because she and Jason used to pray together, when they were dating and engaged. The promise felt good, too. She was alright with them talking more often; it raised her spirits and gave her the strength to carry on. She wondered if she would ever *not* need Jason to keep her balanced and focused.

While she was heating some soup for her dinner, the phone rang. This time it was Sheriff Jones. "I tried to call all afternoon, but your line was busy," he said. Isobel explained that she'd been talking to an old friend, and he accepted her explanation. "Well, I thought you might like to know the results of the investigation into the barn burning..."

Isobel's heart dropped. What would the investigation show? Was Dr. Fitz at fault? If so, why would he do such a thing to her? Sheriff Jones suggested he come over, if it wasn't too late, and that he bring Dr. Fitz with him, and Isobel agreed. She quickly ate her soup and sandwich and was just clearing the table when they drove up in the Sheriff's cruiser.

"Hi…Sheriff Jones… Dr. Fitz. Come on in," Isobel welcomed them at the kitchen door.

The two men followed each other into the now familiar surroundings, each taking his usual seat at the table. They declined her offer of coffee and cookies, so Isobel sat at the table and looked to Sheriff Jones. He took the cue and anxious to tell her of the investigation and what had been done in an effort to determine the cause and blame for the fire. First, he took a few minutes to update her on Old Jake and Josh's situation.

"So, initially, they just wanted to chase you off, make you feel it wasn't safe to stay on the farm. That's when Josh took it on himself to damage your car. But it seems they also heard rumors that your aunt had some old paper or bond that was worth something. That's why Josh broke into her bedroom and trashed it. 'Course he wouldn't know a bond from a bill, so he really didn't know what to look for. Anyway, it seems the judge wants to know if you want to press charges or not. Have you given that any thought?"

Isobel had not considered that her opinion might be needed. "No, I haven't thought about it. I didn't realize I would have to do that. I guess I just figured they would be charged, tried and sentenced. Let me think about that for a while, if that's ok."

The sheriff indicated that she had about a week to ten days to decide, and then the matter would be dropped. All this time, Dr. Fitz sat quiet, not entering into the exchange. He seemed thoughtful and Isobel wondered what was on his mind. She didn't have long to wait; he had strong feelings about Josh and Jake.

"You need to press charges, Isobel! Those two have tormented Betty for years, trying to find some way to get this farm away from her. If you let them off too easy, they will just be back to their old tricks until they get what they want."

"But they are just leasing the farmland. I could cancel that lease so they wouldn't have access to the farm. I probably need to do that anyway if I plan to list it for sale. Surely, they will move on if they don't have land to work?"

"I wouldn't count on it. Jake is pretty spiteful. I think the only way to get rid of them is to press charges and maybe stipulate that they relocate out of the area as part of the sentence." These words of wisdom came from the sheriff, whose opinion Isobel valued.

"I just don't want revenge. That's not my way. All I want is to move forward with my life. I need to sell this place pretty soon; I've already talked with the realtor in town."

Dr. Fitz looked at her inquisitively. "Sounds like you already have plans. I thought you couldn't make plans until you paid Betty's debts and cleared the estate of encumbrances?"

Isobel wasn't sure how much she wanted to share until she had made a firm decision about school. She was pretty sure she would go back for a graduate degree; she didn't know if it would be in business or law. Considering all the options had her mind in a muddle. This was one time when Aunt Betty would have advised her to make it a matter of prayer. Isobel thought she might take the suggestion to heart. Perhaps, if she began to ask for God's help, the whole decision would be easier. She always heard that's how it worked from her more devout friends in college, like Maddie and Taylor.

"I do have some options," she replied to Dr. Fitz's query. "I have seen a lawyer in Omaha who has given me some advice and offered options for my future. I haven't made a decision, yet, but hope to soon."

Once again, Dr. Fitz looked surprised and curious. He didn't ask any more questions, but Isobel could sense that he wanted to. Sheriff Jones wanted to move on to the subject of the barn investigation.

"We have determined what caused the barn to burn," he started. "We do not think there was another party involved…"

"So you think Jake and Josh did that, too?" Isobel asked, surprised that he hadn't said so earlier.

"No, little lady, that isn't what I'm saying. What I started to say was that the barn wasn't set afire on purpose. It was a coincidence that it happened 'round the time when Josh was up to his mischief. No, we found some old wiring in the barn that had frayed and sparked. We believe the barn burned as a result of the hay catching a spark… pure accident, that's what it was. An electrical fire, ya might say."

What a relief! Isobel thought.

Sheriff Jones got up to leave. Dr. Fitz held back as Sheriff Jones headed for the cruiser. "Isobel, I need a chance to talk to you before you leave town. I need to tell you what I know of your birth mother. You might want to look for her, and I might be able to help."

Isobel was speechless. She never told him of the items she found, or Aunt Betty's letter. *So this WAS the secret he knew I would have questions about.*

Noting her surprise, he followed the sheriff's path to the car, got in and waved his good-byes. Isobel was left with several questions. Should she press charges, and if so, what type of punishment did she hope for Josh and Jake? Did she want to look for her birth mother? If she did, should she do it before she goes off to school, or let it wait? She sat down with Aunt Betty's Bible in her hand once again and closed her eyes in prayer. "Lord, help me know what to do. If you are real, find some way to tell me what direction to go. In Jesus name. Amen." It wasn't much, but it was all she could do for now.

Chapter 31

K.C. headed straight home after dropping Isobel off, wondering if he should have checked things out on the farm before he left her there. Was there a danger, an imminent threat? He wasn't sure. He wondered if those who targeted Isobel knew of her inheritance. Not just the farm and all that entailed. He wondered if they were aware of the municipal bond. Perhaps word had gotten out of Betty Kirk's investment all those years ago.

He didn't have much time to worry about Isobel's situation. He knew when he got home that more challenges awaited him. He needed to convince Ma that Talitha should go to the hospital. Tali was still not talking or moving independently when he left in the morning, although Ma and Shyne were doing alright with the children. He just hoped nothing had gone wrong while he was in Kansas City.

Ma met him at the door with a smile on her face, wiping her hands on her apron. "Kwsind," he loved the way she said his name, like a breath of air, "come, let me feed you, son."

He gave her a warm embrace and asked about his sisters. She told him that Tali remained the same; she hadn't done anything without prompting for the whole day. Ma's ability to smile despite the challenge was encouraging, when just weeks before she was not much better than Tali. Perhaps it was like looking in the mirror and seeing what she had been. Ma was back to depending on her faith and her former joy shone from her eyes.

Shyne was playing with the children as if they were all hers. K.C. smelled the stew cooking in the kitchen, recognizing the spices Ma always used when cooking. The children were clean and seemed happy, although Kerron looked anxiously at his mother from time to time. Tamila tried to show her mommy a picture she had drawn but got no response. Her disappointment hurt K.C.'s heart, so he tried to help by showing excitement over her childish artwork.

After dinner, K.C. pulled Ma aside to discuss Talitha. "Ma, Dr. Pearson thinks she needs to be in the hospital."

"Now why would she need that? Just get her some medicine, like he gave me, and she will be just fine, son."

Not wanting to be too forceful, yet understanding the seriousness of Talitha's situation, K.C. spoke more firmly to his mother. "Ma, listen to me. Tali is sicker than you ever were. She isn't responding. You did. We were able to communicate with you at least a little. You did some things on your own. Please, Tali is sicker. She needs to be in the hospital."

Ma looked at him, her eyes glistening. "You're sure? You don't think we can help her here? You're sure, K.C.?" He nodded to her, hurting for her pain.

"We need to do it soon, Ma. We don't know how long she's been like this, and she needs help soon or she might not get better."

"Tomorrow, then. You take her tomorrow for me, and you make sure that Dr. Pearson makes her better. Promise me that, K.C., promise."

He gave his word, and punctuated it with another warm hug for her mom. "Ma, we will get through this. I promise, Tali will get better, and this family will get better!"

Talitha stayed in the hospital long enough to stabilize her medication, and then she was transferred to a nearby rehabilitation center especially for those with mental health issues. The majority of the clients were Native Americans from the reservation and the head of the facility was a well-respected psychiatrist from the Lakota people of Pine Ridge up north. Tali remained at the rehab center for nearly two months. When the doctor began to mention a transition to home, K.C. wondered if she was really ready. He had kept in touch with Dr. Pearson throughout her treatment and knew she was communicating and functioning on a daily basis, but he worried that the pressures of home would set her back. As a test, Dr. Pearson suggested she have a few weekend overnight visits rather than experiencing the drastic change of full discharge from the program.

Talitha was quiet on the drive home for her first visit. She seemed much like she was before her admission, and K.C. wasn't sure what to expect for the weekend. He tried to trust the doctor's assessment of her condition, but she was so quiet. She stared out the window as if seeing the prairie for the first time.

"It's so big." It wasn't much more than a whisper, barely audible over the road sounds and car's motor. "So big."

K.C. didn't respond. He wanted to see if she initiated conversation rather than just answering questions. He was rewarded with quiet for the rest of the trip. When they got home, however, he was surprised that she got out of the car on her own. *She obviously knows where she is,* he thought. She walked toward the house. Before she got to the porch, the front door burst open and two little people squealed as they ran out to hug their mother.

K.C. nearly stopped them, thinking it was too much stimulation for Tali. But then he saw tears rolling down her cheeks as she kneeled in the dust to give her babies a hug. They returned her hug until Tamila said, "Mommy, too tight!" and Talitha released her hold and leaned back to look at her daughter. Kerron clung to Talitha's leg as she stood up and, holding Tamila's hand, she made her way onto the porch.

"Ma, I'm home," K.C. heard her soft voice. Although Ma was sitting in her usual chair, it was seconds before she and Talitha were also hugging. They held each other as if they would never let go. Shyne had Taddy on her hip and Brya and CeCe on either side of her, standing in the doorway. "Hey, sis. You look better." Talitha nodded over Ma's shoulder giving Shyne a brief smile.

The weekend went well overall. Tali's medication seemed to be working well, and as she relaxed, she became more interactive with the family. She still wasn't herself, but K.C. could see improvement.

When Monday morning came, and it was time for him to take Tali back to the center, Ma began to cry.

"Aw, Ma, why the tears? You see she is better. In a few more weeks, she will be able to stay home and not have to go back."

"Why can't we keep her here if she is better? What do they do for her that we can't?"

"Counseling, for one thing. And adjusting her medications if necessary, for another. She could have a setback, and they are trained to help her through those. It's only a few more weeks." He touched her arm and she nodded. She seemed reassured, although none too happy, as they drove off toward Omaha.

Less than a month later, K.C. was making the return trip with a new Talitha. She was talkative, smiling and animated. It was as if the last few months had never happened, with the exception of one major change. Tali was talking about salvation. She had been reintroduced to the Lord while going through her counseling, and decided to allow Him into her heart.

K.C. knew how overjoyed Ma would be with the news; now he needed to pray that Skyla would find someone in the prison that would lead her down that same path. She was on his mind constantly, especially when he looked at her little children, and he was still searching the law books for some way to help her get out of prison earlier than her sentence would allow. There had to be some exception that her lawyer could use in her appeal.

Since the trip to Kansas City, K.C. and Isobel had spoken several times on the phone. He was somewhat puzzled by her tone when he called. Sometimes she sounded friendly and listened to his advice and guidance, especially as it related to her legal affairs. Other times she seemed reserved, stand-offish as if she was afraid of getting too close. He wondered if it had anything to do with her old boyfriend. *The guy must be a fool to have let her get away,* he thought. *If she were my...* and he stopped his musing. He couldn't allow himself to go down that road. He needed to maintain a professional approach and only offer friendship when she seemed open to it.

Chapter 32

She finally returned the papers to Judy Harrison. She needed to move the property, and was not as concerned with how it got done as she was before the news of her windfall. Somehow, she needed to trust Judy. After all, she was the only realtor in town. Otherwise, the next nearest realtor could be several towns away, which would be both inconvenient and complicated.

The sale of the farm happened quicker than she anticipated, but Isobel was happy to be moving on. She said her good-byes to all except Dr. Fitz. She hadn't yet decided if she wanted more information about her mother. What if he knew her as a drug addict or alcoholic? What if she had some terrible disease that Isobel might inherit? So Isobel postponed that good-bye until all her possessions and those of Aunt Betty that she held onto, were packed into a truck and sent on to Omaha.

She had decided to take K.C.'s suggestion of law school seriously. K.C. had promised to help her with his old study materials and with coaching to help her study for the LSAT. Isobel had secured a nice condominium in Omaha where she felt safe and secure. Surrounded by neighbors and in a building with security, she felt less vulnerable than she had on the farm.

Before setting off to follow the truck, Isobel took a drive to Dr. Fitz's office. There didn't appear to be any patients in the waiting room, and his truck wasn't in its usual place, although Dr. Fitz's old car was parked beside the building.

"Is he in?" she asked the office assistant.

"Yes," she stood to her feet, "just a moment while I let him know you are here..."

"I can show myself into his office, thank you," Isobel brushed past her, not meaning to be brusque or unkind. She didn't want to waste time, and having worked there, she knew her way around.

"Oh, well, ok then, I guess!" the receptionist seemed shocked that Isobel would be so assertive. She was used to the respect of the patients in the area; she had acted as Dr. Fitz's gate-keeper for a number of years, and nobody questioned her authority.

"Dr. Fitz!" She needed to get on the road and put all this behind her. "I'm getting ready to leave town. You said you needed to tell me something before I left."

He looked up from his paper and gazed at Isobel over his glasses. Isobel realized how old he was, and that he looked as though he had aged tremendously in the last months since she arrived at Aunt Betty's. When she first met him, Dr. Fitz seemed like a father figure. Now, however, he appeared more like a grandfather, tired, graying in both face as well as hair.

"Ah, Isobel. Come in, my dear. Have a seat," he motioned for one of the chairs in front of his desk. She sat despite wanting to make this a quick visit. Somehow, she felt awkward refusing to do what Dr. Fitz asked.

"Now, remember when I told you I'd be here when you had questions? I thought you might have some questions about your birth mother. But you never came to me for information, so I thought I should share what I know before I am unable to."

"Are you sick or something?" she asked with alarm.

"No, no, nothing like that. I just am not as young as I used to be," he chuckled at his self-deprecating joke. "I am getting more in touch with my own mortality, shall we say. I just realize that you may not come back to this area any time soon so, before I am gone, I wanted to talk to you."

Dr. Fitz began telling Isobel the story she already knew from Aunt Betty's missive. She became impatient. So she had no new questions. Why was Dr. Fitz rehashing old information? Then she heard something she hadn't learned before.

"Yes. I was the doctor that delivered you. Delfina came to me for help. She already had a little boy and had just lost her husband. Then she found out she was pregnant. The man with whom she had relations gave her a ring as a commitment between them, though they hadn't married." Now Isobel understood the significance of the Air Force ring she found in the package with the dream catcher and doll.

"She said she could not marry him because he wasn't of her people. He did not know that she had become pregnant, but she wanted her child to know its father and his heritage, so she needed to find him. She told me his name, and I immediately knew that he was Betty's brother, my best friend, who had recently left for a tour in Japan. Your mother stayed with a family in town until the child, that is, until you were born."

Isobel choked up, but didn't want Dr. Fitz to see. She cleared her throat to get control and spoke for the first time in his story. "I knew most of that already," she said. "I didn't know that you delivered me. Was I born at home or in a hospital?"

"Oh, it was at the hospital listed on your birth certificate. But she brought you back here, to stay with the same church family that hosted her during your pregnancy. She did the best she could to take care of her son and you, but you were a failure to thrive. For some unknown reason, you didn't gain weight or size, and became increasingly susceptible to upper respiratory infections. One good thing came out of her stay here in town. She gave her life over to the Lord."

Why do I keep hearing stuff about the Lord? Isobel wondered. *It's almost as if God is trying to tell me something.* And she smiled.

"What is it, Isobel? What's behind that smile?"

"It just seems that God is at every turn of my life, these days."

"That He is, I'm sure," Dr. Fitz agreed. "After all, a lot of prayers are going up on your behalf."

She looked at him in surprise. "What do you mean? Nobody cares about me and God!"

"Now that is where you are wrong. When Betty was dying, she made me and several of her lady friends promise to keep you in our prayers. She was so concerned for your salvation; she had hoped to see the change before she died, but was content to leave it in the hands of the Prayer Chain and God."

Isobel looked at her hands, ashamed of how she had blown off her aunt's attempts to talk about Jesus. But she had done the same with her friends at college. And with Jason, she had just acted the part; she prayed with him and went to church, but her heart wasn't into it. Now, she felt sad that Aunt Betty had worried so, when she should have been taking care of herself and her health.

"Anyway, back to your mother. She said, if ever you were looking for her, to go to the Omaha Reservation. She was going home to her people. Living off the rez just wasn't for her. She was proud of her heritage and longed for the familiarity of tribal customs and traditions."

Omaha? What a coincidence? Isobel considered the possibilities. Of all the tribes her mother might come from, of all the reservations, what chance was there that she would be moving near the very area that her mother came from? "I'm moving to Omaha." She said quietly to Dr. Fitz.

"Are you now? Well, I hope you stay in touch. What have you planned for your future? Can I help you in some way?"

Finally, Isobel's renewed trust in Dr. Fitz allowed her to tell him all about the municipal bond, about K.C.'s suggestions for her career, and her decision to prepare for law school. She actually felt excited as she told him that she wanted to become a lawyer. It felt so right! They talked for a while. Dr. Fitz assured her that he knew Betty wouldn't have left her without means to resolve the estate issues. He promised to help her whenever and however he could. It was what he could do as part of his promise to Betty.

Isobel left with the promise of staying in touch with Dr. Fitz. As she drove away, it was with a sense of nostalgia. She came to think of this town, these people, as family. The way they had rallied around not only her, but her aunt, and now, according to Dr. Fitz, her mother had also been a beneficiary of the love in this little community. She would continue her career path, but would always think of Kansas as her home.

Isobel arrived in Omaha just as the sun was setting. She already had her condo key and knew where to park. Prior arrangements allowed her to get there ahead of the delivery of her goods. She was pleased to see the furniture that she bought had been delivered and set in place. She had a new bed and living-room and dining-room furniture, but without her personal items, the condo felt like a hotel room. She looked forward to receiving her boxes.

The moving company arrived about an hour after she called to confirm delivery. It didn't take long for them to off load the boxes, and to unpack the few kitchen items that she wanted out of the boxes. The remaining containers were placed in the two bedrooms to wait for her to find time to delve into them. The task of unpacking was just as daunting as going through Aunt Betty's personal items had been. She started with those in the front room and kitchen. It didn't take long.

As she began settling in, she saw the boxes of items she had brought from Aunt Betty's house, including those with the letters and other items related to her birth. She packed those boxes deep in the closet, intending to pull them out later when she was ready to work on finding her mother. At least she was living in the right area to do that research when the time was right.

Chapter 33

With Tali back home, life settled into a routine for the Fox family. Ma ran her kitchen like a sergeant in his chow hall. She ordered her dishes and pans, reorganized the spice cabinet, and took Shyne's suggestion to go grocery shopping. Mrs. Charbanneau kindly agreed to take them in her car. She needed things from the market, too, so it worked well for all concerned, especially for K.C. Any other time, he would have tried to find time to act as chauffeur.

Finally, in the mail one morning in early spring, a couple of months after taking the bar exam, K.C. was rewarded with the results in the mail. He held the official-looking envelope gingerly and Ma noticed his hesitation.

"What are you waiting for, son?" The warmth in her voice sent joy to K.C.'s heart. "I have every confidence in the Lord, that He will provide a way for you to reach your goal. If not this time, then there is always another chance."

He looked at his mother, marveling at the change since Dr. Pearson placed her on an antidepressant. The whole family responded to Ma's improvement, and especially Tali felt revitalized by studying the Scriptures and praying with her mother. She also had a renewed strength of purpose, a determination to improve her lot in life.

He looked at the envelope again and took a deep breath. Using his thumb, he lifted the corner of the back flap and the lightly glued seal released easily. He glanced at his mother and she nodded encouragement. Opening the flap, he pulled out the paper…

He let out a whoop equal to that by any proud warrior returning from a successful buffalo hunt! "I passed, Ma! I passed on my first go round!!!" He jumped up and down and grabbed Shyne's hands dancing in circles of joy. Finally, he could take care of his family in a way that would make Ma proud! "Praise the Lord!" Cried Ma and the children joined in with the dancing and cheering. Even Tali came out of her room and smiled at the obvious happiness that welcomed her.

To celebrate, K.C. told Ma that he wanted to treat them all to dinner at a restaurant, but both Ma and Tali declined. They wanted to prepare a feast for K.C.'s celebration, not go to eat at a white man's establishment. They had their traditions, and they wanted to throw a party for as many as could attend that afternoon. It was K.C.'s job to go to the neighbor's houses to spread the word.

Ma and the girls cooked for several hours, and then people began to arrive, even more than they anticipated. The word spread once K.C. told his nearest neighbors and many from the tribe dropped in during the course of the evening. Some women brought dishes of traditional foods to add to the food that Ma, Talitha and Shyne prepared. Elders came with their congratulations. They had not seen a tribal group member become a lawyer in many years, so this was truly a reason to rejoice. Every family that came brought with them cousins, children, aunts and uncles. Some were distant relatives that K.C. hadn't seen since childhood.

Fortunately, the weather cooperated and the party spread from inside out onto the land surrounding the house that K.C. and Shyne had spent so much time grooming last year. Music played from boon-boxes and the children ran wildly playing games and snacking their way into the evening. When the stars came out, and the full moon shone bright enough to provide outdoor lighting, the elders called all together into a circle. They enjoyed a period of sharing and singing.

As the darkness grew deeper, clouds began gathering indicating a change in weather, and the evening celebration came to a close.

The highest elder of the tribe stood to speak, and all were respectfully silent. He praised K.C. one final time and thumped his back in approval. Then the party dispersed as quickly as it had started. The women ensured that trash was picked up and their dishes removed so Ma wouldn't have additional work to do. Only the Fox family plates and leftovers remained and K.C. told Ma he would bring those in.

As he finished the cleanup, he considered his choices for the future. He recalled the offer from Mr. McMillen and wondered if he should take him up on the idea. He still yearned for something bigger, not for the money, but as a means to his end. He wanted to help the indigent, but on a larger scale than just a little office in Omaha, Nebraska. He saw himself as some kind of activist, like Jesus was, fighting for the greater issues that faced Native Americans.

But K.C. still had Skyla on his mind, too. Her appeal process wasn't going well; postponement after postponement seemed to be ensuring her time in prison wouldn't be shortened. Now that he had his law license, maybe he could assist her lawyer in that process. He needed to find what agency to contact and what procedures were already in place but, somehow, he needed to help.

He looked around the yard; all was back in order. Looking upward, K.C. saw that the moon was totally obscured by clouds and no stars were visible, and then he felt the first droplets on his face. He went inside planning to get a good night's sleep and look into his options over the upcoming days.

K.C. was ready to drive into Omaha the next morning, once breakfast was done. Ma and Shyne worked well together, keeping the children rounded up and out of trouble. Tali still was somewhat withdrawn, although she watched from the sidelines. *Her medication needed better adjustment*, he thought. She was better than before her hospitalization. At least she was out of her room on her own, carrying on conversations and taking care of herself. K.C. was certain that it was only a matter of time before her medication was at a good level and working well.

Today Tali had a follow-up appointment with Dr. Pearson, so K.C. planned to take care of his own business while they met. He wanted to visit with Mr. McMillen again, to see if his offer was sincere, and if it still stood. He also intended to ask if he knew of other firms that might be hiring, just in case the spot with Mr. McMillen was not available or didn't work out.

Tali didn't talk much on the drive to Omaha; she stared out the window watching the landscape. K.C. attempted conversation, but she seemed uninterested (or unable) to say more than yes or no. If his question was open-ended, she just said, "Hmmm?" or "Ahhhh… hmm." It was as if she couldn't put words to her thoughts. He often wondered what it was that had set his mother into such a spiral and whether that same issue bothered Tali or if she had other problems. Unfortunately, because of patient privacy and the sensitivity of counseling, he couldn't ask Dr. Pearson. Someday soon, he needed to ask Ma once again, what it was that Dr. Pearson wanted her to share with him.

Pulling up to Dr. Pearson's office, Talitha seemed to slump into her seat even deeper. Her hooded eyes made her expression difficult to read, but once the car stopped, she opened the door on her own and got out. She lifted her eyes to the sign advertising his counseling services, and then dropped her chin to her chest. *Perhaps it was the idea of needing counseling that saddened her*, K.C. thought. *But what set her off in the first place?*

K.C. escorted Tali into the building and informed the receptionist that he would be back to pick her up in about an hour. She indicated that Tali would wait until he returned. They didn't often allow patients to leave unless accompanied by whomever had brought them in, unless they were far enough along in therapy that they came alone. Reassured, K.C. made his way toward M. McMillen's office.

When he pulled down the side street to Mr. McMillen's office, his heart thumped in his throat. On the window, next to the hand-painted sign they saw the first time, was a piece of paper with a message scrawled on it: "Temporarily Closed due to Illness. In case of emergency, call (402) 555-9876."

So much for the guaranteed job, K.C. reflected. He stood on the sidewalk looking at the sign for several minutes, trying to decide what to do next, where to start in his job search. He heard a voice behind him and was startled. He was so deep in thought that he hadn't heard anyone approach, and realized it wasn't the best part of town for daydreaming. He turned to the anonymous voice and saw a diminutive lady, maybe 45 years old, conservatively dressed and shy in appearance. His eyes must have shown confusion because she repeated herself.

"I said, are you looking for my husband?" in the same soft-spoken voice that had roused him from his thoughts.

K.C.'s smile lighted up his face and glowed from his eyes. "Mrs. McMillen?"

"Do I know you, son?" She appeared surprised by his use of her name, despite the fact that she had identified herself as the wife of the 'Attorney at Law - Sean J. McMillen', the name on the sign in the window. Then she realized her blunder, and laughed at herself. "You must think I am silly!" and she giggled again.

"I was coming to see Mr. McMillen, ma'am. I just received a passing score on my Nebraska Bar Exam, and he had indicated he might have a job for me. I guess that's out the door from the looks of this," indicating the closure sign with his thumb.

"Well, now, we may be able to work something out. My Sean has work waiting for him, things left unattended and he won't be able to get back at it for about six weeks… had gall bladder surgery, don't ya know."

Again, K.C. smiled. Her old country accent came through ever so slightly in her expressions. "How can I be of assistance, Mrs. McMillen?"

"Well, I'm not sure. Sean keeps his business in the office, but he is well enough for visitors. If you could come by the hospital later this evening, maybe we can discuss his outstanding cases." She raised her eyebrows into question marks, and K.C. nodded in agreement.

"I need to take my sister on home, first, so could we say about 6:00pm?"

She agreed on the suggested time, and gave K.C. the information he needed to find the hospital and the room number where her husband was. He drove around Omaha, exploring the area and making sure he knew how to find the hospital that evening. He also stopped by the Legal Aid Office where he found a warm welcome.

They were thrilled at his good news and worried if he would continue his volunteer work. He promised them that he would still put in several half days each week. He visited for a short time, but when he looked at his watch he was surprised to see the hour almost gone.

He went back to Dr. Pearson's office to meet Tali. She met him in the waiting room with a brighter look to her face, in spite of her red rimmed eyes indicating that she had cried during her therapy session. K.C. spoke with the nurse and found that Dr. Pearson had increase Tali's medicine, and called the prescription in to the pharmacy near their home so they could pick it up on their way home.

Tali was more talkative on the way home, and she even told K.C. some of the problems that led to her breakdown. Financially, she was not making it; emotionally, she felt ill-equipped to care for her children; and spiritually she felt vacant. She had no foundation on which to build her life, and felt adrift. "K.C., you just seem to have it all together. How can I ever measure up? I've made a mess of my life and can't do a thing about it!"

He understood her frustration, but also knew she was young enough to change the direction of her life. He tried to comfort her, and pledged to help her get her life back on track. With her living back at home, K.C. knew her expenses were manageable on her limited income from the tribal allotment. But if she wanted to further her education or go to a technical training program, he would find a way to help her. Right now, her future, Shyne's, and Skyla's all sat squarely on his shoulders and he knew he needed income to solve some of the more pressing issues.

After taking Talitha home and getting something to eat, K.C. headed back to Omaha. As much as he would rather not make the drive twice in one day, he needed to explore the employment opportunities more. If Mr. McMillen still needed his assistance even for the six weeks he was recovering, at least he would have one foot in the door to practicing law in the Omaha area.

Mr. McMillen was sitting up in his hospital bed when K.C. got there. In front of him sat his rollaway table with an all liquid dinner on his tray. Mrs. McMillen was trying to encourage him to eat some of the green Jell-O or to sip the beef broth. One sip and he put his face up with disgust. He was obviously yearning for a real meal. Sheepishly, Mrs. McMillen reintroduced K.C. to her husband. "I asked him here to talk about helping, just until you're back on your feet," she said.

He remembered their conversation, and was happy that K.C. had followed through and returned to his office. "I would be glad to let you take a gander at my case files." He filled K.C. in on the most pressing outstanding issues and talked to him as one professional to another. Not once did K.C. sense any condescension from Mr. McMillen. He wondered if the man even recognized that he was Native American. After all, not all clients would welcome a tribal lawyer replacing their regular attorney.

They talked for over an hour until Mr. McMillen showed signs of tiring. K.C. realized that at some point in their discussion, Mrs. McMillen had slipped out of the room. Evidently, her interests did not run in the direction of law, but then, few women shared the same career interest as their husbands. K.C. decided it was time to leave when Mr. McMillen laid his head back on his pillow and closed his eyes. He poked his head out the door of the room, looked up and down the hallway, and caught the attention of a nurse.

"Mr. McMillen is ready to settle down for the evening, I think. His wife went off somewhere, and I need to leave now." The nurse nodded. He left knowing he had a job to go to in the morning, and volunteer work to fill in the gaps. Future plans could be determined after Mr. McMillen returned to the office. Until then, K.C. vowed to serve the community with the same caring attitude he saw in the McMillens.

Chapter 34

Isobel set her sights on taking the Law School Admission Test and focused totally on studying toward that end. She hardly left her condominium, except to go to the local library to study. She worked on her application for law school and was disappointed when she found out that she would miss the cutoff for applications to start in September. Having missed the February test date, she was aiming to take the LSAT at the next cycle, in June.

Applications for most law schools were supposed to be in by March, although some accepted them until May. But she had not found one accepting later applications; most had waiting lists for spaces that opened up from the first picks. She didn't let that deter her, though, because she finally had a goal. She felt in her heart that becoming an attorney was just what she needed. She had the funds, now that the money from the bond had been deposited into her various accounts, and she had nothing but time, since she and Jason were still at an impasse.

One day, several months after resettling in Omaha, she got brave and decided to go to the Law Library at Creighton University. She wanted to see what it was like, to explore the School of Law and get a feel for her future. She wandered the halls, smelled the mustiness of the old library, and generally enjoyed the experience. Isobel remembered when her father dreamed of having his daughter go to college, and here she was now considering a professional career.

No longer satisfied with a Bachelor's Degree, Isobel dreamed of the day she would earn her Jurisprudence Doctorate. She blushed at the thought. Just the name sounded grandiose and pretentious. *What was she thinking? Did she deserve this?* A thousand doubts ran through her mind when she saw the law students filing out of lecture halls.

Suddenly, Isobel looked up and saw a familiar face. "K.C.?" She smiled at him.

"Isobel, what are you doing here?"

"I might ask you the same… I was just visiting, thinking about my future. I am studying for the LSAT now, thanks to you, you know!" The surprise on his face was replaced with a look of satisfaction.

"So, we accomplished something with all our talk?" he asked her. "You're really going to do it, then?"

Isobel and K.C. walked together to a bench outside near the library. They sat and chatted for a while; K.C. told her about his new employment for Mr. McMillen, as well as his continuing volunteer work. Isobel told him of her new condominium and her resolution to score high enough on the LSAT to ensure her a spot in the law school of her choice.

Isobel had found that law schools were ranked, with Harvard at the top, and some of the public universities not registering on the ranking system. A lot of it had to do with what type of job the person wanted after finishing their law school education. If all they wanted was a basic job, any law school would prepare them for the bar exam. But if the student was looking at a prestigious job with a high powered law firm, then Ivy League was the way to go. Isobel had yet to decide where she wanted to go, so she needed to score high enough to keep her options open.

She knew that Jason hoped she would choose Harvard so they could be near enough to rekindle their romance. She seriously considered that option, but couldn't get past the look on his mother's face when they met at the airport or the words said when they didn't know she could hear, and how those words hurt her heart.

Then Isobel thought of the law school she had just walked through. Creighton University was a Jesuit school in a quiet mid-western town, and that appealed to her. She was used to the cold winters, the hot summers, and the storms that blew across the prairies. She also liked the idea of being near the reservation where her mother might have come from. If she was ever going to find her mother, she knew she needed to be near the area of her birth, the area of her conception. She couldn't move far from this part of the country until she had explored her resources for finding a Native American parent. All she had to go on was the name of her mother when she was born. She didn't know if her mother had remarried and how many times she might have married or divorced. So it was the first name that was her real clue, and Isobel didn't know if it was a common name in this region or not.

Isobel was brought back to the present with a question from K.C. "I'm sorry; I didn't hear your question…" They stood to walk toward K.C.'s car.

"Yeah, you must have been a thousand miles away. The old boyfriend maybe?"

Isobel shook her head. "No, I have another issue on my mind. But that doesn't matter right now. What did you ask me?"

"I was just saying that I'd be glad to help you prepare for the LSAT, if you want help, that is. I could find time when my work is slow and give you a call to come down to study at the office."

Isobel wanted to jump at the chance, but thought of Jason and his jealousy. She wondered if she should talk to him before agreeing to study with K.C. "Can I think about it for a couple of days?"

"Sure, take all the time you need, Isobel. No pressure from me. I just wanted to offer, because I know the path was lonely when I traveled it several years ago."

She smiled at his kindness, and realized how silly it was to worry about Jason's reaction. After all, the only commitment they had was that of friendship. They were no longer engaged; they weren't even a committed couple. Just friends. That's where they'd left it, and that left her able to agree to whatever chances came along.

"You know what? I don't need to think about it. I would appreciate any help you can give. Honestly, I don't know what I was thinking. Here's my number and address. Feel free to call, and

I'll pop over to your office. I do know where it is, and I am getting familiar with public transportation, such as it is."

K.C. and Isobel parted ways when they reached K.C.'s parked car. He still had a long drive home ahead of him. "Do you need a ride…?"

Isobel declined his offer. She needed to walk off her confusion. She wasn't sure what she was feeling. She liked K.C., his openness and his honest approach. He didn't seem to be hiding any deep dark secrets, although she hadn't met his family, yet.

She wondered if all parents were as protective of their sons as Jason's had been. Then she felt her heart race. How was she going to explain to Jason that she would be studying with another guy? Did she need to tell him? He was supposed to be calling this evening, and she would need to decide before he called, whether or not to tell him, and just how much to share.

By the time she got home to her apartment, the sun had gone down, and just after she got settled, the phone rang. Looking at the clock, Isobel saw that he was right on time.

"Hi, Jason," she answered with a sigh.

"Hey, there. You sound a bit annoyed, Izzie. What's up?"

"Nothing, really. Just a bit tired, I guess." She rolled her eyes. *What am I going to tell him*, she wondered.

"You're not getting sick, are you?"

"No, Jason. I'm just a bit tired from a walk I took. I'll be fine once I've rested."

"Hey, Izzie. Have you thought any more about coming here to do your law school?"

"That's part of what I need to talk to you about, Jason." Isobel went on to tell him about missing the deadline for applications. She shared with him all that she understood about the application process, which didn't differ much from what he had gone through for medical school.

Jason understood her disappointment and tried to encourage her. He knew she needed to focus her energy until he finished medical school. Then, he thought he would be able to convince her to give up the whole idea and marry him. After all, what need was there for her to be a lawyer, if he could provide for her? Isobel could sense in his voice that he wasn't convinced of her desire to pursue her career goal. He sounded half-hearted in his words of comfort.

"Jason, I also want to be honest with you. I don't know where our relationship is going in the future, or if we even have a future," she took a deep breath, bracing for his arguments, but he held his peace. "I consider you a good friend, and I always will. But I want to be sure that you are not expecting me to be waiting for us to happen again."

"But, Izzie…"

"Please, Jason, hear me out. I am not sure we could ever get past the pain I experienced in your home. I am not sure I will get past it. At least, not unless your parents have a remarkable change of heart…"

"They'll come around, Izzie, you'll see…"

"Jason, stop. Just so you know, I have met another young man who has been quite helpful to me. He is a lawyer, and has agreed to help me study for the LSAT," again, Isobel took a deep breath, anticipating the explosion.

"No, Izzie, don't tell me this! I suppose it's that guy you consulted about your aunt's will… Izzie, I love you! Please, don't turn your back on us!"

Isobel looked at the phone as if Jason was about to jump out of the receiver. She could hear him going on, panic-stricken at the thought of them not having a future. *What else can I say to him? What else was there to say?* They weren't breaking up; there was nothing left to break, other than hearts. Isobel knew they both would hurt, but that time would make it better, unless God saw fit to work it out for them. Just the thought of God intervening in a personal way took Isobel by surprise. She never considered God to be a real person who could solve real problems.

"Izzie, are you there? Are you listening?"

"Yes, Jason, I am still here. I don't have energy to argue right now. I just wanted to be up front with you. No secrets, right?" With that, Isobel tried to get off the phone without more fuss. She had had more than her share of tragedy in her short life, and didn't need to add to it with more drama. When she was finally able to get off the phone, she was exhausted.

Isobel took her shower and fixed a hot drink before making it an early night. She wanted to be fresh for studying the next morning, just in case K.C. called to invite her to the office. The thought brought a smile to her face and joy to her heart. They had no history like she and Jason and there was no crisis to deal with when she was with K.C. She fell asleep feeling like her life had taken a turn for the better.

Chapter 35

Her heart said she was still in love with Jason, but she didn't know if they could ever resolve the problem of his parents. She was attracted to K.C. in a strange way. It didn't feel like romantic attraction, despite the fact that he was very handsome and appealing both in looks and personality. He had a peace about him, almost like the peace that Aunt Betty had, that Isobel attributed to her relationship with the Lord. Isobel wondered. Could K.C. be a Christian? She was only just beginning to soften toward God.

The distraction of moving, studying and refocusing on a career had eased some of the pain Isobel felt because of her losses. She still suffered from a sense of solitude; with no family left, she wasn't sure where she fit in. At times, Isobel wondered if her desire to marry right out of college had more to do with needing to be a part of a family, than it did with being ready for marriage and all it entailed.

She found herself daydreaming more each day about her birth mother. She had a picture in her mind of a young Native American girl, widowed with a small child finding herself pregnant and unmarried. What a tragic start to her life! She was thankful that abortion went against the beliefs of most within the Native American community. And, after all, according to the story from Dr. Fitz, her mother wanted to keep her, but because she was sickly, she gave her up to Aunt Betty. *So,* Isobel thought, *at least she really wanted me.*

Her wandering thoughts began to interfere with her concentration on her studies. Isobel reminded herself to stay focused, but ultimately, when tired or bored, her mind wandered. She knew that, sooner or later, she needed to delve into the search for her mother. But she didn't have a clue where to start. Who could she ask for help in exploring her heritage; who could ask the right questions and who would know the right people to ask?

K.C. immediately came to mind. No, it was enough that he had helped her so much with Aunt Betty's estate. And now he offered to help her study for the LSAT. She couldn't impose on him again. Isobel considered it several times a day, and each time discounted it as a bad idea. Isobel finally got the courage to call the home phone number that K.C. had given her. She was greeted by a soft female voice, "Hello, Fox residence."

Isobel wondered about the young lady. Could she be his wife? He never said if he was married or not. As a matter of fact, what did she really know about him? Absolutely, nothing! She had only seen him in three situations: on the airplane, at the Legal Aid Office, and on the campus of Creighton University. And he probably knew more about her, about her financials after handling Aunt Betty's estate, and about her personal life, since she had opened up to him about 'the former boyfriend'.

"Hello? Is someone there?" the gentle voice prodded the silent phone line for a response.

"I'm sorry… Uh… Hello. Could I speak to K.C., please?"

"K.C. isn't here right now. He's at his office in Omaha. Can I help you, or take a message?" She sounded so nice that Isobel almost liked her without seeing her.

"No, that's ok. I can go to his office. I am calling from Omaha, anyway."

"Oh, you must be Isobel! K.C. told us about you, and that you might call him. He's gonna help you get ready for law school, right?"

Isobel was taken aback by the young lady's unabashed friendliness. She didn't sound like a wife; there was no hint of jealousy or concern. "Yeah, at least I hope he will. I was just calling to make arrangements..."

"He is all set to help you. It's all he's talked about for a couple of weeks since you two ran into each other at that law library. I think he is proud that he talked you into going for that degree in law!" Shyne didn't hold back. Little did she know that she was letting Isobel get a peek into K.C.'s personal life.

"I guess I will get with him at Mr. McMillen's office or the Legal Aid, then."

"Well, let's see... um... today, he's at the Legal Aid. He goes there every Tuesday and Thursday. Hey, would you like to come to my birthday party?"

The unexpected offer had Isobel looking at the receiver in her hand like it was a snake about to bite her, "Pardon me?"

"Well, as much as he talks about you, I thought you could come to the party, so we can meet you... It's in two weeks, so you have time to think about it!"

"I don't even know your name, or who you are..."

Shyne laughed a tinkling, joyful giggle. "I didn't think. He says I do that a lot." She chuckled again. "I'm his little sister, Shyne. I turn eighteen on my next birthday, and we are going to have a great celebration!" Her enthusiasm made Isobel smile, recalling when she turned eighteen.

"Thank you for your invitation. Let me think about it, alright? I will talk to K.C., and if it is ok with him, I might just come." She heard a shriek at the other end of the phone. "Hello?"

"Sorry! I am so happy that you might come! K.C. hasn't had a date in so long that I thought he had forgotten all about women until he started talking about you! I can't wait!"

Isobel got off the phone and decided to make her way to the Legal Aid Office to talk to K.C. face to face. She couldn't risk another excited conversation with an unknown voice on the phone. She just needed to set a schedule for reviewing for the LSAT. Then she could refocus.

She walked into the office and the young lady at the reception desk was the same one who had been there when she first visited the

Legal Aid Office. She was about to ask for K.C. when she saw him at a table with a young couple. The woman held a small baby on her shoulder, patting the baby's back as if burping him. K.C. looked up and caught her eye. He indicated with a motion of his head that he would be with her in a few minutes, so she took a seat on one of their old, plastic and chrome chairs.

When he was done with the duo, he walked with them to the front of the office and shook hands with them as he opened the door to help them leave. When K.C. turned to Isobel with a grin Isobel blushed.

"I wondered if I scared you off with my offer, but I am glad to see you, again."

Isobel put her hands to her cheeks to cool them. She hated that her face revealed her emotion so easily. "No, actually, I would like to take you up on the idea of helping me prepare for the test. I have other stuff on my mind that keeps interfering with my concentration. I thought you might have methods for improving recall and memory."

K.C. was taken by surprise; he didn't expect to see Isobel again, so soon. She seemed so hesitant when he offered his help that he was sure she would never call.

"When would you like to get together?" he said, smiling at her nervousness. "And where is good for you?"

"Well, I am open, since I don't work. You choose the time, and I think the law library would be a good place, don't you?"

"Yeah, sure. How much time do you want to put into each session?" K.C. wondered how he could fit her in between the volunteer work and Mr. McMillen's office. Thankfully, McMillen didn't have any pending court cases; all his work was paperwork, briefs, and estate planning. He definitely wasn't an ambulance-chaser type of lawyer. So far, everything he saw in Mr. McMillen's files indicated an honest man of integrity.

"Well, maybe two hours... *if* that's not too much to ask?" Isobel read his face and realized that his calendar might be crowded. After all, he did have his family. She wasn't sure how much responsibility that added to K.C., but sensed that, quite possibly, he was man of the house.

They talked for a few more minutes, and then K.C. asked if she would have a cup of coffee or tea with him, so they could make more solid plans. Isobel agreed, although her stomach rolled with nerves; she felt unfaithful to Jason, even though it was only coffee. K.C. excused himself and talked to the receptionist to let her know he would be out for about a half an hour. They walked to a small coffee shop around the corner; the fragrance of fresh espresso greeted Isobel's nostrils and she realized she was even a bit hungry. Once inside, K.C. gave his order of a large caramel macchiato to the barista and then he asked Isobel what she wanted.

"Oh, I can take care of mine," she started, but he cut her off.

"I invited you, so I pay… this time, ok?"

Isobel nodded agreement and told him she liked the vanilla latte. The barista rang up their order and, before she totaled it, K.C. added in two scones. Isobel looked at him in surprise.

"Oh, sorry, but I am a bit hungry, and thought you might be, too," he apologized.

"Actually, I am, but I didn't expect you to pay for more than my drink."

The roll of his eyes, silenced Isobel, and she moved to find them a table near the window. *Nice and public.* She reflected. *It isn't a date; it's a business arrangement, that's all.*

K.C. joined her at the table, and looked out the window. He, too, seemed to be working at keeping it casual. "I come here pretty often," he spoke as if to himself as he gazed outside. Then he looked at her. "So, where were we?"

Once again, they discussed possible times and days to meet. Isobel had her cell phone out, looking at her schedule while K.C. pulled a small, spiral notepad out of his pocket. Evidently, he hadn't moved into the cell phone era, yet. She smiled to herself.

"What?" he had seen the little smirk, "Are you laughing at me still using pen and paper?" Then he grinned. "I do know how to use technology, you know. I just choose not to."

Their shared laughter broke the ice. They started talking more easily and before long the half hour break turned into an hour. K.C. looked at his watch.

"Oh, man! It's a good thing I'm not clocking in. I'd be docked for taking a long break," he chuckled, but got up from his chair preparing to leave. "Feel free to sit tight," he said. "But I gotta get back. I'm not sure how many are on the schedule today and it is only two of us volunteer lawyers." He liked the sound of that title. *Lawyer! He had finally made it!*

"No, I need to be heading back to my place to put in some time studying. I feel like I've been playing hooky with you." They joined in another laugh as they disposed of their trash and headed for the door. "So, we meet again on Thursday?"

K.C. nodded in response, "I'll see you at the law library… six o'clock sharp."

Chapter 36

Isobel and K.C. started meeting at Creighton University School of Law library each Tuesday and Thursday evening after that. K.C. kept his schedule open; he didn't want anything to get in the way of Isobel's success. He heard her talk about her ex-fiancé, Jason, every now and then, and he didn't think much of the guy. Although she said he was a Christian young man, his possessiveness despite their break-up said he had issues. K.C. wondered if Jason had ever read the Love Chapter in the Bible. If he had, perhaps his attitude toward Isobel would be different.

K.C. found her to be a woman with a deep love for people. Although she voiced her doubts about God, her life spoke of one who previously had been influenced by a Christian family member, probably her Aunt Betty. She also appeared to be holding back some secret pain that she wouldn't discuss with K.C. Every once in a while, he noticed a faraway look in her eyes and glistening in the corner of one. Then she abruptly perked up and came back to the discussion or topic. It was almost as if she had to consciously push aside sorrowful thoughts to refocus.

Surprised that Shyne had invited Isobel to her birthday celebration, K.C. offered to drive her there and back, because their home was off the beaten path and not the easiest to find. He was pleasantly taken back when she agreed. He had become accustomed to her arguing for her independence. *She will make a good trial lawyer one day,* he thought wryly. *She forms valid arguments like the best of them.*

The afternoon of Shyne's party, K.C. drove to the address Isobel gave him for her condo. *Impressive,* he looked up at the tall building. *But why not with the amount she inherited?* He wondered if he would ever see earnings that could compete with this style of living. Then K.C. reminded himself that he did not go into law for the financial rewards; he still wanted to serve his community, even if it meant pro bono work. Isobel had told him of Jason's rich heritage both in birthright and money. K.C. figured that someone with that pedigree and financial stability was more suitable for Isobel than he could ever be. And once again he reminded himself that he was not looking for a life partner. All he and Isobel had was a friendship and that's probably all they would ever have.

K.C. was greeted at the double glass door entrance by a uniformed doorman who opened the door widely and smiled. "Can I help you, sir?"

"I'm supposed to be meeting Ms. Isobel Kirk."

"Ah, yes. Our young miss. So she has finally decided to date? We wondered about the little lady, always in her place alone…"

"No, sir. This isn't a date…"

Just then Isobel came off the elevator and waved at K.C. "Oh, George, you met my friend?" she spoke to the doorman as if he were her equal.

"Yes, ma'am. Now you young folks enjoy yourselves." With which he opened the door for them to leave the lobby.

K.C.'s hand naturally went to the small of her back to guide her into the car. Isobel didn't pull away, which again surprised him. She sat in the passenger seat and fastened her belt before he closed the door safely. He hurried around to the driver's side and within minutes they were on the highway headed south toward Macy. They chatted casually about the weather and about her upcoming test. *Just another month, then we won't be working together.* K.C. just realized that their study time would have an end-point. The thought saddened him, but he tried to remain upbeat so she wouldn't notice.

Isobel did notice a pause in their conversation; K.C. seemed momentarily distracted. They were turning off for Macy, so she didn't have an opportunity to question him about his mood change. Perhaps it was none of her business. She considered how close they had grown in just the couple of weeks studying together. He quizzed her to test her skills at logic and reasoning and had her write out answers to practice on the spot composition and her ability to form arguments and present reasons for her deductions.

Through all of this, she realized that he was a remarkable man. But he wasn't Jason. Her heart yearned to be sharing this adventure with the love of her heart, the one she wanted to spend her life with. Sadness enveloped her every time she thought that they might never be husband and wife.

Just then they pulled into a long, overgrown, dusty driveway. In the distance she saw a house, but couldn't make out details. As they bumped along, the house came into clearer view, and Isobel was stunned to see the apparent poverty in which K.C. grew up. Obviously, she had little chance to go on a reservation, and the fact that this was the Omaha reservation, the very one her mother came from, intrigued and dismayed Isobel. She wondered if her mother's life had been this difficult, or if she met a man who lifted her out of poverty and provided for her.

"K.C." A shriek from within the house startled Isobel, and then she smiled at the unbridled joy and love in the face of the petite brown-skinned girl, carry a little boy on her hip. *He looked about two years old, and she must be the sister who was having her birthday, so this could not be her child*, Isobel thought.

"Hey, Shyne." K.C. tickled the little boy, "Taddy, my little man, come to uncle." And he took the child from Shyne's arms. Shyne turned to Isobel shyly.

"You must be the one I spoke with… K.C.'s friend?"

"Yes, I am Isobel." She replied, equally bashful in the face of such exuberance. She saw something familiar in Shyne's eyes. *It must be the fact that my mother was from this same reservation,* mused Isobel. *I wonder how closely related folks are around here?* Then the thought came to her that K.C. might have an idea on how to look for her birth mother. She pushed the thought to the back of her mind, promising to talk to him during one of their review sessions.

An older lady watched from the porch just as Shyne gave K.C. and Isobel each a warm hug. As Shyne pulled Isobel along into the house, the lady moved to the side of the porch and gave a strange look in Isobel's direction. Shyne acted like they were old friends, and Isobel glanced back helplessly at K.C. He had stopped to talk to the neatly groomed woman, and Isobel realized she must be his mother.

"K.C., who is this you brought with you?"

"Her name is Isobel, Ma. She's the one I told you about, the one I helped with some problems with her aunt's estate… Lately, I've been tutoring her for the test to get into law school."

"Isobel?" His mother's demeanor changed. "I once knew an Isobel."

"I'm sure there are more out there, Ma." K.C. jokingly replied. He turned to go inside and drew Ma along with his arm around her shoulder. "Who knows, maybe someday we will have one in our family." Ma looked shocked, and he realized he spoke aloud. He touched her on the top of her head, "Don't worry. It's not like that!"

Inside the house, Shyne, Ma and Tali had set out a feast for Shyne's celebration. She didn't invite all the neighbors like the last party. She was content to have immediate family plus Isobel and her best friend who was supposed to arrive soon. The table was neatly set in a buffet style with the plates, flatware, and napkins at one end, several large bowls of food in the middle, and an interesting looking drink in a large pitcher with glasses at the other end.

When Cassie Charbanneau arrived a few minutes later, she brought a joyful spirit into the house. She wasn't crass or crude; the laughter and fun was borne of a young woman with a brilliant sense of humor. It wasn't long before she had them all laughing heartily. She was the perfect opposite to Shyne's quieter disposition.

Talitha and Ma stayed in the kitchen for the most part during the evening. The two seemed equally uncomfortable with the party atmosphere. Isobel felt K.C.'s mother's eyes on her more than once. She wondered if his mom felt imposed upon. After all, never having met Isobel before, it must have come as a surprise to see K.C. bring someone home.

Overall, Isobel enjoyed her evening with the Fox family. She noticed there was no other male figure in the household and concluded that K.C. was the sole provider for his family. She wondered at his ability to juggle so much responsibility at such a young age. *He will make someone a wonderful husband someday,* she thought.

The time came to a close too soon, but with the long drive looming, Isobel knew they needed to get on the road. She said her good-byes and was happy when Shyne and Talitha invited her to come back anytime. She went into the kitchen to find Mrs. Fox to thank her, and found her in tears.

"Are you alright," Isobel asked tenderly. She wasn't used to elderly folks crying, least of all after a party.

"Oh, I'll be just fine, I imagine," replied Mrs. Fox. "Guess it's just seeing my baby grow up, is all. Seems like just yesterday, I held her in my arms…" and her voice caught in her throat.

Isobel gave Mrs. Fox a warm embrace and thanked her for the lovely food. Mrs. Fox clung to her a bit long, so Isobel pulled away to ensure the older woman was truly alright and wished her good-night.

She and K.C. drove through the dark in companionable silence. Since neither was accustomed to parties, they were both spent after an evening of fun and laughter. Soft classical music played on the radio as they made their way back to Omaha, and shortly before they arrived, Isobel dozed with her head against the window.

She was embarrassed when K.C. nudged her to awaken her. She gathered her purse and wrap and declined K.C.'s offer to escort her to her condo. The doorman stood his position as faithfully as the Queen's guard, and Isobel felt quite safe as she went up the elevator and into her place. As she prepared for bed, she reflected on the contrast between the Fox family and Jason's.

Her visit to the Armstrong's revealed a pretentious, autocratic and unfriendly group. On the other hand, the Fox family gathering was warm and welcoming; it was exactly what Isobel expected from a loving home. She wanted to talk to K.C. to discover what made the difference, *if* even he could explain it.

Chapter 37

The next time they studied together, Isobel asked K.C. the burning question she had the night of the party. What made the difference between his family and the Armstrong's? Jason's had all the money they needed and K.C.'s obviously didn't, yet the Fox family showed more joy and love than the Armstrong's had. K.C. told her of the one thing that kept his family strong, faith in God.

Isobel was no longer as 'anti-God' as she had been when Aunt Betty died. She had started reading the old, dog-eared Bible and was realizing that God was more important to her than she thought. She did not want to find herself old and dying before she accepted Jesus as her Saviour. She just wasn't sure how all that worked, and she was too self-conscious to ask K.C.

The weeks after the party quickly passed as Isobel prepared for the scheduled LSAT. She came to look forward to each Tuesday and Thursday study session with K.C. Their friendship flourished after Shyne's birthday party; it seemed that the laughter and relaxed atmosphere had removed some of the angst they each had about their closeness. Isobel was especially touched by the short prayer K.C. would say before they began each time. He asked for wisdom and prayed that Isobel would have the recall necessary to remember what she was learning.

They even found themselves taking a snack at the little coffee shop before they went on to the library. That way there was no need to interrupt their studying for a dinner break. K.C. explained how the LSAT was broken into several sections of multiple choice questions as well as an essay which, although not graded, would be sent to any law schools to which Isobel might apply.

"I decided where I want to go," Isobel told him, "and I won't be applying to other schools."

"Really?" K.C. was almost afraid to ask. He worried that she would choose to go near Jason. She still spoke of him often, and K.C. could tell she was still in love with Jason.

"I want to go right here," she indicated a broad circle with her arm. "I love this place, and if I can get in at Creighton, it would thrill me. I don't need an Ivy League education to prove anything. I just need preparation to become a lawyer!"

K.C. smiled at her enthusiasm, but inside he was smiling at her decision. He welcomed the chance for them to spend more time getting to know each other. If she stayed in Omaha there was a greater chance of that happening. He just needed to have a plan for after the study sessions were done and her LSAT taken. And that day was coming very soon.

Butterflies took flight in Isobel's stomach every time she thought of the test until she thought she would be physically ill on the day of the test. The night before, she had turned in early hoping to get her full eight hours of sleep. Instead, she tossed and turned throughout the night and got up feeling more tired than she was when she turned in the night before. She found herself saying a little prayer over her scant breakfast of orange juice and a toasted English muffin with cream cheese spread on it.

The test took the best part of her day, which wasn't a problem since Isobel had nothing else on her plate. She was pleasantly surprised when done; the test wasn't nearly as difficult as she had expected. Whether it was the test or her preparation that made the difference was of little concern to Isobel. The fact was she left the test center feeling confident and happy. She wanted to call someone, anyone, as soon as she got back to her condo, but Jason would be studying, and K.C. was probably at home since it was Saturday. She sat and stared at the phone trying to decide what to do, when suddenly it rang and startled her. She laughed at the way she jumped at the sound, and then she picked up the receiver and answered.

"Isobel, this is K.C. I was hoping you would be there. I came in to McMillen's for a couple of hours today. I needed to get my mind busy because I was thinking of you taking your test. Uh… how did it go?" he asked tentatively.

"K.C., I am so glad you called! It was OK! I mean, I feel like I did real well, thanks to all your help!"

"You could have done fine without me helping," he replied, but Isobel wouldn't let him off so easily.

"I would have been adrift without you showing me what to focus on. No, I could NOT have done as well if you had not tutored me!"

Isobel's intensity took him off guard. Although in the past she had stood her ground on certain issues, he had never heard her so forceful and passionate. They talked for a bit longer. Then K.C. broached the reason he had actually called. "Would you go out to dinner with me? I mean, we ate at the coffee shop, but I'd like to take you to a real restaurant to celebrate."

"You mean… like… a date?" He heard the hesitation in her voice.

"No strings attached you understand; just a nice, dress-up for dinner type of date. Think of it as a business dinner if that makes it easier for you to say yes."

Isobel hesitated for just a moment, and then she agreed to go with him, but she wanted to go Dutch. K.C. was having none of it, so in the end, they agreed on the restaurant and time and got off the phone. Isobel looked at the clock and realized she only had an hour and a half to get ready, so she hurried to take her shower.

K.C. smiled at the dial tone emanating from his telephone. Finally, Miss Isobel Kirk had agreed to go out with him. Maybe now he could get to the bottom of her mysterious, faraway looks. He hoped her secret didn't have anything to do with her ex-fiancé. But why else would she be so enigmatic when he asked her what was on her mind?

Fortunately, he didn't have to wait long for his answer. Isobel was more talkative than he'd ever seen her. She prattled on about the test from the time she got into his car until they arrived at the restaurant. Even after they were seated at their table, Isobel continued talking about various facets of the exam. Finally, when the waiter came to take their order, she went quiet long enough to look at her menu and quickly make her choice. Once their waiter left, she sat quietly across the table with her hands folded, looking intently at K.C.

"What are you thinking about?" he asked softly. He fully expected her usual answer of 'nothing', but instead she took a deep breath and started on a different subject.

"You know so much about me," Isobel started. "And I really don't know much about you, except what I saw when visiting your family for Shyne's birthday." He nodded to encourage her.

"Well, there is something I haven't told you..." *Here it comes*, thought K.C, but he didn't want to say anything for fear of interrupting her revelation.

"As a matter of fact, I haven't told anyone, yet." K.C. took that to mean that she had not shared it with Jason, but he wasn't sure.

"I don't even know *how* to explain it because I only found out since the death of my aunt." Isobel paused, sighed, and began again. "I found out that I wasn't who I thought I was!"

K.C. was puzzled. How could someone not be themselves? "What do you mean?" he asked cautiously. He wasn't sure if she was speaking in some type of allegory or if she actually meant her statement.

"What I mean to say is... I grew up believing that my mother, who died when I was three years old, and was from Japan, was truly my mom. Then I found paperwork and letters that said otherwise."

K.C. let out the breath he was holding in. "You had me worried there for a minute. So you were adopted? What's the big secret there? Lots of folks are adopted and don't find out until later in life. I mean, I know it was a surprise, but..."

Isobel cut him off. "I wasn't adopted. Not really, that is. There are no adoption papers to go through or records to search."

"What, you were, uh, kidnapped and raised as theirs?"

"No. My dad was my father. At least that part was true. But my mom wasn't my mom. Which means I am not Japanese-American like I always thought. As a matter of fact, I found out from the local doctor that delivered me that my biological mother was of the Omaha Native American tribe, your tribe."

K.C. didn't say anything for a long moment. He contemplated what to say. Was she disappointed to find out that she was Native American? There was a stigma in some cultures to admit to Indian bloodlines. Or was she happy about it? In recent years it was somewhat of a fad to claim to be 'part Indian'. He couldn't read her expression other than to see that she was confused and concerned about his response.

"How do you feel about that?" A question was always safer than expressing an opinion right off the bat.

"I don't know. I feel like I've been living a lie, like when I joined the Japanese-American Club in school. I really didn't belong, and they told me so, although their reasons were different. They didn't welcome ethnically mixed students; they wanted the club to be 'pure-blooded' Japanese."

He nodded. He had heard of cultural clubs that wanted the full-blooded. Welcoming racially mixed individuals diluted the cultural aspect, or so they seemed to think.

"I always wondered why my eyes were large with full eyelashes. I thought I should have inherited a bit of my mother's Asian looks, but instead the only real thing from her, or so I thought, was my straight black hair. Now I realize that even that wasn't hers." Isobel smiled wryly, the sadness apparent in her eyes.

Just then the waiter brought their order, so they sat back and waited for the food to be placed on the table. He made sure the presentation was lovely, and asked if they needed anything else. When K.C. indicated they were fine, he left them to get back to their conversation.

"So how do you feel about the Indian part?" He used the expression that most Native Americans avoided because of its historically negative connotations. He deliberately did that, watching to see her reaction. If she didn't react, it could be that she still lived in that mindset. But if he saw any kind of cringe or discomfort, he would know that she too realized the term's impact.

Isobel blushed. Then she gulped before she began to speak. "I need to admit that I was taken back. Not because of any negative feelings about Native Americans, mind you." Isobel was quick to try to reassure K.C. that she wasn't prejudiced.

"I just know so little about them, about you, which is why I started this conversation the way I did. I really did mean that I knew little about you as a people group, not you as an individual. As a person, I think you are an open book. But I need to learn about the tribe, about the Omaha tribe, in particular. I need to understand my heritage. I was proud to be part Japanese, but now I need to familiarize myself with your...our culture, so I can regain my ethnic pride. Does that make sense to you?"

"Perfect sense," K.C. replied. "So how can I help?"

"Now that the pressure is off for the LSAT, I was wondering if I could spend more time with your family, more time on the reservation. I want to immerse myself in the culture and discover what I've missed for all my life. Later on, when I feel ready, I thought you might have some clues as to how to search for my mother. Right now, it's all about figuring out who I am. Once I feel comfortable in my skin again, so to speak, then I'd like to try to reach out to her, if she is still living. I don't even know where to begin, so I need to let that rest for now."

They continued discussing this turn of events and gradually their conversation turned to less emotional topics. The dinner was delicious, and by the time they finished, both had eaten their fill. They decided to walk around downtown for a bit, to work off some of the food. The evening air was warm and humid; it felt to K.C. like tornado weather. He hadn't watched the weather forecast lately, so he didn't know what was coming up over the next few days.

They began to head back to his car when a large raindrop plopped on the sidewalk in front of them. Hurrying, they almost outran the rain, getting to the car just as the downpour started in earnest. His shirt and hair got wet, and her hair hung limply from the rain, but they smiled as they shut it out and started the car on the path home.

Chapter 38

When Isobel opened the door to her condo, she was surprised to hear her phone ringing. She hurriedly put her purse down and went to the phone, but the ringing stopped just as she was about to lift the receiver. Figuring it must have been a wrong number, she turn to go to her bedroom, to prepare for a quiet hour and a warm drink before turning in for the night, when the phone began ringing again. This time she hurried to pick up the handset on the second ring.

"Where have you been?" On the other end, Jason's voice was sharp with irritation.

"I went out for dinner to celebrate finally taking the LSAT." Isobel's voice sounded defensive in response.

"I know! I was trying to call to see how it went!" His tone hadn't softened. "Who did you go to dinner with?"

Isobel did not think she should feel defensive; she and Jason had no binding agreement preventing them from dating, even though she avoided calling the evening a date. "What makes you think I went *with* someone? I might have decided to go out to celebrate on my own, you know!"

"Nobody celebrates alone! It was *him*, wasn't it?" No longer sharp, Jason sounded deflated, as if he had lost a battle.

"Yes, Jason, it was K.C. He invited me for a business dinner as a celebration of the end of our student-tutor relationship. You needn't worry. We probably won't see much of each other now that we are done preparing me for the LSAT." She answered him quietly, still hating that she had to explain herself.

"Izzie, I'm sorry! I just worry, with you so far away from me that you might fall out of love with me, and in love with someone else. I don't want to lose you. We were so close to getting married… to committing to each other for life. I just can't bear to think of my future without you by my side."

She nodded as he spoke, reliving their dreams for their future. Then, realizing she hadn't responded to his statement aloud, she said, "Jason, has anything changed? You know the issue that has us separated. Unless your family can accept me, I cannot place myself in that situation. Either you and they would not have a relationship, or I would feel their displeasure each time we visited them. And what about our children? Would they treat them as they do you? Or would they, because their skin would be golden, be treated as outsiders? I can't imagine that. Please, I want to maintain communication with you, because I do still love you. But if it is going to be accusatory and confrontational every time, then…"

Jason interrupted her discourse. He saw that he had gone too far this time. Isobel was seriously considering breaking off their phone conversations and cutting him out of her life. He couldn't let that happen. Even if all she would agree to was a friendship, at least he would know where she was and how she was doing.

"OK, Izzie. I'm sorry once again. I know I seem to be saying that a lot lately, but I mean it. I promise, I promise, I won't interfere in your life. I just need to know that we can still talk. I need to know you are doing ok."

Isobel accepted his apology although reluctant to believe his promise. She decided to change the subject and asked him if he still wanted to know how the exam went and he said he did. They talked for nearly an hour with the details of the test first, then Jason talked of his program and how he was looking forward to the final two years with more rotations and less class work. Isobel decided this was a good time to tell him of her decision about where to attend law school.

Jason wasn't thrilled with the idea of Isobel staying in Omaha, but when she went on to tell him about her heritage issue, he understood. "I could help you search for your mother…" he began to offer, but was quickly cut-off.

"Jason, just how do you think you could do that from out there on the east coast? I can't have you interrupting your studies for me. No, K.C. said he may be able to help since it seems she originated in this area, or so the story goes. I don't plan to search until sometime in the future anyway. I want to focus on school. I will already be behind the curve for getting into law school this fall, since I only just took the LSAT. I need to work hard to get in next September. In the meantime, I plan to volunteer at the Legal Aid Office to get a feel for the law profession. Of course, I can only do clerical work and some research assistance, but at least it will get me into the right frame of mind."

He agreed that her plan seemed good, despite his misgivings about K.C.'s intentions. He couldn't believe than any man of their age group could look at Isobel and not find her attractive. She was beautiful in looks, but also in personality, and he knew what a treasure any man would find in Isobel Kirk. He aimed to prevent that from happening. So for now, he agreed to call her several times a week 'to just chat' and keep in touch. But in his heart, he prayed that God would intervene and allow them to become husband and wife in His time and according to His plan.

Chapter 39

When K.C. got home that evening, Shyne and Tali were thrilled to hear that Isobel had finally gone to dinner with K.C. His misery over the way things were left between them made the whole family unhappy. They could see that he had feelings for Isobel, and wanted him to find happiness. Only Ma seemed content to let things be. She did not encourage the girls to intervene on his behalf, and outright rejected the idea of calling Isobel herself. Shyne and Tali didn't understand Ma's resistance, but complied with her restrictions out of respect. Both Tali and Shyne were enjoying new experiences and joys in life.

Tali continued her therapy and her medication was adjusted to just the right levels. She was able to see her life through a different lens, now, and had opened her heart to the Lord. Recognizing her poor choices in the past, helped Tali select better options for her future. She decided to study for her GED and possibly go on to college. For now, she was content to take it one step at a time and focus on her mental health and the health of her children. Despite the crowded conditions, she decided to stay with Ma and Shyne rather than moving back to the city. The bustle of city life held too many temptations, and she was determined to improve her children's chance at life by changing the course of her own.

Church attendance was no longer an obligation for Tali. She found support and encouragement from the other mothers at church, and had become very involved in helping with children's church and the outreach program aimed at other young mothers. Ma was thrilled to see her daughter's enjoyment of worship.

For years she had prayed for each of her children, and now she saw the promise fulfilled: *'Train up a child in the way he should go and when he is old he will not depart from it'*. She only had to remind herself that the promise says 'when…old' but doesn't say just how old 'old' is. *It might take one longer than the others* and she thought of Skyla. *But sooner or later the promise will be fulfilled.* It only took faith enough to stay the course. She was equally please to watch Shyne's growth as a Christian young lady.

Since her eighteenth birthday, Shyne had blossomed with her own new romance. Since she had also committed herself to living a Christian life, she thought she might never find a young man willing to go along with her new commitment to purity and Christian living. She vowed to keep Jesus at the forefront of every decision made that impacted her children and herself. But the Lord had blessed her vow and brought a young man into her life through Pastor Jim. Pastor Jim invited her to attend a youth meeting at his home, and she immediately found common grounds with a handsome young Lakota man named James CrowDog. She happily reported that he, too, was a Christian.

Shyne and James began dating, infrequently at first, but since Labor Day, they saw each other several times a week. They always met in public places, or he came to their home and visited with the entire family. James seemed at ease with the children, not at all put off by the idea of a ready-made family, although that would be a ways down the road. Both he and Shyne stood firm on the idea of a long courtship before making any permanent commitment.

K.C. happily saw his family becoming whole once again, and wondered if it was time to move into Omaha, to allow them the space needed for all the children. He knew it wouldn't make Ma happy; she depended on him to be the stabilizing force in the house. But K.C. also knew that they could manage during the week, and he could come home on Fridays and return to the city Monday mornings for work. Especially, now that his and Isobel's relationship seemed to be blossoming. He wanted to be available for her, and for exploring the possibilities.

First, he needed to get past Ma's reservations about his friendship with Isobel. She appeared almost angry when he spoke of Isobel. Ma started moving things around that didn't need rearranging, and clearing her throat – a clear sign of her annoyance. K.C. tried to talk to her, but she avoided eye contact and continued cleaning and straightening the house. "Ma, what is it? Why do you get in such a mood when I mention Isobel?" But she didn't reply.

Shyne and Tali both noticed Ma's change in attitude, also. They looked at each other and then at K.C. with questions in their eyes, but didn't ask anything for fear of setting Ma off. Although she had been stable on her antidepressants, occasionally her mood shifted to one of melancholy and withdrawal. They noticed it when K.C. broached the subject of getting a place in town, near his job, around the July Fourth holiday. She pulled inward, away from all of them, unwilling to discuss the subject, so he let it drop at that time.

"Ma, please. Sit down so we can talk," he took her hands and led her to the nearest chair. She allowed him to lead her, but made no attempt to look at him or to engage in conversation. Ma kept her eyes downcast even after being seated. K.C. took a finger and lifted her chin so he could see her face; he needed to read her eyes. He was surprised to see her deep brown eyes pooling with tears. "Aw, Ma, what is it? Please tell me what is wrong so I can help."

His gentle tone and tender touch was Ma's undoing. She began to sob, holding her apron to her face to hide the shame of tears, but her shoulders shook as she wept. He held her close, not asking any more questions, just comforting the mother who once dried his little boy tears.

Tali indicated to Shyne that they should leave Ma and K.C. alone, and they gathered the children from their various play areas to take them for a treasure hunt in the fields. The toddlers liked nothing more than running through the tall prairie grass looking for various flowers or insects. They gathered treasures to take home every time they went on their searches. Once little Kerron proudly found an arrowhead, which he kept safely in a shoebox under his bed.

Once the commotion of the children subsided enough to indicate they were out of hearing range, K.C. took a chair and pulled it in front of his mother. He held her hands as she composed herself, and waited for her to speak first.

"Kwsind. It is too hard. I cannot bear the pain when I hear the name 'Isobel'. I knew an Isobel once who died… it grieves me to this day."

"But, Ma. This is not the same Isobel. You must realize that. We cannot treat her poorly because of her name. She did not choose her name; it was given to her; she had no control over that. Please, Ma. Give Isobel a chance. She is the first young lady with whom I felt a closeness that could develop further. I need to see where our relationship goes."

Ma nodded, although reluctantly. She listened to what K.C. had to say and understood that her own reaction was not reasonable. She agreed to allow him to make his own choice, and to be cordial when the young lady came around. However, when K.C. began talking about moving to the city, she again protested. "We need you here, son. The city is too far away."

K.C. continued explaining his decision, rather than asking her permission. He shared with her his original plan to practice law on the west coast, and how his plans had changed. He told her of his ultimate goal of helping their people, especially his own sister, Skyla. In the end, Ma came around to his decision. When he told her it would be weeks before he was ready to move out, she softened even more, and gave in to his choice.

That evening spent with the family, K.C. felt more at peace than he had in quite some time. Finally, he would be moving into his own place, setting off to his own destiny, and he looked forward to those challenges. He also daydreamed while the family visited. He thought of his meeting with Isobel, set for the next day, and wondered how it would go. He had high hopes that they could renew the relationship they had earlier in the summer. As the evening closed, and the young women prepared their children for bed, K.C. decided he would make it a matter of prayer. And as the family came together for evening prayers, he asked his family to include his decisions in the prayer requests placed on the altar. He turned in that night hopeful and excited for the future.

Chapter 40

Isobel arrived at the coffee shop early. She took a few minutes to order her usual latte and a sweet roll and took her seat at the table where she and K.C. were accustomed to sitting. She still wasn't sure of how much she wanted to share with him; what she was sure of was that she wanted to learn more about her heritage, about the Omaha people. Isobel knew she had a big learning curve to make up for the 25 years of not knowing her birthright.

K.C. got there a bit later than planned because parking was scarce, and he came from Mr. McMillen's office, not the Legal Aid just around the corner. He saw Isobel seated near the window and smiled and waved at her as he went inside. He stopped to get a black coffee and made his way to where she was seated.

"Hey, good to see you again," he grinned like a schoolboy with his first girlfriend. Isobel never noticed before that he seemed almost shy in his approach.

"Good to see you, too," she replied sincerely. Isobel was happy that they had reconnected, although she worried that he may feel encouraged in the wrong direction. She didn't want to send mixed messages; she needed to be sure he understood that they had a friendship and nothing more.

He looked up then, and saw the genuineness in her eyes, "So you called for me to meet you...?"

"K.C., I do cherish you as a friend, and I appreciate all you have done for me both personally, with Aunt Betty's estate, and with respect to my career goal." Isobel paused to be sure she wasn't hurting his feelings, but K.C. seemed alright with what she had said thus far.

"Jason and I are talking again. I don't know if it will take us back into the relationship we once had, but for now I feel I need to be honest with both of you. I don't want to give you false expectations, and I need to be honest with myself and Jason. I hope you understand." She reached out to touch his hand and he placed his other hand on hers.

"Isobel, I don't know what I was hoping for. I never had feelings for a woman like I have for you, so I can't give a name to them. I just know that from the day I met you, I felt a connection, and I don't want to lose that. So if it is to be a friendship, I will accept that." Once again, his white teeth shone against his golden skin in a broad smile.

They continued talking for over an hour. Isobel shared her desire to learn more about the traditions of her birth mother, of K.C. and his family. K.C. told her of some of the celebrations held on the reservation, powwows and various family galas, and suggested that she might enjoy participating in some of them. He also thought she might like to attend church with his family sometime to meet other families on the rez with whom she might find friendship and maybe information helpful to her search for her mother.

Isobel loved the idea of spending more time with the Fox family, but wondered about Mrs. Fox. She sensed coolness from his mother, and didn't want to be the cause for problems for him, any more than she was willing to be the nuisance in Jason's family circle. K.C. did his best to reassure her, although he knew his mother still had her concerns.

By the time Isobel and K.C. went their separate ways, they had gotten past any uneasiness felt at the beginning. K.C. promised to call her to make arrangements for her to attend church with them, and to share dates of any celebrations as they arose. Isobel also told K.C. that she would help him in his search for a place in town.

Despite wanting to maintain an emotional distance from K.C., Isobel welcomed having him nearer so she could eventually ask him for more specific help in finding her birth mother. She also knew he would help her once she started law school, if she needed tutoring or advice.

Chapter 41

By the time Halloween rolled around, Isobel had helped K.C. find an apartment near the law office of Mr. McMillen. She joined him on shopping trips to find furniture for his place and assisted in decorating it with curtains and a few well-chosen pictures for the walls. He was starting from the beginning with no dishes or pans, no linens or bedding, so Isobel took time to find good quality items that would be both durable and pleasing to the eye.

K.C. enjoyed the time spent with Isobel and had to constantly remind himself that they were only friends. It wasn't easy, because he found himself growing increasingly fond of the elegant and self-assured young woman escorting him around the various shopping areas in Omaha. He noticed admiring glances in their direction acknowledging that they were a handsome couple. But he knew it took more than looking good together to make a couple. He couldn't compete with Jason for Isobel's heart, so he had to be content with her companionship.

Throughout the remaining part of autumn and on into winter, they avoided the one subject that weighed heaviest on Isobel's mind: her application for law school. K.C. wasn't sure that applying to only one school of law was a good idea. When he put in his application several years earlier, he and his classmates all applied for multiple schools in hopes of being accepted by at least one of them. But

Isobel was putting all her eggs in one basket by applying only to Creighton.

K.C. even tried to encourage her to consider other schools of law such as Southern Illinois University in Carbondale or Gonzaga University in Washington State. Since she had an aversion to the Ivy League, he thought she might consider one of these highly ranked law schools. But Isobel was adamant. She would be going to Creighton. She was convinced this was the school for her, and would not even permit consideration of another.

Isobel began spending two or three afternoons a week helping at the Legal Aid. Although she couldn't work as an advisor, since she had no professional training in law, she could assist with filing and telephone follow-up calls to free up the attorneys to meet with clients. Every Tuesday and Thursday afternoon became her routine, with the occasional Wednesday thrown in, and it helped make time pass quicker. She had put in her application, and needed to keep her mind occupied so she wouldn't sit and worry over her acceptance.

Autumn gradually gave way to winter and the cold winds cut across the prairies. Snow, ice and every other variation of precipitation pelted the Omaha area over the Christmas season making it difficult to get into a joyful spirit. Isobel spent time over the Christmas season with the Fox family, enjoying their unique traditions. She spent time watching more than asking questions, and was soon a full participant in celebrations.

She attended weekly church services with the Foxes, too, from her first time at Thanksgiving, and had made friends with many of the young women. Isobel surprised herself with her immersion into the activities of the church. Isobel recalled her teenage days when she resented church attendance and only went because it was required of her. But now, as she listened to the sermons with a more mature perspective, she realized what she was missing in shrugging off the faith of her aunt. "*the heritage of those that fear (God's) name...*" she thought, and once again wondered if her birth mother was still a practicing, committed Christian.

As the New Year approached, Isobel, like many others, considered her resolutions for the New Year. She wanted to make changes that she could keep, not temporary goals that fall to the wayside before January is done. She thought of her growing connection with Jason. They continued talking weekly and sometimes more often, and found the same love connecting them as they had previously. Her anxiety about his parents was tempered by their agreement to keep their commitment informal until Isobel finished her schooling. Jason was looking at about 18 months left in his medical school, but then he still had three years of residency. Meanwhile, Isobel awaited word about her application and hoped and prayed she would be starting law school in the fall.

New Year's Day arrived wrapped in a magnificent robe of about four inches of snow, topped with a thick layer of ice. The surface cracked and crunched under the feet of those brave enough to attempt walking out of doors, and Isobel decided she would stay home rather than try to go to New Year Services with K.C. and his family. Although he offered to drive, Isobel felt compelled to remain indoors for the day, and was glad she did. News of car accidents and cars abandoned due to treacherous driving conditions came across the TV, and Isobel worried whether K.C. had made it to his family that morning.

Mid-afternoon her phone rang insistently, urging her off of the couch where she had cuddled with her blanket for a brief nap. "Hello?" she answered, wondering who would be calling her that day.

The warm, rich, familiar voice greeted her, "Hello, Izzie. It's Jason."

"Jason, I didn't expect you to call! I thought you were spending the holidays with your parents and wouldn't be in touch…"

"Izzie, I have some news for you that just couldn't wait." The excitement in Jason's voice was contagious and Isobel's heart did its usual responsive thumping. She waited for him to continue, unable to choke out a response to his energy. "Izzie, it's my parents…"

"Has something happened to them? Oh, Jason, what…?"

"No, dear, nothing like that. They are fine…more than fine, they are wonderful."

His description of his parents seemed a far cry from the normal way he talked of them. Ever since their rejection of Isobel, although he still visited and maintained a relationship with them, their bond was strained, tenuous at best. He respected them as his parents, but had lost his youthful unconditional admiration. It had been replaced with a healthy dose of reality-based recognition of them as his mother and father. Where once the child thought of them as infallible, Jason now saw his parents with all their shortcomings.

"Izzie, you won't believe it. I couldn't believe it. If I hadn't been there, I might still not believe it…!"

"Believe what, Jason? What is going on? What happened?"

"Isobel, we attended midnight services to welcome the New Year. My mother, my father and I all went together to our traditional church service. It was such a common practice that I didn't have any expectations for the unusual. But we had a guest pastor talk to us, and Izzie, he was magnificent! He spoke with fervor and enthusiasm about prophecy and end times. His professed joy at the soon coming of Jesus inspired nearly everyone there to draw closer to the Lord! What was most amazing, though, is that my parents responded to his altar call!"

Isobel dropped into the little chair beside her telephone table. What could this mean? Hadn't his parents always professed to be Christians? When Isobel put the question to Jason he was quick to respond. "There's a big difference between calling yourself a Christian because you attend church every week, and being truly converted. Christianity isn't about ritual; it's about relationship…a loving relationship with Jesus. And I believe my parents finally came to realize that! Izzie, I think they are truly changed. They have asked Jesus into their hearts and have repented for their past sins."

She took a moment before speaking again. "Jason, are you saying that they are sorry for the way they treated me? Do they consider that one of their 'past sins'?"

"That's exactly what I am saying, Isobel! They would like permission to come and visit with you, to talk with you and apologize for their small-mindedness and bigotry."

"But Jason, all that happened when they thought I was part Japanese. Now that I know my true ethnic background, are they willing to accept it? Many people have more difficulty with accepting Native Americans into their families than those of Asian roots. And I was supposedly only *half* Japanese, not even full blooded. I don't know if I can subject myself to their abuse again."

Jason tried to reassure Isobel that his parents had truly changed, but the hurt she felt from that first encounter was so deep that she couldn't open herself to another episode. She told Jason she needed time to absorb the information about their conversion. They talked a bit longer and, as usual, Jason ended the call with a prayer. This time he didn't just pray for Isobel, though. He prayed for her acceptance of the Lord into her life, but also for her to be able to see past the pain of the past and look toward the future for the two of them.

Isobel wasn't sure how she felt about his call or his prayer. Although she had become accustomed to hearing him pray for her relationship with Jesus, at the same time it felt like pressure, too. Never was one for emotional altar calls or the old-fashioned, 'hellfire and brimstone' type scare onto the road to heaven, Isobel had a healthy skepticism of his parents' conversion experience.

When I make the commitment to follow Jesus… She smiled wryly because she had thought the word *when* rather than *if. OK, so* if *I make that commitment…* She continued in her musing, *it has to be because I really understand and know what I am getting into. Not just because I want Jason as a husband, or because I want to live a* good *life.*

In the following days, life settled into a routine not unlike the old year's pattern. Isobel returned to her volunteer work, Jason continued calling between his studies and classes, and K.C. and she returned to the camaraderie they had developed. Life felt easy and comfortable, but in the back of her mind, Isobel wondered about her application for law school. She knew that they began making their selections in December and she had yet to hear anything. Days settled into weeks which became months and March arrived with gusto.

Wind whipped across the prairie and the wind chill factor dipped lower than Isobel could recall. Then, just as suddenly, the weather changed to rain and storms. Spring flooding was discussed and the temperatures were erratic. One day it would feel like snow was returning and the next felt balmy like tornado weather. Nebraskans knew that anything was possible in March; winter wasn't over until it was over, and they could still have freezing temperatures well into April.

The afternoon of April first found Isobel checking her mailbox after a morning at the Legal Aid office. A large, official-looking envelope with Creighton School of Law in the return address corner was the only piece of mail in her box. She turned it over in her hands as if somewhere on the outside she would see a hint of what was inside. Then she looked around her, wondering if she looked silly standing there examining an envelope instead of opening it or taking it on to her condo to open it. Nobody was looking in her direction so she had nothing to be self-conscious about, but still she blushed.

Taking her letter to the elevator with her armload of other items, she pushed the button for her floor and relaxed against the wall of the elevator. She felt as if she would faint; her legs shook and her heart thumped wildly in her throat. In her mind, Isobel urged the elevator to hurry, knowing all the while that it was going its usual speed. It hadn't stopped on any other floors, but still the ride seemed to take forever.

Dear Isobel A. Kirk,

Congratulations! We are pleased to accept your application for Creighton School of Law. You are invited to attend beginning in the fall semester which will start August…

Isobel sat heavily onto a chair that she hadn't realized was behind her. The letter went on with all the pertinent information about enrollment and orientation, tuition and fees, and the timetable for various tasks to be accomplished. Isobel stared at it for what seemed like hours, but was probably a matter of minutes, and then she jumped up and started squealing, screaming and jumping up and down like a child at Christmas. It was a dream come true after all her hard work, and the first to hear this news had to be K.C.

K.C. would be at the Legal Aid office that afternoon; they rarely volunteered at the same time or on the same days. Whether to purposely avoid the discomfort of closeness or to slow down any possible relationship, Isobel wasn't sure. She only knew that she had decided to volunteer opposite his schedule once she committed to the work at the Legal Aid Office. Isobel looked at the clock and saw that it wasn't yet one o'clock, the time when he would start his volunteer time, so she would have to wait to share her news.

She thought of calling Jason, but realized the futility in trying to reach him during the day. He was busy with medical school and she usually heard from him whenever he could get a few minutes between studies and classes, so Isobel quickly dismissed the thought of trying. Then sadness came over her.

She thought of her Aunt Betty and how proud she would be of Isobel's successes. She reflected on her father and his desire for her to go to college; law school was so much further than the aspiration he had for her that she knew he, too, would feel pride in her accomplishment. Then her mind went to her birth mother. *What would she think, if she knew?* Isobel pondered. *Was she the kind of person to begrudge her daughter's continuing education? Or would she also be pleased to see how hard her little girl had worked?* Tears filled Isobel's eyes as she considered whether she would ever know the answers to those questions. She wondered if she would ever find her mother and if so, how long before she did?

Chapter 42

Spring melted into a hot, hazy summer and Isobel enjoyed every minute of every day. She absorbed everything she could about law while doing her volunteer work, listening to the various cases brought to them, and discussing them with the lawyers afterward. During her own time, she spent time getting familiar with the campus of Creighton University, absorbing the atmosphere and watching students, imagining herself as one of them in the not too distant future.

Isobel had become a fixture in the Fox home on weekends. She attended church with them, and often drove Tali and Shyne to church functions aimed at young women of their age group. Tali and Shyne accepted Isobel as their brother's friend, but also came to think of her as their friend. Mrs. Fox maintained a safe distance in her relationship with Isobel, always watching, but not initiating conversation or closeness. She seemed content to watch and ensure that K.C. and Isobel did not become more than friends.

Isobel attended powwows and other celebrations with K.C., Shyne and Talitha ever learning about the Native American traditions of various tribes. She was amazed at the differences, having been taught only of similarities in 'Indian' cultures. Every gala was a new experience, and every festival an exciting revelation of her heritage. She saw items at some of the bazaars that reminded her of the few articles left for her by her mother: the doll and the dream-catcher.

She continued to long silently for her mother, for the opportunity to find her biological connection to all of this culture around her. But she knew that the time wasn't right. Isobel needed to stay focused on her career goal and set aside the search for her mother until another day.

Although Jason wasn't happy she spent so much time with the Fox family, he was thrilled with the news of Isobel's acceptance into law school. He was still vocal about his preference to have her closer to him and continued to prod her to give his parents a chance, but Isobel was adamant. She needed to focus on school and her career, and worry later about their opinion of her. Until she and Jason were ready to take the next step in their relationship, Isobel saw no reason to open her heart to his family.

The days seemed to drag as it approached the middle of August and the date for school to start. Isobel organized her condo for studying and made sure it was clean and tidy. She spent time shopping for clothes and supplies: a feminine yet professional briefcase, a new laptop and legal pads for taking notes in class. Then she wondered if she was going overboard. Maybe she just needed normal notebooks and simple clothes like jeans and T-shirts.

Finally, the first day of the school year arrived and with it came cooler temperatures indicating that fall wasn't far off. The crispness in the air was invigorating as Isobel walked toward the lecture hall and her introduction to law school. She smiled tentatively at others already seated in the theater-like hall and made her way toward the front. Throughout her years in school, she always sat in one of the first few rows so she could see and hear the instructor without distraction, and this would be no different.

Despite living off campus, Isobel found herself spending a lot of time on campus either with her study group or on her own doing independent study. She sometimes arrived hours before lectures started so she could be sure she finished up her required reading. At lunch, while eating, she read over her notes and wrote down questions to ask her classmates or the instructor. In the evenings, twice or three times a week, the study groups met to work on projects. Totally immersed in learning all she could about the practice of law,

Isobel felt at home in the law library, and quickly became a leader in the classroom. Her study group relied on her for stability and mediation whenever they reached an impasse in their discussion. She never felt more confident and sure that she was heading down the correct path for her life.

K.C. began to worry about Isobel's withdrawal from the family. The Fox home felt empty on weekends without her, but more than that, he worried that she was once again pulling away from God. Where she had been leaning more toward church attendance and dependence on the church family for encouragement, she now found that in her school and classmates. He asked Shyne and Tali to join him in praying for her on a regular basis.

Jason, too, noticed that Isobel didn't have as much time for him and seemed uncomfortable with his closing prayers when they did talk on the phone. She totally rejected any idea of meeting with his parents, which he had come to accept, although he didn't agree with her logic. He tried to appeal to her spiritually, but she only pulled away more, saying she needed to stay focused on her schooling and career. Law school became the driving force in Isobel's life and everything and everyone else was pushed into second place or, worse yet, discarded altogether.

Chapter 43

By the time Isobel's second year of law school began, the Fox family had stopped hoping she would return for weekend visits. They continued remembering her in their prayers, but Isobel hadn't called or contacted them in months. K.C. felt it the hardest. He missed the friendship and camaraderie they had developed when he was helping her prepare for law school.

Suddenly, out of the blue, K.C.'s phone at the office rang and when he answered, it was Isobel on the line. "Isobel, it's so nice to hear from you! It's been a long time; the girls miss your weekend visits." Isobel was silent for a brief moment, and then K.C. heard what sounded like a sniffle or a sob. "Are you ok?"

Hearing the concern in his voice shook any resolve Isobel had. She broke down for a few minutes and K.C. waited patiently for her to regain her composure. He couldn't recall a time when Isobel lost control; she always seemed able to maintain a resolute exterior despite whatever she was going through. When the weeping subsided and all that was left were sniffles, K.C. once again attempted to open the conversation. "Do you want to talk about it?"

On the other end of the line, K.C. imagined Isobel nodding her head, wiping her nose, and he heard her take a deep breath. "K.C., I've been ill. I thought it was just a flu bug, but it got worse really fast. And then, I ended up in the hospital because I began to lose the feeling in my feet and hands. I was really scared."

K.C. wanted to hang up the phone and go to her, to comfort her, but he waited to hear what more she would tell him.

"They called it Guillian-Barre Syndrome." (Isobel pronounced it like Geyan-buhray.) "I guess it's a virus that attacks your nervous system and kinda paralyzes you. It can be so bad that they put you on a ventilator to breath for you. At least it didn't get that bad for me. But I was so scared as the paralysis climbed up my body…"

K.C. interrupted her. "Isobel, what can I do for you? Are you alright now?"

"Yes, I'm back at home. I still have to do some Physical Therapy because I had to relearn walking and writing. My arms and legs just need to be retrained and strengthened. The problem is…" she paused and took another deep breath. "The problem is that I have missed too much school. I had to withdraw for this semester, but they say I can pick up again next semester, if I am well enough. It's just a matter of being set back that upsets me. I know I should be grateful that it wasn't worse, but it's hard to look at the bright side when I was so focused on finishing school with my class."

"Again, I'm going to ask, what can I do for you?"

Isobel seemed hesitant to ask for assistance. It was almost like they were starting over in their friendship because it had been so long since they had talked. Once again, K.C. wished he could just hang up and go to her condo to talk in person. "Isobel, can I come over? Would it be easier to talk in person?"

Isobel agreed to him coming to her condo later that day. She had her Physical Therapy appointment and an appointment with the neurologist that morning, so K.C. arranged to stop by after work. He had difficulty getting back into his research for the case he was working on because his mind kept drifting back to their conversation. Thankfully, his last appointment for the day cancelled at the last minute, and he was free to close the office early. He put away his documents and cleared his desk, readying it for the next day. Turning over the OPEN sign to CLOSED, K.C. locked the door and, with a deep breath and a prayer, headed for Isobel's condominium.

K.C. was shocked when Isobel greeted him at the door. She was thinner than he recalled and looked shorter than her 5'10" frame because she was leaning heavily on a walker. Under her eyes dark shadows contrasted with her sun-starved complexion; she looked as if she had spent the entire summer in the hospital. Isobel had obviously been ill, without notifying anyone, for longer than she had let on. His first inclination was to wrap his arms around her and help her to a chair, but he knew her independent spirit would reject any attempt on his part. And if he showed the slightest sympathy, he would certainly open himself to a severe rebuke from her.

It took restraint to not help Isobel to the couch when K.C. watched her labored efforts. They made their way into her living-room and he took a chair next to the recliner that Isobel sat in. K.C. looked at her breathing heavily from the struggle to walk such a short distance and she gazed at him with a helpless look and moisture in her eyes. She wasn't encouraging sympathy; she was just exhausted to the point of tears. It was quite evident that she had used every ounce of strength in her body.

When she was able to relax back into the chair, K.C. took her hand between his. "Isobel, I'm so sorry I didn't know you were ill. I would have visited..."

"See, that's just it." Isobel cut him off. " I didn't want anyone to see me like that...like this! I hate this! I was never helpless, not when I lost my mother, not when my father died, and, as you know, NOT when Aunt Betty died. I have always managed somehow! Now, look at me. Just look at me! I am like an old lady, with a walker, barely able to lift my feet, writing my name in shaky, illegible script. Oh, K.C., what am I going to do? I so want to finish law school, but I don't know how long my recovery will take. They say it's different for everyone with Gillian-Barre Syndrome. Some recover quickly while others, like me, go through a lot to get back to normal. AND, they tell me, it could relapse! Can you believe that?"

K.C. just nodded in acknowledgement. He had no answers for her; as a matter of fact, he had more questions, but didn't want to bother her with them. He would talk to doctors he knew and research the illness on his own. For now, all he could offer Isobel was his support. They talked for a long time with Isobel sharing how her schooling had progressed prior to getting sick, and what they had covered in lectures. K.C. brought her up to date on all the news from the Fox household.

Shyne and her beau, James CrowDog, had become engaged and were happily planning their marriage. Tali had settled in to life at home with Ma, caring for Skyla's children, as well as her own. They were both doing well in counseling and on their medication. Tali and Shyne loved attending the young women's meetings at church, and Ma had become involved in several aspects of outreach sponsored by their church family.

At the mention of church, K.C. noticed a grimace on Isobel's face. At first, he thought she might be in pain, but when she turned her face away as he continued talking, he thought he saw a longing in her eyes. "How are you doing spiritually, Isobel?" he asked softly.

Isobel looked him in the eyes and asked a pointed question, "How do you think I'm doing? Why should I serve a God that allows this kind of suffering?" She gestured toward her legs and K.C. nodded.

"I get that you don't understand why bad things happen to good people. You know that it isn't God that gives us these challenges, but He can use them to help us grow spiritually, *if* we let Him."

"You've got to be kidding! How can I know that? I've heard it time and again, 'God gives us tests to try us like gold tried by fire'." The bitterness in her voice cut K.C.'s heart like a steak knife cutting through butter. He prayed for the right words to say to help her understand the love of God.

He picked up the dusty Bible laying on the end table by the couch. Brushing off the dust, slowly and carefully, K.C. opened the Word to Isobel, using the very Bible her aunt had left for her. He showed her verse after verse, all underlined by Aunt Betty with blue ink as promises, showing the love of the Lord for His chosen. He shared the creation and fall, and how bad things came into the world as a result of sin of mankind, not because God wanted to hurt his people.

Isobel remembered reading all the same verses when she attended church school and college, and in the kitchen with Aunt Betty, and could even recite some from memory. She leaned in as K.C. shared more with her about the gift of salvation and how God makes *all* things work out for the best for those called according to His promise. K.C. explained how that referred to those who chose to believe in the gift of God's Son and who chose to ask Him into their hearts and lives.

They must have studied the Bible for two hours before K.C. noticed it was growing dark outside. He made a move as if to leave, and Isobel reached out to him, touching his arm to stop him. "Please, would you help me ask Jesus into my life?"

They were the sweetest words K.C. thought he would ever hear. His heart leapt with joy and right there, without wasting a minute, he knelt beside her chair. Together they prayed for Isobel's healing for her physical body. Then he helped her pray the sinner's prayer of repentance and acceptance of Jesus as her Saviour. When they finished praying, tears poured down both K.C.'s and Isobel's cheeks, but this time they were tears of joy, not frustration.

He gave Isobel a warm embrace as he prepared to leave. She returned his hug as best she could despite the weakness in her arms. Where there was once discomfort in closeness, they were now comfortable in expressing affection. Now, technically, brother and sister in Christ, Isobel and K.C. began a new phase in their relationship. Before he left, he invited Isobel to come to their home for the weekend. K.C. offered to drive her there Friday evening and bring her home on his way to work on Monday morning. That way she could attend church with them as well as catch up with Shyne and Tali.

Isobel was happy at the thought of being with the Fox family again. Her illness had left her once again alone and lonely. None of her classmates had time to visit her, or the inclination. They were too focused on their goal of completing law school. She recalled how she had cut everyone out of her social sphere in favor of those associates in law school. And now where were they? She felt abandoned and out of touch.

But rather than dwell on that, Isobel thought of her upcoming weekend with joy and excitement. It would be the first time she spent the night at the home of the Fox's. Although a little uncomfortable at the thought of such closeness to K.C., she quickly discounted any problems related to staying at his home. She knew he was a man of principle and he knew that her heart still leaned toward Jason.

She hadn't spoken with Jason in over a week. He knew that she had been in hospital and had even offered to come to Omaha to be with her during her recovery. But he was so close to completing his training, that she wouldn't allow him to suffer the same fate she had in postponing her education. Her heart still did somersaults at just the thought of him, but now that she had asked the Lord into her life, she felt even more hopeful for their future.

Then Isobel recalled the many times he pleaded his parent's case with her. She knew that she needed to make that right; she needed to see Mr. and Mrs. Armstrong and accept their apology. After all, they claimed the same birthright: salvation through Jesus. How could she not forgive when He had forgiven her for so much? Isobel decided to call Jason and make the arrangements as soon as possible.

Chapter 44

Isobel was excited at the thought of renewing her friendship with Shyne and Tali, especially now that she, like them, had turned her life over to Jesus. Before, her church attendance had been a nice social outlet, but it took on a whole new meaning now that she had truly accepted Jesus as her Saviour. She looked forward to sharing her testimony with the other young women at church. Her thoughts and conversation had changed to a new vernacular. Suddenly, all the talk she overheard at college and academy made sense; what once seemed like 'speaking in tongues' now became an understandable dialect.

Talitha and Shyne were equally thrilled to see Isobel again. At first, they were surprised to see her physical condition as K.C. helped her out of the car. Watching her struggle with the walker and seeing how thin she'd grown touched their tender hearts and both reached out to her in love. The three went into the house and shared precious moments of commiseration over her illness and current health condition, but rejoiced with her conversion experience.

Only Ma maintained her distance. She watched the young women and their interactions, but did not join in the conversation. She also seemed to be monitoring K.C.'s communication with Isobel. Although he only spoke briefly to let Isobel know where he was putting her overnight case, Ma leaned in to hear every word, as if to ensure they were not talking on too personal a level.

K.C. remained puzzled at Ma's continued resistance to Isobel. In her weakened condition, Isobel was no threat, and he had no intention of taking advantage of her frailty. For now, K.C. only saw Isobel as a sister in Christ. He was happy that she had finally accepted the gift of salvation, and would do nothing to cause her to stumble as a babe in Christ. But he didn't know what he could say to Ma to reassure her that he and Isobel were not involved romantically.

Isobel didn't notice the tension between Mrs. Fox and K.C. She settled into the Fox household as easily as if there was no time gap between her last visit and this. Talitha shyly invited Isobel into her room where K.C. had placed Isobel's personal items. Sharing a room with Talitha opened a new line of communication with the usually quieter of the two sisters. Tali sat on the bed and indicated to Isobel to sit near her. Isobel slowly moved her walker through the door and into the tiny room, but appreciated the tidiness of the quilt on the old bedstead and hand-braided oval rug beside the bed, offering a soft, warm spot against the colder wood floor.

"I love your room," Isobel opened the conversation with a complement, hoping to help Talitha relax. She could tell that Tali felt unsure how to act with a guest in her room.

Tali nodded her thanks and softly, almost in a whisper, said, "Thank you, Isobel. I never told you, but I love your name. It is pretty."

The returning complement took Isobel off guard. "Uh... thanks. I guess I don't think much about my name. But I like the names your family members have. They are so unusual! Do they have special meaning?"

"Some do; some are just nice sounding, like water over rocks or wind through the prairie grass."

Her speech was so poetic and touched Isobel immensely. More than ever, she wanted to learn more about her heritage.

"Did K.C. explain to you that I, too, have roots here on the Omaha reservation?"

Talitha nodded, "he said you don't know your mother." Her face reflected her sympathy; she couldn't imagine not knowing her heritage.

"That's true, but I hope to find her one day. I just need to get stronger before I can put out energy in that direction. It seems that every time I decide to try to find her, some crisis comes up to distract me from those efforts. But I know that I will search and find her one day soon."

"Do you know anything about her?" Talitha turned to Isobel, her eyes bright with thoughts of solving a mystery. "I'm pretty good at solving puzzles; I love mystery stories!"

Isobel told Tali about the few items she had found on the farm: the dream catcher, the doll and the ring. Tali nodded at the first two, understanding their significance within her culture. Tali told Isobel the legend of the dream catcher, although her own dream catcher had long since been discarded after falling apart. She also showed Isobel her own collection of dolls: Kachina dolls from the Hopi, corn husk dolls similar to the one Isobel owned, and a multitude of tiny dolls frequently found in dollar stores. One particular doll caught Isobel's eye. It was almost identical to her doll.

"My mother made that one for me when I was still in the womb." Talitha explained when she noticed Isobel's look of recognition. "Is it like yours?"

Isobel nodded. "Almost exactly! Why, if I didn't know better, I would say it *was* mine!"

They talked long into the night, with Isobel asking questions and Tali gladly telling her all she could to satisfy Isobel's need to learn about the Omaha people. Shyne had already taken care of all the children and, respecting the bonding time for Isobel and Talitha, went to her own room.

The next morning Ma was up early to fix a hearty breakfast for the children and Shyne helped her get them fed and cleaned up before the others rose from their beds. It took Isobel a bit longer to clean up and get dressed on her own, but she managed to join the rest of the Fox family in time for pancakes and scrambled eggs. She smiled at the sight of the family sitting around the table and the little ones playing together across the room.

After breakfast, when they normally had morning worship, Ma raised an eyebrow in surprise at Isobel's eagerness to participate in the Bible study. Isobel was like a sponge, trying to soak up every ounce of knowledge about her newly found Savior. Despite all the years of Bible classes in high school and college, it all seemed new to her. Back then, she hadn't truly listened. She wasn't interested, at that time, in applying Biblical principles to her life, but now it was different. Isobel yearned to make up for all the lost years of not understanding the Gospel. She had even brought Aunt Betty's Bible with her for the weekend. Dog-eared and marked up, it spoke of the love her aunt had for Jesus and His love letter to the earth.

It seemed the weekend would follow the typical pattern of previous weekends. But when a call from the prison interrupted their peace, the whole family was thrown into action and prayer. Skyla had been attacked in the prison and was in the infirmary in serious condition. K.C. wanted to go to her immediately, but he worried about leaving Isobel.

"Don't worry about me," she said. "I will be fine here with Tali and Shyne…"

No one even wondered whether Ma would go with K.C.; it was assumed she would, and she was already gathering her things to head out the door. She kissed the little ones, patting Skyla's two children gently on their cheeks as well. K.C., too, took little time to get out to the car and they headed off to the prison to try to see Skyla.

Once they left, Isobel, Shyne and Tali gathered the little children in a circle, and they all began to pray for Skyla. Brya and CeCe looked worried when they heard their mother's name in the prayer, but they joined their little voices in the prayer, asking Jesus to take care of Mommy. They prayed for some time, then allowed the children to return to their play, while Shyne, Tali and Isobel sat at the table and quietly discussed Sky's situation. They waited for word from K.C. to tell them how serious it really was, but the waiting was as exhausting as if they had been working hard. Worry took its toll, so they prayed again and laid it at Jesus feet, asking for peace to replace the fear of the unknown.

K.C. and Ma were unprepared for what they found when they reached the prison infirmary. Skyla was pale, bruised about the face with scratches and cuts on every visible area of skin. Her right arm lay in a white, plaster cast and a blood-stained gauze bandage wrapped around her head like a halo. IV fluids flowed through a needle taped to her left hand from the bag hanging at the head of her bed. Skyla didn't stir when they got to her bedside and spoke her name. Her lips, cracked and caked with crusts of blood, moved as if she were attempting to speak, but her eyes remained still and closed.

"She hears our voices," the nurse spoke in the quiet of the room. "She is aware that we are here; she just isn't ready to wake enough to look around."

K.C. nodded; Ma hung her head, her lips moving, and K.C. realized that she was praying for her oldest daughter. He looked around and saw only one other inmate in the infirmary and he asked the nurse if they were equipped for Skyla's type of injuries.

"Actually, if she doesn't awaken soon, Dr. Johnson is considering a transfer to the local hospital for further tests. He doesn't want to worry you unnecessarily, but she may have suffered a brain injury. Depending on how she comes out of it, she may need more specialized care than we have here." The nurse excused herself, but sat at a nearby desk to watch their interactions. It was, after all, a prison, and Skyla was an inmate.

K.C. pulled up a chair for Ma, and sat on a nearby stool on wheels like doctors have in their exam rooms. The two sat together, quietly in their individual thoughts, watching for any sign that Skyla would rouse from her beating-induced slumber. After an hour and a half, K.C. needed to stretch his legs, so he asked the nurse where they were allowed to go, and she directed him to a day-room just outside the ward.

He mused about what life within the correctional facility must be like for a free-spirited young lady like his sister. It wasn't a pleasant thought. K.C. shook his head and walked back to the nurse's desk to check in, but she wasn't there. He saw a commotion near Skyla's bed; the nurse was talking excitedly to Ma who had tears streaming down her cheeks. His heart sunk with the fear that Skyla had taken a turn for the worst, but then he saw Skyla's face, smiling up at them.

"Son!" Ma cried out to him as he approached. "It's a miracle! Our girl has awakened and is going to be just fine!" She reached out to give him an embrace, and he warmly returned the hug. Then he turned to his sister and saw happiness in her eyes.

"Skyla, you look different..." his voice made the statement sound like more of a question.

Her face was flushed, and her eyes shone with delight. "I accepted Jesus!" Just the one sentence gave voice to the joy he could see in her eyes. "Praise God!" Ma exclaimed. "I've been praying for this day!"

They visited with Skyla while the nurse called Dr. Johnson to report on her improvement. Visiting hours, although extended for the infirmary, were still limited because it was a prison setting, so they had to leave by five that evening. After hearing the story behind her conversion experience, and the report of the attack that had put her in this condition, K.C. decided that Ma and Sky needed time alone to reconnect. He allowed Ma to visit with Sky while he went to call home with a progress report. He hoped that Isobel would answer the phone, although he knew it would be either Shyne or Tali.

It was mid-afternoon before K.C. called. "She is going to be alright," he said quietly when speaking to Tali. "She was jumped in the laundry, evidently because she wouldn't claim loyalty to a gang. It seems that our Skyla turned her life over to Jesus, and decided to stand up for her beliefs. There were some that didn't like her choice and wanted to force her to choose sides...to make an alliance with one gang."

Reassured by his call, the young women prayed together once again, this time to thank the Lord for answered prayers. Although subdued without Ma and K.C., the children and women managed to get through the day in relative calm. K.C. and Ma arrived home late that evening, just as they were readying to turn in for the night. K.C. asked if they could talk in the morning; he was tired from the drive and the emotions of the day, and just needed to sleep. Ma was also worn out and just wanted to go to bed, so they all said 'good-night' and went to their rooms.

The next morning, while Shyne helped the children prepare for church, K.C. told Tali and Isobel what he and Ma learned about Skyla's time in prison. Evidently, she was involved in a prison ministry, helping lead others to Christ, and had come to grips with the fact that her lawyers had exhausted appeals for her case.

She would remain in prison, but vowed to serve God while she served her time. Ma cried tears of joy when Skyla told her, and K.C. had a hard time holding back his own tears. It was a true miracle, but it also showed that God keeps His promises. He said, "All things work together for good…" and He had truly made good come out of her incarceration.

By the time K.C. took Isobel home on the Monday morning, the weekend had become a turning point in her life. The time she and Tali spent discussing the Omaha heritage and history helped her claim 'the heritage of those that fear (God's) name' and as a member of more than an earthly people; she was adopted into the family of God, and never had she felt more at home.

Chapter 45

Isobel called Jason the Monday afternoon, when she was certain he would be back from classes and study groups. He was overjoyed to hear the news of her conversion. When she talked about being 'totally forgiven' and the need to forgive his parents, he was even more thrilled. To hear that she was willing to meet with his parents was one more step toward convincing her to marry him.

They talked long into the evening until Isobel said she was tired. Knowing that fatigue could worsen her symptoms and weaken her recovery, he instructed her to get off the phone and get to bed, as if she were a child. She reminded him that she had been taking care of herself throughout the ordeal, but wasn't unkind in her response. She laughed at his concern, enjoying hearing the love in his voice.

Promising to talk again soon, they closed their call with prayer, but this time it was a shared event, rather than the one-sided petition from Jason. Isobel spoke from her heart, asking the Lord to help her forgive those who had hurt her in the past, and Jason knew she meant his parents. But he heard no anger or animosity, only an earnest, sincere request for assistance.

Several days later, when Jason spoke with his parents, they were overjoyed at the prospect of finally meeting with Isobel. For them, it was one more step toward reconciliation.

Catherine Armstrong booked a flight to Omaha at the next opportunity they had for travel. Unfortunately, they couldn't get a flight for nearly a month, so it would be a while before they could meet with Isobel. In the meantime, Catherine tried to decide what the best way to show contrition would be. She felt mortified when she recalled how small-minded and bigoted she was back then. But now, with God's help, she would find forgiveness and possibly love in Isobel's heart.

After Jason told her his parent's travel dates, Isobel also had time to consider how unforgiving she had been. She had held onto her grudge like a dog holding onto a bone, unwilling to give even a little from her end. She needed to ask forgiveness of the elder Armstrongs, too. It shouldn't have taken all this time for her to come to her senses. *But then, without true conversion, it is hard to see beyond one's selfish feelings and motives*, she thought.

Unfortunately, because of school responsibilities. Jason was unable to join his parents for their visit to Isobel's. At one time, this might have caused Isobel anxiety and concern. She used to be so insecure, so self-conscious. But now, through the grace of God, she was assured that their second encounter would go much better than the first.

Isobel's rehabilitation slowed during the weeks prior to the Armstrongs' visit. Whether the natural course of the illness, or a side effect of her nervousness and anxiety, it was hard to say, but for whatever reason, she found herself still walking with a walker on the day they were scheduled to come. Sad that she could not meet them at the airport, she called K.C. and asked him to greet them on her behalf and bring them to her condominium. He agreed without hesitation. Isobel had told him of her first meeting several years earlier, and he understood that both she and the Armstrongs were reaching out in faith and forgiveness.

When he stood at the airport holding his homemade sign with ARMSTRONG in big letters, he wondered if they would be taken back seeing a Native American man waiting for them. He didn't know if Isobel had prepared the way for him, or if this would be like a blind date...a total surprise. He didn't have to wait long for his answer.

Mr. Armstrong saw him first as they came down the corridor from their arrival gate, and he touched the elbow of his wife to draw her attention to K.C. Then he saw them both smile and wave, and with relief, he walked toward them with outstretched hand. James Armstrong would have none of the hand-shake offered. Instead he took K.C. into a strong embrace, as if he was a long lost son.

"You must be Isobel's young man, K.C., whom we heard so much about!" His booming voice echoed in K.C.'s ear, and then he pulled back and thumped K.C. on the back. "Yep, you are as we imagined!" He motioned to Catherine who immediately stepped in and kissed K.C. on the cheek, leaving red lipstick behind.

"Oh, I'm sorry…" she pulled out a handkerchief and wiped the smudge off his face. "I am so happy to meet you, K.C." She gave him a motherly hug and patted the redness left on his cheek from her rubbing it.

K.C. was almost speechless at the warmth of their greeting. Then he remembered his mission. "Isobel is not doing as well as hoped, so she asked me to bring you to her home. She is hoping you have not made other arrangements for hotel…" His question hung in the air for only a second before Mrs. Armstrong replied.

"Well, we wondered whether to make reservations, but decided to 'play it by ear' as they say." She giggled at what she thought was a cute little quip. "I look forward to talking with Isobel, and then we will see what we shall do. Isn't that right, James?"

Mr. Armstrong straightened his tie and cleared his throat. "Um… yes, dear, whatever you decide." He smiled at K.C. and winked. "You gotta let the little wife *think* she is in charge occasionally." And he chuckled at his own witticism.

They made their way to K.C.'s car, and he was surprised there were no negative comments about the age or model of his ride. He had yet to upgrade, although his job was paying fairly well. He could see little point in buying another car when the current one ran just fine. He loaded their luggage into the trunk and ensured they were both settled before he pulled out and headed toward Isobel's place.

Isobel was on pins and needles knowing the plane had landed and that the Armstrong's were on their way. She didn't doubt their sincerity of purpose, but it was hard to rid her mind of the images of their first meeting. At times the pain felt as fresh as yesterday, and she prayed for the strength to get past her own feelings and find forgiveness in her heart. She also hoped they would forgive her stubbornness in resisting their prior attempts to put to rights the behaviors of the past.

Then Isobel heard the elevator doors ding, and she knew they had arrived. Laughter rang out as they exited the elevator, but she could not tell who was laughing, or at what. She slowly made her way to the door and opened it widely to allow them to enter past her walker. But as they approached, Catherine Armstrong handed her purse and carry-on to James and rushed to Isobel. Tears flowed down her cheeks as she embraced Isobel tightly. She pulled back to look into Isobel's eyes and saw weariness mixed with relief and joy.

"Oh, my dear. Look at you… you've been through so much, you should be sitting down… come, let me help you to a chair." As was her custom, Catherine took charge and allowed no room for argument, so Isobel did as she was told. She was actually relieved to sit down because her legs shook from both effort and emotion.

K.C. and James Armstrong brought in the various pieces of luggage and stood them by the door, but Isobel protested. "Please, K.C., would you take their luggage into my guest room?" Both men did as requested, acknowledging once again, that the women needed to *feel* that they were in charge. She heard them laughing over the shared joke, and smiled wryly thinking how different this meeting was.

Isobel and Catherine sat quietly, unsure as to how to begin their conversation, but before long they were chatting like old friends. Isobel offered her apology for delaying this reunion, and Catherine insisted that they fully understood her hesitance. They talked and cried over past hurts and shame, and by the time the men returned to the living-room, they were on to a neutral subject…Jason.

The men joined them, although K.C. made it clear that he could not stay. He had the long drive home, since it was Friday afternoon, and his family would worry if he was too late. Isobel sent her love to the Fox family as he left, and he assured her that they would miss her presence for the weekend. They had grown accustomed to the weekly visits of their new 'sister'.

Mr. Armstrong interrupted the women and asked for the chance to apologize directly to Isobel. After volleying back and forth over who should feel sorry for what, Isobel and James settled their differences and hugged like father and daughter. Isobel held the embrace for a few seconds, recalling what it was like to have a father hold her close. They separated with tear-stained faces but happy that they could resolve the ache left from their history and move on toward a future as friends and family in Christ.

They continued talking for hours, sharing their experiences from the last several years, including how each came to accept the Lord as their Saviour. Finally, as the evening grew late, they made ready to turn in for the night. Both were pleased to find everything at their disposal in the guest bathroom; Isobel had taken great pains to prepare a spa-like area where they could relax and feel at ease.

The three days passed quickly, and the Armstrongs left with a promise of seeing Isobel again before long, the next time with Jason. No longer did his parents hold onto the class conscious attitudes they once guarded. They knew of her heritage, and totally accepted her. They even offered to help her find her biological mother, but she declined their assistance. That would be a task she would have to undertake on her own.

Chapter 46

James and Catherine Armstrong flew back to Boston early Monday morning, and Jason wasted no time. He called Isobel during his lunch break to see how their visit went.

"Hey, how was it… visiting with the folks, I mean?"

"Jason, I am so pleased. We really connected!"

Jason rejoiced in his heart when he heard the happiness in her voice. "I'm glad it went well." He restrained himself from taking anything for granted about their relationship, though.

Their conversation was brief because he needed to get to the Grand Rounds presentation scheduled for right after lunch. Jason was enjoying medical school more than he had expected. Now in his fourth year of medical school, he was looking into possible residencies. James Armstrong no longer urged him to go into a Surgery residency. Now, instead, he offered to use his connections to help Jason find a good Family Practice residency. Jason declined his father's offer, despite the fact that it would have made his job easier. He wanted to accomplish his goals based on his own merits, with only God's help.

He listened to Isobel talk of her dreams deferred by her illness, and wondered if she felt the same. She sounded content with the path God had her on. As a matter of fact, Isobel seemed more accepting of God's will in her life, than he was, despite Jason's acceptance of the Saviour many years before. As that initial 'first love' effect of conversion wore off, Jason had lapsed into a comfortable Christianity: not pushing religion at others and not being too dogmatic in his own faith. Jason realized that he needed to reconnect with the Lord; he missed the close relationship he once had where he could feel God guiding his decisions. He even began wondering if the choices he had made regarding his medical practice where truly from the Lord or from his rebellious nature, resisting his father's desires.

Jason wanted to talk to Isobel about his concerns. She always knew how to read his motives; perhaps she could help him reevaluate his intentions. They once had such altruistic plans, and now Jason needed to figure out if he would still work for underserved communities, or return to his father's area of practice to establish his own. Maybe he should consider Omaha and the reservation. If there were opportunities for residency in that area, he could be closer to Isobel and have a chance at renewing their relationship and commitment. Isobel once told him that medical services were somewhat limited for Native Americans. That could be a way of helping her, too. Then he wondered what help he could be.

Would she resist offers to help her when she returned to law school? *She would probably let K.C. help her,* he thought, then chastised himself for his jealous streak. Anyway, it seemed her return to school would be delayed longer than she thought. Isobel said she would be back in school for the spring semester, but acknowledged that she needed more time for rehabilitation and physical therapy. To Jason, it looked as though she would have to wait until the fall to reenter school, and would graduate a year behind her class.

Isobel persisted with her rehabilitation, but true to Jason's prediction, she was unable to return to law school for the spring semester. Disappointed, but determined, Isobel threw herself into the physical therapy, and supplemented it with extra time in the gym. Gradually, as her strength in both her arms and legs returned, she began to feel like herself again. She volunteered one day a week at the Legal Aid Office and saw K.C. even more often, socially.

Isobel was well enough to travel to Boston to attend Jason's graduation from medical school. She no longer walked with a walker, although she moved more timidly than before her illness. James and Catherine Armstrong met her at the airport, but this time their encounter was warm and loving…totally the opposite of the first time she arrived in Boston more than four years earlier. They ushered her to their waiting limousine that carried them to a five-star hotel near Harvard School of Medicine. The weekend was full of planned activities, but they understood that Isobel tired easily and would need rest after her flight from Omaha.

She dozed for an hour or so before dinner, then Isobel changed into a suitable and stylish dress, although she knew Catherine wouldn't mind her dressing casually. She wanted to look nice so she wouldn't embarrass Jason around his friends and instructors. Despite her time in law school, and her increased self-assurance, she still realized the value in making a good first impression. For both she and Jason, their careers would be boosted by opportunities to network with others within their chosen professions.

"Isobel," Jason took her hands and stepped back to look at her, "you look lovely!" She could see the love in his eyes, just as when they were engaged. She yearned for those early years of innocence when all they talked about were their plans for the future.

Isobel blushed at his admiration. "You clean up pretty good yourself," she laughed nervously. She never felt ill at ease with Jason before, so what had changed?

Mrs. Armstrong broke the tension by suggesting they take their seats for dinner. The dining room was filled with other students and parents, but the Armstrong's had a reservation, and were seated immediately. Like any good gentleman, James Armstrong held the chair for Catherine and Jason followed suit, helping Isobel get situated in her chair. Isobel took her time unfolding the napkin and placing it in her lap. Her thoughts were muddled, and feigning concentration on such a simple task gave her time to think. K.C. came to mind as she looked at the lovely crystal and china setting on the table, flanked by actual silverware, not the cheap kind of flatware generally used in restaurants.

Wow! How self-indulgent we are, even when claiming to follow our 'Servant King'! Isobel thought of the irony. *I wonder if Jason still thinks of caring for the impoverished… or has he moved on to more concrete career plans?* Isobel glanced at him out of the corner of her eye. He carried on talking with his parents, occasionally looking in her direction, but not forcing her participation in the conversation. As usual, they talked about everything and anything… current affairs, how political campaigns affected the Christian community, and how they should respond as Christian doctors, now that Jason would have M.D. behind his name.

Once again, K.C.'s face was in Isobel's thoughts. His honest, altruistic way of helping others on the reservation and the volunteer time he put in at the Legal Aid office spoke to the strength of his character. Since she had been spending more time with him, she felt she knew him better than she did Jason. Despite their frequent phone calls, she had had little interaction with Jason for the last four years, except the rare visit. She wondered if love could survive such long separations as she and Jason had had.

"Don't you think so, Isobel?" She was pulled from her daydream with the question from Mrs. Armstrong. She shook her head to clear it, and looked at Catherine, "I'm so sorry. I was off somewhere in my thoughts."

"We could tell, my dear. But I thought you might like to weigh in on such an important decision as the one Jason is about to make."

"I'm sorry. I totally missed everything." She turned to Jason, "What decision were you discussing?"

"I was telling my parents of the two offers I have for residency. One is here in Massachusetts; the other is in Omaha." He waited for her reaction. When she didn't immediately respond, but kept her eyes downcast, he worried he was forcing their relationship.

"What do you think, Izzie? My parents think the one here in my home state would better prepare me for Family Medicine, but I think Omaha would be better for working with low income communities. Although Boston has its share of inner city poverty, they do have access to emergency rooms, etc. But out there, on the reservation, like you told me, the care is sporadic and limited. So Omaha might be the better choice for me, don't you think?"

Isobel sat quietly contemplating the two options. If she agreed with Jason, he might get the wrong message and think she was ready to recommit to their engagement. And if she agreed with his parents, *would* that choice truly prepare him for his future in helping the impoverished? She did not want to be responsible for his choice, so she finally looked up and met each pair of eyes gazing at her.

"I don't think my opinion is important, Jason. I think you need to follow your heart and where God is leading you. Don't let anyone sway you from your path of faith; pray about it and I will keep you in my prayers, too."

His parents both nodded in appreciation that Isobel had not taken the easy route and chosen for Jason. They respected her all the more for her wisdom and faith. Jason, on the other hand, had hoped for a more concrete response from Isobel. He had hoped to cap off his graduation weekend with a renewal of their engagement, but now that did not seem possible.

Jason's graduation went off smoothly, and the weekend sped past. Too soon it was time to say good-bye to Isobel (and his parents) and see them drive off to take Isobel to the airport. He had decided on accepting the residency in Omaha. The Omaha program would meet both needs: preparing him for rural practice with Native Americans, and take him closer to Isobel to explore their relationship possibilities. Despite their qualms, Mr. and Mrs. Armstrong both understood and supported him in his choice.

Isobel, on the other hand, left Boston with more doubts than answers. She saw Jason relying on his own mind to make important decisions, rather than taking the time to pray about them. She wondered at his spiritual life and commitment and whether he was truly following the Lord, or following a tradition of practicing Christianity.

Chapter 47

Isobel returned to Omaha with a renewed desire to search for her biological links to the Omaha people. Seeing Jason with his parents gave her a sense of nostalgia for what might have been had her father not died. Since that could not be undone, however, she needed to focus on the possibility of finding family through her biological mother.

She thought of the closeness of K.C.'s family, and the special doll that Tali had, so similar to her own. Tali treasured the doll as a symbol of the love her mother had for her *even* while she was still in the womb and she wondered if that was the lesson she was meant to learn from her own doll. Tali told her the legend of the dream catcher and, although Isobel thought it was a sweet gesture for her mother to have left that for her, it had less sentimental attachment than did the doll.

She needed to find her mother to answer the question, since her father was no longer able to do so. So many unanswered questions about her father and mother's relationship and plans haunted her mind. Where was she to start her search? She needed to talk to K.C.

"K.C.? It's Isobel. I'm back in Omaha and was wondering if we could meet for coffee."

Of course, K.C. recognized her voice, although he was surprised to hear from her. He would have been less surprised to hear that she was staying in Boston and getting married. He fully expected Jason Armstrong to convince her to become Mrs. Jason Armstrong before he went off to do his residency, wherever that would be.

"Sure! Do you want to meet at our usual place? Is this afternoon alright for you?"

Isobel agreed to join K.C. at the coffee shop around the corner from Legal Aid at two o'clock. She wanted to ask his assistance and suggestions on how to find someone on the reservation. Or, if they no longer lived on the rez, how she could locate them elsewhere? She wondered if there were a database somewhere that kept track of Native Americans living off the designated homelands provided by government treaties. This was all so new to her that she wasn't sure what controls were still in place and how much freedom was afforded American Indians. From the perspective of white America, Isobel knew she had preconceptions that were way off base. From just the short time of knowing the Fox family and attending church on the reservation, Isobel had a different understanding of the culture and traditions of the Omaha, at least.

K.C. arrived at the coffee shop earlier than they agreed on. He was anxious to hear of her time in Boston, to hear if she and Jason were renewing their commitment or not. He was also curious as to what she needed to talk to him about, although he had a clue that it might be related to her need to find her mother. Over the couple of years he had known Isobel, she had made several references to searching 'when the time was right'. Since she had a break until she could return to school, he figured she might think this was the right time.

When he saw her pass the window heading for the entrance, his heart skipped a beat. They had not spoken of the possibility of any relationship, ever since she made it clear that Jason had control of her heart, but she looked so elegant and regal as she walked into the shop, gazed around and finally caught his eye. Isobel smiled at him and made her way to 'their' table, the table they occupied each time they shared a coffee or pastry.

K.C. stood to greet her and held her chair as she sat down. She moved much better than even a month before, and he was thrilled to see the improvement. She seemed nearly back to her original state of health and vitality. K.C. wanted to kiss her cheek, but resisted the impulse.

"So, did you want to make small talk first, or discuss the real reason for this meeting?" he asked with a smile to soften the question.

Isobel grinned. She understood K.C. much better than when they first met, and appreciated his down to business approach. However, this time she wanted to visit before she opened up the subject of her mother. Somehow, just jumping into questions about how to search for her seemed too abrupt. She did not want K.C. to think she took their friendship for granted. She was also concerned that he might resent being used to find someone within his tribe. *Am I assuming too much?* Isobel wondered.

Isobel started the conversation asking about the family...how Tali and her children were doing, Shyne and Taddy, and Sky's two little ones. She hesitated to ask about his mother because, like K.C., she sensed Mrs. Fox's resistance to her. Then she asked anyway. After all, she cared about Mrs. Fox as a sister in Christ, if nothing else. And there was the fact that she was the mother of Isobel's best friends: Shyne and Tali *and K.C.*, she thought shyly.

K.C. shared what little news there was from the home front, and then he asked about her trip to Boston. Despite wanting only the best for Isobel, his heart sunk a bit as he watched her face light up talking about the time spent with the Armstrong family. Now that they accepted her without conditions, it seemed her life was back on the path she originally planned. She spoke of Jason in glowing terms, but was quick to clarify that they still were not engaged. "We really need time to rebuild what was lost..." Isobel tried to explain. "That is hard to do with school and distance separating us."

K.C. didn't know if to rejoice that they had those barriers or express support that they would overcome them. In the end, he realized that he had to allow Isobel to choose her way, so he told her what he thought she wanted to hear. "You guys will come through stronger in the end," he said, noncommittally.

Finally, Isobel got down to the real reason behind their meeting. "K.C., you know how I want to find my biological mother, right?" He nodded.

"Well, I was wondering if you could help me... or at least give me some ideas how to start. I mean, I've been going to church on the rez and spending time with your family, but I'm still no closer to breaking through the natural reserve that seems to be directed at outsiders. How do I get the others, not your family but the others in the tribe, to understand that I come from the Omaha Nation, too?"

"Perhaps, once we are able to find your link to our community, it will be easier for them to see you as a tribal member." K.C. responded.

Isobel heard him say 'we' and immediately her heart rejoiced. She realized that K.C. had already committed to helping her. She squealed a bit, then stifled the noise with her hand over her mouth. "Sorry! I just realized that you were going to help me!"

"Of course! How could I not help you? What would make you think that I wouldn't?" he asked. "Ever since you first mentioned it, I've just been waiting until you were ready to start."

They exchanged smiles and K.C. touched her hand. "Now, as for where to start... Just what information do you actually have that might help us?"

Isobel told him about the birth certificate with the strange name on it, the letter from her father, and the baby book with messages in it from her mother, as well as the packet with the doll and dream catcher, but held back on telling him about the man's ring. Somehow, that ring seemed to apply more to her father than her biological mother. K.C. asked if he could take a look at the items, but Isobel hadn't brought them along. The package and papers, letter lay on her table back in the condo.

"Would you like to stop by my place and take a look at them?" she asked hesitantly.

K.C. looked at his watch. It was already nearly 4:30 so he wouldn't be going back to work or heading to the Legal Aid Office. "Sure. Did you drive or walk?" When she indicated that she had walked as part of her physical therapy, he asked if she would want a ride home.

"I'd love a ride. I was worn out when I got here; I just didn't want to let on to you how tiring the walk had been. I'd really appreciate a ride home."

They cleared their table and headed for K.C.'s car parked just around the corner. Driving the short distance in companionable silence seemed so right to K.C. He always looked forward to the weekend for just that reason and missed their drive together last weekend with her being out of town. Once they got to her condo building, he pulled into the parking garage and parked as close to the elevator entrance as possible. Noticing his efforts, Isobel appreciated his consideration.

Helping her out of the car and gently guarding her steps by his light touch on her elbow, K.C. felt both protective and annoyed. His protectiveness related to her fragility, however minor, was understandable. What he didn't understand was his annoyance. Was it because she continued loving Jason despite the pain that relationship had caused her? Or was it the fact that Jason, if he truly loved her, should be protective and watchful rather than K.C.? K.C. struggled to understand his own feelings.

Together they made their way to her condo and Isobel invited K.C. to get comfortable while she went for the items she wanted to show to him. He sat down and looked around, admiring the artistic hand used in decorating her condo. He took in the fact that both her art and the less expensive bric-a-brac reflected many cultures. Obviously, she showed items with Asian/Japanese influence since she had been raised believing that was her heritage. She also had traditional American items reflecting her immigrant ancestry on her father's side. What pleased K.C. the most was seeing Native American influences: in her color choices, in the statuary by renowned artists, Michael Ricker and Christopher Parnell, and in gentle touches, such as the Morning Star quilt laying loosely on the back of the sofa and the painted buffalo hide hanging prominently in the wall.

Isobel came out of her room with a puzzled look on her face. "I know it's been a long time since I looked at the baby book and birth certificate, but somehow I misplaced them. I can't imagine how, though, because I've guarded them so carefully since finding them at Aunt Betty's place…?" She seemed to be questioning her own mind, whether she was thinking clearly or not.

"You know what? They will show up just when you aren't looking for them. Don't worry! I can always look at those later… let me see what you do have." He reached for the yellowed envelope she held close to her chest as if protecting it from her absentmindedness.

She loosened her death grip on the package and handed it to K.C. with a wry smile on her face. "Probably won't tell you much…" she said as he took it from her hand.

Removing the dream catcher and doll from the envelope, he immediately recognized them as authentic Native American, most likely Plain Indian, items, not knock-off, tourist souvenirs. He handled them respectfully, acknowledging their legitimacy and cultural significance. Turning first one, and then the other over and inspecting every aspect, he looked for anything that might identify the creator, but didn't until he looked under the leather garments on the tiny doll. Embroidered into an undergarment were two initials: D and B in capital letters. He raised his eyebrows as he showed them to Isobel. "Now this is *not* typically done, by the Omaha anyway. What's going through your mind?" He saw her react when she saw the initials.

"Those are the same initials as my mother on my birth certificate." She paused and looked frustrated. "I wish I could remember where I put that thing! I can't remember the name on it… it was kinda strange, like French or something. Oh! My memory has been terrible ever since my illness. The doctors say it will come back, just like my strength and balance, but I get so annoyed at myself."

K.C. tried to reassure her, but the mystery of the two letters had him puzzled. He looked forward to seeing the baby book and her birth certificate to find more concrete clues to her mother's identity. Two letters could apply to any female on the reservation with those initials. He needed a better starting point. He asked Isobel what she knew about her mother, and she shared what little she had: that she was young and from 'the rez', that she had a little boy before Isobel, and that she lived for a while in Kansas City, where she met Isobel's father.

K.C. assumed her mother's age to be somewhere between forty and fifty. She was already a mother when she met Randolph Kirk, but on the rez that could mean anything from sixteen up. However, she probably wouldn't have left the reservation for the big city unless she was eighteen or older. And since Isobel was nearly twenty-seven, that would make her mother at least forty-five years old at this time. He could start with asking around, but the subjects of prior children and children left off the reservation were not openly discussed. He needed a name to work with, and until Isobel could find the documents, he was stalled.

Suddenly Isobel recalled where she had placed the book and certificate, and excused herself to get them from the storage area in the guest room. She brought them to K.C. and saw a strange look pass over his countenance when he looked at the name on the birth certificate. And when he read some of the writing in the baby book, his eyes welled with tears. Isobel was amazed as his tenderness regarding her heritage.

"May I hold onto these items for a while? I promise to care for them and not misplace or abuse them while they are in my care." His plea and promise both touched Isobel as she agreed to let him have possession of her treasures. He left her with a promise to help her locate her mother, and Isobel knew he would do all in his power to keep that promise.

Chapter 49

K.C. held onto the cherished items well into the New Year. He took time to think through his suspicions before testing them. He even wondered at the wisdom of confronting the past. Was it worth the pain it could cause? Or would it resolve old sorrows and relieve the hurt? Such a decision could not be made lightly, and despite Isobel's frequent inquiries as to his progress, he determined in his mind that he would take it slowly.

As Isobel neared the end of her schooling, she thought less about the mystery of her heritage, and more about her future. Although Jason continued to urge her to commit to their relationship, she felt the need to assert herself professionally before getting married. She felt led by the Lord to find a way to reach the Native Americans, similar to what called K.C. into the profession.

She was pleased to see Jason's devotion to helping the indigenous in Omaha and in the surrounding region. He traveled to the Rosebud Indian Reservation in South Dakota for part of his training, and talked openly with her about how he hurt for the problems he saw among the Lakota. Jason was even more understanding of her search for her mother. He knew she felt adrift without family to support her and could not imagine how he might feel in the same position.

As Mother's Day approached, K.C. decided to act on his suspicions. For Isobel, he wanted her to meet her mother either before or on that momentous day. And for her mother, he hoped the meeting would be cathartic, helping her heal a hole in her heart left by an absent child in the home. First, he needed to have a serious discussion with his mother, so he invited her for an outing to shop in Omaha, as his gift for Mother's Day.

He picked her up early on the Saturday morning. "Ma, let me help you," he said as he opened the car door for her. He felt protective of the women in his home.

She waved him off. "Do I look disabled to you, my son?" she asked in a joking fashion. "I am quite able to get into a car by myself." But she allowed him to close the door once she had taken her feet into the car.

As they drove toward Omaha, he made small talk for part of the way, until Ma interrupted him. "I can tell you have something on your mind, Kwsind. What is it? You have been thoughtful and distant for a couple of months. As a matter of fact, I do believe you have been quieter than usual since this New Year started."

He nodded, confirming her observations. But he was uncertain as to how to open the subject with her. Then he decided he needed to confront it head-on.

"Ma, Mrs. Charbanneau has always called you DeeDee, hasn't she?"

Ma nodded and looked at him with a question in her eyes, but said nothing.

"You told me once that your real name was something different..."

"Delfina, yes that was my given name."

"Do you know anyone with a name similar to yours?" he asked quietly.

"No, I have never heard my name given to another. My mother said it was a name of a flower, delphinium, and she just shortened it to Delfina. Why do you ask about my name? What has you so worried?" Mrs. Fox was becoming more concerned with his line of questioning. It made no sense to her that her son should wonder about her true name.

"Ma, I have another question. I know that Fox is not my correct surname; that it was given me by your second husband. What was my father's real last name?"

His mother hesitated. She had never spoken of her first husband. She was married at such a young age, and he had abused her when he was drunk. He died young, because of the alcohol, of kidney failure, and she hadn't spoken of him in years. When her second husband accepted K.C. as a son, and provided well for them until he left unexpectedly, she had put the past behind her, determined to not raise that specter from the graveyard of her memory.

"Son, I do not wish to speak of him. He has been gone these many years, and you have made a new, strong name for yourself. I choose to not give you that information." Her face set in a stubborn profile showed K.C. that this discussion would be harder than he anticipated. To force the issue he decided to get right to the point.

"Ma, was his name Beaupre?" He could tell by his mother's reaction that he touched a nerve. When she didn't speak, he asked again, "It was Beaupre, wasn't it?"

Ma nodded as if ashamed to admit she had once married such a cruel man. She wondered how her son had discovered this facet from her past. She had taken great pains to destroy any papers carrying his name, and when her second husband adopted K.C., they took Beaupre off his birth certificate, as was the custom of the day. In that way, K.C. would never know the truth, or so she thought until now.

"I won't ask why you kept this from me, Ma. I know you had your reasons, but now I must ask an even harder question. It gives me no pleasure to ask you this, and I know it may open a painful memory for you, but I have to ask… Did you give birth to another daughter between me and Skyla?" Ma nodded again. "And was the Isobel of who you spoke so long ago, the one that died… was that the name of the child, the girl you gave birth to?" the question nearly stuck in K.C.'s throat.

By this time, tears streamed down his mother's face. She did not need to give him an answer. In his heart, he had known the truth from the time he saw the name on the birth certificate. She wept brokenheartedly so he pulled off the road at the next available exit. Pulling into the parking area of a strip mall, he turned off the engine. He waited briefly and then he pulled her to him, embracing her as if he was the parent and she the child. He held her until she worked through the tears and was able to talk again.

Ma's mind began to run through how her other children might react if he decided to tell them, and how she could lift her head again once word got out on the reservation. Because of the historical removal of children from families and tribes in attempts to 'anglicize' them, the modern day trend was to hold tightly to all children regardless of the circumstances of their birth. Would anyone understand her choice all those years ago?

Finally, without too much discussion, K.C. restarted the car and they went on to Omaha for the shopping trip. They enjoyed walking around in the stores for about an hour, had a light lunch at a nearby café, and then they headed to his apartment. K.C. wanted to share the documents with her in privacy. Ma realized that their day had not gone as planned, when they arrived at his home. Visiting his apartment had not been in their original plans. She looked at him questioningly.

K.C. got out and went around to the passenger side of the car to open the door for Ma. This time she did not protest his assistance. She leaned on his proffered arm, needing physical aid as much as she needed emotional support. They walked silently to his apartment door and went inside quietly. He helped her get comfortable on the couch with the coffee table at her knees. Then he excused himself to get the package and papers from his office.

As he started placing them, one by one, on the coffee table, Ma gasped in recognition. She fingered the leather garment on the homemade doll tenderly and touched the dream-catcher gently. Looking past the handwritten letters she saw the baby book she had taken great pains to make and saw the birth certificate with the name Delfina Beaupre written on the line for mother.

"It's her, isn't it?" Ma asked, looking deeply into his eyes. "Your Isobel is my Isobel, isn't she?"

It was K.C.'s turn to tear up. With glistening eyes, he nodded affirmation to his mother. "Yes, *my* Isobel is yours too." The realization that he was Isobel's brother suddenly became a reality, and he understood why God had blocked the development of their relationship. It still saddened him, but not for long. He realized that she was his sister, and would always be family, and his heart rejoiced. When Ma saw him make the transition from sadness to joy, she, too, was able to smile.

"Have you told her? When can I go to her as her mother?"

K.C. told Ma that Isobel would be driving home with them that evening to spend Sunday with them at church, as was her custom. They decided to wait until the whole family was together to share the news of K.C.'s discovery. Hopefully, it would be well-received by all concerned. If not, they would work through it as a family, not as strangers. The last to know would be Skyla. Ma would tell her on one of her visits to the prison, but she was sure that Sky's faith would carry her through this challenge, too.

Isobel felt something different in the air when K.C. came to get her. His mother even looked different, happy to see her, which was a bit of a change. Nothing out of ordinary came up in their conversations as they drove back to Macy, and the girls all came out to welcome them as they had on every other visit she made to their home. She waited to hear what was going on, but nothing came up until after dinner. Once the little children were tucked into bed, the adults gathered in the front room. Tali and Shyne usually went to their rooms, but were specifically instructed to return to the front room for a family discussion.

K.C. asked Isobel if he could tell them about his search for her biological family. Tali and Shyne already knew that she was looking for her link to the Omaha nation, so this was not a surprise to them. But when he told them that he had found her mother, both Tali and Shyne were surprised, but not as much as Isobel. She had no clue that K.C. had been working on finding her mother. As far as she knew, he had taken her papers and other items and was still trying to figure out where to start.

She looked expectantly at K.C. who avoided her eyes, choosing instead to look at his mother. Isobel followed his gaze and saw tears in the eyes of Mrs. Fox. She looked back at K.C. with a question in her eyes and he nodded. Isobel mouthed the words, "*Your* mother is *my* mother?" and once again he nodded. She looked back to Mrs. Fox who also nodded, and they both stood moving toward each other to embrace with tears of joy blending from one's cheek to the other's face. Talitha and Shyne took the scene in, watching the silent interchange between their elder brother, their mother and their best friend. It took a moment, but then they too understood what was going on.

Shyne squealed, thrilled with the knowledge that they had another sister. Tali was overwhelmed with emotion, watching her mother and her best friend bonding as mother and daughter. She quietly rejoiced and reached for K.C.'s hand wondering how he was doing. She felt sure that he had fallen in love with Isobel, but he seemed pleased to see Ma and Isobel together. Neither of the sisters questioned how this came to be; they knew their mother was a good woman, and whatever choices she made when young were made out of necessity.

The weekend passed all too quickly, but Isobel chose to stay instead of leaving with K.C. on Monday morning. She needed more time with her family, now that she could truly claim them as her own, not just in spirit, but in reality. Finally, God had heard her pleas and shown her the heritage that was truly hers.

When she finally did go back to her condo later in the month, she called Jason to fill him in on the changes in her life. At first, Jason wasn't sure how he felt about learning that K.C. was actually Isobel's brother. He struggled with the demon of jealousy despite praying for strength to overcome it. Now, God had provided him an easy way out. With the reason for jealousy removed, he no longer had to fight against it, and yet, he knew he had not overcome that temptation. He yearned to be able to say that jealousy was no longer an issue, no matter who Isobel chose as a friend, and he prayed that God would help him continue to grow in that area of his spiritual life.

Isobel returned to Law School with a new determination to excel. Her illness and challenges had indeed strengthened her. She continued to be amazed at how the Lord worked miracles and made good things come from bad events. She finished her studies while Jason continued his residency in Family Medicine in Omaha.

Isobel, happy to be done with law school, looked toward taking her bar exam and hoped to pass on her first attempt just as her brother had done. Meanwhile and beyond, she decided to devote herself to pro bono representation of Native Americans unable to afford good lawyers. Some of her time would be through the Legal Aid Office and some would be out of K.C.'s law firm that Mr. McMillen had finally signed over to him. Isobel was thankful that her inheritance gave her the freedom to help others without the need for an income.

Jason decided to add one more year of residency to his training to help him specialize somewhat in the area of cultural medicine. He would study with a Native American physician who also embraced traditional treatments, so he could be more in tune with those he would be treating. He and Isobel agreed that their relationship needed work; they needed to start at the beginning and rebuild. They would take their time and when the time was right, they would be married. Of that they were both certain!

Epilogue

Two years later…

Isobel sat at the vanity to make her final touchups on her hair and make-up. Out of the corner of her eye, she saw the tray sitting on the vanity which held cards from well-wishers. On top was an unusual envelope. The icon for her college sat in the return address corner. She picked it up, turned it over and saw a return address for the college she had attended. Opening the seal, she found an invitation to a class reunion later that year. She sat back in surprise, wondering at the timing of the invitation.

She knew immediately that she and Jason would attend, but she wondered about her girl gang. Over the years, she had thought of them often, but never took time to contact Ashley, Taylor or Maddie. *What must they think of me?* She wondered. *I just dropped out of site when we graduated.* Then she thought of all the dreams they had for the future and wondered how many had come true for her friends. She breathed a prayer that they had found happiness in their endeavors and joy in the Lord. Isobel gazed at her reflection in her vanity mirror and realized how much she had changed since last seeing her friends and how her plans for her life had been altered according to God's plan.

The peace she felt was mirrored in her eyes, the window to the soul. She looked closer at her reflection, realizing that she had little time for daydreaming. She needed to be ready in just a few minutes.

Isobel was pleased with how her veil and gown looked together. With her 'new' mom, she had taken great pains to be modest in her appearance while pulling together all facets of her heritage. Her 'something new' was the sparkling tiara that sat gently on her upswept hairdo. It was created from silver by a Native American artisan and suite her perfectly. Attached to the tiara was the delicate, lacey veil that represented her 'something old'. After all, it was the veil Aunt Betty planned to wear for her own nuptials. In her face, Isobel saw the joy that she felt in her heart. Gone was the old Isobel who felt sorry for herself and bemoaned her loneliness and poverty. A new person was reflected in the mirror; a new creation!

Thank you, Lord, for carrying me across the wilderness of loneliness and into Your family and the fullness of joy! She breathed this final prayer as she stood to straighten her dress. The beaded bodice and beaded full skirt incorporated her Native American heritage, although the beads were pearly white rather than colorful, as would be more traditional. Her gloved hand reached up and touched the precious bridal gift from her future in-law - her 'something blue' the sapphire necklace and earrings. In her other hand she held 'something borrowed'. A silver wire twisted into a nest for her bouquet and dotted with the occasional pearl, it held her wild flowers into a neat bundle easily carried in one hand. Talitha had made it for Isobel who told Tali she would only borrow it. She wanted her sister to use it for her own wedding in the not too distant future.

It was almost time! She smiled as she heard the organist begin the last song. The next would be the music to announce her entrance, and she needed to be in place. Her gown fit her perfectly; she looked like a princess. She took one final look in the mirror and called to her maid-of-honor who was in the attached room of the suite. Shyne came into the room looking equally beautiful in her aqua-colored gown. She was so thrilled to be an honored attendant for her older sister. This was the first wedding in which she had participated and she was a bit nervous.

Shyne's two children stood beside her. The tuxedoed ring bearer, Tad, now a young man of nine years old, held his pillow with the rings snugly tied in the center. And Shyne's daughter, Alyvia, the flower girl in her gauzy, full-skirted pink dress rocked from one foot to another, dangling her basket filled with rose petals. They adored their newly found Aunt Isobel, and were arguing over who would do the best job for her wedding. After Isobel assured them that they would both do great, she and Shyne and the children went into the hallway where they were greeted by K.C.

He gently lifted the veil from her back and over her face while Shyne straightened the train of her dress. Isobel took K.C.'s proffered arm and they made their way to the ballroom, waiting for the Bridal March to begin. The children began the procession with Taddy walking a bit fast and Alyvia focusing on dropping petals one at a time, all the while falling further behind Taddy. Shyne went next with the Best Man accompanying her to the front. Separating to their positions on either side of the groom and pastor, Shyne gave a stern look to her children to ensure their good behavior. The ballroom had been tastefully decorated for the occasion, and all the family and friends stood to welcome the bride's entrance. K.C. proudly escorted Isobel down the aisle to her waiting groom. She glowed as she saw the smiling face of her beloved.

He stood at the front with the pastor and groomsmen and framed by the large window behind them. The sun was just setting and painted the sky a delightful blend of blues, pinks, and purple, with golden rays emanating upward from the horizon. She wondered at the Lord's handiwork and saw that He was as much a Participant as all the guests in the hall.

As the two stood facing each other, the mother of the groom and Isobel's birth mother walked forward to the altar. They each lifted a flickering taper carefully from its stand and tilted it over the larger unity candle, jointly lighting its wick. Then, after replacing the tapers, the two mothers embraced as an indication of the two families joining as one. Isobel was amazed at the true friendship visible in their hug; there was a time when she never thought it possible.

Talitha's clear, sweet voice sang the words to '*Wind Beneath My Wings'* with feeling and passion. The sentiment expressed in the words mirrored Isobel's feelings for her fiancé. He stayed with her throughout her journey even when she pushed him away. Despite family pressures and distance, he supported her in the search for her family and encouraged her to lean on the Lord and to find strength in Him. He didn't press her for a commitment until he knew she was ready, until she finished her quest.

Finally the time came for the pastor's sermonette and their vows. The words spoken by the pastor passed in a blur as Isobel gazed at her beloved through tears of joy. She wondered that they had reached this point, finally, and praised the Lord for his goodness to them. *I know the plans I have for you…* was truly brought to life in the whole process. Who could have predicted this nine years ago, when her journey began? She thought back to the tears shed over lost love, lost family and lost relationship with God. Then she fast forwarded to this moment, where she had the connection with her Lord and Savior and had a whole new family to love and cherish, and who loved her. And this day…the day in which she would join her heart and life with her true love.

Isobel joined hands with her future husband as instructed for the blessing. The prayer was traditional, but then the couple broke from tradition. Rather than repeat memorized, overused words, they decided to write their own or to speak spontaneously from the heart, whichever they chose.

"I, Isobel, take you Jason; to be my best friend and companion for this journey we call life. I want you to walk beside me through whatever trials life might present and to leap with joy at the wonderful blessings God has in store for us…."

"I, Jason, take you Isobel, just as you are. I fell in love with you before I even knew what was happening. As a teen you captured my eye, as a young adult you captured my heart, and now you have my life. You are 'the wife of my youth' spoken of in Proverbs 5:18 and I promise to be your husband in our golden years, as well…"

As they exited to the tune of the Wedding March, Isobel saw Talitha with Kerron and Tamila proudly standing with their mother. Beside them, Brya and CeCe stood with Ma Fox. The only missing member was Skyla who was hoping to get out in just one more year on good behavior. *My family*, she thought. *I am blessed with a proud heritage of many generations!* Isobel and Jason continued up the aisle, smiling and nodding to friends and family, holding hands as if they would never again let go of each other.

Congratulations rang out as they stood in the greeting line as Mr. and Mrs. Armstrong. The reception hall was decorated with Native American tradition emphasized. Isobel's mother had gladly overseen this portion of the preparations, joyful to have a role in her daughter's celebration. Happy also that Isobel embraced her heritage, rather than discounting it. Although Jason's family claimed history back to the Mayflower, Isobel's heritage extended that far and beyond, and they both wanted to honor that part of their life. After all, their children would have the blood of many tribes running through their veins.

The banquet was catered (another gift from her parents-in-law) and a DJ played appropriate Christian music for the occasion. An opportunity for dancing came after the meal. K.C. stepped in to dance with the bride, since her father could not be there. After a few segments of the first tune carried them around the dance floor, K.C. handed her off to her husband with a flourish and a thump on Jason's back. The music was calm, restful, just as they wanted it. Despite pressures from the wedding planner, they held fast to their standards and used joyful Christian tunes for the dances. Then the final dance for the couple began: Keith Green's '*Unless the Lord build the House*'.

Isobel excused herself to change from her wedding dress into a travel outfit. They would be flying to Barbados for their honeymoon, so most of the clothing packed was light-weight and summery. Her travel outfit was a combination of khaki pants and a colorful, floral blouse. She was pleased at the effect when she let down her hair, using the flat iron to smooth it. Isobel gathered her cardigan sweater over her arm and looked back at the wedding dress and all the fixings around the room. Memories of the wonderful celebration flooded her heart. Her family and friends would clean this mess left behind while they went off on their honeymoon. *I am so blessed!* She thought and lifted her eyes skyward.

Their luggage was already in the car, so she picked up her purse and closed the door on her painful past. Isobel went down the hallway to join her new husband to look through God's window for their life together. They left for the airport with the usual tin cans tied to their car and white writing on the windows: JUST MARRIED!!! Smiling and waving to their friends as they drove off, Isobel and Jason began their life together. Today was the start of a new journey, a new path for the three of them: Isobel, Jason and their Lord and Savior, Jesus Christ!